YELLOW LINE

KRISTAL STITTLE

To Julie, Judy, and Dominique,
For teaching me so much, without even trying.

1

"I GOT THE INTERVIEW."

The responding squeal that came out of Jodie's phone was so loud that she had to hold it at arm's length, a huge smile lighting up her face. Jodie knew she could count on Sandra for a much more enthusiastic response than her dad had shown. Sure, her dad was super proud of her, but he was a lot more reserved with his emotions. When the squealing stopped, Jodie felt it was safe to return the phone to her ear.

"When is it?" Sandra asked.

"Tomorrow. 2 p.m."

"I'm so excited for you!"

"Thank you." Jodie never quite knew how to respond to a remark like that with anything other than a polite thanks.

"So, when you get the job, can you give me an in?"

"It's just an interview," Jodie laughed.

"Yeah, which you'll kill!"

"*If* I get the job, and *if* there's an opening for a position I think you can do, then I'll drop your name."

"You're the best."

"I know."

"Tomorrow is really soon for an interview."

"Well, they just called me like half an hour ago and asked when I was available. I said whenever, and they asked about tomorrow."

"Only gives us one night to celebrate."

"You read my mind," Jodie snickered. "Do you work tomorrow?"

"Not until the afternoon shift."

"So we're good for staying up late, just no heavy drinking."

"You're no fun," Sandra joked.

"Hey, if you want to show up for work with a massive hangover, be my guest." Jodie gave her voice a false air of self-importance. "I have an important interview to think about."

"Where are we going?"

"I was thinking the usual spot."

"Lame. This is an occasion! We should go downtown!"

"It's not *that* big of an occasion. If I get the job, then we can go celebrate some place nicer."

"I'll hold you to that. By the way, you waited thirty minutes to call me?"

"Had to call my dad first."

"Right, right. Should have known he'd come first. Have you called your sister?"

"Not yet."

"Excellent, I'm above her on the relationship scale!"

Sandra had been Jodie's best friend since their last year of high school together, and she could always make her laugh. They were a year apart, but Jodie had stayed an extra year while Sandra didn't. They met when they were in the same marketing class and found out they were both interested in the fashion world. From there, they learned they had a bunch of other things in common, and, in that mysterious, undefinable way, just clicked. It was one of those easy friendships that Jodie so rarely found. When they took the same program at college and lived in residence together, it only solidified their friendship into the rock hard gemstone it was today.

"Don't get too excited," Jodie told her friend. "I only called you first because I know you're not working right now and Amber is."

"Drat!" Sandra wasn't offended in the slightest by this remark, just as Jodie knew she wouldn't be.

"I'll probably send her an email shortly, letting her know. What are you doing right now?"

"Sketching and watching *The X-Files*."

"Again? How many times have you seen that show?"

"I love watching it while I sketch."

"Can I come over and join you?"

"Sure, but bring *Sherlock*."

"Deal."

"See you in a couple then?"

"Yup, bye."

"See ya."

Jodie hung up her phone and rose from her chair, suddenly remembering that she was only half dressed. She had been in the middle of changing when she had gotten the call to set up an interview with an up-and-coming fashion company based downtown. The position was merely a lowly intern spot that probably paid peanuts, but it was a foot in the door and a step toward Jodie's dream of becoming a fashion designer.

Drifting around her cluttered room, Jodie located her socks and a clean T-shirt. Earlier, she had put on her bumming-around-the-house pants and didn't bother changing them now. She knew Sandra wouldn't mind and would probably be wearing something similar. Once fully clothed, she hunted down her backpack of travelling art supplies and made sure everything was in there. Moving out into the living room of the apartment Jodie shared with her dad, she went to the media shelf beside the TV and found their *Sherlock* Blu-rays. She then travelled into the kitchen and wrote down where she was going on the whiteboard stuck to the fridge. It was unlikely her dad would get home before her, but she always left a message about where she was, just in case. Ever since Jodie's mom had died ten years ago, he worried. She was about to leave the kitchen when she realized she was kind of hungry. Not knowing what Sandra would have in the way of food, she grabbed a box of Kraft Dinner that she could cook once she got there. Sandra should have everything else needed to make it.

Ready to go, Jodie used her phone to send her sister an email, while sticking her feet into her shoes.

From behind her, Rusty meowed.

"Yeah, I'm going out for a bit," Jodie told the only other resident of the apartment. Amber had moved out several years ago.

Rusty stood in front of the door, waiting for it to open.

"No, you can't come with me," Jodie said, not even looking down at the fat cat as she finished her email.

With that done, Jodie pocketed her phone and retrieved her jacket from the tiny closet next to the door. After pulling it on, she shrugged into her backpack of stuff and then bent down to pick up Rusty. He meowed again, wanting the door to open so that he could run out into the hallway.

"You know you're not allowed out there," Jodie

reminded her cat as she kissed his head and then gently tossed him toward the living room. He hit the floor on all four feet, producing a heavy thump. "I'll be back later."

Jodie carefully squeezed out of the door, opening it only as much as she had to and keeping her leg in the way, so that Rusty couldn't get past her. He stood there, staring and sulking, as Jodie closed the door in front of him.

Sandra didn't live that far from Jodie. She and her boyfriend shared an apartment just a few blocks down from her. It was an easy walk.

As Jodie strolled along the street, she realized she hadn't needed to bring her jacket. It was an exceptionally warm, spring day, and the sun was out in full force. She had forgotten that the forecast was calling for a hot spell. Maybe she could convince Sandra to get up off her butt and go for a walk. It had been awhile since they had done any adventuring together. Not that there was much left to explore in the area, as most of it they had already seen. Still, it seemed like a waste to spend the day indoors.

Upon reaching her friend's building, Jodie let herself in. She had a set of keys, so that, on the rare occasion Sandra and Lucas took an actual vacation, Jodie could get in to walk and feed their pair of Pomeranians, as well as sprinkle some food in the fish tank. Despite being able to get in on her own, and being fairly certain the door wasn't even locked, Jodie still knocked on the apartment door. She was always afraid of showing up at the wrong apartment one day, that somehow she would end up on the wrong floor and not notice because they all looked the same. She even felt that way about her own apartment, but thankfully, some chipped paint on her door always confirmed for her which one it was.

"Come in!" Sandra's voice called from inside.

Jodie stepped into the apartment prepared for the rushing of the dogs. The two little fluff balls came barrelling towards the door, ready to happily greet whoever was coming in.

"Hello, Flash. Hello, Dance." Jodie bent down to scratch each dog behind the ears. She then headed into the living room where Sandra was sitting cross-legged in a big, over-stuffed chair with her tilted drawing table pulled right up against her. Jodie was right about Sandra wearing comfy clothes; she had on a tank top and a pair of yoga pants.

"Have some pizza." Sandra pointed to the open box on another table next to her chair. "It's leftover from last night. I'm eating it cold, but you can stick it in the microwave if you want it warm."

"Great, thanks!" Turned out Jodie didn't need to bring any food after all. "You sure Lucas won't mind?"

"You know, he doesn't really like leftover pizza."

"I find that hard to believe considering he ate a whole box of it that one morning."

"I think that's why he doesn't like it anymore," Sandra chuckled.

Jodie grabbed some pizza and carried it to the kitchen to put on a plate. Sandra's place was her second home, and she knew where everything was.

"I thought we could go for a walk later," Jodie called out as she put her plate of pizza into the microwave.

"Sure. Maybe we can plan out an hour or two before we hit the bar. Work off this pizza and the future booze."

"Is Lucas going to come with us tonight?"

"I doubt it. He's been really busy at work lately, and all he wants to do when he comes home is eat, watch some TV, and sleep."

"That's a shame." Jodie returned to the living room with her pizza, now reheated, and claimed a seat on the couch.

"Yeah, but it's looking like his hard work is going to pay off. He'll probably get a raise after this."

"Nice!" Jodie knew that Lucas worked like a dog, even when he didn't have to. He had some sort of programming position with a bank and was always researching new techniques and languages and stuff Jodie didn't know much about. Thankfully, Lucas was always willing to fix her laptop when something went haywire.

Looking at the screen, Jodie quickly identified what episode was playing. It was an early episode, probably from season two.

"I brought *Sherlock*," she said, as she started to unpack her supplies on the couch.

"Perfect. We'll put it on when this episode ends. It's been awhile since I've watched *Sherlock*."

"Didn't we watch it, like, three months ago?"

"Yeah, that's awhile," Sandra grinned.

Jodie settled in on the couch, letting her mind wander. She tried not to think about tomorrow, as it would only make her nervous. This interview was very important to her. Ever since she'd been a little girl, she had dreamed of creating the kinds of dresses that actresses would want to wear on the red carpet.

Who are you wearing tonight? the fictional host in Jodie's mind would ask.

Jodie Grey, the actress would answer, going on to explain what she liked about Jodie's designs.

What Jodie couldn't possibly know was that she was never going to make it to that interview.

2

JODIE AND SANDRA walked toward the bar, arm in arm. They had both changed their clothes and put on proper makeup and were feeling a lot prettier.

When Jodie's phone chimed in her purse, she pulled it out and checked the message.

"Looks like my dad is pulling another all-nighter," Jodie told her friend.

"Difficult case?"

"Must be. He hasn't told me much about this one, which means it's frustrating him."

"I'm sure he'll figure it out in the end."

Jodie shrugged. Being the daughter of a police detective, she knew that not every case *could* be solved. There were times her dad had nothing to work with and had to drop the case early on, but there were other cases, like this current one, that left behind just enough crumbs to keep him hanging on.

"You know what?" Jodie looked at Sandra. "I'm going to take advantage of this."

"Oh?" Sandra raised her eyebrows, guessing what Jodie

was planning, but letting her reveal it on her own.

"I'm going to bring a guy home with me tonight."

"Usually you don't decide that until you've had a few beers. Or shots."

"Well, I'm celebrating, and the apartment will be empty, so why the hell not?"

"You go, girl." Sandra snapped her fingers and bobbed her head. They both broke down laughing at how ridiculous she looked doing it. Some women could pull it off, but Sandra wasn't one of them.

"Pub-ho!" Jodie called out as it came into sight. It was a small joint, and on a Wednesday night it somehow became smaller, but it sold beer and was within walking distance of where they lived, so Sandra and Jodie visited it frequently.

Tonight, it was a little more crowded than they had expected it to be, because a game was being televised. This was to Jodie's liking, as it meant there were more men to peruse.

While Jodie attached herself to a group of guys, getting to know them, Sandra spent most of her time watching the game. Sandra was very dedicated and loyal to Lucas, and wasn't about to give these guys a single suggestion that she might be interested in them. Of course, during every commercial break she kept a sharp eye on Jodie. Although they had been here many times, and most of these guys they had seen before, suggesting that they were local, you could never be too careful. Women had to stick together.

Once the game ended, many of the men went home, but a few stayed. One in particular had caught Jodie's interest, and she seemed to have caught his. Deciding he was the man of the night, she focused all her attention on him.

"Jodie, I have to go to the bathroom," Sandra whispered in her ear.

Normally, Sandra would just go on her own, but by telling Jodie, it meant she wanted company, probably so that they could talk.

Jodie excused herself for a moment, making sure to bring her drink with her. After hearing stories about what happened to some girls in college, Jodie had learned to never leave her drink behind, or if she did, she would order a new one instead of finishing it. As a matter of fact, Sandra had probably been watching their drinks more than the game or Jodie.

"Conference?" Jodie asked, as they entered the women's bathroom. Since it was a weeknight, there weren't too many women still in the pub, and the bathroom was empty.

"So, I guess you're going with Steve?" Sandra asked.

"Yeah. He's good looking and is acting really nice. Thoughts?"

"He's certainly a better pick than some of that bunch. How old is he?"

"Twenty-eight. He's only got two years on us."

"And you're sure he's single? A guy like that doesn't look like he'd be single for very long."

"Broke up with his girlfriend last month, according to his more rowdy friends."

"Well, if you're sure you want to do this, then you have my approval."

"Excellent. Then it's time to land this fish before it gets too late."

Jodie and Sandra finished up in the bathroom and headed back out into the pub. The guys had ordered another round of shots, but, being the cautious things they were, both girls declined theirs.

"Oh come on, we bought them for you," one of the drunker men complained.

"It's fine," Steve told his friend. "Technically, *I* bought them, and they don't have to drink them if they don't want to."

"Look, it's white knight Steve!" another man mocked, as if that were somehow an insult.

Steve let it roll off his back and found other people to drink the shots. He offered to buy something else for both Jodie and Sandra, and so they followed him to the bar.

After fresh drinks and a round of pool, in which Steve let Jodie kick his butt, it was time to go home.

"Where abouts do you live? Want me to call a cab?" Steve offered.

"We're both within walking distance," Jodie told him.

"Walking, eh? You know, it's probably not safe for two fine women such as yourselves to walk home alone. Allow me to escort you." Steve held out his arm to Jodie.

"Well, if you insist," Jodie giggled, hooking her arm through his. So far, everything was going as planned.

Steve had to return to the table briefly to get his things, and no doubt, a few words of hearty encouragement from the other men. Jodie and Sandra waited by the door, getting their coats on. Although it had been a beautifully warm day earlier, the nights were still rather chilly once the sun departed.

"Ready?" Steve returned, offering his arm again.

Jodie accepted it a second time, and the three of them headed out.

Even though Sandra's place required a detour, they went there first. Steve sang sports songs a large portion of the way, which made Jodie laugh. When they reached the entrance to Sandra's apartment building, they stopped outside.

"Text me tomorrow about the interview," Sandra said as

she gave Jodie a hug goodnight. Jodie knew that Sandra actually wanted to be texted the moment Jodie got into her building and the next morning, as well.

"I will. Have a good night."

"You too," Sandra said with a certain gleam in her eye.

A flash of lightning and peal of thunder startled them all. Jodie reflexively squeezed Steve's arm, but stepped closer to Sandra.

"What was that?" Jodie looked around. "They didn't even call for rain tonight, let alone a thunderstorm."

The three of them waited for another strike, but nothing happened.

"Weird," Steve commented.

"You two be careful out there," Sandra said sincerely.

"We will," Jodie told her. "Maybe it was just a transformer exploding, or something."

"Could be. Well, goodnight again."

"Goodnight."

"Which way?" Steve asked, once Sandra had disappeared inside her building.

Jodie pointed dramatically, acting a little more drunk than she was, and putting the flash of light completely out of her mind. She was having fun.

During the walk to her apartment building, Steve became a lot more touchy-feely. He wrapped his arm around Jodie's waist and held her close, leaning his head against hers. By the time they reached her building, he was whispering in her ear and even kissing her cheek.

"This is me," Jodie said as they arrived outside her building.

"A magnificent castle for a magnificent princess," Steve commented, although it looked like every other boring building in the area.

"Would the kind sir knight like to see the inside of the castle?" Jodie asked.

"He would, m'lady," Steve grinned.

By the time they got into the elevator, they were making out. Jodie rebuffed him a little, knowing that a few of the residents in the building were night owls, and she would rather her neighbours not see them, but at the same time, Steve was really hot. She managed to break away just long enough to send a message to Sandra.

Once they got through Jodie's door, they stumbled around, still pawing at one another and undressing as they headed for Jodie's room.

When Steve started talking dirty, Jodie got the giggles. She often got the giggles during times like this, and knew there was nothing she could do about it. Usually, she'd have had more drinks, which got rid of them, but not tonight.

"What's so funny?" Steve whispered in her ear while his hands explored her.

Jodie just shook her head and tried to muffle her laughter. Steve was trying to be sexy, but it only made her laugh more.

"No seriously, what's so funny?" he asked, growing a little offended. Some guys could handle the giggles, some guys couldn't.

"It's nothing," Jodie said between snickers. "I just..."

"Go on."

"I just find the act of sex to be kind of funny. You know, the whole dance leading up to it, the dirty talk. The act itself is kind of funny when you think about it."

"You're laughing at me." Steve sat up.

"No, no, no. I'm most certainly not laughing at you." Jodie tried to save the situation. She wrapped her arms around his neck and kissed him hard.

Steve relaxed, but as he ran his hands down her back, she giggled again, partly because of her wandering mind, and partly because it kind of tickled.

"If you're not going to take this seriously, I'm leaving." Steve got off the bed.

"Oh come on. What's wrong with a little laughter in the bedroom?"

"I'm going."

"Mister serious," Jodie mocked. "Lighten up." She knew there was nothing she could do now.

Steve silently gathered up his clothes and quickly dressed himself.

"Can I at least offer you a cup of coffee?" she called out as he exited the apartment.

Meow. Rusty had been sitting in his cat tree, watching the whole thing like the creeper that he was.

Jodie sighed. "Guess it's just you and me now, Rusty, my boy." She slid off her bed and gathered up her clothes. She threw them into her laundry hamper, then put on her pajamas. Ah well, at least the rest of the night had been good.

After drinking a lot of water, Jodie used the toilet, brushed her hair and teeth, and washed her face. She sent Sandra a text message telling her the giggles happened, and that Steve was the serious type. Sandra understood what Jodie meant when she talked about the giggles, and how she found everything surrounding sex to be funny.

Climbing back into bed, Jodie straightened out her blankets and fluffed her pillows. Rusty jumped up next to her, claiming a spot where he could share her warmth without being rolled on in the middle of the night.

"I'm sure tomorrow will be a lot better," Jodie told her cat, as she turned out the light.

3

THE SUN WAS SHINING, the birds were singing, and it was another beautiful spring day. Jodie's internal clock woke her up before her alarm. She could have used a few more hours of rest, but on the other hand, she now had plenty of time to get ready for her interview. She checked her messages first, replying to Sandra's comments about last night, and then her dad and Amber's good luck wishes. Rusty followed her around during her entire morning routine, even sitting on the toilet while she took a shower.

"What do you think I should wear?" Jodie asked the cat, as she opened her closet.

Because the interview was with a fashion company, she felt her usual interview clothes, which consisted of a plain white blouse and black slacks, weren't good enough. Then again, she didn't want to overdo it either.

"What to wear, what to wear?" Jodie muttered as she sifted through her garments. "And how should I do my hair, for that matter? And my makeup? Ugh, I should have thought about this stuff yesterday."

Rusty had no comment on the matter, he was too busy

investigating the inside of the closet, a place he rarely got to explore.

In the end, Jodie went with a knee length, black skirt cut in a slightly frilly yet simple pattern, and a white, short sleeved blouse with a pattern stitched into the collar. The blouse was a little too thin, so she added a white camisole beneath it, making sure that her bra wasn't visible. According to her phone, the weather was going to be the same as yesterday—apparently the whole week was looking sunny—and so a coat shouldn't be needed. For her hair, she pulled the dirty blonde mess into an up-do that was both fun and practical, being careful to get her fringe of bangs just right. When it came to her makeup, she went with a nude style, using mostly concealer and a pale, muted lip gloss. The makeup around her eyes took more time, and she was very careful with it. She had sky blue eyes that she wanted to emphasize without unbalancing the rest of her look. While applying the mascara, she wished Amber was still living at home. Everything Jodie knew about makeup had come from her, and so she was seen as an expert in those regards. As for jewellery, Jodie selected only a delicate, small watch, and small, silver stud earrings. Looking at her nails, she judged they were still good from the manicure Sandra had given her yesterday before they went out. They matched her eyes.

Once she felt pretty, Jodie went to the kitchen to get some breakfast. Rusty raced her there and sat in front of the fridge, hoping to get some milk, or margarine, or perhaps the fabled tuna. Today, he got nothing.

"You're supposed to be on a diet," Jodie told him as she cooked herself some eggs sprinkled with bacon bits.

Rusty was basically a ball with feet. He lived for food, especially people food, and often got what he wanted. Jodie refused to give in today. Her dad would probably give him something later.

It was still early, but Jodie thought that leaving now would be a good idea. She could go downtown, figure out where the building was ahead of time, and then spend some time sketching. Jodie liked it downtown during the day, even though she so rarely went. If she got this job, she'd be down there nearly all the time.

Hunting through the cupboards for her old lunch sack, she eventually located the bright yellow thing behind her dad's unusually large collection of thermoses. Thinking she might even spend some time downtown after the interview —depending on how it went and how she felt—Jodie packed more food than she usually ate for lunch. Slapping together a BLT and a PB&J sandwich, she fit them in the sack with two apples, two of the little boxes of grape juice that she loved, and a Swiss cake roll for dessert. Once her lunch sack was full, she jammed it in with her art supplies. Her water bottle was much easier to find, as it often sat next to her bed at night, ready in case she woke up coughing from an attack of dust, or Rusty fur, or even just really dry air. After refilling it to its full one thousand millilitres, she slid it into the elastic mesh pocket on the side of her bag.

"What do you think, Rusty? Am I ready to go?"

Jodie had been taking her time getting ready, going over everything carefully to keep her hands and mind occupied with busy work. A slow, creeping feeling of sickness was filling her stomach, and it had nothing to do with the alcohol she had drunk last night. She was nervous, anxious even, about the interview. She was experiencing a weird mixture of wanting to delay the interview, and of wanting it to be right now.

"I'll feel fine once I get downtown," she lied to herself.

She wouldn't feel fine until the interview was over. Thankfully, her anxiety wouldn't externalize itself. She had had interviews before—although none as important as this one—and each time she spoke calmly, thoughtfully, and didn't fidget. She thanked her dad for that. Not only was he always rock-steady, but he had taught her a trick to keep from fidgeting when doing something that made her nervous: wiggle and flex her toes. Usually her feet were beneath a table during interviews, or behind a podium if she had to speak publicly, and no one would notice her feet. By wiggling her toes, it kept her hands from searching for something to occupy them.

Thinking of her feet, Jodie realized she needed different footwear. She had been going to wear her nice sandals, but they were open-toed, and she wouldn't feel comfortable using her trick in them. The solution came easily as she spied her simple flats sitting on the top of the shoe pile in her closet. The moment she put them on, she wanted to run out the door and get downtown. She reined in her eager emotions, using it as practice for the interview, and calmly put on her backpack. From under her bed, she pulled out the full-sized version of her portfolio, safely contained within a slim, canvas bag that was slightly larger than the average briefcase, and slung the strap over her shoulder. As part of her job application, she had included a digital version of the same portfolio, but she decided to bring this one in case they wanted to see a hard copy. The portfolio case also contained an extra copy of her résumé. Taking several deep breaths, she looked around her room, thinking there might be something she was missing. There wasn't.

"Now Rusty, don't go breaking anything while I'm out," Jodie told her cat. "You be a good boy while I'm gone, okay?"

Rusty just hung around the door waiting for her to open it, not making any promises. Jodie shooed him back with her foot. She wanted to pick him up and give him a big hug, but didn't want to get his hair all over her clothes. With the warmer weather, he had begun to shed like a mad bastard.

Using the same trick she used every time she exited the apartment, Jodie kept Rusty from escaping. Seconds later, she was waiting for the elevator to pick her up. Jodie nervously checked her phone, trying to occupy herself. There were no messages on any of her social sites, or emails to distract her. Instead, she opened up a mobile game she tried not to play too often because of its addictive nature, and fiddled with that all the way down to ground level. Once outside and on the street, the sights and sounds of the traffic were enough to keep her attention. At least, for now.

Although Jodie had intended to walk to the subway station, a bus arrived at a stop just as she was passing it. Thinking it was good luck, she decided to hop aboard, flashing her monthly TTC pass in the process. The bus was neither crowded nor empty. At the front, a cluster of mothers blocked the aisle with their large buggies, and not all the children were restrained inside them. A particularly rowdy child managed to kick Jodie as she squeezed past, his legs swinging wildly. If he noticed what he had done, the kid didn't say anything about it, and his mother was busy cleaning up a juice mess her other child had caused. Cursing them in her head, Jodie squeezed past to where several other people were sitting quietly. Normally, she liked the back of the bus, but she chose to sit in one of the single seats in the middle after she saw what appeared to be a homeless man muttering to himself back there. Jodie was a veteran of the TTC, and had learned a few things during her travels, the first being never to argue with parents about their kids' behaviours, and the second to never sit near someone muttering.

As the bus rumbled along Sheppard Avenue West, Jodie realized what she had forgotten. She could picture her headphones sitting on the edge of her desk, where Rusty could swat at them and chew the ends if the mood took him. It looked like there wasn't going to be any music for Jodie.

Since it was only a short bus ride, Jodie didn't bother to pull out her small sketchbook. Once they arrived at the station, she hopped off the bus and headed for the subway, which would be the last of the public transit she'd have to take. The building where her interview was scheduled was within walking distance of a subway stop. Frankly, that was a miracle considering how puny the subway system was in Toronto.

Standing on the platform, waiting for the train, Jodie gazed up at the map that marked out the system. It was only four lines if you included the little blue one tacked onto the end of the Bloor line. Most people used only two: the green Bloor line, which ran east/west through the city, and the big yellow U that handled north/south traffic. Jodie was at the very end of the west leg of the yellow line. Her plan was to ride the subway all the way down to the bottom of the U, past Union station which marked its centre, and then up a short distance on the other side to Queen station. It would be a fairly long ride, but Jodie never minded the subway. It helped that, because she boarded at the end of the line, everyone had gotten off the train leaving all the seats empty. If she had had to stand, she was sure she would think differently about it.

A girl about the same age as Jodie waited not far from where Jodie stood. She wore a black top and a jean skirt with black pantyhose. Jodie was taking note of the way the folds of her skirt hung, when the girl took a pair of scissors out of her ratty messenger bag. She bent over and snipped a small hole near the knee of her pantyhose, revealing a tiny star tattoo, which she rubbed a bit before straightening back up. Jodie wondered whether revealing it was a stylistic choice, or whether the tattoo was a fairly recent addition to her skin and was too sensitive for the hose.

When the train finally arrived, Jodie was the first passenger to enter the lead car. She was disappointed it wasn't one of the slick, new trains, which were open the whole length of the train instead of being separated into cars, but at least it appeared to have been recently cleaned. Jodie went straight to the front and took the seat in the corner, her back to the forward facing window. From there, she could see a good portion of the car, and could hide her sketchbook behind the backs of the seats in front of her. Sometimes she used other riders to make gesture drawings, and she preferred it if they didn't know that. Even when she was doodling something from her head, people tended to get curious, and she frequently caught them trying to glance at her sketchbook. A few would even ask what she was drawing, which actually bothered Jodie more, because she didn't like to talk to strangers while in transit. Having a cop-father had deeply ingrained stranger-danger into Jodie. Hearing about some of the cases he worked on had made her a very cautious person when travelling alone. Although it had never stopped her from going places by herself, she was probably a lot more alert than she needed to be.

The ride was going smoothly. So far, no one had started a fight with anyone else which was always a plus. They weren't frequent, but heated arguments on the subway put everyone on edge. Most people stared out of the windows while riding this section of the subway as it was all above ground, but Jodie studied the people as they got on and off. One woman in particular fascinated her. She was an older woman, possibly Pakistani, but Jodie was awful at telling apart ethnicities. She suspected it was because she grew up in such a multicultural city, that she never bothered to ask where people's families were from. The woman was clothed in layers of formless, flowing white fabric, with a shawl thin enough for her dark hair to be visible through it. What really caught Jodie's attention was the thick black cross tattooed on her forehead. Jodie had never seen anything like that before, not in person. The woman took a forward-facing seat, her somewhat grim expression set in a face of stone. When the woman turned her head toward her, Jodie quickly looked back down at her sketchbook, not wanting to be caught staring.

At the stop after the one the woman got on, a really good-looking guy with chiselled features, wearing a dark suit with a loosened tie, and carrying a briefcase, boarded the train. Jodie silently hoped he would take one of the empty seats near her, but he didn't. When Jodie saw people as gorgeous as he was, she often wondered if she was seeing a movie or TV star she just wasn't recognizing. Despite living in Toronto her entire life, she had never had a star encounter. Perhaps, if her interview went well, all that would change.

At the same time as the gorgeous man got on, a kid who looked like he should be in school also boarded. It was possible he just appeared young for his age; Jodie had met several people who were like that, Sandra included. Everywhere Sandra went that had an age restriction, she got carded. She told Jodie that being carded didn't bother her, it was that most people felt the need to say "you'll love it when you're older." Sandra understood that, and didn't mind the words themselves, it was just the fact that she had heard them so many times from so many strangers. This kid probably didn't have that problem. He wore a fairly heavy-looking black jacket despite the day's warmth, and, combined with his black hair and the dark circles under his eyes, he came across as potentially dangerous, someone to whom most people wouldn't make off-hand remarks. Jodie thought he was the sort of guy who would pick fights over nothing, and was glad when he sat at the other end of the car.

The next stop brought on a man with a bicycle, wearing cyclist's clothing, and an elderly woman with a dog. The dog was a happy little corgi that immediately brought a smile to Jodie's lips and prompted her to draw him.

Their train cruised over the highway and reached the Yorkdale station. Several people got off, and a few people got on, likely going to and from the mall. It pleased Jodie that the gorgeous man stayed on, although the punk-looking kid also stayed put. A woman came aboard with a little kid who couldn't be older than three, and who tottled along with his flyaway hair wearing an orange *Diego* shirt. The woman walked straight to the front of the train, picking up her little boy so that he could see out the window in the door.

"Do you want to sit here?" Jodie offered her seat. She had seen many parents bring their kids to the front of the train and found that, for most of them, it was easier to sit backwards on the pair of seats under the window, than stand next to the conductor's booth.

"No, it's all right, thank you." The mother gave her a smile. "We're getting off at the next stop."

"All right." Jodie released the tension in her leg muscles, no longer preparing to stand.

"Yay!" the little boy cried as they began moving.

Small children on public transit could be the most annoying things in the world, while at other times, they were the most adorable. While the kids on the bus had fallen into the former category, this one was of the latter.

"Choo, choo!" he cried out, his tiny hands pressed against the glass as they picked up speed.

Jodie couldn't help but chuckle.

Everything that happened next came as a series of violent noises, punctuated by a single sharp image for Jodie. The mother gasped, the sound nearly drowned out by a heavy *thummp*. Jodie barely had time to register it before a horrible squeal of metal grinding on metal filled the entire car. People screamed and Jodie's head was whipped back, but she was still able to see the mother turn and curl around her little boy, protecting him as her own head was thrown into the sturdy window with a barely audible but unforgettable crack.

4

THE CHILD WAS CRYING. No, crying wasn't the right word. The child was *wailing*.

Jodie, her neck feeling like it was on fire and her head swimming, shoved everything off her lap and slid sideways into the next seat. Beside her, the mother was crumpled on the subway floor, partly on top of her little boy.

"Ma'am, are you all right?" Jodie pointlessly asked, knowing she couldn't be, based on her lack of movement.

She got off the seat and carefully knelt on the floor beside the mother, freeing the child from her arms. Big, fat tears rolled down the boy's face. Jodie sat him on the seat she had just vacated.

"Momma!" he shouted between red-faced wails, reaching his arms toward the fallen woman.

"Your momma needs help right now. I'm going to help her," Jodie told the boy, as she turned back to the woman. "Just stay there."

During her final semester of college, Jodie had taken a first aid seminar. It wasn't much, just the Heimliech manoeuvre and CPR stuff, but it was better than nothing.

While trying to clear her head and think about what to do first, the subway driver's door opened. The driver had a large belly, which he held with one arm, clearly injured in some way.

"Oh jeeze. Oh jeeze. Oh jeeze," he said looking down at the mother.

Jodie carefully placed her fingers on the woman's neck to search for a pulse. She found one, but it was very weak.

"She's alive," Jodie told the driver.

"Oh jeeze. Oh jeeze. Oh jeeze," he just kept repeating.

"Momma!" the kid cried out again and feebly pushed on Jodie's back.

There was another strange *thummp*, and the driver flinched.

Jodie decided there wasn't much she could do for the mother. Not knowing the condition of her spine and neck, she didn't want to touch her. Standing up, she finally noticed the strange blue substance covering the front windows.

"What happened?" Jodie asked the driver, but he just shook his head.

Looking down the length of the subway train, Jodie saw that everyone was still recovering from what had just occurred. Based on appearances, there were a lot of sore necks and limbs, but everyone seemed to be moving. The woman with the dog was gasping and holding her chest. Jodie quickly ran over to her.

"Are you all right?" she asked. "Is there something I can do to help?"

The woman pointed toward her purse and wheezed, "Pills."

The purse had fallen onto the subway floor and slid away under some seats. Jodie quickly dropped to her knees, not caring what the condition of the floor was, and grabbed the red leather bag. She opened the purse and rifled through it, as she returned to the woman. There were at least three pill bottles in there, all of them different.

"Which-" before Jodie could finish, the woman snatched one of the bottles out of the mouth of the purse, opened it, dumped a pill onto her palm, and then dried swallowed it.

"Will you be all right?" Jodie asked instead.

The woman nodded.

Thummp.

The whole car shook, the lights went out, and people screamed. Jodie managed to stay on her feet, thanks to years of practice travelling on buses and subways. She glanced toward the mother and child, and saw that the driver was sitting next to the mom and keeping the kid from doing something unsafe like shaking her. The driver was silently crying in harmony with the wailing child.

The heavy sound and the shudder had been accompanied by more strange blue stuff appearing on the side of the subway car. Jodie didn't know what it was. She thought that maybe it was something leaking out from inside the train, like coolant, and that the lines had exploded. Everyone was gawking at the curiosity when there came another *thummp.*

Out on the Allan Expressway, which ran level along both sides of their above-ground subway tracks, cars were squealing their tires and crunching into one another. Great big globs of the blue substance were on the road. Some of the globs were taller than the train and were slowly settling. They seemed unaffected by the cars that couldn't swerve around or stop in time, which, upon hitting the stuff, dramatically slowed and seemed to become trapped, as if they had just driven into a wall of thick glue.

Thummp. Another glob landed on the road. It had clearly come from the sky, like some absurd raindrop that was far too big and far too solid. Most of the cars had managed to stop by now, but the glob had landed on many of them, burying them within the blue mass.

Thummp. A blue glob hit the back of their subway car, quickly filling in the space between it and the car behind them. That's when the panic kicked in.

"We've got to get out of here!" a woman screamed. "We're going to be buried alive!"

People rushed toward one of the doors that hadn't been touched by the mysterious blue gunk. Jodie didn't know what to do. She was frozen in place as another heavy *thummp* drew their attention to a large mass that had fallen on the expressway, this time on the northbound lanes on the far side of the subway tracks.

The old woman's hand wrapped around Jodie's wrist. Jodie wheeled around, startled and frightened, to face her.

"Stop them," the woman wheezed. "Stop them." She weakly gestured with her hand toward the people prying open one of the side doors. Jodie's eyes widened with under-standing, as more strange *thummps* were heard from all directions.

"Stop!" she called out, moving closer to them. "Don't go out there!" but it was too late.

The frightened people got the door open and spilled out onto the tracks.

Thummp.

Everyone already outside was covered instantly. Jodie could only watch in horror. The glob was massive, covering most of the train car's side that wasn't already encased. Those trapped within it slowly thrashed. It looked like they were trying to swim in extremely thick liquid. The gorgeous man had been standing in the doorway when it happened. Those who had been behind him quickly backed up, but he had no choice. The oozy substance sucked him in and knocked his feet out from under him with the force of its fall. The man's hands quickly reached back out, grabbing the subway floor and pulling until his head was free. Unfortunately, the blue stuff was slowly pushing into the train at about the same speed he could pull himself out.

The punk-looking kid reacted then.

"Get out of my way!" he bellowed, pushing people aside. He grabbed the handsome man's shoulders and pulled with all his might. There was a strange suction sound as the trapped man was slowly freed from the goo, his body being rotated in the process. The kid's hands slipped, and he fell onto his back at the feet of the ring of people who were just watching.

"Help me!" he shouted at them, as he rolled back up and grabbed the man's shoulders again.

Jodie realized she was one of the people who were just watching. Before she could do anything, a burly black man stepped up beside the kid. Together, they heaved on the downed man, who was emerging even slower out of the goop now. They succeeded in pulling him out, down to about his waist, but then suddenly, their efforts seemed unable to budge him any further.

"Stop! Stop!" the entrapped guy called out. "You're going to rip me in half!"

The efforts to free him ceased.

Thummp.

The car shook again, and everyone inside trembled with fear. No one knew what was happening. Everywhere she looked, Jodie saw large chunks of goo sliding down the windows and doors. She had no idea what the hell it could be. It was a kind of turquoise-blue, like pictures she had seen of the ocean in the Caribbean. And like the ocean, it wasn't opaque, she could see through the blue stuff fairly clearly. She could see as more globs submerged almost everything around them, trapping cars and people alike. Inside the blue stuff, the people who had jumped out of the train weren't moving anymore. The dozen or so who had tried to escape were frozen in a tableau of terror, their poses eerie, flailing gestures. Looking back at the gorgeous man, Jodie noticed that the goo was no longer slowly entering the train. It had stopped.

"Okay, try again," the trapped man panted, having been completely flipped over onto his back due to the way he had been pulled.

The kid and the black guy grabbed his arms and heaved. He didn't move an inch.

"Stop, stop, stop!" he ended up crying out once more. "It's no use. I'm stuck."

Picking up a pen that had spilled out of someone's pocket or bag, the big guy, who had helped pull on the gorgeous man, used it to test the blue stuff. He tapped the end of the pen on it, revealing to everyone that it seemed to have solidified. Glancing around at all the worried faces, the black man then touched it with his bare hand.

"Solid as a rock," he commented.

"That stuff's covering all the windows and doors," a woman with a trembling voice observed. "If it's all solid, we're stuck!" It was impossible to say for sure, but Jodie thought the voice might have belonged to the same woman who had caused the mad rush for the door in the first place.

"Calm down, everyone." The big black man who had tested the goo rose to his feet. "We'll be all right."

"Speak for yourself," the gorgeous man grumbled from where he was trapped on the floor.

Jodie stared out at those who were even less fortunate than he was. Were those people trapped in the blue still alive? And if they were, how long could they last like that?

"Just remain calm. Obviously, rescue services will hear about this shortly, if they haven't already, and will be putting together crews as fast as possible. They'll be here in no time."

"How do you know?" one dissenter spoke up.

"I work for Toronto Hydro. Remember the big ice storm that happened at the start of the holidays? We gave up our Christmases to bring back everyone's power, and had people working all day and all night. I'm certain that for this emergency, everyone will be working just as hard."

A lot of people grumbled and walked off, most of them pulling out their cell phones to contact loved ones. Jodie thought that was a good idea, but another thought kept nagging at the back of her mind. The ice storm that the hydro man was referring to, had kept people in the dark and the cold for days, some even as long as a week, and more for those outside the city. How long were they going to be trapped in here? And how far had this spread? And just what the hell was it?

5

"I'M OKAY, POTATO," Jodie's dad spoke over the phone. "Tell me about your situation."

"I'm stuck on the subway with a bunch of people."

"Are you hurt?"

"No. Well, my neck kind of hurts, and I think I have a lump on my head, but I'm okay. But, Dad? There's a woman who won't wake up. Her head took a really hard hit when she tried to protect her little boy."

"Is she breathing?"

"Yeah, I checked for a pulse, she's alive." Jodie glanced down at the mother as she spoke to her dad. She had returned to her seat. The driver was sitting across from her in his dark control booth, keeping the child calm. "I didn't move her. I don't know if her back or something is broken."

"Anything look like it's on an unnatural angle?"

"No."

"Well, best to leave her for now, just to be safe. Anyone else hurt?"

"I don't think so. Except for the people who tried to get off the train. One of these globs landed on them and hardened. I don't know if they're even still alive," her voice hitched.

"Shh, it's okay, potato."

"I'm scared, Dad."

"I know. A lot of people are, myself included. It's okay to be scared, but you also have to be strong, right?"

"Right."

"Can you be strong?"

"Yeah. I can be strong... Dad?"

"Yes?"

"Where are you?"

"In the car with Lucky, I told you that."

"No, I mean... Where's the car?"

Silence from the other end of the line. Then, "It's bad, potato. Real bad. From the reports I'm getting over the radio, this shit has hit the entire city and then some. One guy said there's a glob hanging off the CN Tower like a giant booger."

Jodie didn't know if that was true, or if her dad was just trying to give her a visual that would make her laugh. It didn't work. "How long might we be stuck for?"

"I don't know. No one seems to know what this stuff is yet. I suspect it won't take too long. It seems to have stopped falling, and they've already called a state of emergency. Crews from surrounding regions, even as far as Quebec and Manitoba, and who knows where else, are already being organized to come help us out."

"Okay."

"Guess you're not going to make that interview."

It took a second for Jodie to realize what he was even talking about. "Yeah, I guess not. Think I should call them?"

"When a state of emergency has been declared? I don't think you need to, potato."

"It would make me stand out from the other candidates."

Her dad chuckled. "Whatever you think is best. I should go. I need to check in on your sister."

"Okay. Be careful, all right?"

"Oh, I'm fine here, so long as Lucky doesn't start passing gas."

Jodie could hear her dad's partner laughing in the background.

"You stay safe," he said, becoming more serious. "Don't do anything stupid, or anything that seems remotely dangerous."

"I'll be okay, Dad."

"I'm sure you will be. Watch out for that little boy and his mother for me."

"I will."

"I love you, potato."

"I love you too, Dad."

There was a silent pause as neither of them wanted to hang up, but eventually, there was a soft click as Jodie's dad finally cut off the connection. Jodie stared at her phone for a bit before putting it away, her wallpaper of Rusty gazing back at her. She hoped Rusty would be okay for awhile. More important than her wallpaper was her battery charge. There was seventy-nine percent left. Knowing it could be awhile, Jodie thought that she should turn her phone off to save the battery, but couldn't bring herself to do it, not right now. Her dad might try to call her again, or one of her friends could reach out. No, she would leave it on for the time being.

"How's he doing?" Jodie turned in her seat to face the subway driver, whose round face was way too large for its small features and thinning hair, making his whole head appear larger than it actually was. The little boy was sitting on his lap, ogling the controls before him. There was no power, so he was free to touch them, but so far, it seemed like he hadn't.

"I think I have him distracted, at least for the time being," the driver told her.

"And you? How are you doing?"

"Stomach's sore—it got hit against the control panel during the collision—but I think I'm all right."

"So what happened?"

"What do you think happened?" The driver gestured out the window, which was covered in the thick layer of blue stuff. "This... Whatever this is, fell on the tracks ahead of us. Drove right into it before I could stop."

"What do you think it is?"

"How the hell should I know?"

"I'm Jodie, by the way." She held out her hand, carefully leaning over the child's mother.

"Simon." He reached over with a meaty paw and shook with her.

His hand was sweaty, and Jodie tried to hide the fact that she wiped hers off on the edge of the seat as soon as he let go.

"Do you think I should go out there?" Simon gestured with his head down the length of the car, and then gave it a furtive peep.

"I don't know. People probably have questions."

"I don't have answers."

"You might have some."

"They don't expect me to be some sort of leader, do they? I can't do that."

"What would we need a leader for?"

"That's just it, I don't know. Here, take him. He told me his name is Paul."

Paul looked around as Simon stood up, shuffling the kid off his lap and standing him on the floor. Once the big guy made his way out of the booth, carefully stepping around the mother, Jodie went inside. She had never been inside a subway control booth before. It was rather dark in there compared to the rest of the subway. Its windows were tinted, letting less of the sun through. Because of the blue stuff, most of the train was filled with blue light.

"Hi Paul, I'm Jodie." She crouched down in the doorway.

"I'm not Paul," the kid said.

"No? What's your name then?"

"Apollo."

"Apollo?"

"Yes."

"That's quite the name. There's a Roman God named Apollo."

"A Roman God?"

"Yup. If I remember right, he rides in a chariot and pulls the sun across the sky."

"The sun?" Apollo stood as near to the window as he could get and looked up through its tinting and the blue gunk. The sun was above them, though, where it probably couldn't be seen. "Is Momma seeping?"

"Seeping?"

"Yes."

"Oh, do you mean sleeping?"

"Yes." He was overly articulate with that single word.

"Yeah, she's sleeping."

Apollo stepped away from the window. "Let's wake her up."

"We can't wake her up."

"Why not?"

How do you explain 'unconscious' to a little kid?

"How old are you, Apollo?"

"I'm..." he paused for a moment as he thought it over, studying his fingers. "I'm four," he figured out, holding up all his fingers without the thumb on one hand.

"Four! Wow, that's a good age."

"How old are you?"

"How old do you think I am?"

"Umm." Apollo studied her closely. "I think twelve."

Jodie laughed. "Sure, I'm twelve."

Apollo started to climb into the driver's seat.

"Let me help you." Jodie shuffled forward.

"No! I can do it myself. I'm a big boy."

Jodie sat back and watched. After much squirming and kicking, he got up onto the seat.

"See? I did it!"

"That you did."

"Can I push buttons? The man said I could."

"If he said you could, then you can."

Apollo leaned forward and pressed the largest button he could reach. Nothing happened. He tried other buttons, but none of them did anything either.

Jodie stood up and stretched, taking a single step out of the conductor's cab and looking down the length of the car. Simon, the driver, was walking back toward her, his head down and his feet shuffling. No one appeared happy.

"How'd it go?" Jodie asked him as he returned.

Simon shrugged. "People are upset. I can't do anything because we have no power. A lot of them had questions about her." He nodded his head at Apollo's mother.

Jodie stepped over the woman again and climbed back

into her original seat. Simon sat on the floor beside Apollo, who now seemed to be playing some imaginary game and talking quietly to himself. Rediscovering her sketchbook, Jodie picked it up from where it had fallen to the floor. Looking at her doodles, she didn't much feel like sketching anymore. She wanted to do something physical. She wanted to be proactive about getting out of the subway train. Instead, she tidied up her art supplies and returned them to her bag, including a few things that had spilled out during the crash. She noticed her lunch bag as she put it all back. Knowing that they were going to be there awhile, Jodie was glad she had packed extra food. In fact, she was glad she had decided to spend some time downtown and had packed any food at all. But what about the others? Who else on this train had packed lunches? Had snacks? Had water?

With an effort, Jodie shoved those thoughts from her mind. They'd be fine. It wouldn't take *that* long before they were rescued. They were on a subway next to a major artery for the city, surely the work crews would come through those areas first. They would enable their own ability to mobilize, and then move onto the less frequented and populated areas. Well, maybe they would de-gunk hospitals first, but surely major transportation routes would come after that. No, they weren't going to be there too long.

Looking out the window next to her through the blue layer, Jodie could just make out the upper edge of a building peeking over the side of the valley they were in. It had a glob of blue gunk clinging to it. For some reason, it made her think of Rusty alone in her apartment building. No one was home to feed him. He should be all right for awhile, but a seed of worry planted itself in Jodie's belly. Taking out her cell phone, she decided to call Sandra.

The line rang and rang until it eventually went to voicemail. She tried four more times, hoping that Sandra was just having trouble finding her phone. Eventually though, Jodie had to give up. Sandra probably just got separated from her phone. Maybe she forgot it when she went to work. Although Sandra had never forgotten her phone before, there was a first time for everything.

As Jodie began to think about how Sandra would most likely have been heading to work when the blue came, the seed of worry in her belly sprouted.

6

JODIE CHEWED ON HER THUMBNAIL. It was a terrible habit that she had, and it had been her New Year's resolution to stop doing it, but she broke that resolution now. Thinking of New Year's Eve made her stomach clench again. They had had a quiet celebration to ring in the year. Sandra and Lucas had come over, as well as Amber and her fiancé. Gathered in the small living room with Jodie's dad, they drank Champagne, and flipped back and forth between the Toronto and New York TV programs. Rusty was happy they didn't have noisemakers this year, and was able to put up with their shouting without having to flee in terror. Once the fireworks around the city started, they had all gone out onto the balcony to watch several displays going off in the vicinity. Jodie, Amber, and their dad sang a version of Auld Lang Syne that had incorrect lyrics, but that they sang every year, while the other three tried to sing the normal version, but couldn't remember the majority of the words.

"Fuck!" The shouting of a man brought Jodie out of her memories.

She quickly pinpointed who had shouted by following the eyes of the other passengers. It was the man with his legs trapped in the blue. He had his arms splayed out in either direction, and was staring angrily up at the curved ceiling. He offered no explanation for why he shouted, and no one asked him for one; they all just turned back to whatever they were doing. Jodie had seen him trying to wiggle free earlier, but for the moment he was lying still.

She climbed out of her seat, finding it safer to scramble over the backs of the ones in front of her than to step over the mother again. She walked up to the good-looking man who was trapped in the second set of doors from the front. Conscious of the fact that she was wearing a loose skirt and that he was lying on the floor, Jodie knelt down beside him before saying anything.

"Can I do anything for you?" she asked, knowing that asking if he was all right would probably only piss him off.

"I think the tail of my jacket is caught in this stuff," he grumbled. "I was hoping to take it off and use it as a pillow or something, but noooo," he rolled his eyes, "my upper body has to be as uncomfortable as the lower half."

"Sit up, let me see."

The man struggled to push himself up on his hands, allowing Jodie to look under his back. He was right, the tail of his jacket was stuck in the blue stuff just like his legs, and he tried to sit up, it pulled on his shoulders. Jodie told him so, and let him lie back down. Curious, she placed her hand on the blue gunk. It felt smooth, like moulded plastic, or maybe acrylic. She noticed little bubbles trapped inside, although not many. Then she saw the people trapped just a few feet away and quickly withdrew her hand. The height of the windows kept them out of sight most of the time, but through the door they were easy to see.

"I have some scissors," she croaked. She cleared her throat and tried again. "I have some scissors in my bag, if you don't mind having your jacket cut a little bit."

"I don't mind. If you could help me, I'd be grateful." He had calmed down, and wasn't quite so angry anymore. He just sounded tired. Jodie couldn't blame him for being angry, she didn't know what she would do if she was half trapped in a mysterious substance.

"All right, I'll be back in a second." Getting up to her feet, Jodie went to return to her seat where her bag was sitting. She didn't get far before she was stopped by the elderly woman she had helped earlier.

"Miss?"

"Yes?" Jodie stopped in front of her, wondering if maybe she needed help finding some other pill. Like the trapped man, she appeared tired. Her lined face had managed to age further since Jodie had helped her get her pills. The bright red of her purse and her lipstick—now a shade of purple in the blue light—seemed even more vibrant as her thin skin had paled.

"I wanted to thank you again for your assistance earlier."

"Oh, you're welcome. I should be thanking you. I might have run outside the train if you hadn't grabbed my wrist."

The woman patted her hand. "I'm Roxanne."

"Jodie."

"Nice to meet you, Jodie, despite the circumstances."

"Likewise. I'm currently in the middle of something, but if you need anything I'd be happy to help."

"Thank you, deary."

"Is your dog all right?" Jodie spotted the corgi lying underneath the seats.

"He's a little shaken up, but he'll be all right." The

woman leaned down to pat the tailless rump poking out. Jodie took the opportunity to slip away.

Her bag was lying on her seat at the front, so, not wanting to disturb the downed mother, she lifted it up and over into the next row. These two seats weren't much different from the ones against the front. They were the same hard plastic, with the same thread-bare red fabric inlaid into the seat and back. The moulded curves of the seats discouraged passengers from taking up more than one spot, and their arrangement was an attempt to maximize space. While there were four, rear-facing seats in two rows opposite the driver's compartment, beyond the side doors immediately behind them, the rest of the seats followed a pattern: two or three sideways facing seats beside the doors with a row of forward and rear facing seats back-to-back between them. The pattern ended at the rear of the train car with forward facing seats against the wall on either side of the door that connected to the next car.

After locating her scissors, Jodie returned to the trapped man. As she knelt back down beside him, she thought of the elderly woman, Roxanne, and held out her hand.

"I never introduced myself. I'm Jodie."

"Eric." The man awkwardly shifted himself to shake her hand.

"All right, Eric, if you could try to sit up, I'll snip your coat free."

Once he'd propped himself up on his elbows, Jodie quickly set to work beneath his back. His jacket was a nice one, not some crazy expensive thing, but of good material, and Jodie felt badly for slicing off a piece.

"I have to shift to the other side to get the rest," Jodie told Eric as she withdrew the scissors from under him.

Eric sort of nodded his head to the side, telling her to go

ahead. Jodie moved around him and performed the final snips. Once the jacket was free, Jodie helped him get it off, then folded it up into something he could use as a pillow.

"Thanks," Eric said as he laid back down, the jacket under his head. "Those guys are idiots."

"Who?"

Eric gestured with his head toward the back of the train. Jodie turned to see what he was talking about. The big hydro guy apparently had some tools with him. He and a few others were investigating the windows and doors, trying to find a spot where they could create an opening and potentially escape.

"Why do you think they're idiots?" Jodie thought they were being proactive and couldn't see a problem with that.

"They're not going to find a way out of here. Even on the off chance they do, where are they going to go? I can't get much of a look outside, but this blue stuff is practically everywhere."

"And?"

"You felt it, right?"

"I did."

"Did you notice how smooth it is? Think it'd be easy to walk on, or even climb over?"

"I see your point." Jodie stroked the blue stuff again. It *was* remarkably smooth, slick even. "But it wouldn't be impossible, and there could be a way around it. We're not too far from the next station. At least they're trying."

Eric made a scoffing sound.

"So, you don't think you'd be helping them if you weren't trapped, mister runs-for-the-door even when this shit was still falling?"

A sour look crossed his face, and Eric turned his head away. A thought had crossed Jodie's mind at the same time, possibly explaining Eric's attitude toward the hydro guy and his helpers.

"Look, if they do find a way out of here, I won't leave you."

Eric turned his pale blue eyes back up at her. "Why would you do that?"

"I'm pretty sure I can't make it home from here, and I was heading to an interview that's probably even farther. Where would I go?"

Staring up at the ceiling, Eric turned within. Jodie sat down next to him and leaned against the nearest pole. She thought about leaning against the blue stuff, but decided against it. Although nothing bad happened when she touched it, constant contact sounded unappealing.

"So, where were you interviewing?" Eric turned his face back toward her.

"It was for an intern spot at Charliese."

"I have no idea what that is."

"A fashion company."

"Oh."

"What do you do?"

"I'm a real estate agent." Eric saw in her expression that she knew as much about that as he did about fashion. "I know, thrilling, right?"

Jodie gave him a smile. "Were you heading to, or from a house?"

"Neither. I was meeting with a prospective client. He owns a store in Yorkdale mall, and it was easier for him to meet me there for a quick lunch. I think the meeting went well. I expected to hear from him before the end of the day."

"I guess everyone's plans got screwed up today."

"Hers especially." Eric's head was past the barrier on either side of the door, leaving him with a mostly unobstructed view down the length of the car. He looked over at the mother, still crumpled beside the front door. "I guess we don't have a doctor with us."

"I'm sure someone would have spoken up if they were when Simon explained to everybody what happened to her."

"Simon? That the driver's name?"

"Yeah."

"He didn't really give the best explanation, at least not within hearing range of me. He mumbles a lot."

"Basically, she cracked her head on the window when we hit the blue stuff." The sound of it played sharply in Jodie's mind, causing her to pause. When she blinked, she could see the mother rolling her body to protect Apollo, taking the force of the impact to her head. Then she blinked again, and it was gone. "She's unconscious, but alive." Her voice wavered a bit, but Eric didn't seem to notice. "I thought it would be best not to move her. It's impossible to tell if her neck or spine have been injured."

"Makes sense."

"You two okay over here?"

Jodie turned to see the hydro guy striding up to them, his long legs not requiring many steps. He hunkered down near Eric, his dark, hooded eyes watching the blue stuff more than at them, as they peered out from his wide, flat face.

"Do you need anything?"

Eric rolled his eyes.

"We're fine, thank you," Jodie replied, giving him a smile.

"I'm Denzel, by the way."

"Jodie." She shook hands with the man, feeling the calluses on his palms and fingers.

"Eric." He didn't bother to shake hands because Denzel was squatting in a spot that made the angle too awkward.

"Mind if I check out this crap?" Denzel gestured to the glob covering Eric's legs.

"My blue stuff is your blue stuff," Eric sighed.

"Great."

Denzel stood back up and stepped next to the uneven blue wall. As he ran his hands all over the surface, Jodie suddenly imagined it becoming soft again. She could picture Denzel's dark and callused hands suddenly pressing through the goop. The motion would cause him to lose his balance and plunge headfirst into the stuff, where it would then solidify once more and kill him. Jodie tried to hide the shudder that ran up her spine.

The blue didn't soften, though. Once Denzel felt satisfied, he left to collect his tool bag from the back of the car. Jodie watched him as he went, and noticed that the people who had been helping him search the train had stopped. Apparently, they hadn't found anything good, and so they had split back up into individuals and appeared to be moping in their seats. When Denzel returned, he dropped his tool bag beside Eric, which hit with a heavy thud and a clang.

"Watch it!" Eric flinched, the tool bag having landed unexpectedly close to him. It sounded heavy enough to do some serious damage if it were to drop directly on top of a person.

"Sorry," Denzel said as he knelt down to search through his tools. He stood back up with a hammer, while sticking a file and a chisel into the back pockets of his jeans.

Running his free hand over the surface of the stuff again, Denzel picked a spot that wasn't too close to Eric.

"You might want to shield yourself as best you can. Just in case," Denzel spoke down to Eric.

"Great," Eric muttered. He took his jacket out from under his head and made a sort of tent out of it using his arms. It would only somewhat protect his face, but, unfortunately, there wasn't much else he could do.

Jodie got up and moved to the seat next to Eric's door. The top half of the panel that separated the door from the seats was transparent, so she could see what was going to happen from a safe location. As she moved, she noticed several other curious people watching. A few had even moved to closer seats to witness what might occur.

Denzel tried the hammer first. He swung it hard, as if to drive in a stubborn nail, and struck the blue. An odd sounding *thwok* was all he got. The blue was unmarked. He tried a few more times, just in case, but those weird *thwoks* were all that happened. Realizing it was no good, he turned the hammer around and tried the claw end. A slightly different *thwok* reverberated around the inside of the train. Pulling the chisel out of his back pocket, Denzel carefully set it against the blue, then smashed the hammer into its end. The chisel skittered across the blue stuff, moving so quickly that Denzel lost his grip on it, sending the chisel flying. Eric flinched as it struck his arm and then bounced off along the floor, coming to rest under a seat.

"You okay?" Jodie asked Eric.

"I'm fine, just lost my grip," Denzel answered, thinking she was talking to him.

"Well, your lost grip just gave me one hell of a bruise," Eric spoke bitterly up at him. He had lowered his coat tent and was holding his injured arm.

Denzel walked over to the seats and retrieved his chisel from beneath them.

"There is no way in hell you're trying that again," Eric said, as the hydro man came back over.

Denzel strode up to the blue and ran his hand over the surface where he had attempted to chisel it. With a sigh, he turned and put the chisel and hammer back into his bag. The action confirmed what Jodie's eyes told her: he hadn't made a scratch.

Lastly, Denzel tried his file. As he ran the serrated metal bar across the surface of the blue stuff, an awful squalling sound filled the train. Everyone but Denzel quickly covered they ears against the aural assault. He didn't stop, just kept filing, becoming more and more fierce as he went. A sort of manic energy filled him as he ran the file back and forth, back and forth, faster and faster. Just as his dark skin began to redden and sweat beaded on his forehead, Denzel stopped.

When the file was moved away, Jodie was excited to see a sort of powder on the blue, but then Denzel ran his hand over it. The powdery substance fell away, revealing an unmarked wall.

"What is that?" Jodie asked of the fine particles.

Denzel held out his file bar toward her, his eyes locked and staring at the blue before him. Jodie got off her seat and stepped closer to see. The file's teeth were worn down. Apparently the powdery stuff was metal shavings from the bar.

"What are we going to do?" a woman moaned.

"Calm down, the rescue workers will save us," a man replied.

"But that stuff is stronger than his tools!" a second woman retorted.

"The rescue workers will have better tools." This time it was the guy with the bike answering. "They'll have jackhammers, and blowtorches, and such. They'll be able to get us out."

"How can you possibly know that?" the first woman wailed.

"How can you know they can't?" the biker answered.

Several people started bickering at once. Jodie tried to block it out as she sat down next to Eric.

"Is your arm okay?" she asked. "Can I take a look?"

Eric held out his arm. Jodie undid the button on the cuff of his sleeve and rolled it to his elbow. A red welt had formed on his forearm.

"It's probably going to bruise, but it doesn't look too bad."

"Thanks."

Jodie had been holding Eric's hand to get a look at his forearm. When he lowered his arm to the floor, he continued to hold hers. Jodie felt her face redden, and quickly turned away to hide it, pretending to be more interested in the shouting match. She had been with good looking guys before, but never as attractive as she considered Eric, and only while pumped up with alcoholic courage. Last night's Steve couldn't hold a candle to him. Eric didn't hold her hand for long, as he soon gathered up his jacket and placed it under his head again.

"Everyone shut up!" Denzel the hydro worker bellowed, his voice echoing off the sides of the train.

Those that had been arguing, quickly shut their mouths.

"Bickering gets us nowhere, but pissed at each other," he said in the silence. Without another word, he returned his file to his tool bag, picked it up, and headed back toward his original seat.

Sulking, everyone followed suit.

Jodie reached up and let down her hair. She gave up on

having an interview today, and thought she'd be more comfortable with her hair free. The arguments of the others rang inside her head. It appeared there was absolutely no way for them to get themselves out of the subway train, and it wasn't going to be easy for rescue workers to get to them. This wasn't like a flood, or an ice storm; no one had dealt with this stuff before. They knew nothing about it.

Clasping her hands tightly in her lap, Jodie fought back tears.

7

APOLLO CAME RUNNING down the train toward the wall of the blue stuff.

"Sorry," Simon said as he trundled after the boy. "I thought letting him come see the... whatever it is, would distract him from his mom."

"Watch where you step, kid," Eric spoke to Apollo, who had come close to running him over.

Apollo *wapped* his hands against the surface of the wall, peering up through its almost transparent side. "It's like where the fishes are."

"The fishes? You mean like an aquarium?" Jodie wondered.

"Yes."

That felt kind of accurate, except they were the ones in the tank. Adding to the feeling was the fact that the light coming from outside was predominantly blue. A few small spots on the windows weren't covered, letting in regular sunlight, but most of it was filtered through the blue stuff, giving it a similar tint.

"You sure that's a good idea?" Jodie got to her feet and spoke quietly to Simon. "I mean, with the..." She didn't finish and just gestured toward the blue wall where the dead were still suspended.

"I told him there were statues in the blue stuff," Simon explained. "That it was art. He seems to have understood. Apparently, there's some statues in the mall he and his mother had been to."

Jodie wished she could picture them as just statues or as performance art.

"Could someone tell this kid to move over? He's practically stepping on me," Eric pleaded up at them.

"Apollo," Jodie moved up behind the child, "you have to watch where you're going. It's not nice to step on people."

Apollo looked down at Eric and moved away. "Sorry. Why are you lying on the ground?"

"Come on, Apollo. Eric's tired, we should leave him alone." Jodie took Apollo's hand and began to lead him away.

"He's got his legs sticking through the window wall. Can I stick my legs through the window wall, too?" Apollo asked, as Jodie sat him down across from Roxanne.

"No, you can't."

"Why not? Does he not want to share?"

Jodie held back a giggle. "You felt how hard it was, right? Well, you can't get your legs through something that solid. And Eric is stuck. He can't get his legs out."

"Stuck?"

"Yeah."

"Like when Muffin got stuck in the crawl space? And we had to call a man to come get him out?"

"Sure, like that."

"Have you called a man to help him get out?"

"Yes, someone is coming to help Eric." Jodie stood up, intending to leave Apollo again. She thought that now might be a good time to go through his mother's things. A quiet thought had been nagging at the back of her mind; she was wondering if Apollo might be allergic to something, or have asthma. If he did have a medical condition, they should try to find out before something serious happened.

"What's the boy's name?" Roxanne asked before Jodie could go anywhere.

"Apollo."

"He reminds me of one of my grandsons." Roxanne leaned over so that she could see Apollo who was blocked by Jodie. "Hello, Apollo."

"Hi," Apollo said shyly.

"Would you like a bit of candy? I think I have some in my purse."

"I'm not suppose to take candy from strangers."

"Well, my name is Roxanne. Would you like to talk a bit? And then we won't be strangers anymore."

Apollo's face scrunched up comically as he thought. "Okay," he eventually said, the lure of candy probably being too much. He slid off his seat and then climbed onto the one beside Roxanne.

While he was distracted, Jodie walked to the end of the train where his mother was still collapsed in an uncomfortable looking heap. Maybe she should be moved, but Jodie still thought she shouldn't try.

"What are you doing?" Simon had followed her and sounded mildly concerned when Jodie crouched down.

"I'm going to go through her stuff. I want to make sure Apollo doesn't have a medical condition. I mean, what if he has type 2 diabetes and needs to take a shot of insulin or something? What if he has a puffer?"

"You're thinking of type 1," Simon corrected her. "I see your point, though. Need any help?"

"No, I'm fine, thank you." Jodie then realized that while he stood there, his large body blocked off the view from the rest of the train. "Although, you can supervise. You know, verify that I'm not stealing or anything in case someone asks."

"Okay."

With Simon blocking her, people probably wouldn't even notice that Jodie was about to go through the woman's personal effects. But before doing anything, Jodie felt for the woman's pulse. It was weak, but she was able to find it after a moment. She also placed a hand near the woman's mouth to feel for her breath. It was as faint as her pulse.

The woman wore a backpack, which was probably what had kept her on her side, rather than flopping over onto her back when Apollo had being trying to squirm free of her protective hold. Jodie decided to start there and carefully unzipped the outer pockets first, and then moved into the main compartment. There were a variety of things in her bag. Jodie came across spare clothes for Apollo, a small blanket, a bundle of tissues and baby wipes, a few packages of crackers, cookies, and health bars, two juice boxes, a kind of sippy-cup half full of water, a trio of toys, some cosmetics, a bottle of aspirin, a few pads and tampons, far too much partly-used lip balm, a nail file, and a wallet. The wallet was the most interesting item.

"What are you doing?" Simon whispered as Jodie made to open it.

"I want to know her name. Also, she might have Apollo's health card in here."

Simon shifted his weight from foot to foot. He had gotten more and more uncomfortable with this, the longer it took. Nevertheless, he gestured for her to continue.

Jodie opened the wallet and, ignoring the cash, went straight to the card slots. She located the woman's driver's license and read the name on it.

"Olivia Foster," she told Simon.

Simon gestured impatiently for her to hurry up.

Looking through the rest of the cards, Jodie had been right about the mother carrying Apollo's health card. It seemed his name really was Apollo, he hadn't been lying about it. He also didn't have any illnesses or allergies, or at least nothing the card mentioned. The fact that aspirin was the only medication Jodie had found in the backpack also suggested that there was nothing to worry about. She told Simon as much.

"Okay, now put it all back." Simon glanced over his shoulder. He was sweating. Maybe they would be questioned about what they were doing after all.

Jodie returned everything to the backpack except for a toy train engine that she thought Apollo might like to play with. While she was zipping up the bag, she noticed a square lump in Olivia's pocket.

"What are you doing now?" Simon whined as she reached for it.

"She has a phone." Jodie didn't know what useful information she could get from the phone, but she pulled it out of Olivia's pocket anyway. Apparently, Olivia had missed seven calls since this blue crap had come down. The phone was set to silent, which would explain why no one had heard it ringing. Jodie looked at the missed calls and saw that they were all from someone named Bruce. Jodie couldn't be sure, but she thought that he was probably her husband, Apollo's father.

"What are you doing?" Simon asked again.

"I think her husband has been calling." Jodie showed him the phone. "Should we call him back? Tell him what happened? He could tell us if there's anything about Apollo we missed."

Simon shifted his weight back and forth again. "Go on, go on."

Jodie pressed the few buttons needed to call back the number that had been trying to reach Olivia. It was picked up on the second ring.

"Olive? Are you okay? Is Apollo okay?" a frantic male voice answered.

"Is this Bruce?" Jodie asked.

"Yes, who is this?"

"My name is Jodie."

"Why do you have my wife's cell phone?" He now sounded both frantic and angry.

"Your wife has hit her head and is unconscious."

Silence filled the line.

"Bruce?"

"Is Apollo okay?"

"Yes, he's perfectly fine."

"Are you a nurse, or a doctor?"

"Uh, no."

"Who the hell are you then?"

"I'm not really anyone?" her unease about how to answer turned her tone into a question. "I'm just another passenger on the subway train. I was next to your wife when she hit her head."

"Subway train?"

"Yes, we're between the Yorkdale and Lawrence West stations. This blue gunk has us trapped inside."

"*Mother fuck!*" The voice was distant, away from the phone, but even if Bruce was covering the microphone with his hand, he had shouted loudly enough for Jodie to hear him quite clearly. "My son is okay?" the voice came back.

"Completely fine. He doesn't have any medical conditions, or allergies, or anything like that, does he?"

"No, no. Nothing like that. He's a perfect little boy." His voice was stressing through a variety of emotions that Jodie was having trouble keeping up with.

"We're taking good care of him, sir."

"Don't call me sir!" he snapped. "Sorry. Sorry. He's okay."

"Yes." Jodie wondered how many more times she'd have to reconfirm that. She thought about telling him how his wife had been injured protecting his son, but then thought better of it.

"You said you're between Yorkdale and Lawrence West?"

"We are."

"Okay, I'm coming to you then."

"We're trapped in the train. There's no way in or out."

"I'm coming there!" The line suddenly disconnected.

Jodie pulled the phone away from her ear, confirming its disconnection by checking the screen.

"He's-"

"I heard," Simon nodded. "Now put her phone back."

Before she did, Jodie turned the device off. Its battery might come in handy later. Once it was back in Olivia's pocket, she stood up, and then she and Simon returned to where Apollo was sitting with Roxanne.

"Hey, Apollo. I thought you might want this." Jodie held out the toy train.

"Thomas!" he cried, quickly taking it from her.

"What do you say when someone gives you something?" Roxanne scolded him.

"Thank you," he said without looking at Jodie.

Roxanne stroked the boy's hair affectionately just before he dropped off his seat to play with the toy on the floor.

"Look, Happy! Thomas didn't crash!" Apollo showed the shy corgi his train.

Jodie walked the few steps needed to reach Eric and sat down next to him again.

"Find anything interesting?" he asked her in a quiet voice.

"What do you mean?"

"I could see you going through the woman's stuff." He gestured with his head. "The fat guy's legs aren't as fat as his stomach."

"Don't call him fat, his name is Simon."

"Doesn't make him thin. So, find anything interesting?"

"I was checking through her things to make sure Apollo doesn't have any medical issues we should know about," Jodie informed him.

"And?"

"He doesn't."

"Who'd you call?"

Apparently Eric had had quite the view from his position on the floor. "The mother's husband. He says he's going to come here."

"Yeah? What's he think he's going to do?"

"I don't know. Just be here, I guess."

"I would give anything not to be here right now."

Jodie shifted and straightened out her skirt. Although she felt the same way, in the back of her mind she was somewhat hurt by that remark. There was no reason to be, it wasn't aimed at her at all, but logic had never been able to change her emotional temperament.

"I hope we get out of here soon," Eric sighed up at the ceiling.

8

WHRANG! *Whrang! Whrang!*

Jodie had been lost in her thoughts, thinking about the bar last night, when the sound of metal striking metal solidified her spine, shocking her into an upright position.

"What's that asshole doing now?" Eric wondered, looking down the length of the train.

It was hard to answer Eric's question without getting up. All they could see from where they were was a group of people hovering around the last set of doors.

"I'm betting it's that Denzel guy," Eric said, clarifying which asshole he was talking about.

Apollo had crawled out from under the seats and was sitting next to Roxanne, his eyes wide, with her protective arm wrapped around his shoulders. Simon, the driver, was sitting on the sideways seats in front of them, his sweaty hands wrapped around the pole along the edge of the barrier between the door and the seats. His foot was tapping in an agitated manner.

Seeing that no one else in their little group was going to check, Jodie got up and headed toward the gathering, where the sound was rhythmically continuing. She squeezed herself between the bicycle guy and another tall man, taking up a position in front of them so she could see. Eric had been right, it was Denzel creating the ruckus. He stood before the doors with a hammer, which he was smashing into their lower sections, over and over again. The doors were buckling and warping with every strike.

"What's he doing?" she asked a petite Asian woman standing beside her. The woman silently shook her head. Jodie turned to another woman standing on her other side and repeated the question.

"The stuff we're stuck in doesn't completely cover this door," she said, her large eyes not turning away from the action. "Denzel is hoping he can open a hole wide enough to get us out."

Her fluttering, bird-like voice sounded very familiar. She was definitely the woman who had started the argument earlier, and could even be the panicky woman who had set off the stampede that had resulted in several of the train's passengers being killed.

The noise of Denzel's blows was taking on a different quality now. It began to sound more and more like the times he had hit the blue stuff, directly. Jodie watched as, drenched in sweat, he gave up and collapsed to the floor. The door had been bent out of shape a fair amount, with the ground visible through it, but Jodie could tell it wasn't open enough for anyone to get out, especially the bigger guys like Denzel. That didn't stop the panicky woman from trying, though. She ran up to the opening and attempted to squeeze out, feet first, without any luck. She got jammed half way up her thighs. Crying silently, she pulled herself back out, then retreated toward her seat in the middle of the train car. Muttering and cursing, everyone else drifted back to their own seats as well. Denzel stayed where he was, collapsed against the barrier next to the door, his muscles quivering. Jodie thought about saying something, but didn't know what. Instead, she decided to check out the back of the train while she was there. Walking to the rear door that connected to the next car, she peered into it through the window and the blue. That car was empty. One of its doors wasn't covered which had allowed the people inside to escape.

"It's just a girl checking out the other train car." Jodie heard a voice speak behind her.

Realizing she was the one being talked about, she turned around. It was the punk kid with the large jacket. He was sitting next to a middle-aged man who wore dark sunglasses that hid much of his face beneath his short hair and a flat head. He held a white cane between his feet. The man leaned over and whispered in the younger guy's ear.

"You can tell her that. She's looking right at us," the guy replied.

The blind man became flustered.

"He says you smell nice," the younger guy told Jodie.

"Thank you," Jodie replied, stepping a bit closer.

"What scent is it?" the blind man asked her. "Watermelon?"

"It is." Jodie stood there awkwardly, not knowing what to say or do next.

"Hey, is that guy down there okay?" the kid in the coat asked, gesturing toward the front of the train.

Jodie wasn't entirely sure who he might be talking about. She suspected it was Eric, but it could just as easily be Olivia if he hadn't heard Simon telling people about her earlier.

"The guy trapped in the goo," he clarified when Jodie hesitated. "I saw you sitting with him."

"Oh, Eric. Yeah, he's okay. Frustrated as hell, but he's not hurt or anything."

"That's good," the kid nodded. "I'm Troy, by the way." He held out his hand in a gesture of politeness that Jodie hadn't expected. His facial features were also softer than she had thought, when he first entered the train. Apparently, it was only the expression he had worn at the time that made him look hard. With his slightly too long, floppy hair he could almost look dorky. Almost.

She shook his offered hand, "Jodie."

"And this is-"

"Ed." Tthe blind man also held out his hand in Jodie's direction.

"Nice to meet you both." She shook it as well.

"Troy, here, is a good kid. Been spending all his time filling me in on what's going on," Ed told her.

"I told you to stop calling me a kid," Troy rolled his eyes.

"You're twenty-one years old, that makes you a kid in my eyes."

Troy opened his mouth as if to retort, but then after a quick glance at Jodie, he shut it again.

"Well, I should head back to my end of the car. I'm sure the people I'm sitting with are wondering what's happened over here."

"All right. Maybe we'll come by later and see what things are like over there," Ed smiled at her.

Jodie reflexively smiled back, then made to return to Eric, Simon, Roxanne, and Apollo. As she walked away, she heard Troy whisper something to Ed, but couldn't make out the words.

Since she was travelling the length of the train, Jodie

decided to make the trip more useful. As she walked, she counted how many people there were on board. By the time she reached Eric and had counted those in the front, she discovered that there were twenty-six people still on the train, including Olivia. Twenty-seven if she wanted to include the dog.

"So what was Denzel doing?" Eric asked, as Roxanne and Simon looked on curiously, also wondering what the answer was.

"He was smashing his hammer into a door, trying to bend it outward enough for us to escape."

"I don't suppose he succeeded?" Simon asked hopefully.

Jodie shook her head. "He made an opening, but it's not large enough for anyone to squeeze out." As she said that, her eyes fell on Apollo. He might be small enough to fit through the opening. But even if he could, what then? The boy would be alone out there, and there was nothing he'd be able to do to help them.

Without anything else to do, Jodie went to the front and sat with her bag. She wanted to be alone for a bit, or at least as alone as she could get in this train. It was all just too much. Taking out her phone, she called her dad again. She told him everything that had happened on the train since her last call. There was nothing new on his end, or at least nothing he was going to tell Jodie. It was likely he had heard something over his police radio. If he hadn't heard anything, that was bad, but if he had heard something and wasn't telling Jodie, it was worse.

"How's Amber?"

"She's fine. One of the doors at her office wasn't covered, so she's free to move around. Her house is buried though, and Todd's trapped inside."

"What was Todd doing at home?" Todd was Amber's fiancé and would normally be at work this time of day.

"I don't know. Maybe he forgot something and had to go back for it."

"What's Amber doing? Still at work?"

"No, the power's out there. She was heading for our place last I heard."

"That's a long walk."

"She has nothing else to do."

Jodie was glad. She hoped Amber would be able to get into their apartment building and take care of Rusty.

"We shouldn't be wasting our cells' batteries anymore. I want you to turn off your phone until tomorrow, okay? That's only if you don't get out, of course. If you're freed, try to call me right away."

"Okay," Jodie sighed. Her mind wanted to reject the idea of being trapped overnight, but also knew to be realistic. With this stuff all over the city, clean up wouldn't be quick.

"I'll check in on you in the morning, say, nine a.m.? If you get out of the train, leave me a text message."

"All right. Dad?"

"Yeah?"

"I wish you were here."

"I wish I was there too, potato. I love you."

"I love you, too."

"Talk to you later."

"Bye."

Jodie reluctantly hung up her phone. She then held the power button down until it turned off, the screen going dark. To resist the temptation to turn it back on, Jodie stuck her phone inside the big pocket of her bag, instead of the small side pocket where she usually kept it when she had no pockets in her clothing. Seeing her lunch bag, Jodie decided it was probably a good idea to eat something. She wasn't very hungry, and her stomach felt like it was tied up in knots, but putting something in there might help her feel better.

Looking down the train, Jodie again wondered how many of these people had food. Did Simon have anything? Did Roxanne? Should she share, or just keep everything for herself?

After taking out the pair of apples, Jodie located one of her small art scalpels and used it to cut both apples in half. It was tedious work with the tiny blade, but the scalpel was sharp and the work was something to focus on. She had wrapped the apples in a paper towel before packing them, and now used the towel to carry them in a bundle once they were cut. Thinking Apollo might also be hungry, Jodie knelt down beside Olivia and went through her bag again.

"What are you doing?" Simon called to her, getting up out of his seat.

Jodie held up the snack bar she had located. "Just getting this for Apollo," she replied. "Thought he might be hungry."

Walking back over to the others, Jodie handed the snack bar to Apollo.

"Thank you," he replied, shredding the wrapper.

"Apple?" Jodie turned to Roxanne and offered her a half.

"No, thank you, dear," Roxanne waved her off with a smile.

"Apple?" Jodie turned to Eric next.

"Yes, please. Thank you." Eric reached up and Jodie handed him a half.

"Simon?"

"Thanks," Simon accepted the offering.

Wrapping up the extra half in the paper towel, Jodie sat down near Eric again, and set to work eating her own half. The train was almost silent, with everyone lost in their own thoughts. Jodie thought about her apple core, and whether she should try eating it.

9

WHUMP-WHUMP-WHUMP-WHUMP-WHUMP-WHUMP.

The sound wasn't coming from inside the train this time. Everyone who could, got to their feet and pressed their faces to the window.

"There!" a woman with a massive mane of red hair pointed out the east facing windows.

The people who had been searching out the west side, Jodie included, moved quickly to the other side of the train. Eric, trapped on the west side, struggled to find a position which allowed him to see out of the windows behind him.

"It's a helicopter," Simon observed, pointing toward the back of the train.

A helicopter was indeed slowly making its way south, following the Allan.

"There's another one over here," Eric called out.

Jodie moved up next to him and peered through the wall of blue. Over the frozen bodies, she could see a helicopter in the distance, also making its way south. Even farther beyond it, there was a third that could be seen only because it was flying higher than the others.

"There's a whole bunch of them," a man down the train commented.

Jodie returned to the east facing windows and looked back out at the one that was flying close by. There were more beyond it, including one heading east, possibly following the 401 highway.

"What are they doing?" the guy with the bike wondered.

"Checking out the damage, I imagine," a tall man responded.

"Hey! Hey, we're in here!" the panic woman called out and waved her hands as the helicopter approached the train.

"Shut up, he can't hear you!" a male's voice chastised her.

She fell silent, but when Jodie glanced down the train, she saw that the woman was still waving her arms. She was tempted to do the same.

"They must be assessing the damage," said the cyclist who was standing next to Jodie, agreeing with the tall man.

Nobody said anything to the contrary as they watched the helicopter trundle past, its blades filling the air with noise. After it went by them, but while it was still within sight, Jodie switch to the other side of the train again to look at the helicopters there. They had made roughly the same amount of progress and were continuing to head south.

"I wonder where they're from?" Eric spoke up.

"What do you mean?" Jodie assumed they had come from Pearson International airport.

"I was wondering if they're all from around here, or if maybe the cavalry has arrived from somewhere else."

"Oh. No idea."

"Think the States will send in support?"

"The US probably did this to us," the tall man responded.

"Yeah, right," the cyclist retorted. "Why the hell would the United States attack us? We're their ally."

"Maybe they didn't want to test an experimental weapon on their own soil?" a guy about Jodie's age and wearing house painter's clothes suggested.

"Again, why choose us over one of their enemies? Or Mexico?" the cyclist continued.

"Look, whether it was the States or not makes no difference to us," the red headed woman interjected. "The government out there is dealing with the why and the how. Trapped inside this subway train, I think we have more important matters to deal with than coming up with random theories."

"I still think it was the US," the tall man said.

"Then think that all you want, but there's no point in starting an argument over it." The redhead, having had her say, promptly returned to her seat. Others began to do the same.

Jodie continued to watch the helicopters for a little bit, but her eyes drifted downward, away from the distant vehicles and toward the closer ones. Not far from the subway's side was a chain link fence. The lower half of it was covered by a wooden barrier, but the subway's windows were higher than that, giving Jodie a good view of the Allan's southbound traffic. Jodie hadn't looked at the cars much, mentally having compared them to the trapped people outside. If it weren't for the fence that had dispersed those people left and right, a lot more of them would be visible from inside the subway car, but instead, they were below the windows alongside the train. The thought made Jodie shudder, but movement in the vehicles on the road turned her thoughts away. The cars *weren't* like the bodies, but rather, they were similar to the subway train. The only differences were the smaller spaces and fewer people.

One car in particular stood out. The sedan's red side had a more purple tint when viewed through the blue, but that's not what drew Jodie's attention. The car was tilted on an angle, its front wheels no longer resting on the pavement. It wasn't a dramatic incline, but it made it different from the other cars. It was close too, resting in the left hand lane, the lane nearest the train. Jodie could see a man inside, sitting behind the steering wheel, looking up through his windshield at the retreating helicopters. He glanced toward the train and then did an actual double take as he spotted Jodie watching him. He smiled and waved, then quickly grabbed something off the seat beside him. It was a small whiteboard with bold, capital letters written on its surface in black marker.

HELLO

Jodie waved back. The man seemed relieved to have made contact. The fact that he already had the words written down suggested to Jodie that he had tried earlier without success. The man looked down and erased the words on the whiteboard, then wrote new ones upon it. When he held it up again, it took a moment for Jodie to decipher them. Not only were the letters smaller to fit within the space, but he had written with a kind of short hand usually found in internet comments.

EVY1 OK?

I'M A DR.

Jodie didn't know how to respond. She couldn't just

nod, that would be a lie. Not everyone was okay. Coming up with an idea, Jodie held up one finger, hoping the man understood she needed a minute. Then again, it wasn't like he could go anywhere.

Hurrying over to where her bag was, she drew the attention of those sitting nearest to her, as well as a few others. Digging into the backpack, she located her largest sketchpad and a dark pen. She thought about using a marker, but knew it would only bleed through the paper and use up more than just one sheet at a time. She didn't know how many sheets she might need.

"What are you doing?" Simon asked, as Jodie went back to the seat next to Eric, kneeling on it as close to the window as she could get.

"There's a guy in a car out there communicating with me," she said as she wrote her own message. She traced over the letters several times, hoping they were good enough for him to read. "He says he's a doctor."

Simon, who had been sitting on the opposite side of the train, got up and stood next to Eric. Roxanne also looked out the window beside her, as did several other people who had overheard Jodie.

Finishing her message, Jodie pressed her sketchpad against the window. She had more surface area to work with than the doctor had, and was able to write a longer message.

WOMAN HIT HEAD
UNCONSCIOUS ADVICE?

The doctor squinted a lot and pressed his face right up against his window as he read Jodie's words. After a moment, he seemed to understand them, and turned to his whiteboard.

MOVE
HER?

The doctor also pointed at Jodie as part of his message. Jodie shook her head, understanding he was asking if she had moved Olivia. He wrote again.

BLOOD?

Once more Jodie shook her head. Even though she couldn't say she had done a thorough inspection, she would have noticed if the woman had been bleeding a significant amount. She held up her pad again, pointing to the word advice. The doctor shrugged and shook his own head. He then wrote something else.

PRAY

Deflated, Jodie sat back on her heels, her sketchpad sinking into her lap. She had hoped the doctor would have been able to tell her something, anything, that she could do for Apollo's mom.

"We should all take his advice and pray for our salvation," a voice startled Jodie.

She turned around to find what appeared to be almost everyone on the train gathered either behind her or up against the windows. Word of the doctor had travelled quickly from one end of the train car to the other, and they had all come to see.

"Put a cork in it, Nina," a middle-aged black woman sighed at the speaker.

"No, we should listen to him," Nina said, looking around the group. Jodie observed that she was the panicky woman. "We should all pray. This is a plague from God. Clearly he's angry with us."

People started to wander away, many shaking their heads.

"Surely you must understand what I mean?" Nina turned to the woman with the flowing fabric and head shawl who had the cross tattoo on her forehead. Jodie remembered that the woman had been sitting not far from her when the train was moving, and realized she was one of the few who had changed seats after the blue stuff hit.

The woman simply directed her seemingly permanent scowl in Nina's direction, then turned and walked away.

"Wouldn't any of you like to pray with me?" Nina sounded crushed as everyone continued to ignore her.

"I will. I'll pray with you." It was Ed. Troy had led him toward the front of the train.

"Me too," Simon said.

In the end, five people were going to pray with Nina. They formed a kind of oblong circle on the floor next to a subway pole, just a little farther back from where Jodie sat.

"If you're going to stay that close, pray silently," Eric commented. He seemed more irritated than usual. He probably hadn't liked that everyone had gathered around so close, with him not being able to get up off the floor.

No one in the prayer circle answered him, but they kept their prayers to a polite whisper.

"Your end of the train is interesting," Troy commented, taking a seat across from Jodie. "An unconscious woman, a doctor in a car, a guy trapped in blue gunk, and now a prayer circle. All we have is a large dent in a door, and a frustrated hydro guy."

Jodie realized then that Denzel was one of the few people who hadn't joined the group.

"Is he okay?" she asked.

"Fine, I guess," Troy shrugged. "Just really angry. I have a feeling he's going to start punching stuff soon. I don't know if you noticed, but people are beginning to migrate this way, worried about what he'll do."

Jodie leaned forward and looked down the length of the train. Troy was right, a lot fewer people were sitting at the rear of the car. They had gathered their things and moved up, even if it meant sitting closer to strangers.

"Fuck him," Eric commented.

"You watch your language," Roxanne chastised him. "There's a child present."

Eric just rolled his eyes.

"He's trying," Jodie said about Denzel. "You can't blame him for that."

"I can blame him for this bruise on my arm," Eric reminded her.

It seemed as though there would be no soothing Eric, so Jodie didn't bother trying.

"So, where were you all headed before this hit?" Troy asked.

"I was going to an interview," Jodie told him.

Eric kept his mouth shut, and turned his head the other way. He clearly had no interest in talking at the moment.

"I had been on my way to visit my daughter," Roxanne told them.

"The little guy, that's his mom at the front, right?" Troy glanced toward the front of the train at Olivia.

"Yeah."

"What's your name?" Apollo suddenly stopped playing with his train and gazed up at Troy. Maybe he had picked up on the fact that he or his mom were being talked about.

"I'm Troy." He leaned over his knees, bringing his face closer to the child. "What's your name?"

"I'm Apollo."

"So I'm an ancient Greek city, and you're a Roman God."

"What?"

"Never mind."

"Where were you going, Troy?" Jodie asked.

"Downtown to do some shopping."

"Uh huh." Roxanne looked him up and down. "And your school just lets you do that?"

"I'm twenty-one," Troy sat upright. "I'm not some high schooler like everyone keeps assuming I am."

"And you don't have any college courses?" Roxanne challenged him.

"I happen to be between semesters at the moment. The courses I was taking didn't appeal to me after all. And I attended University, thank you very much, not college."

"Oh, what University?" Jodie tried to steer the conversation to a less combative one. "UofT?"

"Yeah. I had been in computer sciences up until the end of last year. Then I hit a sort of wall and couldn't bring myself to go back. I'm currently looking for a job until I figure out what I want to do."

"You don't have a job, and yet you were going shopping?" Roxanne observed.

Troy bristled. "I live with my mom, she was sending me to get something for her."

Roxanne merely rolled her eyes and returned her attention to Apollo.

"What was your interview for?" Troy turned to Jodie. "Anything I can apply for?"

"Depends on whether you know fashion."

"Clothing store? Because I could fake that."

"No, intern position with a fashion design company."

"Can't fake that. Think you would have gotten the position?"

Jodie shrugged. "Impossible to say."

"I would have hired you."

"You haven't seen my portfolio."

"I don't need to." Troy looked into her eyes a little longer than was warranted.

Jodie flushed slightly and turned away, pulling the hem of her skirt a bit lower. It appeared that blind Ed and Troy were of the same opinion when it came to Jodie: they both found something pleasing about her.

"Why don't you show it to us?" Eric suddenly rejoined the conversation.

"Show you?" Jodie flushed a little more, unsure what he was talking about.

"Your portfolio."

"Oh. I don't think it would be that interesting to you guys."

"I'm trapped in a wall, trust me, anything to keep my mind off of that is interesting."

"I like art," Troy added pointlessly.

Jodie sighed and stood up. "All right, I'll show you."

She walked to the front of the train again, carrying her sketchpad with her so that she could return it to her bag. When she got there though, she decided to keep it out, propping it up on her seat. She'd need it again if they were to communicate with the doctor some more.

"I'm sorry if I made you uncomfortable," Troy startled her by speaking from close behind her. She hadn't heard him walk up.

"You're making me uncomfortable now," she told him.

"Sorry." He took a step back, raising his hands. "I realized that my comment could have been taken the wrong way. I meant I'd hire you because you're nice, and non-judgemental." His ears were slightly more pink than they had been earlier. Jodie was already getting used to the blue filter, her mind adapting.

"Okay."

"That's all I wanted to say," he turned and walked back toward the others.

As Jodie grabbed the bag containing her portfolio, she realized she was a bit hungry. Maybe the apple half had set off her stomach. Looking into her backpack, she thought about the sandwiches inside. In the end, she shook her head and picked up the remaining apple half she had dropped on the seat while getting her large sketchpad. This time, she wasn't going to share it with anyone.

Returning to the others, Jodie handed Eric the large, black, folder-like book that served as her portfolio. Troy sat down beside him so that they could flip through it at the same time. Jodie sat in the doorway across from them and unwrapped the remains of the apple. The paper towel had sucked some of the juices out, but it was still good. Even though it kind of grossed her out, she ate the core as well.

"I like this one," Eric commented, holding the portfolio up so that Jodie could see what page he was on. It was an asymmetrical dress that Jodie had made after being inspired by lizards at the zoo. Although predominantly green, it had a colour fade, and the hem was a vivid blue. There were also carefully placed sequins in small groups to suggest a kind of scaly pattern. Her teacher hadn't been that keen on it, but everyone knew he really hated sequins, and all the other students had liked it. In her portfolio were her original sketches, as well as front and back photos of the actual dresses she had made garbed on a mannequin, plus another set of photos of her dresses worn by a model. The model was just another student from the college, and the photography class had taken the photos for her. Nothing she made after graduating had such a nice display, which is why several school pieces remained in the portfolio. At home, she had trouble finding a blank wall against which to take simple pictures of her mannequins, let alone a whole studio of free photographers eager to make something that looked professional.

The guys continued to peruse the portfolio, not commenting on very much. Troy pointed out one to Jodie that he really liked. It was one that Jodie had debated not including. It was a heavy, beige dress, with a symmetrical cut but an asymmetrical pattern of lines criss-crossing around it. The lines were thin, and made of white, faux-fur, which Jodie had also used as trim around the collar and hem of the dress. She had based it on a blanket she had seen at her sister's, but wasn't too happy with the result. Her dad had really liked it though, and Sandra even borrowed it to wear to a winter wedding, so she had used it to fill the hole in her portfolio.

Jodie thanked them when they picked out the ones they liked. Thinking of school, and especially Sandra, made her heart hurt. She really hoped her friend was okay. There were so many people she worried about, not knowing where they were, or if they were okay. She thought of her sister walking around out there, alone, trying to get to the apartment that Jodie shared with her dad. How many other people were out there? How many were able to escape whatever car or building they were in when *it*—whatever *it* was—happened, only to have nowhere to go? To have nowhere they could get to? Where did the people from the train car behind this one go? And would they come back? Would they bring help? Was help even coming?

10

"I HAVE TO PEE," Apollo announced to everyone within hearing range. "Where's the bathroom?"

Roxanne looked around for help. There was no bathroom on the subway.

"What about the hole Denzel made at the base of that door?" Troy pointed toward the back of the train. "Think he could pee out that?"

"It's certainly big enough," Jodie agreed. She had since returned her portfolio and was lying uncomfortably across a row of three seats. The moulded plastic bits between them kept pressing into various points on her body. She had been trying to find out if there was any comfortable position to lie in, but so far hadn't had any luck.

"Take my hand, Apollo." Roxanne stood up, using the seat back to help her. It was the first time Jodie had seen her stand since the accident. Just that bit of effort seemed to wind her somewhat. Jodie remembered the pill she had had to take and wondered if there was something wrong with her heart.

"I can take him," Jodie offered.

"No, no. It's all right." Roxanne straightened her spine, placing her palms against her lower back to do so. "I need the exercise," she laughed.

"I'd like to come anyway," Jodie said as she stood up. "Could use a stretch."

"Do you need any male assistance?" Troy wondered, making no move to stand. He had been sitting sideways on the other row of three, his back against the barrier next to the door, and his feet up on the seats.

"We should be fine." Roxanne gave him a strained smile, still not liking him very much, then held her hand out to Apollo.

Apollo wrapped his fingers around hers, but then turned back at his mom.

"I'll keep an eye on her, buddy," Troy told him.

"You'll get me if she wakes up?" Apollo asked him in a small voice.

"Right away. I'm sure you're the first thing she'd want to see when she's done resting."

Apollo looked at his mom again. "Okay."

Roxanne picked up her dog's leash from the seat and gave it a light tug. "Come on, Happy."

The shiny corgi wiggled his plump body out from beneath the seats he had chosen as his hiding place. His fur must have been a golden yellow, but it really reflected the blue light streaming through the windows giving it a strong blue-green tint. The dog's jaws were split apart as he panted, his face a big grin that was presumably his namesake.

"Can I walk him?" Apollo asked.

"Sure, just don't pull hard." Roxanne handed the boy the dog's leash.

Jodie led the way for Roxanne, Apollo, and Happy.

They passed the prayer circle of people first, who, for the most part, were no longer praying. All but their leader, Nina, had moved to the seats and were sitting quietly. Nina herself was cross-legged, her eyes closed, her lips moving rapidly but silently.

They had to pause briefly when they came to the cyclist and the tall man. They were sitting on opposite sides of the train and tossing the cyclist's helmet back and forth like a ball. As soon as Jodie, Roxanne, and Apollo were beyond them, they resumed their tossing.

The red headed woman had a book and seemed like she was trying to read, but even Jodie could see she wasn't really focused on it. Her eyes kept wandering away. She watched as the group of three plus Happy walked past her toward the back. A few other people were reading as well, but only one looked like she was really into her book. It was the girl that Jodie had seen while waiting at the station, the one with the small star tattoo on her knee.

When they reached the back of the train, they found Denzel sitting next to the hole he had made, his back turned to them.

"Denzel?" Jodie spoke softly to the hydro worker.

The man glanced over his shoulder at her. The skin around his eyes was raw, as if he had been crying or at least rubbing at them, but the eyes themselves were perfectly clear.

"What is it?" he asked a little gruffly.

"Apollo here has to pee." Jodie gestured to the boy. "Do you think that opening you made is good to use as a toilet?"

Denzel looked from the kid to the opening. "Yeah, sure. Go ahead." He stood up and dusted off his pants. Then, taking his tool bag with him, he moved to a nearby seat.

"Don't look," Apollo told Roxanne and Jodie.

"I do solemnly swear not to look," Roxanne told him, holding up one hand while placing the other over her heart.

Apollo handed her Happy's leash, and then looked at Jodie.

"I promise," she said while turning around.

Both Jodie and Roxanne faced away from Apollo, standing shoulder to shoulder to shield the little boy from view, while Happy sniffed at something near the seats. It took at least half a minute, but eventually they heard the sound of a small stream of urine hitting the ground outside.

"I'm done. Where do I wash my hands?" Apollo wondered.

Jodie had no idea. She had water, but she didn't want to waste any of it on hand washing.

"Did you get any pee on your hands?" Denzel asked.

Apollo made his way around Jodie and Roxanne. "I don't know. I don't think so."

"You can probably just wipe them on your pants then," Denzel shrugged.

Roxanne *tsked* him, then dug through her purse. "Just wait a moment. I have some wipes in here."

"Apollo's mom has some, too," Jodie remembered.

"You went through her things?" Denzel frowned.

Jodie remembered that not many people knew she had done that. "I wanted to make sure Apollo didn't have diabetes, or asthma, or something."

Denzel was clearly judging her, but didn't say anything else. Roxanne found the wipes in her purse and handed one to Apollo. He rubbed his hands with it on his own, rather ineffectually, then threw it out through the opening. It was good enough. Roxanne took his hand again and started to lead him and Happy back to the front. Jodie paused a moment.

"Are you okay, Denzel?" she asked.

"Don't I look okay?" he replied sarcastically. "What? You think I'm supposed to be happy with this situation?"

"No, of course not. It's just-" Jodie stopped herself from finishing. She had been going to tell Denzel that he was scaring people.

"It's just what?" Denzel asked.

"Nothing," Jodie shook her head. She then turned and walked away before Denzel could press it further.

Instead of returning to the seats near Eric and Troy, Jodie went all the way to the front of the train and sat next to her bags. She wanted to be alone for a bit. Her mind was raging around from thought to thought. Curling her legs up to her chest, she put her chin on her knees and tried to forget where she was. She couldn't, of course. There was no making that blue lighting disappear. There was nothing she could do about the somewhat odd smell. She couldn't forget the bodies outside the door or the unconscious woman just a few feet away. She felt trapped, because she *was* trapped. The walls of the train seemed to be pressing in. For the first time, Jodie wondered if the weight of the blue stuff might collapse the ceiling.

Jodie lowered her head and pressed her eyes into her knees. It was so quiet. Without the train rumbling over the tracks or traffic rushing by, it was eerily silent. She could hear the cyclist and the tall guy still tossing the helmet back and forth. She could hear the murmuring of quiet conversations being held.

"Jodie?"

Jodie startled. Although she had been listening intently, she hadn't heard Troy approach. He was very good at walking silently.

"Sorry. I just wanted to ask if you were all right." Even

though he wasn't uncomfortably close, he took an extra step back.

"I'm just... feeling the weight of all this."

"Want to talk about it?"

"I'm afraid I'll cry if I do."

"That's fine."

Jodie smiled for him. "I'm not keen on crying in front of someone I've only just met."

"Fair enough." He paused for a moment. "So, Eric said he's got some cards in his briefcase. I was thinking of showing Apollo some card tricks if you want to watch."

"I'm going to sit here a moment longer, but you go ahead."

"All right."

Troy paused for a second before turning around and heading back to the others. Jodie wasn't sure what to make of him yet. Her first impressions of people often proved right, but Troy seemed determined to flip that on its head. As he neared Eric, Troy took off his heavy jacket, revealing a thin, black T-shirt underneath. His arms were equally thin and wiry. Watching him place his jacket on a seat, Jodie realized it was warmer in the train now than it had been when she first got on. Initially, she thought that maybe their body heat was building up, but then stupidly remembered a greater source: the sun. With the sun constantly shining through the blue, it was warming the subway train. Jodie felt bad for those trapped inside their cars.

Apollo giggled. Troy had already started performing tricks by doing some fancy shuffling. Knowing she should stop feeling sorry for herself, Jodie got up and walked over to watch. Troy acknowledged her with a quick smile before turning back to Apollo. He and the boy were sitting on the floor facing one another, close enough to Eric for him to see by propping himself up on his elbows. Roxanne was sitting in a seat that gave her a view over Apollo's head, with Happy up on the seat next to her. Jodie decided to sit on the floor beside Apollo.

"All right, what trick should I do first?" Troy asked himself. "Let's start with something simple. Pick a card." Troy fanned out the deck in front of the child.

Apollo pointed to one.

"Pull it out and look at it. Don't tell me what it is, but remember it."

Apollo pulled out the card. He almost tilted it enough for Troy to see, but Jodie quickly shielded it with her hand.

"Can you remember that card?" Jodie asked the boy, already committing the six of diamonds to memory.

"Yes," he said.

"All right, put it back in the deck," Troy told him.

Apollo put the card on top of the fan. Troy slid it between two cards and quickly resumed shuffling. His hands were quick.

"Tell me when to stop."

Apollo was fascinated by the quick shuffling of the cards and waited nearly a full minute before saying stop.

"Pick up the top card and tell me if it's yours." Troy held out the deck.

Apollo had trouble grabbing just the top card, so Jodie helped him. When they flipped it over, it was the six of diamonds.

"Whoa!" Apollo's mind was blown. "How did you do that?"

"Magic," Troy grinned.

From where he was watching, Eric rolled his eyes but didn't comment.

"Again, again!" Apollo clapped his hands.

"All right." Troy reshuffled the cards and began the trick once more.

This time, he made it even more impressive by having Apollo, Jodie, and Eric all pull separate cards and place them in different locations throughout the deck. The cards blurred as he shuffled them up again.

"Tell me, Eric," Troy looked over at the man, not watching his hands which seemed to know what to do on their own, "why do you carry a deck of cards around in your briefcase? Seems like an odd thing to have amongst all those papers."

"Sometimes my clients end up running late." Eric didn't take his eyes off the shuffling. "It gets boring sitting around the place I'm going to show them, so I play solitaire."

"You could just get solitaire on your phone."

Eric shook his head. "It's not the same as with real cards."

"Fair enough." Troy turned back to the others. "All right, who's ready?"

Apollo's hand shot into the air.

"If I recall, your card is on top." Troy held out the deck and Apollo pulled the top card off by himself this time. Once again, the kid was stunned when it was his card. "M'lady, I do believe yours took up residence on the bottom." Troy turned over the deck and showed Jodie her queen of spades. "And for you." Troy held the deck over Eric and split it in half. A single card fell out of it. "Is that your card?"

Eric picked it up and grinned. "I have to hand it to you, you're not bad."

"He's magic!" Apollo cried out.

"I think your ears are magic." Troy leaned forward and pulled a quarter out of Apollo's ear. Jodie's grandpa used to do that to her all the time, but she couldn't figure out where Troy could've gotten the quarter from. "And..." Troy made the quarter disappear again.

Without sleeves, Jodie had no idea how he was performing the trick. He even showed both sides of his hands with his fingers spread.

"How did you do that?" she wondered.

"Same way I took Eric's watch." Troy lifted the large, silver piece.

"What?" Eric held up his wrist and confirmed that it was gone. "Hey!"

"Sorry man, couldn't resist." Troy handed it back with a grin.

By now, a few people had gathered behind Troy, curious about what was going on. Troy looked back and saw them all standing there.

"Gather round, gather round," he waved at them. "Better if you're all in front of me where I can see you."

"You mean where they're less likely to see how you're doing your tricks," Eric commented.

"Either, or."

Those who had come to see, stepped around Troy and found places to sit on the nearby seats, or on the floor around Jodie and Apollo. Simon and Ed were among them, as was the rest of the prayer group, except for Nina. She stayed kneeling on the floor a short distance behind Troy, no longer praying but watching the gathering.

"Ed, I didn't think you'd be interested in magic tricks," Troy joked as everyone settled.

"I like the atmosphere," he smiled.

"All right, watch closely. *Watch* closely," he grinned at Eric, who flipped him the bird in response.

Troy pulled off several neat tricks with the cards, as well

as making the coin periodically appear and disappear. Apollo was amazed by everything, often crying out an enthusiastic "Did you see that?" to everyone nearby. The majority of the gatherers watched in silence. When Jodie looked around, she felt more like she was attending a fascinating surgery, instead of a simple magic show. Every now and then a smile would tug at the corners of someone's mouth, but for the most part they were expressionless.

"Jodie, I think this is yours." Troy got her attention back to him. He was holding up the watch she had put on that morning, the one with the leather band and the small buckle she always fought with.

Jodie laughed as he returned it to her, but the hairs on the back of her neck stood up. She thought she'd surely feel something if someone was taking her watch, but apparently not. She hadn't felt a thing.

"Hey!" someone in the audience cried out. "Hey, the doctor is trying to get our attention!"

People got to their feet and bunched up against the windows. Jodie took Apollo and stood near Eric where she could see the doctor, and also protect both of them from getting squashed. Troy took up the space on Eric's other side.

"He's writing something," Roxanne's voice drifted from somewhere Jodie couldn't see. A man in a plaid shirt who had been part of the prayer group was directly in the way.

The doctor held up his whiteboard to the window.

AIR?

"Air? What does he mean, air?" a Hispanic woman turned to the man next to her and asked. Jodie thought the two might be a married couple, and they had also been part of the prayer group. Although she wouldn't ask, in case she was wrong, it looked to her like the woman was starting to show her pregnancy.

"He means he's going to run out of air." Troy moved away from where he was watching and pushed into the group of people. "Out of my way! Out of my way, please, let me see him straight on!"

Jodie watched through the transparent barrier and could just make out Troy as he kneeled on a seat, facing the window. He waved his arms until he had the doctor's attention.

"Your blinker," Troy said, carefully mouthing the words. He used one hand to indicate something blinking, and the other to point toward the back of the doctor's car. "Your tail light. Your blinker." He continued gesturing.

Jodie didn't understand, but it looked like the doctor did eventually. He gave Troy a thumbs up, and began climbing into the back of his car. Jodie watched as he pulled on a strap that lowered the back of the rear seat, giving him access to the trunk. The way the car had been buried in gunk, one of the tail lights was still free of it, the blue having globbed its way over the trunk and down the car's side. Not knowing what was going to happen, Jodie watched with interest. Within a few seconds, she saw what Troy had gotten the doctor to do. The tail light jiggled a few times, and then popped out, sliding across the blue until the length of its wires stopped it. A hole was left behind, from which the doctor's arm emerged, giving another thumbs up. Several people sighed with relief.

Once the excitement was over, the onlookers began returning to their seats. A few didn't bother going back to where they had been, preferring to sit down closer to the front doors. No one went beyond the doors though, where

Jodie's bags rested on the seats and Olivia continue to lie unconscious.

"Good job," Roxanne commented to Troy, patting him on the shoulder.

"I wouldn't have thought of that," Simon commented. He was one of the people sitting near the front doors. "What made you think of it?"

Troy shrugged. "I don't know. I just remembered in high school they told us to kick out the tail lights if someone ever threw you in a trunk. I figured it would be as good an air hole as any."

Jodie focused on the other cars. Many of them were completely buried, with no chance of an air hole being created through the blue. She hadn't thought about how they would run out of air in there; she had been thinking about them as being in the same predicament as she was. But the smaller spaces meant less oxygen, and being completely covered meant no air could get in.

Then she remembered that her dad was trapped in a car.

11

JODIE FIDGETED WITH HER PHONE. Should she call him? He had said not to turn her phone on until tomorrow though. He would probably have his turned off. But what if he didn't? Was his car completely buried? Had he thought about the air situation? Were he and Lucky breathing their last breaths?

"Please stop pacing, you're making me dizzy," Eric commented.

He had been watching Jodie walking back and forth, often passing by his head. Jodie didn't listen to him.

"What's wrong?" Troy asked for what must have been the fifth time. They could all tell she had been fretting about something since the doctor had kicked out his tail light, but she wouldn't tell them what.

"Dear," Roxanne was suddenly standing in front of her, holding her shoulders, "why don't you sit down?"

Jodie felt guilty making Roxanne stand up, after she had seen the effort it took her to get to her feet the last time. She allowed the much older woman to lead her to the seats nearest to Eric and sit her down on them. Roxanne sat down beside her, moving her hands from Jodie's shoulders to clasp them around Jodie's hands and phone.

"Tell me what's wrong," she said calmly, looking Jodie in the eye.

"It's my dad," Jodie eventually squeaked.

"What about him?"

"He's in a car like the doctor. What if he doesn't have air? I want to call him, but he told me to keep my phone off and wait until tomorrow. What if he can kick out his tail light like the doctor, but doesn't realize that he should do that? What if he doesn't know until it's too late?"

"Deep breaths," Roxanne continued to speak calmly. "Breathe with me. In, and out. In, and out."

Roxanne and Jodie breathed together until she stopped shuddering.

"There, that's better." Roxanne patted her hands and continued to hold them. "Now, if you're really worried about your dad, call him. I don't think he'll get mad at you for caring."

Being told what to do made Jodie feel a lot better. Somehow, getting permission from Roxanne was all she needed. She turned on her phone. Roxanne released her hands but continued to sit with her while Jodie waited for her phone to boot up. Before she could check the battery indicator and think about changing her mind, Jodie brought up her phonebook and quickly found her dad's number.

It rang four times before the voicemail picked up, an unusual number of rings.

"He didn't pick up." Jodie could feel the tightness returning to her throat.

"Maybe his phone is just off," Roxanne gently suggested.

Jodie shook her head. "If his phone was off, voicemail would have picked up right away."

Her cell chimed, indicating she had a text message. Jodie assumed it was something she had received while her phone was off, especially when it chimed a second time immediately after. Still, she checked them just in case her dad had sent her some kind of instructions. The newest message was from him, and she had just received it. Although she made a habit of checking the old ones first, she selected this new one immediately.

Cant hear. Have to text. Wats wrong potatoe? It was definitely from her dad with its awkward spelling, grammar, and punctuation. He rarely ever read his messages before sending them, and had never gotten along with touch screens.

Jodie quickly responded with, *Do you guys have air getting into the car?*

She waited eagerly for the response, not even registering that it was strange that her dad couldn't hear at the moment. Jodie stared intently at the message screen, waiting for a new one to pop up. It was taking awhile. Did her dad see her message? Did it get lost in the ether? Maybe she should send it again. But what if he got it? Was he checking the car for possible air holes? What were he and Lucky doing?

In the end, it turned out he had just been writing a fairly long response.

Yes as of 5 mins ago. Guys on radio mentioned it. End of hood not covered. Used shotgun to blow hole in floorboard. Getting air from under car. Ears still ringing badly and cant hear shit. You ok?

Jodie sighed with relief.

"Good news?" Roxanne asked her.

"Yes. He's getting air into his car. They had to use a

shotgun to do it and his ears are ringing so badly he can't hear anything right now."

"Your dad has a shotgun in the car?" Eric wondered.

"He's a detective. Sometimes he teams with the SWAT guys, so he keeps the gear in the trunk." Jodie typed up a response to her dad, telling him that she was fine and about the doctor in the car, also making sure to mention that they had their own hole in the train.

He eventually replied, stating that he was happy that she was okay, and that she should turn her phone off again. She said she would. Before actually turning off her phone, Jodie thought she should look at the other message; it could be from her sister.

It wasn't. The message was from Lucas, Sandra's boyfriend. He was asking Jodie if she was all right, and if she had heard from Sandra. Apparently, he had tried her cell several times already, and even her workplace phone, but he couldn't get through.

Jodie replied that she was fine, and that she hadn't heard from Sandra. She told him not to worry, that Sandra was probably at work, and the lines were just down. At least, that's what Jodie kept telling herself.

"Do you get internet on that thing?" the man in the plaid shirt from the prayer group asked Jodie about her phone.

"No, I don't have data," she said as she turned it back off. That wasn't entirely true, she had a little bit of data, but she didn't want to use her battery any more than she already had.

"I have lots of data on my phone," Roxanne told Mr. plaid shirt. "I don't bother much with a real computer."

"Would you mind using it? Maybe we can get some information about the rescue efforts."

"I'm no good at searching." Roxanne got up from her seat—it was less difficult for her now than it had been earlier—and walked back over to her former seat, where her purse was. "I suggest you do the looking."

Once she located her phone, she handed it to Mr. plaid. There wasn't a password on it, and he went straight to work checking the news. Everyone who was close enough to know what he was doing, waited with baited breath for an update. Jodie watched his face as he read a page. The way his expression slowly crumbled into something resembling pain dropped her heart into her stomach. Still, no one asked questions, waiting for him to tell them on his own.

"It says..." he started, but then had to swallow a lump in his throat. "No one knows what it is. If it's an attack, no one knows by who, but there are a lot of accusations being thrown around in the comment section. They're still testing it..." he paused, whether to read something again, or gather his will to keep speaking, Jodie couldn't tell. "Most of the tools they've tried have had no effect on the substance."

"Most tools?" Simon looked up from where he had been staring intently at his feet. "Does that mean they found something that *does* work?"

"Yeah, one second." Mr. plaid scrolled through the news report again, searching for a section he had already read. "Blowtorches seem to do the job. Intense heat apparently turns it back into that gooey state. Unfortunately, it only works on a small area, and once the goo drips out of that area, it re-solidifies. It looks like in most cases they're cutting through walls and things to get the trapped people out. There's a photo gallery if anyone would like to see."

Just about everyone raised a hand. Mr. plaid handed the phone to Simon first, since he was the closest. Ed sat quietly next to him, unable to see the photos.

"Can I watch Thomas?" Apollo looked at Roxanne and pointed to her phone.

"Thomas?" Roxanne was confused by the request.

"The train," Apollo offered very little in the way of clarifying information.

"I think he wants to watch YouTube videos," Eric explained. "I have a nephew, he does the same thing. I swear the kid can work a touch screen better than I can, and he's two years old."

"Maybe in a few minutes, when everyone else is done with the phone," Roxanne told Apollo.

Apollo looked from Roxanne to the phone, and then back to Roxanne.

"Why don't you play with Happy?" Roxanne suggested.

"He doesn't want to play. He just lays there." Apollo sat down on the floor and began pushing his toy train around some more. The kid was clearly getting bored. Jodie had a feeling that he'd soon be begging to go home, or to wake up his mom.

When Simon finished with the phone, he handed it to Roxanne. Although the woman had raised her hand when asked if she wanted to see the photos, she looked only at the first one before passing the phone on to Jodie, who took it and sat down next to Eric where they could both see the pictures at the same time. Troy left his seat to shuffle up on Eric's other side, so that he could see, too. The album came with a warning that a few photos were of a graphic nature.

The first photo must have come from one of the helicopters. It was a high, wide-angle shot of the city, and showed blobs of blue stuff attached to and drooping down the sides of buildings, while more blue globs filled sections of the streets. Some of the blobs were small, no larger than one of the windows on the subway train, while others were monstrous, filling up entire intersections.

The second photo was of the CN Tower. What Jodie's dad had heard turned out to be true; a glob that was reminiscent of a booger hung down from it. Underneath, the dome of the Rogers Centre—or the Sky Dome as Jodie still liked to think of it—was covered in a layer of blue, giving it the look of a monstrous beetle.

Photo three was from street level. It seemed to be a suburb somewhere, although it was difficult to tell. Most of the photo consisted of a hydro pole covered in blue. The lines on one side had been ripped out of the pole, but those on the other side were still attached, covered in a thin layer of the stuff.

The next photo showed a similar, odd contrast. On one side of a street, blue stuff had hit a tree and smashed off a bunch of branches, which were then stuck to the ground below. A tree that looked to be the same species just up the street had also been hit, but none of its branches were broken. The blue stuff just coated the upper section. Maybe there was something Jodie couldn't see due to the smallness of the picture on the phone, but it was really weird that some of the blue blobs had hit harder than others.

There were more photos of blue stuff covering things. A car was completely entombed in a perfectly even layer all around, while nothing else in the photo was touched. Next was the buried cross of a church. An impressive curtain of blue hung from a bridge that crossed the Don Valley Parkway, reaching nearly all the way to the highway. Cemeteries and playgrounds were equal targets for the stuff, as tombstones and swings sparkled in the sunlight. They came across one photo that was very interesting. A few guys in a boat were hauling the stuff toward the shore of Lake

Ontario. Apparently, when it hit the water, it didn't sink, but spread across the surface where it hardened into things that looked like icebergs.

Then came the photos of the relief efforts. In the first one, rescue workers were cutting a hole through the side of a hospital, its emergency entrance buried just a few feet away from them. The next one was one of the blowtorches, melting the stuff away from the side of a car, as a woman inside it shielded her eyes from the bright light.

Eventually, there were photos of people trapped outside. Similar to those beside the train, the ones a few feet away from Jodie right now, they were all posed in odd, torturous-looking positions from thrashing around, trying to swim out of the stuff before it hardened. One picture showed a teenaged girl sitting in the road, crying. Next to her was a large blob of blue, with a woman trapped inside. Only the woman's right arm had escaped interment, and the teenaged girl was holding the woman's hand. Jodie suspected it was the girl's mother.

Then came a picture that squeezed Jodie's heart and throat. A man was trapped in the gunk, with only his eyes, nose, and the tips of a few fingers poking out. Another man had his arms locked around the trapped man's torso, clearly having become stuck himself while trying to save the other.

"I'm not sure I thanked you earlier," Eric said to Troy when they came across that photo.

"I'd like to think you would have done the same if I were in your position and you were in mine," Troy told him.

Eric didn't reply to that.

The next photo came with a caption. A woman had her arm trapped and was being prepared to have it amputated. She had been given the option of waiting to see if they could find a safe way of removing her, but she wanted to get out by any means necessary. Out of focus people were gathered in the background, turning her surgery into a spectator event. The following photo had a pair of shoes stuck in the goo, and Jodie nearly threw up when she realized that feet and ankles were still in them

Eric turned his head away from the phone, tears leaking from his eyes. Even if he was willing to go through with an amputation, it was unlikely he'd be able to get one. He was nearly buried up to his navel, which was far too much to cut off.

Without thinking about the fact that she had just met the man a few hours ago, Jodie reached over and stroked his hair.

"It'll be all right, Eric," she told him. "You're on the floor of a subway. They can probably just cut the floor out from beneath you and then you'll be free."

Eric closed his eyes and pointed his face up at the ceiling. It was clear to Jodie that he wanted to be alone. She stood up and patted Troy on the shoulder to get him to do the same. The two of them left Eric by himself and sat on the seats, where they continued to look through the pictures.

They were all just more of the same. A few stood out, like the one of a group of men travelling through a storm sewer where a small bit of blue oozed through a grate overhead, but most of them began to blur together. It took Jodie a while to realize why she was looking through all these photos. She was looking for her dad, for Amber, for Sandra. She was hoping to see someone she knew, to know that they were safe. There were maybe two hundred photos in this online album, and Jodie scrolled through all of them. Many were barely given a second's glance, before she moved on, but she did get through them all. Troy sat beside her the entire time, also viewing the horror show. By the time they reached the end and handed the phone to the Hispanic couple who were waiting, Jodie was crying.

"Is there something I can do?" Troy quietly asked Jodie, placing a hand gently on her shoulder.

Jodie shook her head. "I'm going to go sketch for awhile." She got up, walked back to her seat at the front of the train, and tried not to look at Olivia before she sat down facing the other way.

Pulling out her water bottle, Jodie screwed off the top and took a large swallow. Once the liquid was in her mouth and going down her throat, she wanted more, but she stopped herself. Conserving water was even more important than conserving food. It had to last longer. Tightly resealing the cap, she returned the water to her bag, then pulled out her small, pocket-sized sketchbook. She wanted to draw in her larger book, where she could use broader arm movements, but knew she should save the paper in case they had to communicate with the doctor again. So many new restrictions she had to follow. There were so many things she wanted to do, but couldn't. She wanted someone to tell her what to do, instead of having to place the burden of decision upon herself. That wasn't going to happen though. Everyone was looking for someone to follow, someone who had answers, but that someone was clearly not on their train. Jodie would use her willpower to obey her own restrictions, something her dad had taught her to do while growing up. Once she decided something, she had to see it through to the end.

Jodie spent the rest of the day with her head down in her sketchbook. She was drawing an intricate pattern. When it filled the entire page, she switched to her pencil crayons and started to give it colour. Sitting sideways, with her feet up on the other seat and her sketchbook propped up against her knees, Jodie blocked out the world. She didn't even pay attention when Simon came by to grab something for Apollo from Olivia's bag.

When Jodie finally pulled her head out of her sketchbook, it was because of the combination of the needs to pee and to eat. She had difficulty deciding which one to satisfy first, until she realized her hunger was making her dizzy. It was well past her usual dinnertime, and the sun was disappearing behind the hills and buildings that flanked the Allan Expressway and the subway tracks, turning the interior of the train into a strange purple. Jodie took out the BLT she had made that morning. The lettuce and the tomato had both contributed to making the bread kind of soggy, and the lettuce had lost some of its crunch. Jodie didn't care as she slowly ate the sandwich. Her stomach was telling her to eat it faster, to chew only enough times to be able to swallow, but she forced herself to eat slowly. She remembered Amber once telling her that eating slowly was good for the digestion and made you feel fuller despite eating less. So, Jodie ate slowly, not exactly savouring each bite, but taking her time tasting all the parts. When the sandwich was finished, she washed it down with one of her little boxes of grape juice. By then, she really had to pee.

Sliding to the end of her seats, Jodie first looked down at Olivia. The only light that reached her had to travel through the windows of the driver's box, which meant that, because they were tinted, she was in a considerable amount of darkness. Looking down the rest of the train, Jodie observed that a lot of people were being quiet right now. Apollo sat on Roxanne's lap, sucking his thumb, while Simon and Mr. plaid sat across from one another, neither saying a thing, both staring up at the ceiling. Ed had his back to her, while

Troy was sprawled across a set of three seats near him. Looking at Troy made Jodie wonder if he had eaten anything since the accident. Her mind had a short but vicious war with itself over whether Jodie should give him any food or not. In the end, she grabbed the Swiss cake rolls before heading for the hole at the back of the train.

"Roxanne?" Jodie spoke quietly, not wanting to disturb the peace that had settled over the train. Even farther down, those who were speaking to one another did so in whispers.

"Yes, dear?" Roxanne looked up at her, shifting Apollo in the process.

"Do you have any Kleenex or anything in your purse I could have? I have to go to the bathroom."

"Of course I do." Roxanne put Apollo down on the seat beside her so that she could rummage through her purse.

Apollo's thumb came out of his mouth with a pop. "Mommy still sleeping?"

"Unfortunately, yes."

"When is she going to wake up?"

"I don't know."

"I want her to wake up, but Simon says we can't."

Jodie couldn't think of a good response for him.

"I want my daddy." Apollo put his thumb back into his mouth.

Remembering the brief conversation she had had with the man, Jodie wondered where Apollo's dad was. He had said he was going to come find them, but was that even possible? Could he even get here, or was the way blocked? Jodie wondered if her sister had made it to the apartment.

"Here you are, dear," Roxanne said, as she held out a small package of Kleenex. "I've already been down there myself. It's not easy to use, but if you lean your back against the dent in the door, you can go without having your fanny touch the floor."

"Thanks. I'll bring back whatever I don't use."

Jodie made one more stop before going the rest of the way to the bathroom-hole.

"Troy?" she whispered, unsure if he was asleep.

His eyes immediately opened and met hers. He wasn't asleep at all.

"I thought you might want this." She held out the Swiss cake rolls.

"You sure?" he asked, while taking the package out of her hand.

"Yeah. I had a sandwich in my backpack, so I'm okay." She wasn't going to mention the other sandwich that was still in there. Apparently, there were now limits to her kindness.

"Thank you." Troy immediately tore open the plastic packaging.

"Eat it slowly," she said, as she turned to continue down the train. Emptying her bladder was starting to become a very urgent need.

"You wouldn't happen to have any more of that, would you?"

Jodie stopped and turned to find panicky Nina looking at her. For once, her voice seemed to match the soft look her face and hair conveyed.

"You mean food?" Jodie wondered. "No."

Nina nodded, then clasped her hands and returned to silent prayer. Jodie suddenly thought that maybe she shouldn't have given anything to Troy. She hadn't given anything to Ed, or Mr. plaid, and the half apples from earlier weren't a lot for the others. Jodie had played favourites by giving the Swiss cake rolls to Troy. It was too late now, though.

It seemed that people had bunched toward the front of the train even more now. Denzel wasn't sitting at the back any longer; he had joined two business men, making the woman with the cross tattoo on her forehead the furthest one back. It didn't take long for Jodie to figure out why. Even before she reached the hole in the door, she could smell it. Apollo had probably been the first, but he most certainly hadn't been the last. Jodie wished she had been wearing a T-shirt that she could pull up over her nose, but neither her blouse nor her camisole were good for that. It was clear that people hadn't been just pissing out of the hole.

Using one Kleenex, Jodie wiped at the door where she thought her butt might press against it, doing her best not to look down. Then, carefully and awkwardly, she hiked up her skirt, pulled down her underwear, and leaned against the dent as Roxanne had suggested, the lower half of the dividers on either side of the door providing barely enough privacy. She could hear her urine splattering against the ground as she relieved herself.

Once done, Jodie used some more Kleenex to clean herself up, then quickly pulled up her panties and threw the used tissue through the opening. The moment her skirt was corrected, she headed away from the vile smell.

That was when a woman screamed.

12

JODIE'S HEART leapt up into her throat and then immediately dropped into her stomach. What could possibly be happening now? The screamer had been the Asian woman, who wasn't far from Jodie. She had jumped to her feet, and was now yelling at the shaven-headed man, who had been sitting next to her, in a dialect Jodie couldn't identify, let alone understand.

As Jodie moved closer to the scene, the woman with the cross tattoo also got up to see what had happened, as did the black woman Jodie had seen earlier, and then Denzel and the business men.

"Calm down, lady!" the guy who was being yelled at said, holding his hands up in front of him as if to block her shouting. "What the hell?"

"What's going on here?" Denzel asked.

"Hell if I know! Ow!" The Asian woman swatted his hands with her purse. "She just started yelling at me for no reason!"

The Asian woman turned to Denzel, still speaking at

lightning speed in her foreign dialect, pointing an accusatory finger at the sitting man.

"Calm down," Denzel told her. "I can't understand you. Speak English."

"Yo, I've been sitting near this crazy woman all day," the shaven-headed man told his audience. "I don't think she *can* speak English. Crazy Chinese bitch. Ow!" She had swatted him again.

This time, the Asian woman turned to Jodie and the cross-tattoo lady. She used more gestures this time, while continuing her non-stop accusations. Eventually, she made a pincher gesture with her index finger and thumb, then patted her behind.

"I think she's saying that he pinched her butt." The woman with the cross tattoo spoke very calmly and clearly, despite her heavy accent.

"Did you?" Denzel turned to the man.

"What? Of course I didn't!"

The Asian lady swatted her purse at him again, but this time he managed to drop his hands out of the way before they were struck.

"Why would I pinch this ugly ass chick's ass?" the shaven-headed guy continued. "You are not my type," he spoke slowly and loudly at the Asian woman.

She replied with a string of words that Jodie figured were curses.

"Everyone, just calm down." Denzel stepped forward so that he was almost between the two. "Maybe you pinched her, maybe you didn't. Either way, she thinks you did. All you can do is just not sit near one another anymore. Got it?"

"I got it just fine, but try explaining that to the chink."

"There's no need for that kind of language," the tattooed woman told him.

"You can fuck off with her," the guy told her.

The tattooed woman didn't dignify him with a response. She walked up to the Asian woman and gently led her away from the scene. The guy was about to get up, when Denzel kept him down with a firm hand.

"You stay put," he told him.

Muttering something under his breath, the shaven-headed guy obeyed.

Jodie wouldn't be surprised to learn the guy *had* pinched the woman's butt. He just had that look about him. He was the kind of guy Jodie instinctively avoided at bars. There wasn't anything specific about his look that set off what Sandra called her creeper-radar, she had been fine with other men who had shaved heads and full sleeve tattoos, but this guy was setting it off.

"What are you looking at?" he snapped at Jodie.

"Nothing." Jodie squeezed her way between the two businessmen and headed toward the front of the train. The Asian woman and the tattooed lady had claimed a pair of seats near the guy with paint splattered clothes and the girl with the star tattoo on her leg. The Asian lady and cross-tattoo hadn't answered any questions about what happened, so Jodie filled in the curious as she made her way back to the front.

"Did we miss something good?" Troy asked when she returned to her usual area.

"Some guy pinched a woman's butt. She wasn't too happy about it." She sat down on the floor next to Eric. "Did I miss anything around here?"

"I pissed myself." Eric was especially sour, and, from the sounds of it, with good reason.

Jodie glanced at the blue encasing his legs. She couldn't

tell he had peed himself, at least not in the quickly darkening light.

"I now have damp pants clinging to my balls and thighs," Eric continued.

"I'm sorry to hear that," was all Jodie could think to say.

"At least it wasn't a number two," Troy commented.

Eric flipped him off.

"I wanna go home," Apollo whined.

"I know, small one." Roxanne stroked his hair. "We all want to go home."

"Why can't I go home?"

"Because we can't get off the train. We're stuck in here."

"Stuck?"

"Yes, it means we can't get out. We can't leave and go home."

"Make us not stuck."

Roxanne chuckled. "I'd love to, little one, but I can't. No one here can make us unstuck, we have to wait for the rescue people outside to come."

"How long?"

"I don't know."

"All night?"

"Most likely."

"So it's like a sleepover."

"It's like a sleepover."

"I'm tired."

"Here, lie down then." Roxanne got up and lay Apollo down across the pair of seats. She took off her nice navy blazer and balled it up as a pillow for him.

"His mom has a blanket in her bag," Jodie remembered.

"I'll get it," Simon volunteered, hauling himself up onto his feet.

"Happy, up! Up, boy." Roxanne patted the trio of seats

in front of the child. The little dog whined and circled, but eventually obeyed his master and hopped up onto the seats. Roxanne got him to lie down on the seat nearest Apollo, where the boy could see him and pet him. Simon returned with the blanket and draped it over Apollo's body.

As darkness continued to descend, Jodie wondered where she was going to sleep. All of the triple seats nearby were taken, and the double seats weren't long enough for her to stretch out on. Without anything to do in the oncoming night, it seemed most people were preparing to turn in early. Troy looked like he had already nodded off, and Eric was going to be close behind him. Eventually, Jodie got up and went to the double seats across from Apollo, next to Troy. Blind Ed was slouched in the seats facing the other direction, looking dead to the world and like he'd have a neck cramp when he woke up. Before she sat down, Jodie peered out the window above the boy, checking on the doctor. Through the blue murk she couldn't make out much beyond a few vague shapes.

Jodie curled up tightly so that her hips and legs were on one seat, and her shoulders, arms, and head were on the other. The annoying rise between them rested against her soft side, which was better than against hard bone, but not by much.

She didn't really fall asleep. Although her mind wandered, Jodie just wasn't tired enough or comfortable enough to completely let go. Her stomach wasn't as full as it wanted to be, her legs were quickly getting cramped and kept falling off the seat, and she was cold. While moving about she hadn't noticed it, but after the sun left them it kept getting colder and colder in the train.

Her mind brought her back to the night before, when she and Sandra had been at the bar. Part of her mind wanted to keep jumping ahead, to when she got attacked by the giggles, but another part kept playing out the memory linearly. Something about it seemed important. She remembered walking with the guy, arm in arm, taking Sandra home. Something about Sandra's apartment... Then it came to her, the lightning bolt. They had thought it strange at the time, but then quickly ignored it. Might it have had something to do with the blue stuff? If so, what? And would it make a difference knowing that? It certainly wouldn't help the people in the train get out. Her mind continued to dwell on it, anyway.

At least it did until the helicopter flew past. The heavy thumping of the blades made Jodie open her eyes and partly sit up. It wasn't near enough to wake anybody up, but close enough for all of those not fully asleep to notice it. Jodie stared out the window above her and spotted it zipping along. Even though it was moving at a fast pace and wouldn't be able to see much, the helicopter had a bright searchlight that swept over the landscape. Maybe they were just using it as a reminder to everyone that people were still out there trying to help them.

Jodie lay back down, but the chill had really gotten to her now. It was downright cold. Her arms shivered, and her teeth issued a quick staccato of chatter.

"Hey," Eric whispered.

Raising her head again, Jodie peered over at him. He was hard to make out in the darkness, but as her eyes adjusted, she could tell he was looking at her.

"Are you cold?" he asked.

"Yeah," Jodie whispered back.

"Me too. Come over here."

Jodie slipped off her seat and went to sit by Eric.

"Maybe we should share body heat," he suggested. "You know, lie next to each other."

"Mind if I join the huddle?" Troy whispered from the darkness. "I'm willing to share my coat."

"Take the boy," Roxanne added. "He's shivering."

Jodie got up again to fetch Apollo. He was barely awake, completely worn out from the day. While moving him, she returned Roxanne's blazer.

"Will you join us?" Jodie asked her.

Roxanne shook her head. "I go down on that floor, I'm not getting back up." She wasn't even lying on the seats, but sitting with her back against the barrier, her legs folded neatly before her.

"Okay."

Jodie carried Apollo over to Eric, and Happy hopped off the seat and followed them. After much manoeuvring, they got Happy to lie down next to the blue, his head against Eric's side, and then Apollo was laid down beside the dog. Jodie curled up around the kid's back, partly sharing his blanket, resting her head on Eric's shoulder, and letting the boy use her arm as a pillow.

"No homo, right?" Troy joked to Eric as he lay down behind Jodie, draping his coat over both of them.

"I just want to be warm, man," Eric replied.

All along the train, people without adequately warm clothing were snuggling up to strangers to fight off the cold. A few were stubborn and continued to sit alone, but the majority bunched up. Before the night was over, the Hispanic couple had settled in on Eric's other side, their heads resting against the blue, and their arms wrapped around each other, while Nina had curled up beside their legs, near Eric's head. Even Mr. plaid had joined them, spreading out his flannel shirt to share with Nina, while Ed lay against Troy's back.

Jodie managed to get some sleep in this huddle, but not much. It was still cold, despite the shared body heat, and uncomfortable. Her legs were still cramped as she curled them up under her skirt, and there was no padding on the floor for her hips and shoulders beyond her thin clothing. At least Troy was polite and kept his hands to himself, folded up against her back. Although she wouldn't have minded the warmth provided by being enfolded in his arms, she wasn't *that* comfortable with him yet. Instead, she wrapped herself even more tightly around Apollo, her hands against Happy's furry side.

At some point in the night, Apollo woke up asking for his mother. He was half-asleep, and Jodie was able to quiet him back down and get him to fall asleep again. She promised him that he could see his mom first thing in the morning.

By the time the sun started to rise, everyone was stiff and sore. Nobody had slept soundly, and they were all still chilly. Jodie would have been content to lie there all morning, but the moment Apollo opened his eyes, he was wide-awake.

"You said I could see my mom now," he told Jodie, shaking her with his tiny hands.

Jodie groaned. She had convinced herself he wouldn't remember that.

"I want to see my mommy," he whined, pretty much ready to climb over Jodie.

"Okay. Okay. I'm up." Jodie sat up and stretched, wincing as several of her joints popped. Her hip felt the worst. Throughout her high school and college years, Jodie had done her fair share of sleeping on floors. She knew that if she kept moving today, most of the pain would work itself out. Her hip, though, felt like it might remain sore all day.

"Then I want breakfast," Apollo told her as she got to her feet. "And I'm cold."

"I know. So am I. Keep your blanket wrapped around you."

Most of the people in the huddle, now awake, remained where they were, unmotivated to move. Troy wasn't. He got up, his knees cracking especially loudly, and went to check on Roxanne. Jodie left him on his own to find out how her night had been and took Apollo to see his mom.

"You should know you can't touch her," Jodie told the boy.

"Why not?"

"Because she got hurt when we crashed, and if you touch her, you could hurt her more."

"Mommy's hurt?"

"Yes."

"Can we kiss it better?"

"Unfortunately, we can't this time."

They reached Olivia and stood at her feet.

"I'm up, Mommy," Apollo told her. "We're still on the train. It's still crashed. Daddy's not here. I miss him and want to go home. Why won't you wake up, Mommy? I'm scared and want to go home."

Jodie wasn't listening as she studied Olivia's face. There was something definitely different about it this morning. It was paler, and her lips had taken on a bluish tint that didn't come from the coloured light seeping in. Perhaps it was just from the cold, but Jodie had a terrible thought.

"Apollo, I need you to stand right here and don't move. Can you do that for me?" Her voice shook.

"Where are you going?"

"I just need to kneel next to your mom for a second."

"I can kneel with you."

"No!" Jodie barked a lot harsher than she meant to. "I'm sorry, no," she said more gently. "Just wait right here."

Releasing Apollo's hand, Jodie stepped around Olivia's body until she could kneel down near her head. Her skin was definitely paler, it wasn't just some trick of the dull, morning light being filtered through the blue. As Jodie reached her hand forward, it shook worse than she had ever seen her hands shake before.

"Don't touch her," Apollo wailed. "You'll hurt her."

His sudden voice had startled Jodie, making her draw her hand back to her chest like a mouse that's narrowly escaped the trap. When Jodie turned to him, she saw that Simon had overheard them and was now lingering behind Apollo, wondering what was going on.

"It's okay, I know how to touch her without hurting her," Jodie told Apollo.

As tears started to fill her eyes and blur her vision, she reached forward again. Her hand was still trembling, however not as much. First, she placed her fingers in front of Olivia's mouth. She desperately wanted to feel breath, but there was none. Jodie's mind tried to convince her that Olivia's breathing was just too weak to feel, that the cold had slowed down her systems. Swallowing a sudden lump in her throat, Jodie placed her fingers against Olivia's neck. It was cold. Much too cold. Her skin didn't feel right. The moment she touched it, Jodie wanted to pull her hand away, but she persisted in searching for a pulse. There was nothing.

Olivia was dead.

13

A STRANGE SENSATION came over Jodie's mind as she confirmed that Apollo's mother was gone. A hollow wind blew through, taking with it all her thoughts and feelings. It was as if a weight had settled upon her soul.

"What are you doing?" Apollo wondered.

Jodie looked up and saw Simon staring anxiously at her, constantly shifting his weight and wringing his hands together. He saw the pale skin and blue lips, too. Jodie slowly shook her head, just once, while meeting Simon's eyes.

"Nothing," she then said to Apollo, quickly standing up. "I'm betting you have to go to the bathroom."

"No."

"I'm certain you do. You just got up. People always need to go to the bathroom when they get up."

"I want to stay with Mommy." Maybe he realized that something was wrong with her. Maybe he saw it on Jodie's face.

"You can come back after you pee. Come on." Jodie held out her hand to him as she stepped back around Olivia.

She made sure to hold out the hand that hadn't touched Apollo's mother.

"Okay." Apollo took her hand, ready to be led away.

"What should I do?" Simon asked her in a strangled voice.

"I don't know. Is there anything you can do?" Jodie then took the boy away, leaving any decisions to be made to Simon.

They stopped by Roxanne to grab tissues and wipes. She'd probably be out of them by the end of the day, but Jodie couldn't worry about that now. Roxanne was still tired, and cold to the point of shivering. She sat wrapped up in Troy's coat, leaning against Troy himself, who rubbed her shoulders. Jodie couldn't worry about that, either. It was clear that Troy wanted to ask questions, and maybe he did, but Jodie didn't hear them over the hollow wind. She took the tissues and wipes, and proceeded with Apollo to the toilet hole.

It was harder to navigate the subway this morning than it had been yesterday. When people had gotten cold, many of them had given up the seats to huddle together on the floor.

"Please tell me you didn't drool on me," Jodie overheard the red headed woman commenting to someone. She didn't look around to learn more about the incident, she just pressed on.

Some people were managing to sleep through the intrusion of the sun and the sounds of others waking. The lady with the cross tattoo and the Asian woman were both in the seats they had claimed after the incident yesterday, leaning against one another, completely out of it.

"It stinks," Apollo commented, stopping in his tracks.

"I know, but there's nowhere else to go. Come on." Jodie gently tugged on his hand.

"It's too smelly."

"Then pull your shirt up over your nose."

"I don't want to."

"If you don't go here and now, you'll end up going in your pants and then this smell is going to follow you everywhere." More anger than Jodie had intended peppered her voice. It seemed Apollo's good behaviour was slipping away with time.

Apollo pulled his shirt up over his mouth and nose and went to the hole. Jodie waited nearby, breathing through her hand, ready to give him the wipe when he was finished.

"I'm hungry," he stated as he washed up.

"So is everyone else. We'll find you something. Wait here for a second while I pee." Jodie sat Apollo down on the nearest seat and went to the hole. Once again, she did her best not to look through it, and tried to keep her skirt bunched up between her skin and the door. Having not had much to drink since the last time she went, not a lot came out. Still, her bladder had been saying it was time to go, just as it did every morning. She cleaned up with a tissue and disposed of it.

Apollo was still sitting where she had left him, swinging his legs and watching the loose strap on his shoe flop around. Jodie reattached the Velcro strap for him, then took his hand. They began their short journey toward the front of the train where Olivia's body was no doubt waiting for them.

"You son of a bitch!" a voice interrupted them. There was no mistaking the slow, heavily accented voice of the woman with the cross tattoo.

Jodie held Apollo closer to her, and turned to look. The

woman was still sitting beside the Asian woman—who miraculously continued to sleep—and glaring back over her shoulder at the accused butt-pincher. The man in question was still half-asleep, having just climbed up onto a seat.

"What's going on now?" Denzel asked the woman.

"She's dead!"

For a moment Jodie was stunned. How could that woman already know that Olivia had passed away in the night?

Suddenly, the cross-tattoo woman stood up, her white folds of material flowing around her as she slid past the Asian lady, who slumped over to occupy the abandoned space, making no movements of her own.

"You killed her!" the cross-tattoo woman pointed a crooked finger at the butt-pincher. "She's been murdered!"

And here Jodie had thought things couldn't possibly get worse.

"Go run to Roxanne," Jodie told Apollo.

"I want Mommy," Apollo whined.

"Fine, just go." She gave the boy a weak push in the right direction, not even turning to check if he was leaving. They were just on the other side of the doors in which Eric was trapped, so she figured he would be fine.

"Whoa, whoa, whoa!" Denzel stepped between cross-tattoo and butt-pincher, holding his hands up in either direction.

"What? Who's dead?" butt-pincher appeared frightened now, waking up quickly, thanks to a sudden flood of adrenaline.

"You killed her!" cross-tattoo shouted at him, remaining behind Denzel.

"I didn't do nothing!" butt-pincher cried in response. "I don't even know what you're talking about!"

"Everyone needs to calm down!" Denzel shouted in a booming voice. All of the passengers on board fell silent, even those who were just whispering confused questions to one another. "Who's dead?" he said in the silence, looking at cross-tattoo.

She just pointed to the slumped-over Asian woman.

"Someone take a look," Denzel ordered, keeping himself between her and the accused.

No one moved to follow his command.

"You," Denzel pointed directly at Jodie, "check on the woman."

Jodie's blood turned to ice. She had already proven one woman had died this morning, and now she was being asked to check on another. The thought of touching cold skin again made her want to vomit.

"I got it," the Hispanic man volunteered, his tanned and squared features turning only slightly paler. He and the probably-pregnant woman had been sitting in the seats in front of the Asian lady yesterday, before they had joined the night-time huddle on the floor. Now, he stepped around Jodie and walked up to the woman's prone body.

The pregnant woman, who Jodie guessed was his wife or girlfriend, made an odd sound in the back of her throat. The man held out a hand to her, silently telling her he'd be all right. Everyone watched as he knelt on the seat in front of the woman, and reached for her head where it was lying on the seat beneath the window. From where Jodie was standing, she could see the man brush strands of hair away from her face and neck. Her ear was revealed where a small, dried-up trickle of blood could be seen coming from it. The man paused for a moment, then searched for a pulse.

"She's dead," he confirmed.

A series of shudders and cries ran through the train.

"There's blood coming out of her ear," the man informed everyone.

"Yes, because that man over there stabbed her in the side of the head," cross-tattoo said matter-of-factly, pointing her accusing finger back in butt-pincher's direction.

"What?" butt-pincher jumped to his feet, more scared than angry, but definitely both.

"She wouldn't give you what you wanted, and so you killed her for it," cross-tattoo continued speaking in a way that suggested no argument would sway her.

"I would never do that!"

"How do we know that?"

Based on people's expressions, they were beginning to believe cross-tattoo.

"He's going to murder us all!" Nina wailed.

"I'm not a murderer!" butt-pincher screeched, his hands balled up into fists, and his eyes filling with tears.

"If he didn't do it, someone certainly did!" the pregnant-looking woman added, her face set into harder lines than her husband's.

Suddenly Jodie found herself standing in the middle of chaos. Everyone began speaking and shouting at once. Many accusations were thrown butt-pincher's way, and those who argued against them were then also accused.

"Did anyone see him do it?" Jodie spoke loudly.

A few people had heard her and calmed down slightly, curious about what she had to say, but most people hadn't.

"Did anyone actually see him do it?" Jodie shouted, trying to be heard by everyone.

It seemed that this time it worked. People started falling silent all around the train.

"Anyone?" Jodie turned a slow circle, looking at them

all. "Anyone actually see him? Or anyone else for that matter?"

Nobody spoke up.

"It was him," cross-tattoo stubbornly spoke, crossing her arms in front of her chest.

"But you have no proof of that." Jodie was thinking of her dad. She was thinking about what he would do in this situation.

"Who else would do it? No one has any motive to kill that poor woman."

"Motive? Look, my dad's a detective, and he sometimes tells me about some of the cases he works on. Not everyone's motive is clear-cut and understandable. It doesn't always fit in a nice little box that you can label 'this is why he did it.' "

"Someone did it," redhead spoke up.

"Who else would have done it?" cross-tattoo challenged Jodie.

"I don't know," she shrugged. "Maybe you did it. You were closest to her and were quick to throw the blame elsewhere. You even came up with a motive for the other person."

The cross-tattooed woman bristled. Jodie spoke again before she could open her mouth.

"It could have been Denzel, for all we know. Or the driver, Simon. Maybe it was Nina, or Troy. It could even be me, for all you know. The fact is, there's zero evidence to implicate anyone. Everyone on this train is a suspect." Jodie watched as all those she named stiffened at the mention. No one liked the idea of being put into the crosshairs.

"I think it's safe to say that I didn't do it," Eric spoke up from his prone position. A few people managed to chuckle at that, whether it was Eric's intention or not to bring a bit of levity to the situation.

"So what do you suggest we do then, little girl." Cross-tattoo gestured for Jodie to go on.

She chose not to rise to the bait about the little girl remark. "We have to work together, for one thing. Everyone keeps an eye out, so it doesn't happen to anyone else. We also have to decide what to do with the bodies."

"Bodies?" Nina squawked.

Jodie sighed, dreading being the bearer of more bad news. She didn't know if Apollo was listening, and didn't look behind her to find out, because she didn't want to see his face if he was. "Olivia, the boy's mother, passed away in the night."

"Was she murdered, too?" someone asked.

"I don't think so. I don't have any medical training beyond basic first aid, but I don't think so. If I had to guess, I'd say her head injury caused a brain bleed, but that is literally just a guess."

"We can put them in my cab," Simon spoke up from behind Jodie. "I was already thinking of putting Olivia in there. The other woman can go in there as well."

"Her name was Lin," cross-tattoo spoke loudly, making sure everyone heard her. "She had a name, and it was Lin."

"Lin," Jodie nodded.

"Aren't we going to do anything to find the killer?" Nina's voice cut like a knife. "We can't just let whoever it is get away with it!"

"I have a suggestion," redhead raised her hand. When everyone turned to her, she shrank a little in her seat. "We search everyone, and all their bags. We look for the murder weapon." She looked at Jodie for confirmation that this was a good idea.

"We'll do that," Denzel spoke up instead, "and we'll find out who has food as well. We all need to share in this crisis."

The hair on the back of Jodie's neck stood up slightly, as she felt the comment was directed at her. She still had a sandwich in her bag, possibly a little stale now, but one she had been hoping to eat soon for breakfast. If sharing was enforced, she'd be lucky to get a bite of it.

"What if someone just dumps the weapon from their bag or whatever before they get searched?" spoke a middle-aged woman with fair hair and freckles who had been relatively quiet up to this point. She sat with another woman who looked like a somewhat younger version of herself, suggesting they were related, perhaps sisters.

"If the weapon has already been dumped, there's not much we can do about that," Denzel answered her. "Right now, everyone watch each other. We'll start at the back of the train and work our way forward. No one is to move from where they are right now."

For most people that was fine, as they had all moved to their seats, but Jodie was stuck standing in the middle of the train.

"You're not performing the searches on your own," Jodie spoke up when she saw Denzel head toward the back of the train.

Several voices murmured their agreement that at least two people had to perform the searches.

"I'll help," the cyclist volunteered.

"So will I," said cross-tattoo.

The two of them, plus Denzel, went to the back of the train to begin their search.

It took a long time to go through everything. They checked every pocket and pouch on every bag. They even came across bags that had been left behind by the people who had tried to flee only to become trapped in the blue, and it took awhile to realize that they didn't just belong to folks refusing to own up to them. Every scrap of food, including a humble stick of gum, was placed in a neat pile in the middle of the train where everyone could keep an eye on it. Jodie grew hungrier and hungrier as the proceedings dragged on. Pat searches were performed on everyone, and seats were temporarily vacated in order to be thoroughly investigated.

"I'd rather she give me the pat down, if you don't mind," Jodie told the cyclist when it was her turn. Although cross-tattoo didn't like her, Jodie didn't want some strange man's hands running over her.

Jodie's bags were the second to last to be examined. Denzel did most of the searching, digging through her pockets and strewing her art supplies all over the floor. When he pulled out a box of Kraft Dinner, Jodie was surprised. She had completely forgotten she had put that in there before going to Sandra's the other day. Others on the subway gave her a dark look, disapproving of the fact that she had food like that and wasn't planning to share. Jodie didn't care about their looks, she was too busy quelling the anger that bubbled in her belly when the cyclist took her water bottle to the food pile. She hadn't even gotten a drink yet this morning, her mouth still full of sleep gunk that was especially bad since she couldn't brush her teeth last night. Still, she had to watch her precious water be added to the pile. The cyclist himself had to give up his water bottle, and he hadn't looked too happy about it, either. No one was happy when their food and water were taken away.

Olivia's bags and pockets were the last to be searched. They treated the body gently, as they had Lin's, but Jodie couldn't watch. After being so careful not to move her at the risk of further injuring the woman, seeing them straighten her out was too much.

When the search was finally completed, they had a pathetic pile of food and drink, and a surprisingly substantial pile of potential weapons. Nothing they found had blood on it, so the killer was either very good at hiding the weapon, or very good at cleaning it. Denzel's tools made up the majority of that pile, but there were also a lot of Jodie's art supplies, like her scalpels, a small bike repair kit the cyclist had, a few pocket knives, and several nail files from women's purses. Pens and pencils were all searched for blood as well, but it was decided that they could stay with the people who owned them. Jodie wasn't the only one who passed the time by doodling or writing.

"So we're no closer to knowing who the murderer is," Roxanne commented grumpily when the proceedings were done, one of her hands covering Apollo's ear, while his other ear was pressed into her bosom.

"We may never know who did it," Denzel told her, "but at least now we've taken away everything that could be used in the future to kill someone else."

"God is punishing us," Nina declared. "He's punishing us for all our sins!"

Groans met her proclamation. Even those who had spent time praying with her, rolled their eyes or ignored her.

"When can I get something to drink?" Jodie asked.

"We should move the bodies first," Denzel told her.

"I'm not going to help with that," the cyclist said, sitting down. People weren't giving him the friendliest of looks for his involvement in going through their things. Even the tall guy he had been so chummy with before, wasn't too happy with him. Jodie felt a little bit badly for him, mostly because she figured he would have been the coldest last night; his tight clothes weren't meant to keep him warm, and he didn't seem to have any fat on his bony frame.

No one volunteered to help move the bodies. In the end, it was just Denzel with cross-tattoo helping. Olivia was put in the driver's cab first, her belongings that weren't in one of the piles, going with her. Lin was to be moved next.

"We should take her jacket," redhead suggested.

Cross-tattoo gave her the most withering stare that Jodie had ever seen one human give another.

Redhead shrank in her seat, but continued. "We don't know if we're going to have to spend another night in this train, but if we are, I don't imagine it'll be any warmer than last night."

Cross-tattoo got overruled as the riders thought about their night shivering in the cold. Once it was determined that no blood had gotten on the woman's light, spring jacket, it was carefully taken off her body and set aside. Denzel picked Lin up under her arms, while cross-tattoo grabbed her feet. Cross-tattoo was stronger than Jodie had thought; she didn't struggle at all carrying Lin to the driver's cab. Once the bodies were carefully settled, and the door closed, they came to the problem of the food.

"How are we going to make sure everyone gets the same amount?" the middle aged woman with freckles asked. She was sitting close to the small pile, and was probably resisting the urge to take something.

"We'll put someone in charge of distribution," Denzel said.

"I don't trust some stranger to be in control of my food," the girl with the star tattoo spoke up.

"Neither do I," Eric added. The only thing he had contributed to the pile was a small pack of breath mints.

"I have to eat more than other people." The apparently pregnant woman placed her hands on her belly. "I'm eating for two." She at last confirmed Jodie's suspicion.

"Then what do you all suggest?" Denzel threw up his hands in frustration.

"I have an idea," one of the bland, generic-looking businessmen raised his hand.

Everyone waited for him to go on.

"We divide the food equally now, and then everyone decides on their own when they eat it," he suggested.

People muttered amongst themselves about this, but no one had a better idea.

"What about water?" Jodie's thirst just kept getting worse until it was all she could think about. "We don't have enough containers to divvy it up."

No one had a solution for that problem.

"I think whoever owns the water, should have it back." It was the tall guy who finally spoke up, drawing a lot of confused and even angry looks. If he had contributed water, people probably wouldn't listen to him, but since he hadn't, people gave him a chance. "They get their water back, but they're not allowed to refuse a drink to anyone else unless more than one person has decided they've had too much. And they're not allowed to keep the water out of sight. It has to be out where everyone can see who has some, and how much is left."

Even more grumbling met this. It forced those who had no water to rely on those who did. Many people had at least a little bit in a water bottle, but there were several who didn't.

"Does anyone have a better idea?" Eric spoke up.

No one did. In the end, it was decided that the tall guy had the best plan for the water, and people were returned their drinks. Jodie immediately took a swallow from hers, conscious of the fact that everyone was watching her. She was careful to drink just enough to rinse out her mouth, and soothe her dry throat.

"I'd like some," Eric told her as soon as she was done.

Jodie knelt down beside him, helped him to sit up, and let him have a small swallow of water. Troy and Ed also wanted a drink each after that, and Jodie watched them closely. She was disheartened to see how much the water level had dropped after only a few people had taken small sips from it.

Turning to Apollo and Roxanne, Jodie saw that Apollo was finishing the last of the water from his sippy cup.

"Did he drink his juice boxes yesterday?" Jodie asked.

Roxanne nodded.

"Here. Give him this if he gets thirsty again." Jodie handed Roxanne her last box of grape juice that had just been returned to her.

"So, how are we going to split up the food?" the kid with the paint-stained clothes and wildly curly hair asked.

"Very carefully, and while everyone watches and has input on what's going on," Denzel said, stepping up to the pile. "Gather 'round."

There was a great shuffling as people rose from their seats to squish into the empty spaces near the food pile, several of them remaining standing and filling the aisle. Troy hung back a little so he could relay what was going on to Eric, Ed, and Roxanne. Roxanne had chosen to stay out of the mess to sit quietly with Apollo, while Ed wouldn't be able to see what was happening, and Eric's line of sight was blocked by those standing around.

The process was long and gut-wrenching. It was disheartening to watch the food get divided up into smaller and smaller parts. By the end, Jodie was given nothing but half her box of dry Kraft Dinner, the other half having been poured into a container for the redhead. Even the cheese powder had been removed and given to someone else. With no way to cook it, she wasn't looking forward to eating it, and didn't expect it to be very filling. Once everything was divvied up, the subway passengers returned to their seats. Jodie went straight to her bags to tidy up the mess the searchers had left behind, making sure to keep her water bottle in sight of the others.

Being so near the empty space where Olivia had lain made Jodie feel light-headed. Someone had died today. Two people, actually, one of them murdered. They had no way of knowing who the murderer was. Did he or she plan to strike again? Was Lin only the first? If someone had already done this now, what would happen once the food was all gone?

14

WHEN JODIE CHECKED HER WATCH, she panicked to see that it was already past nine a.m. She was supposed to have checked in with her dad by now, but after everything that had been going on that morning, she hadn't remembered until it was too late. Dragging her bag to her, she pulled her phone out of its pocket. Jodie had decided to bring her bags with her when she had positioned herself in the doorway across from Eric. She didn't mind the subway floor at all anymore, and liked being able to stretch her legs out without bothering anyone. She was also close to Eric and could help him if he needed anything.

Once her phone was on, Jodie gave it a minute to connect, waiting for any messages that might come through. She discovered she had five texts, and decided to start with the oldest and work her way to the newest.

The first message was from her service provider. As a customer listed in Toronto, she was now receiving unlimited calls and text messaging, as well as unlimited access to Twitter, Facebook, and certain news websites, during the crisis. They didn't want anyone who was trapped unable to get vital information. Jodie was oddly touched by the gesture, and would have been extremely thankful for it had she the battery power to waste. Maybe someone else on the train was with the same provider and would make use of it.

The second message on her phone was a blanket message sent as the result of some sort of emergency effort. It was full of advice. Jodie read through it all, mentally checking off what they had and had not done. A lot of it didn't apply to them, such as filling bathtubs with water in case it became unavailable, or covering windows with any extra blankets and lighting candles at night to reduce the cold. Jodie wished they could cover their windows, or had candles. There were also recommendations concerning food and water consumption. It sounded as though they were assuming people had a fair amount of both. Then again, most people who couldn't be helped right away were trapped in buildings, rather than in transit, and had access to sinks and powerless fridges.

Her phone's third text message brightened Jodie's morning a degree. Her sister had made it to Jodie and her dad's apartment. According to the time stamp, Amber had gotten there around two in the morning, and must have been both freezing and exhausted. It was a quick update, saying she had been able to get inside, and that Rusty was being looked after. Apparently he was being extra snugly.

The next message had the opposite effect. It came at the absurd hour of four a.m. from Lucas. Based on the writing, Sandra's boyfriend was drunk and depressed. Jodie didn't read the entire message. Just reading the start of it bummed her out. It sounded as though Lucas thought that Sandra was dead. If there was actual confirmation of that within the message, she didn't want to see it.

At last, came a text from her dad. It had been written

before nine a.m., and expressed that he wouldn't be able to call. His hearing was still buggered from the close range, confined space shotgun blast. He didn't mention anything bad, but Jodie assumed he'd be both hungry and thirsty by now. It was unlikely he and Lucky had anything more than coffee in the car when the blue came. She hoped his hearing wasn't permanently damaged. Her dad also mentioned Amber's message, stating the same things about Rusty, then went on to say that he and Lucky were going to see if they could dig their way out of the car today. They had no idea how they were going to do it, but if they could get under the car, they might be able to squirm their way out under the hood. He ended by saying he would check for messages from her throughout the day, but that she should only send him one. He'd try calling her around nine o'clock at night if his hearing was better, and if not he'd leave another message. He was able to charge his phone and use it more often than Jodie could thanks to the car's twelve-volt adapter. He mentioned he'd pass on any important information he got from it or his radio.

Her dad's message was the only one Jodie took the time and the battery life to respond to. She debated how much to say about the murder. It would worry him. Hell, it worried Jodie. In the end, she decided that full disclosure was best. She mentioned that Olivia had passed away in the night, and that Lin had been stabbed by something through her ear. At least, that's what they thought. For all they knew, her eardrum could've blown out. After writing about the food and water, and agreeing to the call time, Jodie told her dad she loved him, sent the message, and then powered down her phone.

Thinking about blown eardrums, Jodie began to wonder if that was an actual possibility. Might they have gotten worked up and paranoid over nothing? Could Lin have been suffering some medical condition all this time, and something finally burst and killed her? Jodie could think of only one way she might get answers.

Pulling out her large sketchbook and selecting a few pens, Jodie brought them over to the window. People had been changing seats again. Redhead now sat in the three seats across from Troy, sitting sideways next to Roxanne and Apollo, and playing Patty Cake with the boy. The Hispanic couple had also moved, now occupying the rear facing seats across the aisle. Jodie noticed that the people who had moved were the ones sitting the closest to where Lin and cross-tattoo had been when Lin was killed. Cross-tattoo continued to occupy her seat, making Jodie wonder if they left the area because Lin had died there, or because cross-tattoo hadn't.

"Pardon me." Jodie smiled at the redhead, kneeling on the seat beside her. "Just want to check on the doctor."

"By all means." Redhead's round, smooth face smiled back, as she scooted over slightly to give Jodie a bit more room. "I'm Mandy, by the way."

"Jodie." They briefly shook hands, then returned to what they had been doing.

It took awhile for Jodie to get the doctor's attention. It was hard to tell, but it appeared he had left the rear seat flattened after kicking out the taillight, and had reclined the back of his passenger seat as much as he could. Jodie could make out part of his white shirt as he lay on the far seat, facing the other way. It was impossible to tell if he was sleeping, or doing something else. Eventually, he rolled over and Jodie made a lot of motion in an attempt to catch his eye. She succeeded, and the doctor got up and slid over to his upright driver's seat. He drew a big question mark on his whiteboard and held it up for her to see. Jodie held up her own message in response, using a short hand to save space on the page for future messages. She also stopped printing in all caps, thinking that if she only capitalized the first letter of each word, it might be easier for the doctor to make them out.

How R U?

The doctor squinted and pressed his face to his window, reading the message. He then turned to his whiteboard and responded.

HUNGRY

Jodie exaggerated a nod and patted her chest then stomach, letting him know that they were hungry, too. The doctor redrew his question mark and pointed at her. Jodie wrote her next message.

Maybe Murder Here

The doctor frantically pointed to his question mark several times, seeking more information. Jodie thought hard about what to say next.

Can Eardrum Explode On Own?

The doctor wrote his response.

HIGHLY

NOT

Jodie figured he meant highly unlikely. The doctor once again drew his question mark. Instead of figuring out how to write it, Jodie used a fresh page to draw it. She drew a large, exaggerated ear, switching to a red pen for the blood. Next to it, she wrote *Think Stabbed*.

LIKELY

Jodie sighed, wishing the doctor's response had been different. He wrote something else.

ONE

EAR?

Jodie nodded her exaggerated nod again.

LIKELY

Jodie gave him a thumbs up to thank him, then she remembered her phone messages.

R U Cold? she wrote.

AT

NIGHT

Cover Windows?

The doctor gestured all around him. With what? He had nothing in the car with which to cover his windows. Jodie raised both her hands and shrugged.

There was nothing else for the two of them to say to one another. The doctor eventually put his whiteboard down, but continued to sit in his driver's seat and stare out the windshield.

As Jodie remembered the cold night, she noticed it wasn't cold anymore. Inside the train, it was a pleasant temperature for the moment. It reminded her of walking through the sunshine with Sandra the other day. Jodie closed her eyes and let the warmth flow over her, allowing it to get down to her bones and drive out the last of the night-time chill. Then, she gathered her things and returned to the doorway across from Eric.

"He say anything interesting?" Troy stuck his head around the little barrier that separated his seats from Jodie.

"Not really. He's hungry, and nearly froze to death overnight, so nothing different than here. I wanted to know if spontaneous eardrum-bursting was a thing."

"And is it?" Troy wondered.

"In the words of the doctor, highly not. I figure he means highly unlikely, but needed the writing real estate."

"Or, he thinks it's impossible."

"I prefer to pretend that there's a chance Lin died of natural causes, as opposed to us being trapped on a subway train with a murderer, don't you?"

"I see your point."

Troy grabbed the bar on the edge of the barrier and swung around in a rather slick move until he was seated on the floor beside Jodie.

"So, who do you think it is?" he whispered conspiratorially.

"I honestly have no idea," Jodie whispered back. "I don't even know everyone's names yet. It could be you, for all I know. The only people I know it's not is myself, Apollo, and Eric."

"How do you know it wasn't the kid? Maybe he did it in his sleep, or doesn't understand what he did?"

Jodie gave him an incredulous look. "Besides the fact that that's crazy, he's constantly being watched. Hell, I had my arms wrapped around him all night."

"Could have happened before then. And I'd like to point out that I was against your back for the same length of time you were next to him. You know, maybe it was you. Maybe you murdered Lin before going to lie down next to Eric."

Jodie scoffed. "I didn't. Obviously, I have no way to prove that though."

"You do have a bunch of stuff in the weapon pile," Troy gestured briefly in its direction. After the food had been organized and meted out, all the potential murder weapons had been moved to the seats at the very back of the train. If anyone took a step past the toilet doors, people would know.

"They're just my art supplies." Jodie knew that that was no argument.

"I think it was Denzel," Troy whispered even quieter. "The way he went all Neanderthal on that door yesterday?"

"What about Nina?" Jodie suggested. "She seems pretty insane. Freaks out at the drop of a hat. She might have wigged out in the night."

"Well, we can safely assume it wasn't Ed." Being blind, there was no way he could've gotten to Lin, stabbed her with such precision, and made it back to his seat without anyone noticing.

"True. He can be added to the non-suspect list. Eric, Ed, and Apollo. And Happy. Pretty sure the dog didn't do it."

"That poor dog. He needs more than a walk to the hole to do his business, and nobody included him during the splitting of the food."

"I love dogs, but even I find it's a hard argument to make, taking food away from a person to give to him."

"I still feel bad about it."

"Me too." Jodie looked at her box of Kraft Dinner. *She* wasn't going to share with the dog, and it was unlikely anyone else would, except maybe Roxanne. Hopefully, the squat ball of fur didn't get so hungry that he started attacking people.

"How many peoples' names do you know on this train?" Troy changed the topic.

Jodie thought it over. "Including myself, the dog, and the two dead women, I know thirteen."

"How many people are on the train?"

"Twenty-six plus the dog. I counted yesterday."

"Okay, tell me who you know. I want to know, too."

"Other than us, there's Apollo, the kid. His mom is Olivia, and the other dead woman is Lin. Simon's the train driver, Ed is the blind guy, and Roxanne is the old woman.

Happy's her dog, and Eric is trapped in the blue. I just met the redhead, her name is Mandy. The frail-looking, blond woman who keeps panicking is Nina, and then there's Denzel near the back."

"I've got one more name you can add to your list."

"Who?"

"Anthony." Troy hiked a thumb back toward the front of the train.

"Mr. plaid shirt?" Jodie thought of the burly, hairy man who resembled a lumberjack.

"Yeah."

"Okay, so Mr. plaid is Anthony. That's now fourteen out of twenty-seven names."

"More than half."

"Barely. Pretty much *is* half."

"Still, you seem pretty good with names. I'm awful at remembering them."

"Like most things, I get it from my dad. He taught himself to remember names, and then taught me when I was little. Came in handy at school."

"You've mentioned your dad a lot, but never your mom. What's she like?"

Jodie tried to keep her voice even. "She passed away."

"I'm sorry." Troy suddenly turned away, shuffling awkwardly.

"No, it's okay." Jodie didn't like to talk about it, but she knew she shouldn't avoid it completely. "She was hit by a truck coming home from work. It was winter, the roads were covered with ice, and the truck driver just lost control. Nobody's fault, really. She was killed instantly, no pain."

Troy picked at a string hanging off the hem of his shirt, unsure what to say.

"What about you?" Jodie changed topics. "What are

your parents like? I already know your mom sends you downtown to pick up her shopping."

Troy chuckled to himself, then leaned in conspiratorially again. "I wasn't really going shopping."

"Where were you going then?" Jodie whispered back, curious.

"You know that little show I put on yesterday?"

"Yeah?"

"I can steal more than people's watches without them noticing."

"You're a pickpocket?"

He paused momentarily before answering, as if unsure he wanted to continue. "My dad's a grumpy old bastard in a wheelchair. I mean, like, old-old, to the point of retirement. My mom married him for his money, not expecting him to lose it all gambling on the stock market. She now works two jobs and gives *him* an allowance. She can't bring herself to leave him after all he's done for her. The wheelchair, combined with his age and the I'm-better-than-you personality, have made it near impossible for him to find a new job. With the job market the way it is, I can barely get shifts at the sporting goods store that presumably hired me, although you wouldn't know it based on how infrequently they call me in. So, from time to time, I go downtown and pick the pockets of the richest looking people I can find. If they have cash, I take it, then wipe down the wallets and stuff them in mailboxes. I have no idea if the postal service returns them, but it makes me feel better than chucking them in the trash."

This time, it was Jodie's turn to fidget and say she was sorry. After the heroic way Troy had acted since the blue came, she was surprised to learn he stole from people. Her first impression of him hadn't been a good one, maybe because she was picking up on his intentions. Jodie didn't really believe in psychics, but she did believe that people gave off different kinds of energy, and those sensitive to it could pick it up.

"Everyone has their own crap story, right?" Troy continued. "I swear, in high school, no one was allowed to talk about the good things that happened to them. Everyone was always talking about the bad, and trying to top each other. Whose life is harder, and all that."

Jodie couldn't help but smile. "I used to think the same thing."

"I guess it doesn't matter now, though. We're all in the same shit." He gestured around the train bringing them back to the present.

They sat silently together, neither of them having anything else to say. Jodie nibbled on a few dry noodles, taking her time chewing them. They didn't really relieve the yawning chasm that was her stomach, but it was the best she could do. Filling her belly with water would have helped, but that wasn't an option. Even with everyone taking conserved sips, the amount in the water bottle was diminishing quickly.

The longer they were in there, the greater the threat of something drastic happening. Jodie herself felt weak from the lack of food, and she knew that everyone would be feeling the same, but that wasn't going to stop people from attacking one another as they became hungrier and more desperate. And there wasn't a damned thing she could do about it.

15

"AHOY, TRAIN!"

For awhile now, everyone had been sitting rather quietly. A few conversations had sprung up here and there, but when they turned into arguments, the people fell silent. Now, everyone sat up and looked around, trying to figure out who had just called out. It was an unfamiliar voice.

"Apollo!" the voice called out again, and Jodie realized it wasn't coming from inside the train.

"Daddy!" Apollo screamed, climbing off the seat next to Roxanne. "Where are you?"

Jodie was up in an instant and heading for the back of the train.

"Apollo!" the voice responded louder than ever, reacting to the child's cry.

Jodie wasn't the only one who had gotten up, just about everyone was on their feet. They all crowded to the rear of the train and searched for where the voice was coming from. A man was standing near the subway car behind theirs, in front of the doors from which its riders had escaped.

"Are you Bruce?" Jodie shouted through the glass and the blue.

"Where's my son?" he shouted back.

The mass of bodies parted, allowing Apollo to get close to the windows. Jodie helped him up onto the seat, where he and Bruce could see each other.

"Daddy!" Apollo cried again, in a heartbreakingly happy voice. "I've missed you!"

"Apollo!" Bruce cried back, his knees becoming visibly weak. He got as close as the blue stuff would allow.

"Can you get to the other side of the train?" Denzel shouted. "We have an small opening over there."

"I think so." Bruce looked along the length of the subway, then turned back to gaze up at his son. "I'm right here, Apollo. Daddy's here for you."

People watched through the windows as Bruce climbed aboard the car behind theirs. He investigated the doors on the other side until he found one he could pry open with a large crowbar he carried in a heavy-looking backpack. Once outside on the other side, he quickly found their shit opening.

After making a repulsed expression, Bruce quickly overcame the smell as he knelt down to peer through the opening. "Apollo," he smiled broadly.

"Daddy!" Apollo knelt in front of the opening, everyone on the train crowding behind him.

"Come on, buddy, let's get you out of there."

"Bruce? Sir?" Jodie knelt down beside Apollo. "I'm the one you spoke with on the phone."

"On my wife's phone. Where is she?"

Jodie's throat suddenly pinched and she couldn't find the words.

"Sir, I'm sorry to tell you this, but she didn't survive the night," Troy was behind Jodie and spoke for her.

The pained expression that crossed Bruce's face made Jodie want to throw up.

"I want to get my son out of there," he spoke in a deadpan. What had he seen during his journey to make him accept what he had just heard so quickly?

Jodie nodded. "Do you have something to cover... that up with?" she gestured to their waste. "And maybe something we can wipe the doors with?"

Bruce didn't hesitate. He shrugged off his backpack and pulled out a tarp, quickly covering up the disgust, and then passing them a T-shirt half covered in dried mud.

"Okay, Apollo, you're going to have to squeeze out. Are you ready?" Jodie asked him after wiping down the doors.

"Where's Roxanne?" he asked, looking at all the faces around.

The crowd shifted until Roxanne was brought to the forefront.

"Are you coming?" Apollo asked.

"Sorry, honey, I can't fit. You'll have to go to your dad without me."

"I like you," he said, "and Happy."

"Why don't you take Happy with you?" Roxanne had brought the dog to the back of the train with her, and now held out his leash. "He can fit."

"Can we bring him, Daddy?" Apollo excitedly asked. "Can we bring Happy? Please? Pretty please?"

Bruce looked from his son to the old woman with the dog standing behind him. Jodie was fairly certain he didn't want to bring the dog.

"He's a good doggie. He plays with me and Thomas."

Apollo suddenly whipped around to stare at Roxanne, his eyes full of alarm. "Where's Thomas?"

"I have him right here." Roxanne held out the blue train. "Best you hold on to him tightly, so that he doesn't get lost."

"Is Mommy still sleeping?"

"She is, darling."

"If she wasn't, could she fit?"

"No. She has to stay here with us."

"Okay."

"All right, I'll take the dog," Bruce gave in. "Just get my son out of there. Please." His voice was stressed and impatient. It had taken him over a day to get here, going through who knows what, and now he was so close to what he had come for.

Jodie held Apollo's arms and lowered him through the opening onto the tarp below. His head just barely made it through. As soon as he was clear, Bruce swept him up into his arms and covered his son with kisses. He could have left then, but he did as he promised and waited for them to get Happy out.

"Will you tell people we're here?" Jodie asked, while Roxanne said goodbye to her dog.

"Sure," Bruce nodded, although he seemed distracted, staring at his son's face and brushing his hair back from his forehead.

Happy didn't go through the hole as neatly as Apollo had. The corgi didn't understand what was going on, and squirmed in ways that were counterproductive. He was also a little thicker around than Apollo's head, and had to be pushed to get him all the way out.

"Do you have any food? Any water?" Denzel asked during the proceedings.

Bruce shook his head.

"Can you bring us some? Please. We're starving in here."

Happy was finally free, and Bruce picked up his leash. The first thing the dog did once outside was lift his leg and pee on the fence.

"Can you please bring us some food and water?" Denzel continued.

Bruce looked at all the faces staring back at him, overwhelmed.

"I'm sorry," he said, then turned to leave.

"Wait! Please!" people cried out from behind Jodie. They all turned to follow Bruce's progress back through the train car behind them. "We're starving in here! You can't leave us! Come back! Please, come back!" Their voices piled upon one another.

Jodie could only sit by the opening, another wave of weakness washing over her. As soon as Denzel had mentioned food, and that Bruce could get some for them, her spirits had unexpectedly risen. She could picture it in her head: Bruce travelling away with his son, but then returning later with a team of rescue workers. They would have food, and water, and blowtorches they could use to get them out. She saw it so clearly, that she didn't expect Bruce to just walk away like he did, to make no promises to ever return.

"Come on, Jodie." Troy took her arm and helped her to her feet.

People were still yelling through the window and the blue, but now they were throwing curses and insults. Bruce was probably far enough away already not to be able to hear them. Troy and Jodie walked back to where Eric lay, trapped and unable to watch what was happening. Roxanne had already returned to her seat, disappearing from the crowd shortly after her dog was off the train.

"So the kid is gone, huh?" Eric commented.

Jodie collapsed down next to him, still in shock over what had just happened. How could someone just leave them like that?

"You okay?" Eric pushed himself upright so that he was at eye level with Jodie.

"No." Her voice sounded very small to her ears. Her vision wavered as tears spilled out of her eyes.

Eric didn't say anything, he just wrapped his arms around her, hugging her to his chest so that Jodie had to balance for both of them. Jodie sobbed into his shirt, as everything, the whole situation, washed over her at once. She couldn't pin down a single thought as a tide of feeling brought them all crashing down at the same time. She just cried and let Eric hold her.

It was impossible to tell for how long Jodie had been crying, but eventually she stopped shaking. Eric took that as a sign, and gently held her out at arm's length.

"You okay?" he asked again, already knowing the answer, the same way Jodie had known that he couldn't possibly be okay. "You certainly look a lot worse."

Jodie chuckled despite herself, rubbing her eyes and face with the palms of her hands.

"On the plus side, you gave yourself a nice face wash. Although your makeup could use some touching up."

"You don't look so hot yourself," Jodie retorted, wondering if she should bother using the makeup in her bag to touch up her face. It seemed pretty pointless, especially when it would be a waste of water to wipe away the running mascara. Also, her remark was a complete lie. Eric still looked damned good, even with his hair messed up and going greasy, and stubble making an appearance all around the lower half of his face. Just about all the men were rocking the five o'clock shadow look, or at least their version of it. Troy's wasn't coming in too well; same for the kid in the painting clothes, but his hair was so fine that it was hardly noticeable.

"Actually, I am rather hot," Eric commented, unbuttoning the top few buttons of his shirt.

At first, Jodie mistook his comment for arrogance, but then she realized he was talking about the temperature of the place. All day, it had been getting warmer and warmer. It was no longer the comfortable temperature it had been earlier, but uncomfortably hot. The air was still, and smothering. Looking at the windows, Jodie wondered if a powerless subway train always got this hot in the sunshine, or if the blue was acting like some sort of magnifying glass. She had thought about it being an insulator at first, but then remembered the freezing night, and figured that that couldn't be it.

"I hate this subway map," Eric commented out of nowhere as he lay back down.

Jodie turned her eyes upward to find a subway map above the door, right in Eric's line of sight. It was in the middle of a string of ads, with maps above alternating doors. Jodie had ridden on transit so many times, that she pretty much failed to see them anymore.

"I actually wish I had an ad. At least then I'd have something to read. Like that ad." Eric gestured to a block of white farther down the row. "Have you ever read that one? It's about the struggles of a homeless kid. That block of small text is actually a story, if you've ever taken the time to read it."

"I haven't," but Jodie had seen the ad before, and knew which one he was talking about.

"It would be a lot better than this crap," Eric gestured to the map. "I mean, look at the puny number of stops and lines we have. Compared to places like London and New York, this is pathetic. I've already memorized all the stops."

Jodie peered up at the map again. Her eyes tracked along the yellow U-shape until they located the stops that they were currently trapped between.

"It's Jodie, right?"

She looked back to see the pregnant woman standing behind her. "Yeah."

"I'm Carla."

"Nice to meet you."

"I'd like some water, if you don't mind." She pointed to the bottle near Jodie's curled up legs.

Jodie checked the level, then gave her some. The woman took a long swallow before Jodie knew what was happening. She made a distressed sound in the back of her throat, not knowing what to say, but then Carla finished. She handed the bottle back to Jodie, the level having dropped considerably.

"Thank you," Carla said. "This heat and the baby are just really getting to me." She then walked off to rejoin her probable-husband.

Jodie stared at the water level, her heart squeezing again at how much was gone now.

"Bitch," Eric muttered under his breath. "She's barely pregnant enough to show. She's probably just using it as an excuse to get more than everyone else. Did you see how much food she got? I couldn't see the actual distribution, but it looked like she came back carrying more than the others. More than what I was given."

"Maybe she was holding the food for both her and her husband," Jodie said offhand, still distracted by the low water level.

"No, I saw he had the same amount of food as everyone else."

Whether she was using the baby as an excuse or not, neither of them could refute her comment about the heat. Soon, everyone was going to need water, and they were going to be hard pressed to take small sips.

16

JODIE WAS BACK in the doorway across from Eric, doodling in her small sketchbook. She had trouble focusing on the page for more than five minutes at a time, often giving up on what she was drawing to make pointless squiggles.

The girl with the star tattoo walked up to Jodie and sat down, leaned against the other barrier, and straightened out her short skirt the same way Jodie straightened her own, longer skirt every time she sat. The hole she had cut in her tights, before boarding the train the other day, was now causing a run down most of the length of her leg.

"Hi, I'm Alison," she said, not offering a hand to shake, but waving slightly.

"I'm Jodie. You here for water?" Everyone who had come to talk to Jodie lately was there for water, and she instinctively reached for the bottle.

"No," Alison shook her head. "I was wondering if you have a bit of paper and a pencil I could borrow? I thought I might like to do some sketching."

"Sure," Jodie brightened, turning to her bag beside her.

She dug around inside until she found her second small sketchbook. Originally, she had designated one of the pocket-sized books for clothing design sketches, and the other for gesture drawings and doodling during her travels. There was no point in separating the two now, and handed the other girl her design book.

"It's been awhile since I used a pencil," she commented, slowly flipping through Jodie's book and looking at her drawings. "When I draw, it's predominantly on the computer these days."

"Are you an artist?"

"3D modeller, but I do some painting on the side, especially when I have to texture my own models at home."

Jodie didn't completely understand what she was talking about, but could guess, more or less. "Done reading your book?" she asked, remembering she had been the only one able to focus on reading earlier.

"Yeah," she nodded, finally coming to a blank page.

"You say you have a book you're not reading?" Eric twisted around awkwardly in order to see them.

"I do." Alison glanced at Eric and then quickly looked away.

"Would you mind if I borrowed it? I'm bored out of my skull over here."

"Um, yeah. Sure. I'll get it for you." Alison carefully placed the sketchbook and pencil Jodie had lent her on the floor beside her, then hopped up onto her feet. She was gone for only a few seconds. Upon returning, she handed her paperback novel to Eric, still not looking directly at him.

"Thanks," he said, not even bothering to turn it over and read what it was about. He went straight to the first page.

Alison sat down near Jodie again, their legs stretched out parallel to each other.

"I like your tattoo," Jodie commented, gesturing to the star.

"Thanks. It gets itchy, though."

"So what is it you model?" Jodie asked. She found it funny that in her own line of art, that sentence would mean something very different.

"At home I like to model scenes. Interior sets, mostly. Lately, I've been working on a science lab. Lots of neat equipment."

"And your job is 3D modelling?"

"Sort of. I work at this tiny game company. No one but upper management gets paid, it's all volunteer work. No one really knows what they're doing. The art department consists of me, my friend Ashley, and a bunch of high school students doing a co-op course. There used to be another guy, the art lead, but he quit recently, so everyone is extra lost. The place is a revolving door of artists and program-mers. Everyone there wears several hats."

"Sounds terrible." Jodie thought about the intern posi-tion for which she had been going to interview. She wondered if it was an unpaid position, and if they just burned through people like that.

Alison shrugged. "Maybe. It's a unique learning experi-ence, and everyone past high school level has become good friends. The hours are whatever I want them to be, no one keeps track of who's coming and going. My husband and I moved here a couple of months ago when he was offered a good position at IBM. I'm looking for a properly paying job elsewhere, but this place will fill in the hole on my resume nicely."

Jodie was surprised to hear that she was married, but that was only because she herself was single with no prospects. Alison could easily be older than her, and Jodie wasn't as young as she sometimes pictured herself. Hell, some of her classmates had gotten married right after college, which was nearly four years ago. Her sister was engaged to be married before the end of the year, and Sandra and Lucas were likely to get hitched soon, too. Provided Sandra was still alive.

Returning to her sketchbook, Jodie tried to focus on her drawing. Instead of doodling, she thought she'd try drawing a knight, despite the fact that it would be difficult without references. She used to draw knights all the time before she moved on to fashion. Medieval themes still heavily inspired her work.

She was close to the shading stage when the fluttering of pages distracted her. Looking over, she saw that Eric had dropped the book Alison had lent him and was sitting upright.

"You okay, Eric?" she asked.

"Yes. No. I don't know."

Jodie put her sketchbook aside and crawled over to him. "What's the matter?"

"I can't feel my legs." His voice had taken on a detached quality, as if he couldn't believe what was happening.

"I assume you could feel them before?"

"Yes. I could wiggle my toes and feel them moving around in my shoes. Now I can't. I think I'm wiggling my toes right now, I'm telling them to, but I don't know." His voice cracked.

Jodie peered into the blue, hoping to see some small movement from a fold in his pants or the leather of his shoes.

"Just keep trying to move. Try your legs, too," she told him.

"I am."

"It's all right, Eric." Troy had joined them, kneeling down on Eric's other side. "Remember to breathe."

When Jodie glanced back at him, she saw that Eric's face had turned red, and his chest was hitching spastically. Troy started taking slow, deep breaths, encouraging Eric to do the same, to breathe with him. It was the same thing Roxanne had done for Jodie.

She turned back to the blue. The sun was causing a bit of glare, so she put her face close to it, and cupped her hands around her eyes.

"Keep wiggling, I think I can see movement," Jodie encouraged Eric. "Yeah, it's not much, the blue stops most of it, but I can see a tiny fold under your knee shifting. Your legs are moving, you're not paralyzed. Ah!" Jodie fell back from the blue, her hands held out before her.

"What is it? What's wrong?" Eric quickly asked in a tight voice.

"The sides of my hands went numb." Jodie flexed her pinkie fingers and rubbed them with her thumbs. There was no feeling at all in them.

"Your hands were touching the blue, weren't they?" Troy asked, while placing the entire palm of his hand against it. After a few seconds, with everyone nearby watching him, he pulled his hand back. "I can't feel a thing with it," he announced, poking his palm with his free hand.

"What does it mean?" Eric looked all around, hoping someone had answers.

Nina opened her mouth, about to say something, most likely something about God punishing them.

"You shut your mouth and don't say a word," cross-tattoo cut her off with a snap. She offered nothing herself, while standing in the aisle and watching, but just keeping Nina silent was actually helpful.

"The feeling in my hands is already coming back," Jodie told Eric and Troy, as her fingers tingled. It felt the same as when her leg or foot fell asleep.

"I'm not touching the blue though, my pants and shoes are in the way," Eric whined. "I should be able to feel my legs and feet."

"Maybe it's seeped into the fabric a bit," Troy suggested, flexing his hand. "I mean, it started out in mostly a liquid state, right? Could it have soaked into your pants?"

"Maybe," Eric latched onto the idea. "Yeah, it probably did. Everything was so hectic, I can't recall feeling if any of it soaked through my pants. That's probably what happened."

"All right, everyone back away from the blue stuff," Denzel bellowed, trying to assume control. "No one should touch it anymore."

"No one was really touching it to begin with," redheaded Mandy commented.

That flustered Denzel. "Yes, well, no one should ever touch it again. This shit is changing somehow, and we can't predict what it might do next. So... just keep away from it." He shuffled off back towards his seat after having made his statement, an attempt to keep himself in a position of authority. A lot of eyes rolled behind his back. They had all come to the same conclusion on their own.

Eric reached for Jodie's hand. "I'm frightened," he whispered to her.

Denzel's words probably hadn't helped. If the blue did continue to change, Eric was in the proverbial line of fire.

"Please don't leave me alone." Eric gently squeezed Jodie's hand.

"I won't. I'll sit right here with you." Jodie used her free hand to stroke his hair, trying to ignore the greasiness of it.

"When did you first notice the numbness?" Troy asked him.

"Pretty much the moment it happened, like, a minute or two ago," Eric spoke up at the ceiling. "Since I can't really move my legs, my knees have gotten really sore. As soon as that uncomfortably stiff feeling went away, I noticed my legs and feet were numb."

"So this came on suddenly," Troy was nodding. "There's a lot of these blobs connected together and overlapping right? Basically becoming one giant mass? Maybe someone was testing some blue gunk that attaches to our blue gunk. Maybe they sent some electricity through it, and that's what caused the numbness to come on."

"Yeah. Yeah, it's probably just that." Eric was eager to agree, eager to have it be something unimportant.

When Jodie looked into Troy's eyes, she could tell he was lying. He didn't believe it was anything like someone testing electricity on it. He had recognized Eric's fear and was throwing him a flimsy life preserver to grab onto. Jodie turned her attention back down to Eric and continued to stroke his hair and hold his hand.

"I would like to form another prayer circle," Nina squeaked loudly enough for everyone to hear.

Jodie thought she would be ignored, but apparently, the call to prayer was stronger than their mutual dislike of the woman. The same people who had prayed with her before—Simon, Mr. plaid aka Anthony, the Hispanic couple, and blind Ed—all got up to join her. New members entered the prayer circle as well. The middle-aged freckled woman and her younger companion attached themselves to the outer edge, and one of the businessmen and the black woman sitting farther down the train walked up to be included. They were frightened, and so they were turning to prayer. Curiously enough, the woman with a cross tattooed on her forehead had yet to pray.

"I would like to pray," Eric whispered to Jodie, not wanting to be heard by anyone in the prayer group gathering so close to him.

"You're allowed to pray," Jodie told him.

"Will you pray with me? And you, Troy?"

"I'll pray with you." Troy took his other hand.

"Jodie?"

Jodie pursed her lips. Religion had never been a part of her life. When asked, she didn't believe in God, or a pantheon of gods. She thought that when people died, there was nothing afterward. No deity was watching them, concerned about all they did. Although she sometimes liked the idea of God, she could never bring herself to truly believe. She had never prayed before.

"You're going to have to walk me through it," she eventually told Eric. Even if prayer was meaningless to her, she realized it could help Eric in his time of need. He was helpless in his situation, unable to do anything *but* pray.

"I don't know what I'm doing either," Eric chuckled. "Troy?"

"Not a clue."

"All right, we'll fumble our way through it. I don't think the words matter anyway, just the intention." He closed his eyes, so Jodie did the same. "Dear God... Please help us in our time of need. Please help us get the hell off this train without anyone else getting hurt. I don't know if you sent the blue shit or not, but if you were punishing someone, or all of us, we got the message. We'd like to go home now."

When Eric paused, Jodie opened her eyes. His were still closed, tears escaping from beneath the lids. Jodie looked across at Troy. Troy was staring back, maybe thinking about the same things she was, maybe not.

Eric opened his eyes with a series of blinks, quickly releasing Troy's hand to wipe away his tears. "I couldn't think of anything else to say."

"You did fine." Jodie squeezed his hand.

"Better than anything I could think up," Troy added with a shrug.

The prayer group next to them was mostly silent, with only a few of them muttering under their breath. Eric watched them for a bit, his head twisted around at an awkward angle.

"Do you think they're including me in their prayers?" Eric whispered.

"Of course they are," Jodie frowned. "Why wouldn't they?"

"I've noticed that most people don't like to look at me." Eric turned his head to stare at the blue wall before him, or rather on top of him. "You two are great, but most of them..."

Jodie thought about Alison lending him the book, about how she wouldn't look directly at him for longer than a brief glance. At the time, Jodie had just assumed that that was who Alison was, that she had trouble looking at a man that handsome. Jodie had met women like that before, had been in class with a few. Now, she realized that she could have been mistaken. Eric would notice something like that more than she would. It was hard not to notice when people avoided looking at you.

"They're just scared is all," Troy told him. "Unfortunately, you remind them just how trapped we are. It's also possible that people feel bad complaining about their situation, when yours is worse."

"That makes no sense to me," Eric scowled at nothing.

"I understand it," Jodie admitted. "When you have a problem, but someone has a worse problem, it makes you feel bad about thinking that you have a problem. It's like complaining you're unappreciated at work, and then someone tells you they have cancer. Your feeling of unappreciation doesn't go away, but now you feel bad about feeling that way when you're better off than this other person."

Eric nodded slightly, maybe understanding. Jodie didn't know if she properly conveyed what she meant. It was something she had learned on a deep level within herself just last year, when she was complaining about the part time job she held at the time and then discovered one of her former classmates was being evicted with no place to go. She felt angry about her job, and then felt angry at herself for not feeling lucky to have the job, as well. When she took the time to break down her feelings, she figured it all out, and managed to teach herself it was okay to be angry about her job, even when people were worse off. It made for a happier Jodie.

"Fuck, it's hot." Troy stood up, flapping the collar of his shirt. He had removed his jacket some time ago. "Oh, ah, sorry Roxanne." He glanced in the older woman's direction.

Without Apollo sitting next to her and Happy at her feet, Roxanne looked smaller, somehow. Frailer. Her blazer was off, and a modest top button of her shirt was undone, while her fingers fidgeted with a tassel on her purse.

"No need to watch your language anymore," Roxanne said to Troy, without turning her face away from the window. It was impossible to say what she was looking at. "There aren't any children anymore, not on this train." She was sad. Since meeting Apollo, Roxanne had made it her mission to take care of the boy. Now that he was gone, she didn't know what to do with herself.

Jodie continued to sit beside Eric, holding his hand.

"Jodie, can you help me get this shirt off?" Eric asked her, releasing her hand to undo the buttons.

"Are you wearing something under it?" Jodie didn't think he was.

"No, but this heat is murder, and I can't just move around to where there's better air flow."

Jodie wasn't going to deny his request. Eric could get his shirt off on his own if he wanted to, it was just easier if Jodie helped him. She tried hard not to turn a shade of pink when she saw his nicely sculpted and lightly haired chest. It seemed that no matter the situation, that part of her brain didn't shut down. Once his shirt was off, Jodie placed it behind him so that the bare skin of his back wouldn't touch the subway floor whenever he laid back down. For now, however, he chose to sit up.

"Jodie, is it?" Alison asked timidly.

"Yes?"

"I'm done with your art supplies. Thank you for letting me use them." She offered the sketchbook and pencil back to Jodie.

Jodie scuttled over to her and took them back. "Anytime."

"I like your designs," Alison said, as she got to her feet.

"Thank you."

"See you around, I guess." Alison then turned and departed, carefully stepping over and around the gathered prayer group.

"She seems a little weird." Troy stood up but bent over to comment to Jodie in a low voice.

"She's an artist, of course she's weird."

"Is that an admission?"

"Of course it is. You don't think I'm weird?"

"We all wear Velcro shoes."

"What does that mean?"

"Just something a friend and I came up with. It means we're all crazy."

"Well, she's crazy good. Look at this." Jodie had found the page that Alison was drawing on. It was a surprisingly accurate rendition of the subway train, blue wall included, but without any people.

"How do you do that with so few pencil marks?" Troy peered closely at the drawing. "Like, some of these are just squiggles, but when I look at it as a whole, they're not."

"It's all about knowing where and how dark to make your squiggles," Jodie laughed as she put away the sketchbook. "This one girl in my class, whenever we did life drawing stuff, was a master of the long distance squiggles. If you looked at her page from the distance she drew it, it just seemed to be a mess, but if you stood back across the room, it looked exactly like the thing she was drawing. It was so weird." Once the sketchbook was put back, Jodie decided to take off her blouse. Her camisole wouldn't cover her bra straps, but she had never really worried about that before. Camisoles were her usual top of choice in the summer.

"You're lucky you're in a skirt and not heavy jeans like I am."

"You can roll up your jeans, you know," Jodie suggested.

Troy waved the suggestion off, but didn't give an explanation why. A silence passed between them, the result of having run out of things to say, once again.

"I think I'm going to take a nap," Troy eventually said, turning to sit on the triple seats.

"That's probably a good idea," Jodie agreed. She was

still tired from the rough night last night, and the heat was sapping her energy.

Shuffling around her bags, Jodie made herself a reasonably comfortable spot. She used her backpack as a pillow and her portfolio as a bit of weak padding under her hips, along with her folded blouse. Normally, she didn't sleep during the day, but she could already feel her mind drifting. The soft murmuring of the prayer group seemed to help.

Lying on her back, Jodie held her water bottle against her belly, her fingers wrapped through the plastic loop which kept the lid attached to the rest of it when opened. She wasn't going to let anyone open it while she was napping and unaware, even if they were pregnant.

17

"FUCK, JODIE. JODIE, WAKE UP."

Jodie couldn't tell if she was still dreaming or not. Her dreams had been extraordinarily vivid while napping. One in particular stood out, in which she was trapped in an ice cave with a bunch of other people, unable to walk. Despite the ice cave, they were all roasting, and Jodie had said they should dig into the ice where it would be colder. It was surprisingly easy to dig, but it only made things hotter, and the ice never melted, but Jodie was so thirsty and wished it would.

"Jodie," Troy hissed into her ear again as she had stirred, but then started to drift off once more.

"Wha...?" she raised a hand to her eyes and rubbed them. Her mouth tasted even worse than it had that morning. She really wished she could brush her teeth.

Troy helped her sit upright, his face full of worry. Seeing the fear in his eyes woke her up all at once.

"What is it?" she asked, finally finding her voice. "What's wrong?" Thinking she might have lost her water despite her attempts at safekeeping, she brought the bottle to her face and found it just as full as it had been the last time she checked.

Troy glanced around nervously, making sure no one could hear him. He then leaned over and whispered to Jodie. "I think Roxanne is dead."

Jodie slapped a hand over her mouth, muting a cry before it could escape. She held the air in her lungs while she watched Troy's eyes fill with tears.

"How?" she finally squeaked out, her hand muffling it.

"I think the killer got her." Troy's voice was shaking. "I don't know what happened. I woke up and noticed that everyone on the train seemed to be sleeping. When I happened to look over at Roxanne, I saw blood coming out of her ear. I haven't checked her pulse or anything yet, but I don't think it's good."

Jodie squeezed her eyes shut, and pressed her hand tightly against her mouth, her lips being crushed into her teeth.

"Roxanne? Roxanne?"

Troy turned around so that both he and Jodie could see Mandy. She had awakened facing the old woman and saw the blood right away. Her eyes widened to the point where they seemed in danger of falling out of her skull. Before Troy could make a move to keep her quiet, Simon also woke up and noticed the blood.

"Oh my God!" the large man bellowed. "She's dead!"

Suddenly, everyone was awakened with fright.

"Who's dead?" Nina squalled.

"The old woman, Roxanne." Anthony—his plaid shirt unbuttoned to reveal a hairy chest and belly underneath— moved to kneel on the seat behind Roxanne and check her pulse.

A wave of noise rippled through the train car as everyone seemed to speak at once. Eric had to sit up, and Troy protected Jodie as people hurried to the front in a crowd, needing to see for themselves, to confirm it with their own eyes.

"Did anyone see anything?" the tall guy called out, his voice carrying above everyone else's.

"Where is that man?" cross-tattoo harped, turning back to where the butt pincher had been sitting.

Jodie managed to get to her feet. She was worried that cross-tattoo was going to do something awful to the man, having already pegged him as the killer. Jodie squeezed through the crowd and followed after her, reaching out a hand to try to stop her. Other people were following as well, a cacophony of voices, some of which agreed with her accusation, others that fretted about what to do.

"Bastard can't even get up to look at what he's done." Cross-tattoo's light clothing billowed around her as she gestured grandly at the man.

The accused butt pincher, and now accused killer, was curled up on a set of forward facing double seats, still asleep. Jodie thought it strange that he could sleep so heavily in the middle of the day, so deeply that the uproar hadn't caused him to stir.

"Wait," she said to cross-tattoo, trying again to stop her. "Wait, something's wrong."

Cross-tattoo saw it then and came to an immediate stop, Jodie bumping into her, and the crowd coming to a shuffling, stumbling halt around them. Just like with Roxanne, there was blood coming out of the man's ear.

"Steven?" the black woman, who had been sitting near him, pushed through the crowd. "Steven, if this is a joke, it's not a funny one." She walked up to him and shook his shoulder.

He didn't respond. Everyone seemed to be holding their breath, hoping he'd do something, anything. He didn't.

The woman carefully placed her fingers against Steven's neck, checking for a pulse. She looked back at the crowd and shook her head.

Jodie's world starting spinning. How could this be? Her knees went weak and she found herself collapsing toward the nearest seat. The middle-aged woman had been standing right behind Jodie. She grabbed her shoulders and eased her gently down, sitting in the seat beside her.

"You're all right." She held Jodie, trying to comfort her and perhaps take comfort for herself at the same time. "You're okay."

"How?" Jodie breathed the word rather than spoke it. "How could this happen? They're at opposite ends of the car. How?" She found she was trembling.

"Jodie." Troy appeared in front of her. "Are you all right?"

"She almost fell," the middle-aged woman told him. "I caught her. I think she's just really shaken up about what happened. We all are."

"Thank you. I'm Troy, by the way."

"Sydney."

"Jodie, you forgot your water bottle. I brought it for you."

Jodie took it and held it tightly to her, like a precious stuffed animal. Even though she was still shaking, and her legs still felt weak, she tried to stand. Troy quickly replaced Sydney's arm with his own and supported her.

The train was chaos. Everyone was shouting at one another, accusations were thrown. Denzel was trying to organize them all, to find out where they had been or whether they had seen anything. People answered him when he got up in their faces, but from what Jodie was hearing, no one knew anything. The majority had been sleeping, some reading or staring out the window, and a few had gone to the bathroom but hadn't noticed anything strange.

"Come on, we should get back to Eric and make sure he hasn't been trampled." Troy began to lead Jodie away from the scene, back toward the front of the train.

They threaded their way around worried people, who were beginning to settle back down into their seats, although their hands still nervously fidgeted, and knees bounced with uncontainable energy. Nina was actually quiet for the moment, curled up in her seat, her eyes darting around as they tried to watch everything, while her teeth gnawed on the thumbnail pushed between them.

Eric was fine. He was sitting up, his shirt back on but with the front unbuttoned. He was leaning back just far enough to see Roxanne. Anthony and the Hispanic man were moving her off the seat. They were gentle about it, but Jodie wanted to shout at them to be careful. She managed to hold her tongue. Troy sat down with her on the floor near her bags.

"I think someone drank your water during the chaos," Troy told her, taking her attention away from Roxanne.

Jodie finally looked at the water bottle, easing it away from her body. The level was definitely lower. There was barely anything left. The water line was below the 100 ml mark, which was the lowest measurement on the bottle. She would have cried had she any tears left. Her eyes felt raw and her body hollow. She just couldn't take any more bad news. Her throat was sore, she needed to drink.

"Want to finish it with me?" she spoke quietly to Troy.

He had been watching Roxanne be carried off toward the driver's cab, and now turned back to face her.

"The water. I'm very thirsty, but I don't want to drink the last of it." There was no emotion in her voice. "Will you drink the last when I'm done? I don't want to keep looking at it and worrying."

"Sure."

Jodie screwed off the top and took a large swallow. It was soothing. She wished she could have used some to rinse her face, but even in her off-kilter state she wouldn't do that. When there was barely any water left, she handed it to Troy. Troy paused for a moment, then drank the last of it.

"There. It's gone." Troy handed back the empty bottle.

Jodie placed it nearby, where people would be able to see it and know that it was empty and not ask her about it. A minute later, Denzel and one of the businessmen walked by with butt-pincher Steven slung between them. Learning that his name was so close to the man's whom she had gotten the giggles with, made her feel even worse. He was headed for the death room. Jodie had seen that room. She knew there wasn't enough space to have all of them lying respectfully in there. The bodies were either going to be propped up in some way, or stacked on top of each other. She didn't like to think about either position and didn't want to know which solution they chose.

"I saved her, you know?" Jodie said to Troy.

"Who? Roxanne?"

"Yeah. After the crash, she was having some sort of heart attack or something. I helped her find her pills."

"She was a good woman. You know, I don't think I saw her eat or drink anything since the blue gunk came. She was always giving it to Apollo, and once I saw her slip something to Happy."

Jodie leaned against Troy, and he wrapped his arms around her, resting his chin on her head. It was too hot for such physical contact, but she needed it. She wondered how much longer it would be before someone else died, and whether it would be the result of murder, thirst, hunger, or even suicide.

When Troy sighed heavily, Jodie felt it as well as heard it. She slowly eased herself back out of his embrace, needing to get away from the heat.

"It's too hot for this shit," Troy commented, putting Jodie's thoughts into words. Almost everyone had returned to their seats by now, only a few pacers were still standing.

"I just wish we could do something." Jodie leaned back against the door. "Just sitting here, letting the killer get away with it, it's terrible."

"Unless you have your dad's detective brain and a CSI kit hidden somewhere, I doubt there's anything you can do. We don't have any evidence that we can use with our limited resources."

"It's the devil!" Nina suddenly cried out. "The devil has come to rule the Earth! He is attempting to claim our very souls! We must pray to God for his guidance in this wicked time!"

"Put a cork in it, you ninny!" cross-tattoo shouted at her, rising to her feet. "First it was God, and now it's the devil! It isn't either, so quit your talk! This blue stuff is either Mother Nature having some sort of fit we've never seen before, or we've done this to ourselves! That doesn't really matter right now, because it's certainly one of us that's doing the killing! So put a sock in it before I put one in it for you!"

Nina fell quiet. A few people actually applauded cross-tattoo for her bombardment. Jodie just felt uncomfortable.

No one liked an argument on a subway train, especially one trapped in mysterious blue stuff with no way out, and no foreseeable help coming. Not to mention, the killer on board.

18

JODIE WISHED she could nap again, but after what had just happened, neither she, nor anybody else, dared fall asleep. She sat on the floor, leaning against the door so that she faced the wall of blue that trapped Eric. Troy was next to her, propped up against the other half of the double doors. He had made to return to his trio of seats earlier, but apparently he got seat-scooped. The Hispanic couple had moved from the double seats to the ones Troy had been occupying. Troy didn't seem to mind; he plopped back down beside Jodie with his coat.

In her hands, Jodie twisted her phone around and around. The dark screen tempted her. She knew that calling her dad wouldn't do anything, but she wanted to call him anyway. She wanted to hear his voice. Unfortunately, limited battery power restricted her to turning on the phone only during the agreed-upon call times.

Ten years ago, just before Jodie's mom died, her dad had been working on a particularly difficult case. Jodie didn't know the specifics of it; she was sixteen at the time and wanted nothing to do with murder. She remembered her dad having a hard time of it, though. He would work odd hours, sometimes not coming home at night. Jodie's mom used to joke that he was having an affair; she was like that. She trusted her husband completely, and understood he was driven by his work. The woman never once entertained the idea that her jokes could be true. Jodie didn't, either. Her dad was as honest and loving as they came. Not to mention the fact that his partner, Lucky, was working the same hours and was a close friend of the family. He wouldn't let Jodie's dad step out on her mom.

There was something about the case, though, something that Jodie felt she should remember. All she could recall was that a kid had died. She couldn't remember if other people had also been killed, or if the kid had died during the investigation, or if his death was what started the whole thing. Jodie didn't know why her mind insisted on dwelling upon it, but it did. Maybe because of when it happened.

Before the case was solved, Jodie's mom had her accident, and her whole world fell apart. Her dad may have been driven, but not that hard. He dropped the case, passed it on to someone else, and took time off to pull the family in close. Amber had just started University at the time, and had come home to be with them. They all needed each other for the next week or so. It was a dark time, full of silence and misery. It was the only time Jodie could remember feeling truly, deeply depressed, the kind that kept her from getting out of bed in the morning.

But that case. Jodie had never found out if it had been resolved or not. She didn't know why she cared.

"I have to piss," Troy suddenly spoke into the silence.

"Then go piss." Jodie gestured toward the back of the train.

"I will, but..."

"But what?"

"I'm wondering if I should piss in a water bottle or something."

"Gross. Why?"

"Because we're out of water."

"Wait... You're going to drink pee?"

"We might have to," Troy shrugged.

"That's disgusting."

"Did you ever hear that story, about the guy who got stuck in some canyon by a boulder in the States somewhere? He cut his own arm off to free himself?"

"Yeah, they made a movie about him, didn't they? It was up for a bunch of awards."

"Yeah. Well, he drank his own pee."

"I am not drinking pee. Especially not your pee. I'd rather die of dehydration."

"I have to agree with the lady," Eric chimed in. Because he was always lying on his back and staring up at the ceiling, it was impossible to tell when he was listening. Jodie briefly wondered what happened to the book he had borrowed. "I would never want to drink piss."

"Not a lot of people *want* to drink piss. All I'm saying is that we might not have a choice."

"So you're going to pee in a bottle? Not my bottle." Jodie carefully moved the container farther away from him.

Troy sat silently for a moment, thinking before speaking. "No," he eventually said. "I'm not going to pee in a bottle. Not this time, at least. You might change your mind in the future though." He got up onto his feet.

"When your urine is less refined due to dehydration? I don't think so." Eric twisted his body so he could see Troy's face.

Troy just shrugged and walked off to do his business.

"You know, there's actually an advantage to this numbness?" Eric said to Jodie, after twisting back into his usual position.

"Your knees don't hurt anymore?" Jodie remembered him mentioning that.

"Well, there's that, but there's more. I can't feel the piss in my pants anymore. I don't even know if I've peed myself again. For all I know, I shit myself, but I can't feel anything down there."

"That's lovely."

"I know, right? Aren't you jealous that it isn't you trapped in this wall?"

"Oh, totally jealous."

"Damn straight. This wall is tight." Eric tried to sound like a gangster, but it just made Jodie laugh. She couldn't help but picture the kids who hung around in her apartment building's laundry room, thinking they were cool and bad ass when they were maybe ten years old.

"Are you drunk?" Carla, the pregnant lady, snipped at them, perhaps finding Jodie's laughter disrespectful.

"No, but if you have any booze on you, I'd love to be," Eric retorted.

Carla just huffed, and Jodie could imagine Eric getting an intense eye-roll right about then.

Troy returned, walking a little faster than usual, and sat down beside Jodie again.

"Denzel is up to something."

"Oh? What now?"

"He and those guys in the suits are going through the pointy objects pile."

"What for?"

Troy shrugged. "I asked, but they told me to buzz off. My guess would be to see if something was missing."

"That would be great if they had taken an inventory of things to begin with," Eric told him.

"Then maybe that's what they're doing."

Mandy leaned forward in her seat, her red hair flashing in the light. Apparently, she had been listening to their conversation as well, even though they always tried to speak in low tones that wouldn't carry far.

"What if they're arming themselves?" she wondered.

"That's not fair," Jodie spoke without thinking. "Why do they get weapons to protect themselves and we don't?"

"We should all be able to protect ourselves," Nina spoke up, also eavesdropping. Her voice was shriller and more easily heard by those farther away. "We should all be allowed to."

"What's going on?" Simon asked from the front.

"Denzel and some other guys are going through the weapons pile. We don't know why, but they might be arming themselves," Mandy answered.

"That's outrageous." The Hispanic man got to his feet.

Jodie got to her feet as well, not because she was angry like he was, but because she understood that she had helped, inadvertently, to set something off, and didn't want to risk getting trampled. Looking toward the front of the train, she saw the tall guy and the cyclist get up as well. Soon, a crowd of people was heading toward the back, demanding answers, demanding they be allowed to be armed.

Jodie and Troy followed them. She hoped that a fight wouldn't break out because of what she had said, but she also wanted to hear. She wanted to know why they were sorting through the weapons.

"What's going on back here?" the tall guy shouted to start things off.

Denzel and the businessmen turned to face whoever was confronting them, only to find a mob staring them down.

"I'm organizing a patrol," Denzel told them, "so that what happened earlier can't happen again."

"And you're arming the patrol?" the cyclist spoke this time.

"Yes," Denzel stated bluntly.

"That's something you should have consulted all of us about!" Anthony shouted from just in front of Jodie, his broad, plaid-covered shoulders making it difficult to see.

Peering over the seats, Jodie could see past the crowd. The two businessmen seemed to be extremely uncomfortable, and not just because of the heat. They all but cowered behind Denzel.

"All right then, I'm consulting you now." Denzel held his large hands out toward the people. "Don't you all think we should have a patrol set up? Make sure there's always someone keeping an eye on things?"

"What if one of these patrolmen you're picking turns out to be the killer?" This time it was Nina speaking up.

"That's why we'll always have two people patrolling at the same time."

"I only see three of you here!" the tall guy shouted angrily.

"We should all be allowed to have weapons to defend ourselves with!" Nina continued. Several voices shouted their agreement with this.

"Whoa, whoa, whoa," Denzel tried to calm everyone down. "We can't have everyone running around with sharp objects."

"Why not?" Troy asked reasonably from the back before anyone else could scream the question.

"Because we'd have a lot more accidents then. Every disagreement would have the potential to break out into a knife fight. No, it's better we limit who has weapons. Only those on the patrol. Being on patrol will be a voluntary duty, and once they're off patrol, they hand in the weapons. Will, Stan, and myself were just sorting through this stuff to decide what the best two weapons would be."

Jodie wondered whether Stan was the businessman with the lighter coloured hair, or if that was Will.

"We're not degenerates," middle-aged Sydney spoke up. "We're not going to descend to the level of stabbing one another because of an argument."

"You say that now, but just wait until we're truly hungry and thirsty," Alison spoke quietly but was still heard by all. An uncomfortable murmur went through the gathering.

"And when were you planning on telling us this?" cross-tattoo took a step toward Denzel as she spoke, deciding to ignore the previous comments. Jodie couldn't see her face, but imagined it was as stern and sour as ever.

"Once we had decided on what the patrolmen would carry. Will and I were going to take the first shift and inform people in the process." Denzel turned and put his hand on the shoulder of the businessman with the darker hair, confirming which one was Will. "And then Stan," he hiked a thumb at the lighter haired businessman, "was going to come around with a clipboard and take down everyone's name, as well as note whether they wanted to volunteer for patrol duty or not."

There was a general grumbling.

"Why don't we just do that now, then?" the cyclist asked, looking at the group around him.

"It'd be easier to do if everyone were in their seats.

We're not organized and ready yet. So please, go back to your seats, and think about whether you want to volunteer for patrol duty or not."

"Come on." Troy gently took Jodie's arm and turned her away. Jodie went willingly enough, hoping others would follow their example.

"What's going on? I only caught some of that," Eric asked as they approached.

"I'd like to know what's happening as well," Ed added. He hadn't followed the group, evidently not wanting to be in a mob with his disability. He had, however, moved from the pair of forward facing seats to those facing the tension behind them.

"Denzel is putting together a two man patrol to keep an eye on things," Troy told them. "The patrol is going to be armed. They'll be coming around soon to ask for volunteers."

Troy and Jodie sat down in the doorway, even though Troy could've taken the opportunity to reclaim his three seats.

"I'm going to guess we're not included in that," Eric commented to Ed.

"Can't really keep an eye on things when I can't see," Ed responded with a shrug.

Jodie found it fascinating that he shrugged. It was such a visual form of communication, she wondered how he had learned it when he couldn't see anyone else shrug. Then again, she didn't know why he was blind. He might have spent most of his life able to see, and shrugging was a habit. Before she was able to ask Ed any questions, the others had come back and were streaming by, returning to their seats. Sydney and the younger woman, who Jodie assumed was her sister, were with them. Apparently, they had decided to change seats and moved up to the front section. Jodie leaned into the aisle and watched as they went all the way to the front, taking the seats across from the driver's cab. It seemed not everybody was uncomfortable being that close to where they stored the dead. It wasn't like they could see them or anything. There was space there being unused, so the two of them had decided to use it.

Cross-tattoo also changed seats. She moved from the seats that she had shared with Lin before she died, to the sideways facing seat right next to the doorway in which Eric was trapped. She was the only one still sitting near Nina. It made Jodie uncomfortable, now that she could see the woman's harsh features all the time. She hoped cross-tattoo moved seats again soon, to one farther away. Jodie would have moved to the forward doors, but she didn't want to leave Eric.

"Do you think you'll volunteer?" Troy whispered to Jodie once everyone had settled.

"No. Will you?"

"Yeah, I think I will. I'd like to help. I'm surprised you don't want to, what with your dad being a cop and all."

"That's probably why I don't want to. I already know the kinds of things I might have to deal with while on duty."

Troy nodded. "I wish she wouldn't sit there," he said with the slightest of head gestures in cross-tattoo's direction.

"I agree."

They both fell silent and sat uncomfortably within the peripheral vision of cross-tattoo.

It took awhile, but eventually businessman Stan came around with a folder, a sheet of paper inside it and a pencil in his hand. He went to Nina first, wrote down her name, and made a note that she didn't want to do any patrols. He then turned to cross-tattoo.

"Fatima. F-A-T-I-M-A. Fatima." She spoke like the world's most bitter spelling bee contestant. "And I'd like to volunteer."

Stan made note of these things without saying a word, then nodded and quickly turned away. He seemed relieved to approach Troy and Jodie.

"I'm Troy." He held out his hand.

"Stan." They shook, and then Stan wrote down his name. "Do you want to volunteer for patrol?"

"I do."

"And you?" Stan raised an eyebrow at Jodie.

"I don't, and my name is Jodie."

"Jodie," he said slowly as he wrote down her name. Once he was done, he glanced over at Eric, unsure about what to do. Obviously he couldn't volunteer, but his name should probably be written down.

"That's Eric," Jodie told him. "I don't think he wants to volunteer for patrol," she tried to joke.

Stan grinned for her and wrote down the name, making some special note beside it that Jodie couldn't see.

"What do you know? Maybe I'd make a great patrolman," Eric spoke up. "I would just need you all to sit within my sight lines."

"And if there's a confrontation?" Jodie asked him.

"Well, then my partner's shit out of luck and has to handle that on his own."

Stan moved on to the Hispanic couple, and Jodie finally learned the man's name was Joa. He volunteered for patrol but his wife didn't. Joa insisted that Stan make special note of Carla's pregnancy. Eric mocked Joa while Stan was between the two of them, blocking Joa's view.

"There are only five people on this train I don't know

the names of now," Jodie whispered to Troy, just for something to talk about.

"Oh yeah? Who?"

"There's the woman with Sydney, who I *think* is her sister, but I could be wrong. There's the tall guy, the guy with the bike, the kid with clothes covered in paint, and the black woman sitting near the businessmen near the back."

"I can't help you, I don't know any of their names. Why don't you ask Stan to let you take a look at his list?"

Jodie shook her head. It wasn't that important to her to learn everyone's names. She liked knowing the names of the people she was trapped with, but not enough for her to go around asking people.

The patrol had started, and Jodie watched Denzel walk by, his back straight as he moved with a purpose. She leaned forward so she could watch when he reached the front of the train and turned around. Looking the other way, Jodie saw Will standing at the very back. They both started walking toward each other at the same time, probably trying to time it so that they'd pass each other in the middle. Jodie wasn't sure that was the best way to do it, because once they passed each other, there wouldn't be eyes on the middle until they turned around again, but then Jodie didn't know what a better way to patrol would be.

"I'm going to check on the doctor," she told Troy, as she took her large sketchpad back out of her bag.

"Okay," Troy responded absently. He was staring at the map above the blue wall, seemingly studying it like Eric had.

When Jodie settled in with her sketchbook, beside Mandy and facing out the window, the redhead shifted so that she could see the doctor's responses as well.

"What are you going to tell him?"

Jodie shrugged. "I'm just going to update him on what's happened over here. Ask him how he's doing. Not much, really."

The two of them sat there by the window, waiting for the doctor to notice them. Jodie could make him out in the back seat, moving around, but she couldn't tell what he was doing. Eventually he sat up to take a break, and Jodie and Mandy began waving their arms.

"What are you doing?"

Jodie looked over her shoulder to find that Will had paused in his patrol, standing behind them and fidgeting with the end of one rolled up sleeve.

"Trying to get the doctor's attention. I want to see how he's doing," Jodie told him, then returned to her attempts at signalling.

"Why? It's not like you can do anything."

"It's not like it'll do any harm, either," Mandy snapped at him. "Shouldn't you continue patrolling for a real threat?"

Jodie glanced back again and saw that Will's face had flushed a bright red. He turned promptly on his heel and continued on his way.

"You'd think the people doing the patrol should have a spine," Mandy whispered to Jodie.

Jodie kept her thoughts to herself. Being a good officer was a fine line to walk, between letting small things go and abusing power. It could be hard under normal circumstances, and these were anything but. And there was the fact that not a single volunteer had had any training, whatsoever.

The doctor finally noticed Mandy and Jodie, and climbed into the driver's seat to start up a slow dialogue.

Jodie started by telling him what had happened, how

there had been another two murders, and how they now had a patrol. The doctor informed them he hoped they stayed safe.

Jodie then went on to ask him how he was doing. He responded by separately writing down three words: hunger, thirst, and hot. When Jodie asked him *what* he was doing, it took even longer for him to respond, having to write down one or two words at a time and waiting for Jodie to figure out what he had said. Apparently, he was cutting off the backs of the seats. He was going to use the fabric as blankets when the sun went down, and it got cold again. Jodie told him he was very clever. The doctor's response wasn't so cheerful.

DYING
ANYWAY

19

THE SUN HAD JUST FINISHED SETTING, and Jodie was wringing her phone in her hands.

"You should turn it back off," Eric told her.

Jodie ignored him. Troy placed his arm around her shoulders, then placed his other hand over hers, ceasing her fidgeting.

"I'm sure he's fine," he told her.

"Then why hasn't he called or sent any text messages?" It was well past the time when Jodie's dad should have made contact.

"His phone is probably just dead."

"But he's been charging it through his car's cigarette lighter." Jodie was unsuccessful in keeping the worry out of her voice.

"Car batteries can die, too," Eric reminded her. "It's been at least an hour, hasn't it? You should turn off your phone before it turns itself off."

"But I don't know when I should turn it back on."

"Send another text message to your dad. Tell him when

the next time the two of you should try communicating is," Troy advised.

"And when should that be?"

Troy shrugged, releasing both her shoulder and her hands at the same time.

"Do you think two p.m. sounds like a good time?"

"Sure?" Troy shrugged again.

"Two p.m. is a great time," Eric told her. "Now send the message and turn off your phone."

"You seem awfully worried about the battery life of her phone," Troy spoke to Eric while Jodie typed up her final message.

"Because I like having at least some connection to a real cop," Eric hissed, not wanting to be overheard by the current patrol. At the moment, Anthony and the tall guy were walking the aisle. Unlike Denzel and Will, they didn't time their patrol at all, which allowed them to walk back and forth at their own pace, so that they were staggered and unpredictable. Presently, the moon was the only light, and it was weak. It wasn't easy to see much of anything, which made it even more difficult to know where the patrolmen were at any given time.

Jodie finally turned off her phone, the last electronic on the train to wink out. A small shudder ran across her skin. It was already starting to get cold again.

"Come on, let's join Eric," Troy suggested, having witnessed her shiver.

"We have to be careful not to touch the blue," Jodie reminded him as they shuffled across the train.

It was beginning to look as though tonight it would be just the three of them huddling together. After the murders, people had become mistrustful. They still grouped together for both warmth and protection, but the groups were smaller, made up of only four at the most.

After a lot of fumbling around, they figured out there was no way for all three of them to lie together without touching the blue or being in the way of the patrols. In the end, Troy and Jodie sat up, each leaning against a section of barrier that the blue hadn't swallowed on either side of Eric. They draped their legs over him in a sort of human blanket, and then put Eric's suit jacket on top. When Roxanne was taken away, her things were left behind and Troy had been able to snag her blazer and Apollo's blanket. He let Eric use the blazer under his head, while wrapping the small blanket around his own shoulders and giving his large jacket to Jodie. Jodie also had her portfolio wedged between her and the blue to keep her from drifting into it in her sleep, while Troy used Eric's briefcase. It wasn't very comfortable for any of them, but it was the warmest they could get.

"I hope neither of you kick in your sleep," Eric muttered. "I rather like my face and chest the way they are."

"I don't, but I can't vouch for him," Jodie replied.

"Please, your legs were jittering all through last night," Troy joked

"It's called shivering," Jodie said, putting on a haughty tone, "and it's only because I was cold. You, on the other hand, couldn't keep still."

"Shh." Eric freed one of his arms from beneath their legs and placed his finger to his lips. "People trying to sleep down here."

Jodie suppressed a giggle, but it made her body shake.

"See," Troy whispered as quietly as he could, "she's already jittering."

Now Jodie had to try even harder not to laugh, which

only made the shaking worse. She managed to get herself under control as the tall guy walked by on patrol.

Shifting into a slightly more comfortable position, Jodie prepared to sleep. It was easier than she had expected it to be. At various times throughout the day, she had nibbled on her dry Kraft dinner noodles so that her stomach didn't feel so hollow. The box was empty now, just like everyone else's food stash. The great hunger had begun. Jodie had tried to sleep while hungry before, and found she couldn't do it. Tonight, however, her mind drifted easily. She had no energy to stay awake.

Unfortunately, it wasn't a deep sleep she drifted into. Vivid dreams travelled through her mind, yet she was aware whenever one of the guys shifted or someone walked past, either on patrol or while heading to the toilet hole. As the temperature continued to drop, her flesh crawled with goosebumps. She pulled Troy's jacket as tightly around herself as she could, crossing the empty sleeves over her head like a bad hat.

The things her mind dredged up were strange. She thought about food and water a lot. She dreamed she was in a bar full of good-looking men, but all she cared about was trying to order a drink. The bartender ignored her, serving everyone else, including another Jodie who couldn't stop giggling. Eric was there, but only his upper half, propped up on a stool and chowing down on nachos topped with everything, the basket of them never seeming to get any emptier. She felt a little sick in this dream, like she did whenever she had a fever. It was probably the cold shudders causing that. In her dream, Eric unexpectedly started to choke. He kept eating, but was making awful choking sounds at the same time. Suddenly he fell off his stool.

The loud thump Eric made as he hit the floor caused

Jodie to flinch, her eyes blinking open. It was nearly pitch black, and it took her awhile to realize where she was and why she couldn't see anything. She had thought she was still asleep.

"Joa?" a woman's voice whispered in the dark from the far side of the train. "Joa, did you just hear something?"

It was the slow, accented voice of cross-tattoo, more recently known as Fatima. So Jodie wasn't asleep then, and the thump hadn't come from her dream.

"Joa?"

Jodie wondered why Fatima was awake and talking to the Hispanic man. Her mind was still groggy and tired, so it took her some time to figure out that the patrol had changed.

Footsteps came toward them. Jodie's eyes adjusted as well as they were going to, and she was able to make out the shapeless form of Fatima's flowing clothing, the white practically glowing in the dark.

"What's going on?" Nina whispered from the shadows, sounding as confused as Jodie felt.

Fatima ignored her, kneeling down beside Jodie. She didn't look at Jodie though, didn't seem to give her a second thought. The woman's focus was on something on the floor near Jodie, just past the doorway.

"Everyone, wake up!" the powerful voice of Fatima rang through the train car.

If Jodie hadn't been wide-awake before, she certainly was now. Beneath her legs, Eric jerked and tried to sit up before remembering he was pinned. Jodie quickly withdrew her legs away from him, while Troy did the same.

"What's going on?" a lot of people repeated Nina's earlier question.

"Somebody find a light!" Fatima bellowed above all of the other voices.

A small spear of light pierced the darkness. Jodie peered around the barrier to see what was happening. The girl with Sydney was the one with the light. It was a tiny, single LED flashlight, which she held unsteadily pointed at the floor. The cone of light moved toward Fatima, where it found the prone body of Joa.

"Joa?" Carla, his wife, whispered from the seats beside him, where she was wrapped up in both of their jackets.

The girl with the light stopped when the beam found blood.

"Oh God, Joa, no." Carla's voice twisted with anguish. She struggled to unwrap herself from the coats she had been using to keep warm, her limbs seeming to fight against each other as if her subconscious didn't really want to get closer.

"What happened?" Denzel demanded to know, coming up from behind Fatima.

Fatima shifted to the side to let him see. Denzel bent down and rolled Joa onto his back. He hadn't been stabbed in the ear like the others, but in the throat. It almost looked like someone had attempted a tracheotomy, except this hole was filled with blood. With horror, Jodie realized that the choking she heard hadn't been from her dream. There wasn't enough blood to suggest an artery had been hit, but something in his throat must have bled inside; he had drowned in his own blood.

"No, no, no, no," Carla kept quietly repeating over and over, tears streaming down her face. She had managed to untangle herself, but now her limbs had locked up. She was perched on the edge of her seat, her hand held out before her, the fingers shaking. Her eyes were trying to convince her of the opposite of her words, and it looked to Jodie like they were winning, as she couldn't bring herself to touch the cooling body.

"Perhaps you should sit elsewhere," Fatima advised her, almost kindly but not quite.

Carla didn't move.

The beam of light started to shake, the girl holding it trembling. Fatima got up and took the small flashlight from her, then handed it to Denzel.

"Bailey, come here," Sydney hissed. The girl who had relinquished her flashlight and who Jodie thought of as Sydney's sister returned to Sydney and balled up in the older woman's protective arms.

"What happened?" Denzel stared at Fatima with accusatory eyes. "The patrol was set up just to prevent this sort of thing."

"I don't know," Fatima admitted. "We were on patrol, but I had to go to the bathroom. When I finished, I heard a strange noise, and could no longer see Joa, although we had been having a hard time seeing each other ever since the cloud cover came in and blocked out the moon."

"Did you see anything?" Denzel turned to Jodie, shining the light in her face.

Jodie blinked painfully at the LED. "No, I was asleep. I got woken up by a thump, which I think was when he fell. I..." Jodie glanced at Carla not sure if she should continue, but decided to anyway. "I think I heard him choking before that, but I thought I was dreaming it."

"What about you two?" Denzel shone the light on Eric and Troy next.

Both of them shook their heads.

"I didn't wake up until she shouted." Troy pointed at Fatima. Eric nodded in agreement with Troy.

"Did anyone see anything?" Denzel called out loudly,

shining the small light all around. No one said a word, although a few were creeping closer to the scene, trying to get a look.

Denzel turned back to Joa and just stared at him. Jodie couldn't take her eyes off the blood-filled hole. She couldn't help but think that maybe he could have survived had he not been bleeding on the inside. Surprisingly little blood came out of him.

"How long do you think he could have lived with such a wound?" Fatima eventually spoke. "Can we rule out the people at the far end of the train?"

Denzel shook his head. "I don't know. I don't think so."

"If he was stabbed back there, why would he come up here?" Anthony wondered.

Denzel shrugged. "Maybe he was trying to get away from his attacker. Maybe he knew he was dying and wanted to see his wife one last time."

Fresh sobs escaped Carla in response.

"Come with me." Fatima wrapped her arms around Carla, pulling her up onto her feet. "You don't need to see this. Come with me."

The two women shuffled off into the darkness, out of sight of the body.

"You see?" Nina pointed a pale finger at Joa. "You see? We should all be armed! We should all be able to protect ourselves! Clearly the patrol doesn't work!"

"Put a cork in it!" Denzel snapped at her.

Nina withered into her seat like a blowtorched flower.

"Obviously, having everyone armed isn't going to make a difference. Joa was armed." Denzel located the pocket-knife the dead man had on him and held it up for everyone to see. "Didn't help him much, did it?"

There was some mumbling, but no one spoke up to answer him.

"Someone want to help me move him to the driver's cab?" Denzel then asked, in a much gentler voice.

"I'll help," Anthony volunteered, already standing nearby.

Simon got to his feet and whispered quickly into Anthony's ear. Anthony nodded, and Simon sat back down with a huff.

"I'll take his legs, you take his shoulders," Denzel directed Anthony. "Try to not get any blood on yourself."

While Anthony gently scooped up Joa's arms, Denzel placed the small light between his teeth. He then grabbed Joa's legs, and together they hoisted him up and carried him to the driver's cab.

Jodie didn't know what to think. She was still in a kind of shock. The patrol was supposed to protect them, but instead, one of them had been killed. It wasn't until Troy shifted around Eric and wrapped his arms around Jodie, that she realized she was shaking, and not from the cold. Joa had died right next to her while she slept.

She couldn't cry, there were no more tears left. She couldn't scream either, her throat was too tight. A feeling of claustrophobia closed in around her. Suddenly, her throat wasn't the only thing that felt tight, but also her guts, her lungs, her limbs. An overwhelming urge to thrash swept through her muscles. A certainty that she would die here, in the cold, dark, close quarters of the train car flooded her mind.

Without giving an explanation, Jodie pushed Troy away from her. She shot to her feet and dashed to the door across from Eric, pressing her forehead against the cool glass. Her hands found the window's frame, her nails slowly sinking into the tough rubber.

"Breathe, Jodie," Eric spoke from the floor behind her. "All you have to do is breathe."

That wasn't true, she needed so much more. She needed to eat, to drink. She needed a solid night of sleep in a warm bed, to hear her dad's voice again. Most of all, she needed to feel safe.

"What are you doing?" The note of disgust in Sydney's voice cut through the stale air of the train. Jodie turned her head to look. She had to know what else was happening. She had to.

"She has a jacket she doesn't need," Anthony responded, but Jodie couldn't see him, "and Simon said there are some kids' clothes in her backpack. The backpack itself we can use to help us keep warm."

Jodie drifted back into the aisle on shaking legs, her eyes focused toward the front of the train, where the one source of light still shone. Sydney and the younger woman she had called Bailey were looking through the open door of the driver's cab. Mandy had moved to one of the train's doorways, her back turned to the sights, and her arms wrapped tightly around herself. Denzel was leaning against the train's front door, and it was by following his eyes down, that Jodie spotted Anthony's feet sticking out through the doorway. He was on his knees in there, doing something she couldn't see.

"What's next?" Bailey spoke quietly, but her voice carried through the confined space. "Are you going to start stripping them of their pants and shirts?"

Anthony mumbled something indistinguishable.

"All right, that's enough," Denzel said, pushing off the

wall and standing upright. He still held the flashlight, lighting the scene.

Anthony stood up and stepped out of the driver's cab, Olivia's coat and backpack in hand. Once Anthony was out of the way, Denzel closed the door, sealing the dead back inside.

"I'm going to continue Joa's patrol." Denzel's voice was raised for all to hear. "Will anyone join me?"

"I'll stay on duty," Fatima responded, getting up from the seat and leaving Carla alone. When Denzel pointed the light in their direction, it revealed that Carla wasn't moving. Jodie flinched, thinking the worst, but then the pregnant woman blinked her eyes. She was just in shock, shut down and staring at nothing.

"Can I have my light back?" Bailey asked Denzel.

"I think it's best if the patrol has a flashlight," Denzel told her, keeping it for himself.

Neither Bailey nor Sydney argued. It could have been that they agreed with him, or it could have been that they just didn't want to start a fight with him.

"All of you should sit back down." Denzel gestured to those few still standing, Jodie included. "Try to get some sleep if you can."

Nina made a scoffing sound from close by, but managed to keep her comments to herself for once.

Jodie didn't so much sit back down beside Eric as collapse. She saw Troy wince as her knees hit the floor with a thud, but she felt very little pain.

"You all right?" Troy asked her.

"I'm betting no," Eric responded for her.

"You dropped this." Troy draped his jacket back around Jodie's shoulders, but he was careful not to touch her.

Jodie crawled over beside Eric and curled up next to him, her legs crunching into his side, and her feet against her portfolio. She ignored Eric's wiggling as he tried to get more comfortable. After a minute, Troy went back to sitting as he had before, his legs now draped over both Eric and Jodie.

It was impossible for Jodie to tell whether she was asleep or awake. She couldn't remember closing her eyes, until she was opening them again, with Denzel's light passing over her, Fatima at his side. Denzel didn't use the light all the time, but he used it often enough, and it always woke Jodie up.

When she was asleep, she dreamed of the train and those trapped on board. Some of the times she woke up, or thought she did, it turned out to be just another stage of the dream.

The night dragged on, disorienting now as well as cold and frightening. And yet her dad's case, the one from long ago, kept interrupting her thoughts when awake, and occasionally even her dreams. It was as if there was some relevance to what was happening now, yet what it could be, she couldn't grasp.

Jodie was so thirsty.

20

"JODIE, WAKE UP."

"Why?" Jodie could see no real reason to confront the day. She just wanted to sleep until everything was over, one way or the other.

"Because your knee is digging into my ribs." Eric pushed on her legs, trying to move her.

Jodie scooted back a bit, but refused to open her eyes. She knew the sun must be rising, because there wasn't an all-consuming darkness behind her eyelids anymore, but that wasn't a reason to get up. Despite her stiff legs and neck, and her aching hips and shoulders, she stayed tightly curled up beneath Troy's jacket, which had a faintly pleasant smell to it, unlike the rest of the train that had gone sour. That's when she noticed that Troy's legs were no longer draped over her side.

"Where's Troy?" she asked in her quiet, sleepy voice, still refusing to move her eyelids.

"Taking a piss. You should apologize to him."

"What for?"

"I think you hurt his feelings when you shoved him last night."

Jodie finally cracked open an eye. It was actually a little lighter than she expected. She had assumed the sun was still below the horizon, casting only a faint grey light like it had when she awoke the day before. Based on how well she could see, the golden orb had to have crested the curvature of the earth at least a little bit.

"He didn't do anything wrong," Jodie told Eric once she saw he wasn't kidding.

"I'm not sure he knows that."

Jodie closed her eye again. She didn't want to care about other people's feelings. She just wanted to ignore everyone and everything. To shut down. But she couldn't.

Sighing heavily, she opened both her eyes and waited for Troy to return.

"Think we'll get some rain today?" Eric asked in the meantime, looking out through the wall of blue.

Jodie made to turn her head, but the painful cries from her neck made her stop. Instead, she rolled her entire body onto its back, her feet squished between the blue and her own butt. Her head was almost even with Eric's, and she got a good look at what he stared at all day. The map hadn't changed and was uninteresting, but the sky was different. No longer was it a normal, endless blue. The gunk still tinted it blue, but it was different. Clouds gathered overhead in a grey, shapeless mass.

"Maybe," Jodie said in response to Eric's question.

"I would like it to rain."

"Why?"

"Maybe we could manage to catch some of it. Stick the water bottles out through the opening. The rain might even wash away this gunk."

"I doubt it." Jodie would be surprised if the rescue people hadn't already tried water. There was no reason rainwater would be any different.

"Thank you."

"For what?"

"For not abandoning me like the others."

"I think you thanked me for that already."

"Whether I have or haven't, I'm thanking you again."

"Troy hasn't abandoned you."

"I think he would if you did."

Jodie pursed her lips.

Eric unexpectedly threaded his fingers through Jodie's and squeezed her hand. She turned her head to look at him, but he kept staring out at the sky. She no idea what was running through his mind.

Beyond Eric, Jodie spotted Troy returning. Eric let go of her hand as he got close, and Jodie sat up.

"Morning," Troy said, sitting down on the other side of Eric. "I'd offer you some coffee, but, you know."

"I'm sorry for pushing you last night." Jodie felt she should get that out of the way as soon as possible. "I had some sort of panic attack."

"It's okay. How do you feel now?"

"Sore and emotionally numb." She proceeded to crack and pop several of her joints, and rubbed the back of her neck.

"That's gross," Eric commented on the popping.

"I don't want you to get upset, but..." Troy pointed down the aisle behind Jodie.

Confused, Jodie twisted around to look, a few of her muscles creaking. Apparently, while she'd been sleeping, someone had taken her portfolio bag and moved it. She hadn't noticed that her shoes were now the only things protecting her feet from going numb, up against the blue. It took a second for her to realize that her bag had been placed where Joa had died, where there had been a small puddle of blood.

A red fury rose quickly out of Jodie's gut, obliterating the numb feeling. Her mouth opened and twisted itself around silent words, unsure which ones to use. In the end, she said none of the curses that came to mind and turned back to face Troy.

"They could have at least asked," she eventually grumbled through gritted teeth.

"It was there before I woke up, so I don't know who did it."

"Probably her," Jodie mumbled, pointing a discreet finger at Fatima. The woman with the cross tattoo appeared to be asleep. She was slumped across the aisle from where she had been yesterday, having changed seats with Nina, who had taken over the role of comforting Carla after Fatima went back on patrol.

"Maybe," Troy shrugged.

"You know she could be the killer, right?" Eric whispered between them. "She was sitting next to the Asian woman when she died, she clearly didn't like that guy in the back, and she was on patrol with Joa when he was killed."

An involuntary shudder ran a course through Jodie's body. It was possible.

"But why would she kill Roxanne?" Troy asked.

Eric shrugged. "Why kill anyone, really? Maybe it had something to do with the kid, or the dog."

"I don't think it was her," Jodie shook her head. "I think she's a kind of crazy bitch, but I don't think she's the murderer."

"Why not?"

"I don't know. It just doesn't... fit, I guess. I don't know why."

"Who do you think did it?" Troy asked her.

Jodie just shook her head and shrugged. She could no more make a guess at who it was than explain why she didn't think it was Fatima.

"Maybe you have good instincts like your dad," Eric suggested. "I'm assuming your dad has good instincts."

"He's not some TV cop," Jodie forced a grin. "People get caught thanks to hard work and slip ups on the perpetrator's part, not wild guesses."

"I'm sure wild guesses sometimes work. Where else would the TV shows get it from, then?"

"I don't know, but that's not the way my dad works. He uses something called evidence."

"Which we have no way of collecting," Troy sighed.

"Sort of. We have no way of collecting fingerprints, or hair samples, or any of that stuff. If we knew what we were doing, we could study the wound patterns, angle of attack, maybe even figure out an approximate time of death."

"*If* we knew what we were doing."

"Which we don't," Eric added.

Jodie's stomach rumbled loudly.

"I agree," Eric spoke to it.

"I've had a headache all morning," Troy sighed. "Since yesterday, actually."

"Hunger headache. We probably all have them." Jodie had been trying to ignore hers. She was more thirsty than hungry. Her mind kept wandering off to think about cold beer. Turning back to gaze up at the clouds, she hoped it would rain. She hoped it was a deluge, which flooded the train and somehow swept them all outside, Eric included. It was impossible, of course, but it's what she fantasized about.

The tall guy came striding over toward them and stopped beside their little group. He was probably the most average looking man that Jodie had ever seen. Nothing stood out about him other than his height.

"Are you Troy?" he asked, pointing.

"I am," Troy nodded.

"Cool, my name's Ace. Apparently we're supposed to start a patrol together right now."

"Oh, all right. Better now than the middle of the night, I guess."

"Yeah. Here, this is the knife you're supposed to carry." Ace handed him a small pocket-knife as Troy got to his feet. Jodie briefly wondered whom the knife actually belonged to.

"So how do you want to do this? Split up, or stick together?" Troy asked.

"After what happened, I think we should stick together."

"Yeah, probably a good idea." Troy turned to Eric and Jodie. "I'd say see you later, but I'm not really going anywhere."

"Hang out with you later, then?" Jodie suggested.

Troy shrugged, then he and Ace started their patrol by walking slowly toward the back of the train. Ace was a least a head taller than Troy, and his hair could probably brush the ceiling if it stuck straight up.

"Did you sign up for patrol? I can't remember." Eric turned away from watching them to face Jodie.

"I didn't."

"Cop's daughter not volunteering for patrol duty? *Tsk tsk.*"

"Got anything good in your briefcase?" Jodie pointed at

it over his body. It had become badly scuffed since Eric first boarded the train.

"Besides a deck of cards? Nothing. There's just files and junk. Flyers, forms, business cards, you know."

"Business cards? Do you and the other real estate agents ever re-enact the scene from *Psycho?*"

"Every time the office issues new ones. They're all the same though, just different names and numbers. Buying in bulk is cheaper."

"Wanna play some cards?"

"As long as you don't shuffle like Troy, sure."

"I wish I could shuffle like that." Jodie grabbed the battered briefcase, popped it open, and located the card deck. She also found the book Alison had lent Eric. "You still plan to read this?" she held it up.

"Oh. No." There was something odd about the way Eric answered.

"What's wrong?"

"There's nothing wrong," he replied a little too quickly.

Jodie just stared at him, waiting for the truth.

"I've just been having a lot of trouble focusing on letters lately," he finally admitted

"What do you mean?"

"When I try to read something, I don't know, the words just stop making sense."

"It's probably because you're hungry, thirsty, and haven't been able to move for nearly two days. Come on, sit up while we play cards. Do you have trouble telling the cards apart?"

"No. Single digit numbers seem to be okay. Individual letters, too. It's when they form a bunch of words that I just seem to... I don't know, get lost."

"All right, well, you shuffle, and I'm going to return this book to Alison." Jodie handed him the card deck.

"Okay."

Jodie hoped she was right about it being nothing more than thirst or something similar. With his legs having gone numb in the blue, who knew what else it could be doing to him? She chose not to dwell on it.

Alison was sitting sideways on a section of three seats, the guy in the paint splattered clothes facing her. They were playing some hand slapping game that Jodie thought might be called Concentration, but she wasn't sure. There was a different game she remembered playing as a child that could also be called Concentration.

"Ian, you suck at this," Alison was saying as Jodie approached them.

"I'm getting better."

"Only because my reflexes are getting worse."

"Alison?" Jodie quietly interrupted.

"Jodie, right?"

"Yeah. I just wanted to return the book you lent Eric. He says he's done with it." Jodie wasn't going to tell them why and hoped neither one of them asked about it.

"Sure. You can just put it on top of my bag under the seat." Alison gestured with her head, not removing her hands from their placement under Ian's.

Jodie crouched down and put the book on top of the frayed messenger bag. As she stood back up, Alison pulled her hands out from under Ian's and smacked the tops of his.

Ian's paint-covered clothes shifted around his body as he settled into what he must have thought was a more alert position. Alison smacked his hands again, proving him wrong.

Jodie walked back to Eric, glancing around at the other

train passengers. Some people were awake, performing low-energy activities, while others shifted uncomfortably in their seats trying to sleep some more. One of them was a murderer, but looking at them now, that didn't seem possible. Everyone had darkened, sleep deprived eyes that were fearfully drawn to any major sound or movement, like when Jodie had gotten up. It almost seemed easier to think that a ghost was killing people rather than to imagine someone on the train doing it.

"So, what are we playing first?" Jodie asked Eric as she sat back down beside him. He was using the top of his briefcase as a kind of table to help him shuffle.

"I thought we'd start with the classic round of Crazy Eights."

"Sounds good."

He used the briefcase to deal out the two hands, and they started the game. The two of them played in silence, speaking only to declare when they had one card left. At regular intervals Troy would walk by, occasionally stopping to look at each of their hands before moving on with Ace.

Eventually, Eric lowered his hand with a heavy sigh.

"What is it?" Jodie wondered. "I'm not beating you that badly, am I?"

"Did you know that I have a girlfriend?"

The words threw Jodie off balance; had she been walking, she would have stumbled. "No, is she nice?" A lame question, but it was the first thing to tumble off her tongue. She didn't know why she had thought he was single. A guy that good looking with a solid job? Of course he had a girlfriend somewhere.

"Nice enough." Eric's eyes were distant, staring through the discard pile. "I think she's cheating on me though."

Not entirely understanding what was going on here,

Jodie put down her own hand. "Why do you think that?"

"She talks to her ex-boyfriend a lot more than she should. I called her once, when she was helping out at some community charity thing, and I could hear him in the background. She hadn't told me he was going to be there. I've been cheated on before."

"I'm sorry."

"Apparently, I can only find women on the rebound of a relationship they weren't ready to let go of."

"I'm not on the rebound." Jodie felt incredibly stupid the moment she said it.

Eric looked up at her face, giving her a smile that didn't quite reach his eyes. "No, you're not." He briefly squeezed her hand before looking back down. "Maybe it's because of my dad. I knew my dad was cheating on my mom, but I didn't do anything about it. I didn't want them to break up."

"When someone cheats on you, it's entirely their fault, not yours."

"When I was in elementary school, I once hit a kid with a baseball bat and broke his arm. I can't remember why. I'm not sure I even had a reason."

The sudden change in topic threw Jodie for another loop. "Eric? Are you all right?"

Before he could answer, a disturbance broke out toward the rear of the train.

"Hey! Have you been holding out on us?" one of the businessmen, Stan, shouted.

Jodie leaned into the aisle to see what was going on. Stan was standing before the black woman, his face red with fury.

"I'm going to go see what's happening," Jodie told Eric as she scrambled up onto her feet. Eric just nodded and lay down.

"I've done nothing of the sort!" the black woman shouted back at Stan, her aquiline features remaining composed while anger burned out of her eyes.

Troy and Ace arrived at the scene first and took up flanking positions around Stan. Jodie joined the growing crowd of onlookers, curious to see what was going on. If they were of the same mind as Jodie, they wanted to know what was happening before it became dangerous.

"Then where did you get that, huh?" Stan pointed to a small piece of sandwich that the woman was holding.

"If we could all just calm down here." Ace raised his hands toward Stan.

"Shut up!" Stan responded, practically spitting in his face. "Nadia's been holding back food!"

"Unlike you lot, I managed to save some of mine." The black woman, Nadia, managed to stay calm, but spoke powerfully. Even though Stan had a threatening advantage over her seated position, she held her head high and faced him.

"Bullshit! Give it to me!" Stan lunged for the sandwich.

For a second, Jodie had a clear view of the food in question. She swore it was her sandwich, the peanut butter one she had made before leaving her house. Then all hell broke loose.

Ace and Troy tried to grab Stan, but he began swinging wildly. Ace was shoved violently into the crowd. Jodie was crushed between Bailey and Simon before the crowd shoved back. Nadia had jumped to her feet and was shouting, her words unintelligible over the bellows of Stan. The crowd was yelling their two cents' worth as well, managing only to add to the chaos. The sandwich piece had disappeared. Troy almost had Stan pinned, when the businessman suddenly tripped him up and knocked him on his ass. Ace made to grab him next, but Stan punched him in the jaw. Ace reacted on reflex. His fist lashed out and connected with the side of the businessman's head. Stan flew sideways, tripping over Troy's legs. He went down hard, and Jodie heard a sound she had wished never to hear again.

A solid *crack* rang out as Stan's head met the edge of the seats, similar to when Olivia's head had connected with the front door, but there were fewer other sounds to bury it. He crumpled and instantly ceased to move. Everyone fell into a shocked silence.

Troy crawled over to Stan and felt for a pulse. Based on the angle of Stan's neck, Jodie was fairly certain he wouldn't find one.

"He's dead," Troy announced, staring up at Ace in surprise.

"You killed him," Nadia added, collapsing back down into her seat.

"I... I..." Ace stammered, his fighting fury instantly drained out of him.

"You killed him!" Nina shouted from the gathering.

The crowd suddenly took up her anger and Jodie wanted to get out of there, but she couldn't. The people were packed in too closely around her.

"Murderer!" someone shouted.

"I bet he's the one who's been stabbing people!" another person added.

Ace turned to face the throng, his eyes wide and full of fear. "No. No. It was an accident. I didn't mean to."

"Killer!"

"What's going on in there?" a new voice silenced them all. It had come from outside the train.

21

"WHAT'S HAPPENING?" the voice called out. "Is everyone all right?"

While the group was distracted, Denzel pushed Ace down on a seat. The tall man's knees gave out, and he crashed down with a huff of air whooshing out of his lungs.

"Watch him," Denzel ordered Simon, in all likelihood because he was the biggest. Simon nodded.

Jodie didn't think Ace needed any watching. His eyes were locked on Stan's crumpled form, horrified at what he had done. The crowd split in two, half of them following Denzel to see what the voice was about, while the other half stayed behind, still preoccupied with what had just happened between Ace and Stan. Jodie didn't want to be anywhere near Ace in case they decided to lynch him, and so she followed Denzel.

"Hey, in there!" a man stood between the tracks, where they had first seen Apollo's dad. He wasn't alone; at least five other men plus one woman were with him.

"You can get through that car!" Denzel shouted. "We have a small opening over here!"

The man waved in acknowledgement. His troupe turned to the train car behind them and found the same way through that Bruce had. It didn't take long before they were next to the opening.

"Is that piss?" one of the men commented to another, pointing at the tarp that was still down there.

"Where else do you expect them to go?" the other replied. They were lucky that the lack of food had seemed to stop everyone's bowels, at least since Apollo had left them. There hadn't even been that much urine released onto the tarp ever since the water ran out.

"Hey there." The man who spoke to them earlier knelt down as close as their waste would allow, peering in through the hole.

Denzel sat down as well, looking back out. Jodie made herself a part of the group that clustered behind him.

"Looks like you were having some sort of meeting. Did we interrupt?" the mystery man asked.

"We're just having a few problems due to hunger is all," Denzel told him, avoiding mention of the death.

"Are you here to get us out?" Nina spoke hopefully.

"We would if we could," the man answered sadly. "We would need better tools than we have to get you out of there. The city requisitioned everything they could get their hands on for the relief effort. Sorry to say, we're not the rescue workers."

"Who are you, then?" Denzel asked.

"I'm Liam, and this is Johnny, Chris, Dennis, Nate, Alan, Tyson, and Matilda."

Jodie tried to memorize the names but they came at her too fast, and she wasn't entirely sure who Liam was gesturing to each time. Only Matilda stood out as the single female.

"What are you doing here?" Denzel asked.

"Is there someone in there named Ian?" Liam ignored his question and asked one of his own.

Everyone turned and shifted, locating Ian and bringing him to the front. He seemed nervous.

"You're Ian?" Liam asked.

"Yeah. Who are you?"

"We're from the Sideline Emergency Forums. We brought you some food and water."

Jodie felt her entire soul light up.

"You guys should be thanking this kid," Liam continued. "He found the forums we set up, and told us your situation. It took us awhile to get here, there were others on the list ahead of you, but we're here now. Are there still twenty-seven mouths to feed inside?"

"There're only nineteen now," Denzel spoke up when Ian stalled.

Everyone's good mood turned sour. Knowing exactly how many people had left them was sickening.

"Any of them get out alive?" Liam didn't seem at all surprised that the number had dropped.

"Yeah." Ian perked up a bit, able to answer this question. "We were able to get the kid and the dog out through this hole."

"Do you still want the dog food we brought?"

"Yes," Denzel answered immediately.

"All right. Is there anything under this tarp?" Liam gestured to the blue plastic beneath their hole.

"Shit," Ian told him.

"All right then." Liam turned to the men behind him. "Dennis? We should probably shovel dirt over this if we can. It'll make moving the food easier and maybe help cover up the smell."

"You got it." Two of the men set to the task of moving gravel and dirt to cover over their urine. They even brought out tissues to wipe down the door with, and gave a lot more to the people in the train when Nina mentioned they were out.

"Are you able to get through that fence?" Ian gestured to the chain link and wooden board fence behind him.

"Probably, why?"

"There's a doctor trapped in a car. Just up that way," Ian pointed. "I don't know if you can see it, but it's the one with a rear light kicked out. Could you get some food to him?"

Liam stood up and peered through the chain link barrier, locating the doctor's car. "Yeah. Since you lost some people, we'll give him a bit of yours."

Jodie felt sick for forgetting about the doctor. She communicated with him more than anyone else, and yet she hadn't thought of him and how he must be starving as well.

Matilda got a boost from one of the men and scrambled up the fence, cutting the barbed wire across the top with some small wire snips.

"What's it like out there?" Denzel asked, while the rest waited for their food and drink. They could see it now, as men started to unload it from bags, and pressed closer to the hole. Jodie's stomach made an odd suction feeling, and her head swam for a moment.

"It's rough," Liam answered Denzel. "A state of emergency has been declared. A lot of people are working to deal with this, only taking time off to sleep. Some of them have to be forced to take breaks. Power is out every place that doesn't have a generator, and the roads are blocked, so not much is getting in or out. Crime is rampant. People are coming in from all over the place to help, but often times the police just can't get to where the crime is happening, if they even know about it. People are starving everywhere. Food is being brought in, but getting it to people is difficult. We're from a forum of volunteers who have come in to deliver the food on foot. It's not easy. Often times we have to take detours, or get creative to keep moving forward. And people want our food. They beg, and they plead, and some even try to attack us over it. All we have to defend ourselves with are batons. We've been lucky not to have run into anyone with a gun so far. We'd give up the food in that situation. Soon, someone is going to learn to recognize us and take advantage of that. The head of our forum is hoping to work something out with the police, or even the military, to provide an armed escort, but who knows if that'll happen."

"Where are you stationed?" Denzel wondered

"Barrie has become the central hub, but we came from Markham. They got hit there, but not badly. We can move around out there."

"What happens to the people once the rescue workers get them out of the buildings they're in?" Ian asked next.

"The rescue workers don't do shit after that. If something suddenly tears a hole in that tin can of yours, you have three options: stay put and hope for the best, go some place else, like home, and hope for the best, or start hoofing it. A bunch of people outside the affected zone have opened up their homes to strangers, and the government has been setting up refugee centres all over the place. Some are better than others," Liam shrugged. "It's hard to move nearly three million people."

"I think we got the piss covered," one of the men spoke up. "We can start moving the food in now."

The throng of passengers crushed together trying to get to the opening, reaching out with their hands. Jodie was one of them. The sight of the food had taken over her normally polite instincts, and had her stretching her hands out with the rest of them.

"Get back!" Denzel bellowed. "Get back!" People started listening to him when he began to shove them. His large frame easily moved people aside. "Nothing is getting in if you clog up the hole that way!"

Jodie fell onto her back as Anthony was shoved into her. She had a brief moment of panic, thinking she was going to be trampled down there, but then Troy's hands were locked around her arms and pulling her up onto her feet. He helped Jodie move back with the crowd, all of them fearful of Denzel's wrath.

"We're going to be organized about this," Denzel commanded. "Ian, you'll help me get the food in. Everyone else keep back! No one eats anything until we figure out what we have."

Looking around, Jodie saw that only four people weren't part of the food-grubbing mass: Eric, Carla who still appeared to be in shock, Ace who was in a different kind of shock, and Simon who stood watch over him. Simon, though, seemed like he wanted to bowl his way through the subway car, throwing people left and right, to get at the food coming in. Even blind Ed was part of the mob, his head turning this way and that as he tried to keep track of what was happening, his hands resting on Mandy's shoulders to help him with the ebb and flow of the crush.

Piece by piece, their sustenance was passed through the opening to Ian, who then handed it to Denzel. Denzel proceeded to stack it all up on the seats on the far side of the doors, across from the pile of pointy objects.

"What are these?" Ian asked the men outside. Jodie was wondering the same thing. She could catch glimpses of silver packaging over the shoulders of Sydney and Bailey.

"MREs," one of the men outside, possibly Liam, answered. "I've never tried one myself, but from what I hear, what they lack in taste they make up for in nourishment. You should be able to eat just one per meal."

Along with the silver packages, bottles of water were being handed in. Jodie wondered how heavy the backpacks were for the people who had carried them here. She wondered how much food and water she and the others were getting, and how long it would last them. Eventually, the food stopped, and a few blankets were passed into the train.

"Sorry we don't have enough blankets for all of you."

"We'll make do," Denzel told him.

"Well, that's the last of it."

"Thank you so much for this," Ian told the men outside. "Really."

"You're lucky you found our forums before your phone ran out of juice. Not everyone has been so fortunate."

"Do the rescue workers know we're here?" Nina suddenly shouted out.

"I'm sure they do. Even if they didn't know before, we submit numbers and locations to them as soon as they come to us."

Jodie peered out through the window and saw Matilda scrambling back over the fence.

"You feed the doctor?" Liam asked her.

"Yeah. He was really grateful." She turned toward the train. "Thanks for letting us know."

"Well, we should be going now," Liam said, turning back to the train. Jodie could just make out a few of them as they hoisted their now mostly empty backpacks up onto their shoulders.

"Just a minute." Denzel knelt down by the opening,

shooing Ian away. Whatever he said next was in a whisper that no one heard. Liam's answer was likewise muted. He then stepped back from the train and raised a hand to everyone through the windows.

"Good luck to you all!" Those with Liam also raised their hands.

Jodie didn't want them to go. She wanted them to stay outside, where they could talk about what was going on. Where they could learn what the people on the train needed and go get it. Where they might be able to do something, anything, about the murders that had taken place onboard. But they didn't stay. They had other people who needed food delivered to them. Everyone watched in silence as the group travelled through the train car behind theirs, and then disappeared up the tracks. The moment they were out of sight, everyone's attention returned to the food.

"I'm so thirsty," Bailey said to her older sister.

"Give us our food," Nadia, the black woman Stan had argued with, demanded.

"Yeah, we want our food!" Anthony added.

"Calm down!" Denzel bellowed. "You'll get it. Form an orderly line. Fatima? Could you come over here a minute?"

While everyone shoved and bumped into one another, trying to get the best place in line, Fatima pushed through them to reach Denzel. The line continued past Ace, his tall form curling upon itself and making him appear a lot smaller. Simon had stopped guarding him, using his girth to secure a good place in line for himself.

Jodie got a place in line right behind Troy. They were standing near the still body of Stan, which no one had moved as of yet. Food and water were a lot more important than the dead's dignity. Jodie was so hungry, the body's presence did nothing to affect her appetite, not even Stan's open and blankly staring eyes.

The line moved slowly. Leaning sideways, Jodie could see that Fatima was handing out one MRE and water bottle per person, while Denzel performed line control.

"Why are we only getting one?" Mandy called out, having gotten shoved further back in line than Jodie.

"Because the last way we did things clearly didn't work." Denzel pointed to Stan's body for emphasis. "We're going to hand out one MRE to each person, twice a day. You only get one water bottle once a day."

"That's ridiculous!" Nadia shouted, outraged.

"If we're all getting the same food at the same time, then we shouldn't have any more accidents. If you hadn't kept that sandwich piece, Stan would still be alive."

Nadia blanched as she was accused of being the cause of death. "It's not my fault I was better at rationing than he was," she muttered, the earlier strength in her voice washed out.

"How do we know everyone is getting the same amount?" the cyclist asked politely.

"You're all standing in line watching, aren't you? I'm pretty sure we'll notice someone going through the line twice. There aren't *that* many of us."

"I mean, how do we know no one is stealing anything?" the cyclist continued.

"Myself and Fatima are going to guard the food. I'll probably ask others to volunteer for that as well."

"Between the guards and the patrol, there aren't going to be many of us that *need* watching," Troy spoke quietly back to Jodie.

"That's probably a good thing," Jodie replied.

As the line shuffled forward, Jodie noticed that those

who had gotten their food were clumping up around Denzel. The line took up half the aisle, while Stan's body blocked the other half. No one was eating just yet, but a few water bottles had been cracked open. They all held their silver packages like precious objects that were going to be stolen the moment they weren't paying attention.

"What about Ace?" Alison asked, as she received her food from Fatima. She wasn't that far ahead of Jodie in line.

"He's a killer, he doesn't deserve any food," Anthony scowled at her.

"It was an accident, though." Alison shrank back from him.

"He'll be fed, don't worry about it," Denzel told her, urging her to move on so that the next person in line could pick up their MRE.

"And Carla? She's not in line," Mandy observed, her red hair a frizzy mop about her head from several days without a shower or brush.

"I'll get her food to her," Fatima informed everyone.

The line finally got short enough that everyone with food could flood past the back of it, avoiding Stan's body. They all hurried to their seats where they could eat.

Troy was next in line. He stepped forward and received his water bottle and MRE.

"How are you going to distribute the blankets?" he asked, pointing to the pile on the seats against the back wall.

"We'll hand them out when night comes," Denzel told him.

Jodie was next. She resisted the urge to snatch the silvery package and the water bottle from Fatima's hands, and cradled them to her chest just like everyone else. Looking at the pile, she realized that even with Denzel's strict rationing, the food wouldn't last long.

"Can I get Eric's food? He can't get in line like the rest of us."

Fatima glanced at Denzel, who left his post and grabbed a water bottle that he placed in Jodie's hands. He then snagged a plastic baggy, which Jodie had missed earlier, and also thrust it into her hands.

"What the hell is this?" Jodie asked. She was pretty sure it was kibble.

"Dog food," Denzel confirmed.

"What the hell?" Troy hadn't left yet, waiting for Jodie.

"I don't see why we should waste good food on him," Denzel spoke to them both, and loud enough for everyone still in the vicinity to hear. "He's a lost cause."

"He's a human being!" Jodie shouted back at him.

"Just be grateful I'm giving you an entire bottle of water, or do you want me to take that back?" Denzel took a step toward Jodie, looming over her.

Jodie wanted to stand her ground for Eric's sake, but she couldn't. She couldn't risk losing what she had already gotten for him. More importantly, she couldn't risk losing what she had gotten for herself. She stepped back from Denzel, her eyes dropping to her feet.

"Come on." Troy placed his hand gently on Jodie's shoulder, guiding her away from Denzel. Glancing at him, Jodie saw that Troy wasn't taking his eyes off the large man for a second, not until they were at a safe distance. Once they were, Jodie slipped out from under Troy's hand and hurried back toward Eric.

Apparently, Eric hadn't been watching the line, as his face was turned toward the ceiling, his hands resting lightly on his stomach.

"Eric," Jodie spoke as she got close.

He didn't turn to look at her.

"Eric?"

Jodie dropped down beside him, quickly placing the water bottles and food packets on the floor between her and the blue wall.

"Eric, what's wrong?"

She placed her hands on his chest and shook him. Eric didn't respond.

"Eric!"

22

"ERIC, WAKE UP!" she pleaded.

When he continued to be unresponsive, Jodie checked his ears, fearing the worst. They were fine. Next, she felt for a pulse. It was easy to locate, pumping strong and steady. His chest expanded and contracted as he breathed.

"Come on, Eric," she whispered, and not because she knew that everyone would be watching them right now, but because her throat and her chest had become tight. "If this is some stupid joke, you have to stop. Please. You're scaring me."

When he continued to do nothing, Jodie pulled on the front of his shirt, attempting to haul him upright. Troy quickly dropped down beside her, helping out. He held Eric upright but slumped over, while Jodie searched his spine for injury. There was nothing. As far as Jodie could tell, he was one hundred percent, he was just... gone.

"Lower him back down," Jodie told Troy. Together they lowered Eric so that his head and shoulders rested on Jodie's thighs while she knelt on the floor. "Hand me his water."

Once the bottle was in her hand, Jodie cracked it open.

Carefully tilting his head, Jodie gently used her fingers to open Eric's mouth. She poured a tiny amount of water between his lips. Both Troy and Jodie watched as Eric swallowed. Hope rose up in Jodie's chest as she thought that that was all he needed, but it quickly deflated again when Eric did nothing else.

Pouring a little bit more water into his mouth, Jodie watched him swallow again. She did it three more times, always with the same result. Eric would swallow, but nothing more.

"What happened to him?" Jodie quietly asked Troy.

"I don't know," Troy shook his head.

"Maybe we shouldn't have let the dog food go so easily," Denzel spoke up. He was walking toward them, carrying one half of Stan's body, while Ace, his eyes red, carried the other half. Stan's head lolled unnaturally with every step they took.

"Fuck you!" Jodie shouted. She wasn't usually one for curses, but this was an appropriate time if ever there was one.

Denzel just kept walking, taking Stan to the room of death.

Gently lowering his head onto his folded jacket, Jodie slid out from beneath Eric. She crawled the short distance to where she had put her food down. Whatever had happened to Eric, it didn't change the fact that she was starving. Troy sat cross-legged on the other side of Eric's body, opening up his MRE.

"Is there something in there we can feed to Eric?" Jodie asked him. "I'll eat the dog food if there is."

Troy poked at the contents. "I don't think so. This all seems to require some amount of chewing."

"Maybe he'll chew?"

"Or maybe he won't, and choke. I wouldn't risk it."

"Well, he certainly can't eat the kibble then."

"What if we put the kibble in his water bottle? Let them soak in there, dissolve a bit? Maybe he'll be able to drink the nutrients down with his water?"

Jodie nodded. It sounded like a logical plan to her. After opening the baggy of dog food, she plucked out a few kibble bits, and popped them through the mouth of the water bottle. She would see how well just a few of them dissolved before adding more.

A wash of dizzy-exhaustion swept up through Jodie's body, settling in behind her eyes. She wavered, and tilted sideways, her arm instinctively reaching out to stop her. Her bare hand landed on the blue wall.

-sun was warm on her face. Jodie ran through the shallow ocean water with the joyous abandon that only small children could seem to manage. Ahead of her, Amber's fair hair reflected the light, streaming in the wind. She held a bucket in one hand that she planned to fill with seashells. Jodie held her own bucket, but intended to use it for another purpose. She wasn't interested in the frail shells like her sister was, but the more solid and ancient rocks. If she could find a good one, it would become a prize for her collection back home.

"Jodie! Amber! Come eat some lunch!"

The two girls turned and looked across the beach to where their mother was sitting and waving to them. Jodie wasn't particularly hungry, but Amber immediately changed directions to obey the call. Jodie didn't like being alone, not in a different country like this, and so followed her big sister. Beneath their feet, the hot sand shifted and swallowed their toes with every step. Once they reached their mom, Jodie threw herself down on her towel, knowing the soft sand beneath it would catch her.

"What did you two monkeys get up to while I was gone, huh?" Jodie's dad asked as he handed both girls a corn dog and a little paper cup with ketchup for dipping. Jodie had never eaten a corn dog, but earlier, her dad had told her they were just like hotdogs on sticks.

"We were looking for shells!" Amber crowed.

"Were you now? Just don't go building any sandcastles until I'm ready. I'll show you how a real pro does it."

Jodie's mom laughed, but Jodie didn't understand the joke. She just dipped her dog into the ketchup and took a bite. It wasn't that much like a hot dog. It didn't taste very good, not like the hotdogs her mom made.

"Thanks for planning this." Jodie's mom kissed her dad on the cheek. "I needed this vacation more than I realized."

"You're not the only one," he replied, then turned to his daughters. "Now, when you're done those, who's-

"Jodie! Jodie!"

"What? Stop shaking me." Jodie shrugged out of Troy's grasp. She couldn't remember when he had moved beside her.

"Are you all right?" he asked her.

"Yeah. I mean, I got a little dizzy there for a second, but I'm fine."

"A little dizzy? Jodie, you've been unconscious for five minutes."

"What?" Jodie sat up straight and alert. "What are you talking about? I just got a little woozy, but I'm okay now."

"You touched the blue gunk and then just fell over."

Jodie looked at the blue wall. She was farther away from it than she had been earlier, and couldn't remember how she got there. Everyone was staring at her.

"I... I don't know what happened," she admitted.

"Remember how, when Eric's legs went numb, you

could touch the blue stuff with your hand and it would go numb as well? Well, I think it's changed again, and now it knocks you out. Don't you remember anything?"

"I..." Jodie thought hard, trying to remember if there was anything between feeling dizzy and Troy shaking her. "The smell of the ocean."

"The smell of the ocean?"

"It's all I remember. I was dizzy, then there was the smell of the ocean, and then you were shaking me. I think I should drink something."

"Yeah. Yeah, of course." Troy quickly scrambled around to fetch her water bottle and hand it to her. Jodie cracked open the lid and took a larger swallow than she probably should have, but it felt so good going down her throat.

"So I guess we know what's wrong with Eric, then," Jodie said, recapping her bottle.

"I guess so."

"And you feel totally fine?" Mandy asked from her seat. There was something about the way her hair flashed in the light that prickled Jodie's mind, but she couldn't grasp it.

"Yeah. I mean, I'm hungry, but I feel okay."

"Here, take your food." Troy handed her the MRE she had gotten from Fatima. "I managed to try a bite before you went AWOL on us. It's not great."

"Better than a corn dog?"

"Huh?"

"Never mind. I don't know." Jodie opened the package and looked inside. Like Troy, she poked at the contents before eating. All of it felt kind of rubbery. "What is this stuff?"

"I think that's some sort of dry meat, those are dry veggies, that's some solid bread, and that... I'm not sure. A cheese maybe? To fill out the food groups?" Troy pointed to each item as he spoke.

"Seriously?"

"I have absolutely no idea. I figure it's best not to think about it."

Jodie sniffed at it, but the food didn't give off much of a smell. When she took a bite, she learned it didn't have much of a taste either. The texture was terrible, but now that she was chewing, her stomach started yowling for her to swallow.

As she sat on the floor and forced down the unpleasant food, people stopped looking at her and returned to whatever it was they did to pass the time. Once it was deemed that everything was okay, people stopped paying attention. But not everything was okay, not in Jodie's mind. As she ate, she watched Eric's body continue to lie still. If she didn't know better, she'd think he was fine.

"He was acting weird," Jodie spoke quietly to no one in particular.

"What was that?" Troy asked. He was always listening to her.

"Eric. Before the confrontation with Stan happened, he was acting weird."

"What do you mean?"

"I don't know. He was telling me weird things, like how he thought his girlfriend was cheating on him, and how he'd broken some kid's arm with a baseball bat when he was younger. He also mentioned he had been having trouble reading, now that I think about it."

"How so?"

"He said he could make out individual letters and numbers just fine, but he was having trouble putting them together to make words or sentences."

"That is a little odd. You think the blue gunk was affecting his brain at that point?"

"Yeah. I shouldn't have left him. I shouldn't have left him alone."

"There's nothing you could have done."

"But he shouldn't have been alone."

Jodie took another bite, chewed, swallowed. Troy had been right when he said it was best not to think about what she was eating.

23

WITH THE CLOUD COVER, it wasn't as hot as it had been the day before, but the temperature still got above a comfortable level. Sitting in her doorway across from Eric, Jodie had taken off her blouse again. She had also unbuttoned Eric's shirt, and rolled up his sleeves, wanting to keep him comfortable, just in case he actually was still present but unable to move. She had also closed his eyes, as his empty stare bothered her, and she feared his eyes would dry out because he wasn't blinking enough. They kept themselves closed once she had run her fingers over them.

"It stinks in here," Troy commented, wrinkling his nose. He persisted in sitting with Jodie, even though he could've taken his trio of seats back. With the presence of food and water at the back of the train, another seat shift had occurred. People wanted to sit closer to the source, so that they could get in line quickly when the metaphorical dinner bell was rung. Noticing that Troy was choosing the floor, Sydney and Bailey had eventually moved away from the front seats to camp out on the abandoned trio. With Fatima down by the food on guard duty, Simon had placed himself in the seats on the other side of Jodie's door. Even Anthony had moved from the trio of seats next to the front doors, to sit in the less comfortable, rear facing seat next to Mandy. It probably wouldn't be much longer before they were all jammed up at the back of the train, huddled around the food like cavemen afraid of the dark.

"I don't really notice it," Jodie said in response to Troy's statement about the smell.

"It's a boiling pot situation," Mandy told her.

"A what?"

"Boiling pot situation. A frog thrown into a pot of boiling water will immediately jump out, but put one in a pot of water at say, room temperature and heat it up slowly, it will stay in there until it boils and dies."

"You acclimatize," Sydney added.

"You can do that with smells?" Troy wondered.

"Sure, why not?" Bailey leaned forward in her seat so that she could see Troy. "People who grow up or live for awhile in houses where they cook strong-smelling foods don't really notice, but the next person to move in sure does."

"Speaking from experience?" Troy asked.

Bailey nodded and sat back.

"Do you think I should give him some more water?" Jodie asked Troy, nodding in Eric's direction.

"You gave him some just five minutes ago. I'm sure he's fine."

Jodie wasn't so sure. She was constantly worried that he needed more water, or more soggy kibble. Being unconscious, he couldn't tell them what he needed, and so Jodie worried that she wasn't doing enough. She couldn't help but feel as if she had failed him somehow.

"Is your phone still alive?" Bailey asked Sydney.

"No, it died early this morning, before you woke up. Remember? I told you when I gave you a news update."

"Oh yeah."

"Crap, what time is it?" Jodie muttered to herself, looking at her watch. It was just past two in the afternoon, the time she had told her dad they should try communicating again.

Jodie dug through her backpack and located her cell phone. Powering it up, she waited impatiently to see if she had any new messages, completely ignoring the warning message that she had closed without reading. There was nothing.

It was only about five minutes past two o'clock, so Jodie hoped that was the only reason she hadn't heard from her dad. Quickly scrolling down to his number in her address book, she called him. The phone almost instantly went to voicemail. Wherever her dad was, and whatever he was doing, his phone seemed to be off. Jodie left a message and said she'd try again later. On the off chance that he still couldn't hear, Jodie also decided to send a text message.

Half way through typing it, her phone started making this awful beeping sound.

"No, no, no, no, no," she kept repeating as she typed faster, ignoring all the typos that sprang up.

"What's happening?" Troy wondered. He wasn't the only one curious, as both Mandy and Nina were staring at her.

"My phone's about to die. It's out of batteries." She finished her message at last and hit send. The screen winked out before she received confirmation that it made it through the airwaves. She had no idea if her text got to her dad.

Gripping her phone tightly in her hand, Jodie resisted

screaming at it and throwing it against the wall. That would accomplish nothing more than upsetting a few people, and maybe even injuring someone.

"It's all right," Troy told her, resting his arm across her shoulders.

"I just wanted to hear him again," she whispered, her head drooping. Her skirt was filthy.

"I know you did. And you will, once we get out of here."

"How can you be so sure?"

"Didn't I show you already? I know magic."

"If only your magic could get us out of here, I'd believe you."

"If only."

A general silence had fallen over the train. Everyone was exhausted, not so much physically, but mentally and emotionally. No one wanted to do anything, not even talk to one another. There was nothing to talk about, and it was always possible that the person next to you was a killer. Jodie still couldn't wrap her head around that fact, that she had somehow ended up on a train with a murderer.

Remembering Olivia's phone, Jodie became hopeful again for a brief flicker. Then she remembered that Anthony had taken the dead mother's backpack. The phone was in there and had undoubtedly been found by someone else by now. Jodie didn't even know what Anthony did with the bag, or where it was. Besides, even if she did and could get hold of the phone, she didn't know her dad's number. She relied too much on the address book within her phone, which was inaccessible with the battery dead.

Jodie just wanted to go home. She wanted to go home, curl up in her own bed with Rusty, and sleep. She wasn't even sure she wanted to wake up.

It was getting harder and harder to imagine going home.

The longer she stayed in this train, the more she thought she'd never leave it. Eventually, she would just die here. How she'd die, she didn't know. Most likely, the killer would get her. Who would be next? Who would be the next person found with a puncture in their ear, or their neck?

As she sat there on the floor with Troy's arm around her, she wondered if he could be the killer. He was quick with his hands, able to make things seemingly appear and disappear at will. She didn't think it could be Troy, though. Not when Joa died. If the thump of his body had been enough to wake her, then surely Troy getting up would have done the same. Their legs had been almost interlocked, after all.

It was hard not to think about those who had been killed. It bothered Jodie, and not just because people were dead. She felt like she should be able to figure out who had done it.

First there was Lin, sitting beside Fatima, her ear exposed to the aisle and anyone who walked by. That was the easy kill, when no one knew, and no one was suspicious. After that, however, the killer managed to kill both Roxanne and Steven, who were sitting at opposite ends of the train from one another. That one would have been a lot more difficult. Last, was Joa who was on patrol. He had been awake.

The murderer was getting bolder. Showing off, even. Jodie suspected that he was challenging himself, seeing who he could get away with killing. With a thought that made her feel sick, Jodie wondered if he might be doing it just to alleviate the boredom of being trapped on the train. The planning and execution of murder must fill up a lot of time.

Who was next? What new challenge had the killer come up with? And who could be that sick?

"Jodie? Are you all right? You're shivering," Troy interrupted her train of thought.

"I'm just thinking about the people who've been killed."

"You probably shouldn't."

"I know I shouldn't, but I can't help it. Those poor people will never make it home, just like those trapped in the blue outside." Jodie raised her eyes and stared out through the blue wall. The times she had looked at it earlier, she hadn't focused on the things inside of it: the people forever suspended. Now she did, picking out features, and limbs, and terrible expressions. She began shivering again.

Troy, not knowing what else to do, pulled Jodie even closer, wrapping his other arm around her. "We'll get out of here," he told her. "I promise you, we will."

Jodie didn't think it was a promise he'd be able to keep.

24

AS THE THIRD day slowly became the third night, Jodie sat with her back to Eric and the rest of the train, peering up and out through the windows in the door before her, her empty dinner package crumpled up on the floor. It hadn't rained after all. The clouds were still hanging low in the sky, reflecting the last of the setting sun's light. She wished she could see the colours properly. Sunsets weren't nearly as pretty when viewed through a wash of blue.

"The night should be a little warmer," Troy said, still leaning against the doors.

"Yeah?"

He nodded. "The cloud cover keeps more of the day's heat trapped against the earth, instead of letting it all go back out into space."

"Still going to be cold, though."

"Most likely."

They fell silent again, Jodie still looking through the window while Troy played with one of her pencils, spinning it around between his fingers. They had essentially run out of things to talk about. Whatever they did say to one another, inevitably came back around to something depressing, or something they had already talked over more than was necessary.

Everyone on the train was glum and sluggish, but wary. The closer it got to night, the more tense they became. It seemed they all expected someone to die that night. And why not? Someone had died every night so far.

"Do you have a patrol shift tonight?" Jodie spoke without emotion.

"I don't know," Troy shrugged. "Maybe. They just come by and tell me when I'm on patrol."

Jodie knew that, and was unsure why she had asked. Troy had been with her just about every second since Stan had been killed, and no one had come by to tell him about any patrol schedule. Even when she went to the bathroom, Troy had followed her to make sure nothing happened with Denzel. Due to the location of the food, Denzel and Fatima were essentially also guarding the toilet hole, which was rather inconvenient and uncomfortable.

"How are we going to keep Eric warm?" Troy made another attempt at conversation.

Jodie didn't respond.

"I mean, if touching the blue knocks you unconscious, we probably shouldn't get that close to it, right?" Troy continued.

This time Jodie shrugged. She didn't know and it made her feel unwell to think about it, so she avoided it.

"Do you think we'll get one of those blankets?" Troy kept talking.

Jodie shook her head. They would never give one of the blankets to Eric, and Jodie and Troy by themselves weren't a large enough group to get one. It was going to be another long and cold night.

Once the sun had set, leaving them in the dark, a single flashlight turned on at the end of the train. The current patrol was Simon and the cyclist, who carried the blankets. It seemed it had already been decided who was getting them, and no discussion was to be had. Jodie leaned into the aisle and watched who the lucky recipients would be.

Denzel and Fatima got one, which wasn't unexpected. Now that they had joined forces, of course they'd give themselves the good stuff. The next blanket was given to the paint-covered guy, Ian, who shared with Alison and would probably share with the cyclist when he was off duty. Usually Ace could be expected to share with them as well, but now that he was a killer, Denzel was keeping the tall man by his side. Jodie couldn't begrudge Ian for getting one; no one would have any blankets—or food—if it weren't for him. The third blanket was handed out to Nina and Carla. Jodie wondered if they got one because Carla was pregnant, or because she was still in shock over the death of her husband. Recently, she had started responding to things like food, water, and even simple questions, but she rarely made a sound, and spent most of the time gazing down at her feet. Nina instantly unfolded the blanket and began wrapping it around the two of them. It looked comfortable and warm. The last blanket passed right by Jodie and Troy and was given to the sisters. Mandy immediately moved across the aisle to take the third seat and snuggle up beneath the blanket with them. It was just large enough to cover all three of them; there was no way for anyone else to share.

"Excuse me." Jodie stopped the cyclist before he could follow Simon to the rear of the train where they would probably receive more orders from Denzel.

"I'm sorry, there aren't any more blankets," he told her, misinterpreting her reason for stopping him.

"It's not that. I was just wondering what your name is. I just realized that yours is the only one I don't know."

"Oh." His eyebrows twitched with mild surprise. "I'm Max."

"I'm Jodie."

"I know. Is that all?"

"Yes."

Max turned to hurry after Simon, narrowly dodging one of the center poles that gleamed in the weak light. Jodie liked the light of the flashlight, and wished it was on more often. Since the light wasn't coming from outside, it wasn't first filtered through a wash of blue. Everything was more real beneath its shine. It all appeared warmer, and more comforting, despite the high contrast shadows that were being thrown.

Troy crawled past her, moving toward Eric.

"What are you doing?" she whispered.

"I figured this would be the best time, before the light gets turned out." Troy grabbed Apollo's small, child blanket and tucked it all around Eric. It was just long enough to cover him from chin, to blue stuff. Troy worked very carefully when he was near the blue. Once the blanket was secure around Eric, Troy then readjusted the man's suit jacket-pillow, loosening the arms and using them to wrap around Eric's head. In the end, only his mouth and the end of his nose were exposed. Troy then crawled back over to Jodie.

"Good?" he asked her.

"Good enough, I guess."

"Now for us." Troy leaned against the door and invited Jodie to lean against his chest. She did, no longer uncomfortable with extremely close contact. Her personal space had dropped down to nothing when it concerned Troy or Eric. Once she was comfortable, Troy used Roxanne's blazer to protect the bare sections of her legs from the cold. It wasn't much, and was barely large enough to cover them. As the light went out, Troy draped his coat over both their torsos and arms, wrapping his own arms around Jodie's waist once he was done.

"Sorry I can't do anything more for your legs," he whispered, his breath tickling her ear.

"It's okay. This should be fine." Jodie had to admit that she liked being taken care of. After putting so much effort into making sure that Eric was okay, she hadn't really noticed that Troy was doing the same for her. Although she liked being able to stand on her own, she was glad to have someone watching out for her. It was something to hold onto during the craziness.

"Hope you don't mind sleeping sitting up. I thought it might be better than lying down on the floor."

"It's fine. As long as I don't feel anything poking my backside during the night."

Jodie's attempt at a joke fell flat. Instead of laughing, Troy shifted uncomfortably behind her, pulling his hips away from hers.

"I'm sorry," she said quickly, unable to think of anything else to say.

"No, it's okay. I guess if I were a girl I might worry about the same thing."

"I was just trying to make a joke." Jodie felt highly embarrassed and was pretty sure Troy felt the same way.

"Oh."

The awkward moment led into a silent one. Sighing, Jodie closed her eyes and decided to try to sleep. Troy's arms wrapped a little more tightly around her, and he shifted slightly to the right, leaning his head against the barrier between the doors and the seats.

Minute after minute ticked by, as sleep continued to elude Jodie. Her mind just wouldn't shut off. Every now and then, she would open her eyes to find they weren't heavy in the slightest. There was virtually nothing to see in the dark, except for the occasional shadow of movement as one of the guards walked past. Based on their footsteps alone, Jodie learned to tell whether it was Simon or the cyclist, Max. They weren't walking next to each other, but they weren't leaving much space between them either. Jodie felt certain she'd recognize a foreign pair of footsteps and know if the killer was nearby, but she didn't know what she would do if such a thing were to happen.

Her mind kept circling back to her dad's case, as it always seemed to do these last few days. It was annoying. It didn't matter from what angle she came at her memories, there was nothing new there. She couldn't remember much about that time, only the depression that came afterward. Still, her mind insisted there was something there, something important, if only she could grasp it. It was like recognizing an actor in some movie or show, but not quite being able to place where she had seen him or her before. Unfortunately for Jodie, she couldn't just open up a Google search or check IMDb this time.

Minutes dragged on into hours, while Jodie sat awake. She could tell Troy was sleeping by the way his breathing had changed, and his body had lost its tension. It made her sad to admit it, but she was jealous of him. She wished she could escape into the realm of dreams as easily as he had. Jodie wondered what time it was. The watch on her wrist was her nice one, which meant it didn't have the glow function that her usual sports watch did.

Something made a soft shuffling sound nearby. Jodie opened her eyes, but could see nothing other than the usual soft outlines of a few poles. Whatever light they were finding to reflect wasn't nearly enough by which to see anything else.

Jodie's mind raced. There was no reason to think the shuffling had been anything more than someone nearby shifting their position. Despite her rationalization, her heart rate sped up. The killer was still on the train. There was a chance it had been Stan, but Jodie didn't think so. Whoever the murderer was, he knew what he was doing. He wouldn't have given himself away by being so angry over a small scrap of food.

When no other sound accompanied the shuffling, Jodie convinced her eyes to close again. Her mind went straight back to thinking about her dad's case. It seemed even more important now.

With her added fear, something started to form in her mind. Whatever it was her brain was trying to remember, she knew she was close now.

Something moved closer. Jodie had no way of knowing this, but she did. She hadn't heard anything, and with her eyes closed, there was absolutely no way she could've seen anything, but she knew. Her heart sped back up, galloping in her chest. The presence got slightly closer again.

It's a trick of your mind, Jodie kept thinking to herself. She remembered being a child, lying in bed in the dark, certain that a monster of some kind was creeping out from beneath her bed. There was never anything there. She tried to tell herself that this was no different, just her frightened mind playing tricks on her.

The mysterious presence got closer. There was no

reason for Jodie to risk that it wasn't just some trick of the mind. She opened her eyes.

A black shape was between her and the barely visible poles. It was right in front of her!

Jodie reacted on instinct, her childhood fears realized. Screaming, she pistoned both her legs into the center of the unseeable thing's mass. There was a heavy *oomph* as she knocked it over backward.

Behind her, Troy awoke with a start, trying to get up and forgetting that Jodie was on top of him. The single flashlight snapped on as the patrol came pounding down the train, Simon wheezing along behind Max's athletic body. All around, people awoke, startled, confused, and frightened. Jodie ignored them all and continued kicking her feet, pressing her back tightly against Troy's chest as if to become a part of him.

Max reached the form, which had begun to rise. It took Jodie's mind a second to realize it was a man. Of course it was human, what else could it have been?

"Ed?" She stilled as she recognized the face, but his dark sunglasses were nowhere to be seen.

"I'm sorry," he said, holding his hands out toward her. "I needed to use the bathroom, I didn't mean to-"

A metallic *clank* cut him off. The center of the flashlight beam found the source before Jodie's eyes could. It looked like the handle of Ed's cane, but there was something wrong about it. Instead of the white stick meant to help him walk, the light glinted off a metal spike, tarnished with dried blood.

It suddenly hit Jodie what her brain had been trying to remember, the reason her dad's case was relevant. During the entire ordeal, only one woman had been in the right place and right time to have committed the crimes, but she was confined to a wheelchair and so it would have been impossible for her, especially as there were stairs in the way. Her dad never found out whether she did it or not, if she was faking her injury, but he had begun to wonder about it just before Jodie's mom died.

Here was a man faking a disability. Without his sunglasses on, Jodie could see how clear his eyes were. She could see them dart from the weapon, to Jodie, to Max. He was reading their expressions.

Ed could see, and Ed could kill.

25

THE MOMENT WAS FROZEN in time. Nobody moved or said anything as they all came to the same realization. All eyes were on Ed and his blade. Even he didn't make any movements or utter anything in his defence. He knew there was nothing he could say.

"You murdered Joa!" Carla broke the silence with a shattering scream, her whole body trembling with its force. Those further down the train who might not have been able to tell what was happening, certainly knew what was going on now.

Ed reacted quickly to Carla's shriek. He knew there was no way he could take on everyone in the train. Kicking his no-longer-hidden blade away from himself, Ed swiftly dropped to the ground, lying flat and placing his hands behind his head. Jodie recognized the position as one that cops ordered suspects into at gunpoint. She briefly wondered if Ed had been arrested before.

"You murdered him!" Carla howled again, launching herself from beneath her blanket and landing on her feet beside Ed. Once there, she began kicking him, over and over again, her wild swings missing him as often as they connected.

Max and Simon watched the scene, not knowing what to do.

"Stop! Stop!" Jodie got up, holding her hands out to Carla. Whatever Ed had done, slowly kicking him to death wasn't going to solve anything. "Please, stop! We need to work this out!"

Max finally broke his eyes away from Ed to glance at Jodie. Understanding dawned in his eyes. Passing the flashlight back to Simon, he stepped up behind Carla and wrapped his arms around her. He pulled the flailing woman away, being careful not to step on Eric or touch the blue wall so close behind him. The stillness of the scene then exploded.

"You should have let her kill him!" Bailey shouted, jumping to her feet, her sister right beside her.

"That's not justice!" Nina stood up and shrieked back, for once making Jodie glad to hear her voice.

Everyone began shouting at one another. Some were all for killing him, while others, like Jodie, thought he should just be bound. Opinions were piled on top of one another to the point where it was nearly impossible to tell who was arguing for what.

Suddenly, Anthony pushed his way between the sisters. He held his hand over his head, Ed's deadly weapon clasped tightly within it.

"No!" Jodie screamed, her hands rising to her mouth.

Troy nearly knocked her over as he threw himself in the way. As the blade came down, it brushed along the side of Troy's arm, leaving a bloody furrow. Troy's scream of pain was added to the chaos, but he grabbed Anthony's arm, keeping him from using the blade again.

"Shut up!" the voice of Denzel bellowed. He bowled his way through the crowd, his heavy muscles allowing him to shove even Simon to one side, who fell into a seat with a thump, the beam from the flashlight jumping erratically around the train. As the fuming bull of a man reached Ed, people shut up as he had ordered, all except Carla who cried out hideous, wailing sobs, as she stood crumpled within Max's confining embrace.

For a split second, Jodie thought that Denzel was holding a weapon in his hand. It would have been easy to grab one from the back while everyone was distracted. It turned out to be only duct tape, however. Denzel knelt over Ed, placing one knee on either side of his torso. Ed continued to stay perfectly still. Denzel grabbed the not-blind man's arms and forcibly removed his windbreaker, which he tossed carelessly to one side where it landed on Eric's head. Denzel then manipulated Ed's arms so that the bare wrists were held together, and swiftly wrapped a considerable amount of duct tape around them. Despite how painful the jerking of his arms must have been, Ed didn't make a sound. It seemed he knew this would happen eventually.

Once his wrists were bound, Denzel hauled Ed up onto his feet, but then stopped. He appeared unsure what the next step should be.

"Hand me the blade," Denzel eventually said, turning to where Troy was still holding Anthony.

Troy released him, and Anthony gave Denzel the sharp spike.

"We should kill him," Carla spoke her mind through her sobbing.

"Not now. We'll deal with this in the morning after we've all had a decent night's sleep and time to think things through. Patrols will stay on." Denzel shoved Ed before him, the crowd parting swiftly to let him pass. Simon followed in the opening, keeping the light trained upon the two of them.

Everyone watched as Denzel hauled Ed down the train, all the way to the post nearest to where he was currently camped out. Shoving him against the post, Denzel proceeded to use more tape to bind him to it. Large portions of Ed's body shone a dull silver as Denzel used the entire roll. He bound him in such a way that Ed could barely move, and he certainly couldn't sit down.

"I suggest all of you go back to sleep before Simon turns off that light and you all end up in the dark," Denzel commanded the onlookers.

Not wanting to fumble around in the near pitch black, the passengers were quick to obey.

Troy sat down on the floor, pulling in a sharp hiss of breath between his teeth.

"Is your arm all right?" Jodie quickly sidled up next him, trying to look at his arm while the meagre light lasted.

"It'll be fine, it just hurts," Troy told her.

A bloody line made its way from the front of his scrawny bicep to the back. Jodie pulled off her blouse.

"What are you doing? You need that for warmth."

"I have you for warmth, remember?" Jodie flashed him a quick smile as she rolled up the blouse. She worked quickly, not wanting to do this in the dark. Once her light shirt was carefully folded into a flat roll, she placed the thickest part against Troy's injury.

He pulled in another sharp breath.

"Sorry." Jodie wrapped the makeshift bandage around his arm as tightly as she dared. She then tied the short sleeves together to secure it. "Not great, but it'll do."

"Thank you."

"Thank you for jumping in Anthony's way."

"I didn't think it was right for him to kill Ed. That's not how you solve problems, it's how you make more murderers."

Jodie was nodding her agreement when the light winked out. By feel, Troy and Jodie shuffled around, locating his jacket and Roxanne's blazer. They returned to the corner of the doorway and managed to sit the way they had earlier without too much bumping and knocking. Jodie snuggled down under Troy's jacket, hoping that her shaking would be blamed on the cold.

26

WITH HER MIND no longer running in circles chasing down a memory, sleep came quickly to Jodie. As she woke up in the early morning light, she realized it must also have been a heavy sleep. Somehow, Troy had managed to disappear from behind her without waking her.

As she rubbed her eyes, planning to find out where Troy had gone, she happened to look at Eric. Someone had taken Apollo's blanket from him. Jodie quickly crawled across the gap, noticing that his jacket was gone from beneath his head as well. As she placed her hands upon his skin, she felt that it was cold. Immediately, her mind jumped to the worst conclusion, until she found a steady pulse in his neck. He was alive, just cold. His small but warm wrapping must have been stolen during the turmoil last night. Jodie tried to remember if she had seen anyone pick up Ed's jacket. Whoever it was, would have had the best opportunity to steal from Eric, already being down there, but it was no good. Fear and exhaustion had made her memories of the previous night fuzzy.

"I did the same thing when I got up."

Jodie raised her face to discover that Troy had found her, before she could even go looking for him.

"The blanket is down by the hole. They used duct tape to hang it over the opening to reduce the smell coming in. There's no way we're going to be able to get it back, even if it managed to stay clean."

"What about his jacket?" Jodie asked, wearily. She wanted to fight for Eric, fight for his right for warmth, but she was just too tired to argue with anyone.

"I didn't see it anywhere."

"Ed still alive?" Jodie found it easier to sit next to Eric and ask Troy about the morning, rather than look for herself. She tried to rub warmth into the trapped man's arms.

"He is, although he doesn't look too well."

Jodie's eyes shot up to meet Troy's, wondering if the not-so-blind man had been beaten in the night.

"He's really tired," Troy continued. "Although he hasn't said anything that I've heard, you can tell by his expression and posture that he wants to sit or lie down."

Jodie let out a sigh of relief.

"I think the breakfast call should be soon," Troy said after a moment's silence. "Once we get our mystery meat, we can make Eric comfortable with my jacket and Roxanne's blazer."

"Why not do that now?"

"Do you want to trust that no one is going to steal them?"

"Good point."

Jodie had left both items by the other door. Troy went over and got them, draping his jacket over his arm and handing Jodie the blazer to carry.

"How's your arm?" Jodie asked, gesturing to her blouse that was still tied around his wound.

Troy glanced down at it as if he had momentarily forgotten. "Still stings every now and then. I haven't looked at it. I didn't want it to be still bleeding, and then have nothing to wrap around it again."

"I think if it were still bleeding, that blouse would be completely red by now. Here, sit down." Jodie patted the floor beside her. She had become so used to the floor of the subway train that she didn't give a second thought to the grit that stuck to her palm and fingers. She simply brushed it back off, something she no longer bothered to do with her skirt. Troy sat and let Jodie untie the blouse. He gritted his teeth as she pulled it away from his skin, the dried blood tugging on the wound and on the tiny hairs of his upper arm.

"It looks like it's stopped bleeding," she told him, searching for any new beads of blood. All around the wound his upper arm was a crusted brown. Jodie wondered if they should use a bit of their water supply to wash the area. In the end, she thought better of it. Not only did she not want to waste water, but it would be too easy to rinse away the clot holding the wound closed and cause the bleeding to start again. She didn't think her blouse would make a good bandage a second time.

A bone-jarring clanging filled the train car. Jodie quickly covered her ears with her hands and leaned into the aisle to see what it was. Denzel was striking one of the overhead handrails with a socket wrench. Anyone who had still been sleeping certainly wasn't anymore.

"Time for breakfast," Denzel bellowed.

A few people shot to their feet, wanting to be first in line.

Jodie wished her stomach wasn't encouraging her to do the same, especially when she remembered the texture of the food. She and Troy got up together, but Jodie didn't head for the line right away. Snatching her art supply bag off the floor, she stuffed Roxanne's blazer into it, and made sure that Eric's water and the dog food were still secure inside. She then carefully folded her blouse so that the bloodstains were covered and put it in her backpack as well. Her portfolio bag was a lost cause. She spotted the flat thing underneath some seats to one side, where Mandy usually sat. A trail of crusted brown blood led from it to where Joa had taken his last choking breath. It must have been knocked aside during the scuffle.

Troy had waited for Jodie and let her walk ahead of him, sticking his jacket into her backpack as well.

"Oh, one second." Troy doubled back to where Eric was lying, then returned swiftly with his briefcase. "We shouldn't let anything else get taken."

Jodie nodded in agreement, glad that Troy had thought to grab it. Even though there was likely nothing of value in Eric's briefcase, someone might be tempted to take it anyway. At least now, it was safe with Troy. Jodie wondered if someone would try to steal the shirt off Eric's back.

The line formed in an orderly manner, with Jodie and Troy at the back of it. They all stood single file, with a gap where Ed was bound. There seemed to be an unspoken rule to keep their distance from him. It was hard to look at Ed. With dark bags hanging under his eyes, he slouched as much as he could within his bonds. If the tape were to be suddenly cut, he'd fall on his face. Thinking about what he had done though, made it hard to feel sorry for him.

Jodie remembered the first time they had met, after the blue entrapped them. Troy had been sitting with him, helping him with his disability. She remembered how Ed had identified her perfume. At the time, she had treated it like she would a comment about her clothing, but now she thought it was creepy.

As Jodie reached the gap in the line, Ed lifted his head and looked directly at her. An involuntary flinch caused her to bump into Troy, who placed a hand on her shoulder to steady her. Ed's eyes were unsettling. After being hidden behind those black shades for so long, the clarity and depth in them were unnerving. Jodie didn't like him looking at her.

"It wasn't you," he spoke, his throat dry, giving him a slight rasp. No one was going to share any water with him.

Jodie tried to ignore him.

"I wasn't going to kill you," he continued. "I was going to kill him." Ed's bright eyes shifted to Troy.

A confession. Ed wasn't denying what he had done, but admitting to what he had planned to do. It was only then, that Jodie realized the people who had gotten their food already weren't dispersing. They were gathering together on the seats nearest to Denzel. Had he asked them to stay? Now they were all staring at Ed, soaking in his words.

Behind Jodie, Troy stiffened, his hand clamping harder onto her shoulder. Jodie could picture it, waking up in the morning, Troy's arms still around her but no longer providing warmth. His skin would be cold, and when she tried to wake him up he wouldn't move. Jodie would turn to find a trail of blood running out of his ear. The imagery made her feel dizzy, lurching her stomach sideways.

Denzel stepped forward before anyone could react. "Keep the line moving. We're going to deal with this once everyone has their breakfast."

It seemed as though everyone was accepting his deci-sion; no one said anything, got up to leave, or left their place in line. Jodie wondered if maybe it was the exhaustion that was causing the lack of an outburst. She knew that no one had gotten a good night's sleep, as usual, not to mention the emotional wear and tear. Crap just kept piling on, to the point where people couldn't muster the energy to create another uproar.

Ed didn't say anything more. His head drooped to his chest, his eyes now hidden as they stared down at the floor. Jodie hurried past him once the line gave her enough space to do so. She was glad to be behind Ed, where he couldn't look at her if he decided to raise his head again.

The line kept moving until Jodie got her silver package and water bottle, as well as a water for Eric. After what Ed had said to her, she didn't think she'd be able to eat, but the sudden burble from her stomach told a different story. Once Troy got his package, Fatima told them both to find a seat nearby. Unfortunately, the nearest seats were within Ed's field of view, so Jodie and Troy sat in the doorway opposite the one with the hole. Jodie could see what Troy had been talking about when it came to Apollo's blanket. It was taped to the door just above the hole so that it hung over it. It would be easy to move out of the way to do one's business. Jodie wanted to tear it down, but she resisted. Who knew what had touched that blanket by now?

"So, it's time to decide what to do with this murderer," Denzel announced to the gathering in the train. "Let's try to be calm about this and not turn into the squabbling mad house that was last night, all right? If you have something to say, put up your hand and I'll call on you."

Several hands immediately abandoned their food to shoot into the air, Jodie's and Troy's among them. There didn't appear to be a single person without their hand up.

Denzel sighed heavily. "Okay, seems everyone has an

opinion. We might as well give everyone a chance to say their peace, and then we'll decide."

Carla shot to her feet, taking the first opportunity to speak. "He's a murderer, and so he should be punished as one. My husband is dead, my child without a father. Why should that man be allowed to live while Joa does not? The murderer should be put to death."

As Carla sat back down, Jodie quickly got to her feet to speak ahead of anyone else. She could tell that Denzel was disapproving of this unorderly way, but she wanted to counter Carla before he started picking who could speak.

"Revenge is not justice," Jodie told the group. "Might I remind you all that we don't have the death penalty here? We don't kill people. If you kill Ed—that's his name, remember? He has one of those—you'll only be stooping to his level. It doesn't matter what he's done, he doesn't deserve to die. No one deserves to die. It's disgusting and heartbreaking that other people have died because of him, but one more death isn't going to make them come back. It isn't going to make things better."

Jodie ran out of steam quickly, uncomfortable with all the eyes on her, and so she sat back down.

"I'm going to call the next speaker." Denzel shot glances at both Carla and Jodie.

One by one, everyone got a chance to speak. Far too many people wanted blood, and it made Jodie shrink with fear. There was so much anger. She was angry too, but hadn't they been taught that violence is not the answer? Other people were unsure. One brought up the question of feeding Ed if he were to remain alive. To not feed him would be another form of murder, a slower one, but who would give up their food? Jodie was glad when Troy got to speak. He reminded everyone that Ed could continue to receive his own portion of food, that his guilt hadn't changed their supply levels. Jodie hoped that since he was the person who Ed had intended to kill last night, his voice would carry more weight. Here was the guy about to be murdered saying his would-be killer should be allowed to live.

Unfortunately, Denzel took his say after him. "That man, Ed, if that's really his name, is clearly a psychopath. Think about it, he was pretending to be blind before he even got on this train. I don't know where he was going, or what he intended to do, but I doubt it was to run a charity soup kitchen. He's probably had murder on his mind since before leaving his house, and he clearly shows no remorse for what he's done. Yes, we don't have the death penalty here, but that's because we have a system in place to house these lunatics. Look outside. You think someone is going to be able to get this guy to a prison? A court house? Any sort of jail cell? I think the odds are pretty good that he'd manage to escape, and there's no reason to think he wouldn't kill again. We have a chance to stop him here and now, for good."

Not many others spoke after that, but all who did backed up Denzel's points. There had been a large number of speakers clearly for killing Ed, while far fewer spoke against it. Denzel stepped forward to speak again, once it was clear everyone was done.

"Ed? Do you have anything you want to say?"

Ed turned his head, craning his neck to try to see those who were literally talking behind his back. "I don't think anything I have to say is going to make a difference, do you?"

"Probably not," Denzel answered.

"Tell us why!" Sydney unexpectedly shouted, a look of embarrassment crossing her features after her outburst.

"Why? Why what? Why did I kill those people specifically? Why did I kill anyone at all? Why was I pretending to be blind? Why, why, why, that question is so vague. Why do you get up in the morning? Why do you have the life that you do? Why do you talk to the people you know, like the foods you eat, dance to your favourite song? Why do anything? Because you want to and you can."

A stunned silence followed Ed's remarks. His words didn't really give them an answer, but they also suggested he wasn't going to. They would have to live without knowing why certain people had died.

Denzel cleared his throat, bringing the attention back to him once it appeared that no one else had anything else to say. "So let's get to the voting. There will be no abstaining, you must vote. Those who think Ed should be executed, raise your hands."

Jodie couldn't look. She stared down at the food in her lap, having only been able to pick at it. Every time someone had mentioned killing Ed, her stomach had clamped shut.

"All those for keeping Ed alive, raise your hands."

Jodie shot her arm up into the air. From the corner of her eye, she could see Troy doing the same.

"Well, there you have it," Denzel sighed. "The voting is eleven to six for execution."

An involuntary squeaking sound escaped Jodie's throat as her chest compressed. Only four other people had sided with her and Troy? Even if Eric had been able to vote, or Ed —whom Jodie assumed couldn't vote both because he was the one on trial and because his arms were bound—it still wouldn't have been enough to save him. They would still have been three votes short of a tie.

"Let's get this over with quickly," Denzel said.

"Who's going to kill him?" Simon asked.

"I was going to, unless someone else would rather."

"Let me do it." Carla shot to her feet with fire in her eyes.

Denzel shrugged. "Sure."

"Troy, I can't watch," Jodie managed to wheeze, her chest still tight enough to make her worry about her heart.

Troy helped Jodie up onto her feet by hauling on her with one hand, using the loop on the top of her backpack. He held his food tightly with his other hand, while Jodie tried not to lose hers. Everything felt numb, including her fingers, and she was worried about dropping the open silver package.

While Denzel chose the weapon of death from the pile, Troy and Jodie scurried past, heading for the front of the train. They were quickly followed by Mandy, Nina, Max, and Ian. It seemed likely that they were the four other people who voted against execution. Once they reached Eric, Troy directed Jodie into the doorway opposite where they liked to sit. Instead of taking the seats nearby, the other four sat with them, clumping together as if for protection.

As Jodie sat down, she caught a brief glimpse of the back of the train. Denzel was handing Carla the spike that had been hidden inside the white cane. Ed's own murder weapon was going to be used to kill him. The rest of them were gathering around Ed, almost eager to witness.

That was more than Jodie could stand to see. She buried her face in Troy's shoulder as he did his best to wrap a comforting arm around her, despite her backpack. Someone else placed their hand on her knee, and Jodie felt them all scoot closer. Based on its size, she was guessing the hand belonged to either Mandy or Nina, but Jodie didn't bother to raise her head to check.

"Any last words?" Denzel's voice carried to them easily in the still air of the train.

"At least I stopped you from killing each other sooner," Ed answered cryptically.

There was a pause, then a kind of gasp. Jodie knew that Ed was now dead or dying. When she heard the choking, she knew for sure. Carla had decided not to kill him like he had done most of the others, with a quick puncture through the ear canal, but in the same way that Ed had killed her husband. He was choking on his own blood. Both the arm around Jodie's shoulders and the hand on her knee tightened.

It felt like a long time before the choking stopped, but eventually it did. Everything remained still. After a moment, the shuffling of feet and clothing filled the train as the executioners returned to their seats. They were most likely going to finish their meals. Jodie didn't feel hungry at all anymore.

When finally she lifted her face and opened her eyes, she discovered something perverse. The sun had come out, breaking through the looming clouds that never did release their rain.

27

ED'S BODY was still taped to the pole. No one had cut him down yet. A clear division had formed within the train. Those that had voted against execution sat in the section near the front of the train, none of them farther back than where Eric lay. Those that had voted for the execution sat at the rear. An entire section of seats, between the second and third sets of doors was empty. So far, the only time anyone had crossed the no man's land, was when Max had gone to grab his bike from where it leaned against one of the third doors, and bring it up front with him. Since then, everyone stuck to their ends.

Jodie was slumped in one of the trio of seats that Troy had originally claimed. She leaned heavily against the barrier next to her, the open MRE on her lap. Her instincts made her pick at it occasionally, knowing she needed food, but the taste of it often made her feel sick. Troy sat quietly beside her, his own meal already eaten but in no way enjoyed.

Not only was Ed's body still hanging, the executioners

had used Eric's jacket to catch the blood from the hole they had put in his neck, and then to cover his face afterward.

"We should do something," Mandy whispered to Max. The two of them sat on the trio of seats across from Jodie and Troy.

"Like what?" Max whispered back.

"I don't know. Demand they cut him down or something. It's not right, just leaving him hanging there."

"It's disrespectful," Nina added. She had chosen to sit in the pair of rear facing seats beside them, where Roxanne had been sitting when she was killed.

"Not to mention unsanitary," Mandy continued. "I mean, isn't that why we moved the others into the driver's cab to begin with?"

"I don't like the idea of him being put in there with them," Ian spoke up while picking at a stiff paint stain on his shirt. He was sitting in the seats opposite Nina's location, next to Jodie and Troy. They had all bunched as closely together as they could while still maintaining a comfortable separation.

"I don't like it, either," Mandy told him, "but that doesn't mean he should be hung from a pole. That's the only place we can put him. We should do something."

"You want to walk down there and demand they cut him loose?" Max raised his eyebrows at her.

"Why not?"

"Because they have all the weapons and a willingness to kill, not to mention all the food," Max reminded her.

"So? It's not like we did something wrong; we just happened to vote differently than them. They're not going to attack us for being concerned about the health of everyone on this train."

No one countered Mandy, but no one made a move

toward the back, either, not even her. It was Nina who eventually got to her feet. Panicky Nina stood up as tall as she could, one hand clasped tightly around the cross at her throat.

"I'd rather not go alone," she said to no one in particular.

Mandy immediately stood, followed by Max a moment later. Soon they were all on their feet. Jodie chose to stick to the back of the group, behind everyone else. With Nina leading the way, they crossed the no man's land to where Ed was bound near the edge of it.

"We're going to cut him down and place him in the driver's cab with the others," Nina announced.

Those closest to them looked nervously toward the very rear of the train where Denzel was sitting. He was clearly their leader now. Peering around the others, Jodie could almost see a hierarchy forming, with the leaders sitting the farthest back, next to the weapons and the food.

Denzel waved them on. "Go ahead, what do I care?"

"He doesn't deserve to be put with the others!" Carla snapped.

Nina still had one hand clasped around her cross, but by looking through the gap between Max and Mandy, Jodie could spy that the other hand was trembling at her side. It didn't show in her voice.

"Be that as it may, we should move him there for health reasons. If there was another place to put him, we would, but there isn't."

Carla didn't say another word, but her upper lip twitched as if she were about to snarl. Jodie suspected that if it had been someone other than Nina talking, she would have fought to keep Ed disgraced. Since Nina had sat with her for so long after her husband was killed, she had earned some respect from the pregnant woman.

"We're going to need something to cut him down with," Nina continued, stepping forward so that the rest of them could gather around Ed. Jodie hung back, unable to look directly at him, let alone touch him.

Fatima rose from her seat with a small knife in her hand. Jodie thought it was one of her art scalpels but couldn't see it well enough to be sure. Fatima handed it to Nina, who used the blade to cut the tape securing Ed to the pole, first down one side and then the other. Mandy and Troy held Ed's shoulders and made sure that Eric's jacket didn't slip off his face or the wound. No one wanted to see either. The moment Nina had separated Ed from the pole, Fatima took back the blade and returned to her seat. Ian and Max picked up Ed's legs, and with Troy and Mandy, they began carrying him to the front of the train. Jodie led the way, intent on opening the driver's cab door. She could contribute that much, at least.

Her hand fell on the latch and as she pulled the door open, she wished she had stayed in her seat. A foul air wafted out, making her eyes water and her throat close up. It was the smell of human decay. Without her blouse, Jodie had nothing with which to cover her mouth and nose except for her free hand. She clapped it over the lower section of her face so hard that she hurt her mouth and nose. And though Jodie had turned away from the cab as quickly as she could, she still glimpsed a bit of what was inside. She saw just enough grey and sagging flesh to give her nightmares for the rest of her life.

The four moving Ed held their collective breaths as they entered the small space, where they dumped the body on top of the others. The flies were the worst part of the whole thing, as they couldn't be as easily forgotten as the smell. The entire time they were working, Jodie had to listen to the flies. The driver's cab had a massive swarm of them inside, buzzing and feeding and breeding on the corpses. Her vision began to swim, not just from emotion, but from the power of the stench. Finally, Ed was settled, and everyone hastily backed out of the little room. Jodie threw the door closed, nearly hitting Max who got out of the way just in time. Troy made sure the latch caught, and then they all rushed away from the door, taking great breaths of the somewhat fresher air within the train, although it had been fouled by the air from the driver's cab dissipating along its length. Only Nina stayed behind a moment longer, saying a quick prayer outside the door for those lying inside.

Jodie returned to her seat where the remainder of her meal was waiting for her. She quickly resealed the package as best she could, unable to even look at the food without getting queasy. The others collapsed into their seats, both emotionally and physically drained. None of them had gotten enough rest or food to be carrying a body around like that, on top of the debilitating horror show that was the driver's cab. Once more, a silence settled over them.

"What's the first thing you're going to do when we get out of here?" Mandy asked Max several minutes later.

Max shrugged. "Go home, I guess. Change my clothes. Take a shower."

"A shower sounds really good. What about you?" Mandy leaned forward to speak to Nina around Max's side.

"Me? I plan to find the nearest church and thank God for our release," she answered.

"Ian? Do you have any plans?" Mandy continued.

"Once I let my family know I'm okay, I want to help those forum guys. You know, the ones who brought us food?"

"Give back what you got."

"Yeah, something like that."

"And you?" Mandy looked at Troy next.

"I don't know," Troy shrugged. "I haven't really decided yet."

"Really?" Mandy sounded genuinely surprised. "You have no idea what you want to do when we get out of here?"

Troy just shook his head.

"Jodie?"

Jodie knew her turn was coming next. "I just want to sleep in my bed," she answered honestly. "What about you?"

"I was thinking about eating a big meal, but after we heard about what the city is like, I'm not sure I'll be able to find one. Maybe I'll just sleep, too. A warm bed sounds nice." Mandy's eyes drifted off as she began to think about it.

No one had much interest in keeping up a conversation, so once Mandy stopped talking, things got silent again.

Most of the clouds had broken up and drifted off, leaving behind only a few puffy, white ones. The sun was shining in through the blue once again, slowly heating up the train. Jodie had never hated the sun more in her life. Normally, she loved the sun, with summer being her favourite season. Now, she just wanted it to go away. She wanted the dull overcast skies of early spring and winter. She hated the cold that came when the sun went down, but she couldn't tolerate its midday heat either. Only in the early morning and early evening was she comfortable with the temperature.

As the day progressed, Jodie eventually returned to her food and ate it. She actually felt less sick when she finished, her hunger having contributed to the dizzy spell. With Troy's help, she carefully fed Eric, if that's what it could be called. Dog food mostly dissolved in water didn't feel like enough of a meal. Jodie used the back end of a clean pen to help break up the blobs of dog food. She decided that with tomorrow's water, she would smash up the dog food first, try to make a powder of it before mixing.

The day got hotter and hotter as the sun filled the train. Mandy, Max, and Nina all ended up sitting on the floor, trying to avoid the direct sunlight coming in through the west windows. When Mandy just narrowly missed sitting on Joa's bloodstain, Jodie realized that either no one noticed it or that they didn't care about it anymore. She herself had stepped through it many times. Her portfolio bag lay beneath the seat across from her, abandoned. Neither it nor its contents were of any more use.

Jodie sat with her eyes closed, trying to use as little energy as possible. She thought about her interview, and what it might have been like. She imagined both scenarios, one where she got the job and one where she didn't.

Eventually, Mandy started up a card game, and all six individuals joined in. They sat on the floor, as out of the sun as they could get, and played on the surface between them.

"I can't believe Ace voted for execution," Max eventually spoke during their third round of Crazy Eights. "You'd think after what he did, he'd have some compassion. Things could have easily turned bad for him."

"Ace didn't mean to kill Stan. It was an accident. Totally different," Mandy reminded him.

"I'm not surprised," Troy spoke up. "Have you seen the way Denzel's been lording over him since it happened? Ace is always by his side now, as if Denzel is the only thing keeping him from the same fate. Of course he wouldn't vote against him."

"I thought Anthony would vote against it," Mandy went

on. "The entire time that discussion was happening, I couldn't stop thinking about Roxanne and how against it she would be. I thought with how much time he had spent around her, he would think the same."

Jodie felt a slight pain at the mention of Roxanne's name, but did her best to hide it.

"I think a lot of them voted out of fear. Not just of Ed, but Denzel," Troy said.

"We never should have let him take charge of the food," Ian added.

A lot of heads nodded in agreement.

"Maybe we should do something?" Nina asked hesitantly.

"Like what? One card left." Mandy held up her single card, close to winning the game again.

"I don't know," Nina shrugged, drawing into herself, fidgeting with her cross again.

"You're suggesting we try to take back the food, aren't you?" Ian encouraged her to say more.

Nina only shrugged again.

"I'd be willing to try," Max told them all.

"No," Jodie finally spoke up. "We're not going to do anything but sit here."

They all turned to her, waiting for an explanation.

"Did no one else hear what Ed's last words were? 'At least I stopped you from killing each other sooner,' that's what he said. He had a lot of time to watch us all, and he came to the conclusion that we're going to turn on one another. Also, last card." When Mandy hadn't been able to play her last card, it gave Jodie a chance.

"Jodie, Ed was insane," Troy reminded her unnecessarily.

"Yes, but that doesn't mean he can't be right. I thought

about it. If we hadn't had him to unify against, we probably would have broken up into groups like this sooner and begun fighting one another. I think we should do nothing. We'll pass the time quietly, eat food when we're given it, and let Denzel be in charge until the rescue workers come."

"What if Denzel decides one of us doesn't need to be fed?" Max bristled.

Jodie shrugged. "I'm not sure I have that low an opinion of him. Or the others, for that matter. Deciding to kill Ed is one thing, but to kill one of us, when we're not antagonizing them, would be senseless and the others would know it. So we're going to sit here quietly, and do what we're told."

"What if he decides to do something to Eric?" Troy asked her.

Jodie stiffened. Eric was her weak spot, and Troy knew it. "He won't do anything."

"How do you know?" Troy pushed. "People have already been taking stuff from him. Denzel decided he should only get dog food, and that was before he was in a coma. I doubt you'll get a bottle of water for him in the morning."

"Then I'll share mine with him."

"No you won't, you need yours."

"If we all chip in a little water, he'll be fine."

"He won't be."

Tears escaped Jodie's eyes, as she put her last card face down on the floor, no longer caring about the game. "We're not going to do anything." She did everything she could to keep her voice calm.

"Even if it means Eric has to suffer?"

"What would you do, then?" Jodie snapped at him, but in a whisper to keep from drawing the attention of those at the back of the train. "What would you do? Attack

Denzel? Is that your plan? More death? Does someone else have to die? Because that's all I see in the future. Maybe—*maybe*—you can get someone to come around to our side of things, but what would that do? We're still trapped in a fucking subway train waiting for rescuers to come."

Jodie would have stormed off if she could. Instead, she just abandoned her card, picked herself up, and moved to sit across from Eric. She leaned against the barrier, with her back toward the front of the train, her face turned toward the door beside her.

She just wanted to go home.

The others were whispering. Jodie couldn't hear what they were saying, and didn't want to. She just sat silently, trying to dry up her tears so as not to waste hydration. The heat was already drawing enough moisture out through her pores without her spending precious water on senseless crying.

When Troy came and thumped down next to her, Jodie refused to acknowledge him. She knew it was him though, because only he would sit so close that their shoulders were touching one another.

"You won the game, you know," he said after a moment.

"This isn't a game," she answered bitterly to the door.

"No, I mean the card game. You could have played your last card."

Jodie sighed heavily, but still stubbornly refused to look at him.

"You're right about that other stuff, too. Where would more aggression get us? Nowhere. We're not going to try anything. We're just going to get along quietly until help comes."

Finally Jodie turned her head, needing to see his face to

determine if he was lying. His eyes had a glassy appearance, as if he, himself, were trying to hold back tears.

"I just feel helpless," Troy admitted. "I want to do something, *anything*, but there's nothing. There's nothing I can do to get us out of here. There's nothing I can do." A drop plunged over his lower eyelid and down his face, which he was quick to wipe away.

Jodie turned her body toward him and wrapped her arms around his shoulders. "I know," she whispered. "I wish I could do something, too."

"You don't understand. I've *never* been able to do anything. I lied to you earlier, about why I was going downtown. My family doesn't have money problems. My mom did marry a man who's not my father, but he wasn't some old rich dude. He was just a regular guy who I couldn't get along with. We argued all the time, until I ran away from home. My mom never tried to stop me. I don't think she cared. She was too busy taking care of her two new kids to notice what was going on with me. So I ran away. I was on the train because I knew it was a good place to pick pockets. My entire plan for the day was to ride back and forth until after rush hour, stealing what I could and hoping not to get caught. Then I'd either find a shelter for the night, or maybe go to my friend Bradley's place. He lets me stay there sometimes and store my stuff, so long as I don't make a mess, pay for any food I eat, and his girlfriend's not over."

"And that's the truth?"

"That's the truth. I'm a useless human being and always have been."

"You're not useless." Jodie squeezed him tighter. "Is this why you don't know what to do when we get out of here?"

"Yeah. I have no interest in going home. I have nothing to look forward to."

"You don't want to know if your mom is okay?"

"I'm not sure she even looked for me when I ran away. It's been a few months and I haven't heard anything. I tried to return once, but only my step-dad was there, and he wouldn't let me in. He said they were all doing a lot better since I had gone."

"That's awful."

Troy nodded, quickly batting away another escaping tear.

"You're coming with me, then."

"What?"

"When we get off this train, you're coming with me. We'll go to my place, where you can meet my sister and my dad. They're nice people, they won't turn away someone in need. We'll have something to eat, get some sleep, and then decide what to do."

"Are you sure?"

"Of course I'm sure. You're not useless, Troy. You've been helping me get through this with my mind intact. It's the least I can do to help you out afterwards."

"Thanks."

Troy shifted to place his arm across her shoulders. It was too hot for so much physical contact, but they both needed it. They held onto each other and waited for rescue.

28

WITHOUT ANY PLANS TO make or execute, the day dragged by slowly. Max grumbled a few times, but he didn't try anything. Either Troy had brought them around to Jodie's way of thinking, or they had done it on their own. The only time Jodie went to the back of the train during the day was to relieve herself. It was awkward with so many people so close. Thankfully, Fatima and Nadia were there, and they believed in privacy. Each woman took one end of a blanket and held it up as a curtain, keeping their backs turned to Jodie so that she could do her business in relative peace.

At one point, Jodie thought to check on the doctor, but she couldn't get his attention. It took Jodie awhile to figure out where he was and even longer to determine what he was doing. The hole at the back of his car was just big enough for him to fit his arm through. She could make out flashes of hands and the glint of something metal. It appeared that he was attempting to widen the hole. Jodie couldn't tell what he was using to grind and chip away at the metal framing, but odds were, it wasn't going to do much good.

When the dinner bell was rung, or rather the overhead bars were struck, Jodie joined the back of the fast-forming line with the other five people who had voted against execution. She did her best not to stare at the spot where Ed had been bound and killed, where a chunk of duct tape still clung to the pole. That was over and done with, and she needed to get past it.

Jodie's group of six behaved themselves, collecting their dinners and returning to their area near the front of the train. The sun had started to set, reducing the sweltering heat and allowing them to sit as comfortably as they could on the hard plastic seats.

"Do you think there's going to be a patrol tonight?" Max asked, unable to let them eat in silence.

"I don't see why there would be," Troy answered him, pushing his mystery meat around between bites of rubbery vegetable substitute. They had no utensils and were forced to eat with their fingers. A few people, like Nina, wasted small amounts of water to clean their fingers first, but most didn't. They had run out of wet naps awhile ago, and were beginning to run out of the Kleenex that had come with the food, which was being saved for bathroom trips. Jodie's solution was to scrub her fingers on a relatively clean looking patch of her clothes before eating. It made her feel better even though it didn't do much. Hygiene around the train had rapidly deteriorated. Someone was going to end up very ill if they didn't get out of there soon.

"I don't know," Max shrugged. "They might still have a patrol."

"I don't think they will," Jodie spoke up, siding with Troy. "With Ed gone, what would be the point? No one else has shown any signs of aggression, or an intention to hurt anyone else. There's no need to keep an eye on people."

"We hope," Mandy muttered.

"If it weren't for the cold, I think we'd actually be able to get a somewhat decent night's sleep," Jodie continued, not wanting Mandy's comment to be the last word.

"What do you want to bet they're not going to give us one of those nice blankets?" Max briefly gestured toward the back of the train.

"Oh, I have one of those." Nina shifted to reveal she had been hiding a blanket between her body and the side of the train this whole time. "No one came around to collect them this morning, so I held onto it."

The revelation of the blanket picked up everyone's spirits a little.

"So what did you all do before getting stuck on this train?" Ian asked, changing the topic to something a little lighter. "You've probably figured out by now that I used to paint houses." He gestured to his multicoloured clothes.

"I was going to an interview with a fashion company," Jodie told the group, happy to talk about something that didn't concern their immediate situation. "Before that, I had a part-time job at a fabric store until they drastically reduced their staff. Eric told me he was a realtor."

"I'm between jobs at the moment," Troy answered simply, glossing over all the stuff he had admitted to Jodie.

"What about you, Mandy?" Ian turned to her.

Mandy sighed. "I'm an escort."

Jodie couldn't hide her surprise, and neither could a few of the others. Mandy didn't look like the kind of person who worked in that industry. She was pretty, but down to earth.

"I'm not a hooker, if that's what you're thinking," Mandy added when she saw everyone's surprise. "I just make single, rich guys look good at parties or conventions or whatever when they don't have a date. My night ends after whatever social gathering it is, with the guy, or sometimes girl, dropping me off at our office where my boss arranges my ride home. We have emergency buttons and everything in case something goes wrong." She returned to her food with the obvious intention of saying nothing more about it.

"Max? How about you?" Jodie saved Mandy from any possible questions by redirecting their attention.

"Bicycle courier," he answered simply.

"I didn't think couriers took the subway," Troy wondered aloud.

"Generally, we don't. I was supposed to have the day off, but someone got into an accident and I was asked to fill in. I was on my way to work."

"That's some bad luck," Ian commented.

"I think we have all had some seriously bad luck," Max replied. "Nina? You're the last one. What did you do?"

"I'm a librarian," she told them, not using the past tense in which the question had been asked. "I was going down-town because I had heard of a small book shop that was having a going-out-of-business sale. I was hoping to convince the owner to donate anything he couldn't sell, and perhaps even purchase a few things myself."

"Quite the collection of people," Ian commented.

Jodie nodded in agreement, wondering about the personal stories of those at the other end of the train. She especially wondered about those she could never ask; the ones whose bodies were now rotting in the driver's cab.

"So Jodie, what company were you interviewing with?" Mandy asked as she finished her meal.

"It was for an intern spot with Charliese," Jodie told her.

"I know them. I get to wear their dresses sometimes, provided I act like a walking billboard whenever I'm questioned about them. Do you think you would have gotten the job?"

"I honestly have no idea. I would like to think so."

"I looked through her portfolio earlier," Troy chimed in. "I don't really know anything about fashion, but I think they would have hired her."

"Oh? Where's your portfolio?" Mandy wondered.

Jodie pointed it out behind her feet. "It's pretty much ruined by now."

Mandy noted the bloodstains. "I'm sorry." She looked back up at Jodie, offering her a weak smile.

Jodie shrugged. "Pretty sure I have no chance of getting that job now. After we get out of here, I'll find time to make a new one."

"If you need any modelling pictures, I'd love to help you out," Mandy offered. "I've done a little bit of modelling."

"That would be nice. I'd like to keep in touch with you all once we're out of here."

"Unfortunately, our phones are all dead," Ian reminded them.

"So?" Jodie opened her backpack which sat at her feet. Lately, she rarely let it get farther than direct contact. "I have some paper. We can all write down our Facebook names, or Twitter handles, or even phone numbers and emails if you'd like." Locating her small sketchbook, she tore out a page and then ripped it into smaller pieces. "Here." Jodie wrote her contact information on each piece, then handed them around with the pen and the sketchbook for a writing surface.

The papers went around, everyone writing something on them. When they got to Troy, he paused. Jodie suddenly remembered his situation, and that he may not have any contact information.

"If you don't have a Facebook, we can make you one once we're out of here," she whispered to him.

"I have one, I'm just trying to remember if I used my real name or not." He poked her with the back end of the pen, giving her a smile. "It's been awhile since I logged in." Eventually he wrote something down.

Jodie took all the scraps of paper and handed them out, one to each of them. "There. Now we can all keep in touch."

"Assuming we get out of here," Max grumbled.

Nina glared at him. "Don't be such a negative Nancy. We'll get out of here, just you wait."

Jodie sucked her lips against her teeth to resist saying anything. Panicky Nina telling someone not to be a negative Nancy? It was hard not to find that rather amusing.

As night fell, and the meals were finished, they continued to chat about unimportant things. Ian and Max did most of the talking, telling everyone about weird jobs and customers they had had. The others joined in on occasion with a story of their own, but not often. Mandy never mentioned her customers, but sometimes mentioned her boss or something weird that one of her co-workers had done. For just a moment, Jodie felt like things were normal.

Then the sun was gone, and the blue did something new.

29

EVERYONE HAD GOTTEN USED to the darkness that came with the setting sun. Occasionally there would be a few clouds that covered the moon, but they didn't expect it to be as dark as it had been when the skies were overcast. As it turned out, it would be their brightest night yet.

When the sun sank past the point where the sky was the shade of a purple bruise, the usual darkness fell. It lasted only for about a minute. To the surprise of everyone on board, the blue stuff encasing the train suddenly began to glow. Several people gasped, and many startled out of their seats, moving away from the windows.

"What's it doing? What's it doing?" Nina's voice picked up the usual high-pitched and annoying tone it did whenever something unexpected happened.

"I don't know, calm down," Troy told her. "I don't think it's really doing anything other than glowing."

Jodie and Troy both knelt back down on the seats and stared intently at the glowing stuff. There didn't appear to be anything different that could be causing it to produce its own light.

"The doctor has no idea," Mandy told them.

Jodie glanced over and saw Max gesturing an obvious 'I don't know' with his arms and shoulders in the doctor's direction. She assumed the man in the car was making the same gesture in return.

"It keeps changing." Ian had his face pressed up against the window as he peered at it. Now that their initial reactions of fright had abated, a lot of other people were also up against the windows. "First, it was gooey, then it became solid. After that, it started to numb things that touched it, and eventually it... I don't know, put them in a state of unconsciousness, and now it glows."

"What next?" Nina quietly whined. "Is it going to start moving and consume us all?"

"I really doubt that." Max turned away from the window to speak directly to her.

The same kind of murmuring was going on at the back of the train, as people wondered what was going on.

"If it weren't so eerie, I'd think it was kind of pretty," Mandy commented.

Jodie agreed with that statement. The light wasn't bright, not much more than a kid's glow-in-the-dark star stickers plastered to a ceiling, but there was so much of it, that it was enough to see by quite easily.

Troy leaned back from the window. "It's hard to tell, but I think all the blue gunk is doing this, not just the stuff here."

"I wonder why?" Jodie didn't ask anyone in particular, knowing they wouldn't know.

Troy shrugged and answered her anyway. "Maybe it's been absorbing the sun's energy? Who's to say."

Nobody said or did much for several minutes. They all just sat there and stared at the blue.

"It's going to do this all night, isn't it?" Max eventually said, turning away from the imprisoning oddity.

"Seems like it." Ian also turned away.

One by one, they all stopped looking directly into the glowing blue.

"Maybe it'll leave on its own," Mandy quietly hoped.

Nobody responded. Jodie thought most of them were thinking the same way she was, that that would never happen, but they were keeping quiet to keep from bursting Mandy's bubble.

Jodie didn't keep track of how much time passed with all of them just sitting there quietly. She was deep within her own thoughts, remembering Avatar, a movie that involved a lot of glowing scenery. Movies and TV shows had always been a way for her to escape.

"I guess if it's not going to do anything else, we should probably try to get some sleep," Max eventually stated.

Jodie and the others agreed.

There was much shuffling around as everyone tried to figure out the best way to share their warmth. It was already getting cold, and no one wanted anyone to be left out. In the end, they laid down in a kind of block, with three people on one side and three people on the other, their legs tangled up in the middle. Nina was able to spread the blanket over all of them, so they were all covered up to their lowest ribs at least. Jodie lay in a somewhat crooked position, with her head on Eric's shoulder. If something happened in the night, like Eric waking up or moving in some way, she wanted to know. Also, Troy had placed his jacket on the man, and she had no intention of letting someone steal it in the night.

Troy curled up against her back, wrapping his arms around her. Jodie's backpack, Eric's briefcase, and

Roxanne's blazer were all on top of them, keeping them as warm as they could get. Nina was behind Troy, wrapped up in her own light jacket, while Max, Mandy, and Ian bunched together at the other end of the blanket. Jodie was a little jealous of Mandy, getting body heat on both sides like she was, but wouldn't change her position for anything. Their legs were so entangled, Jodie could barely tell which ones were hers, let alone whose legs were against them. As she closed her eyes, she hoped no one had restless leg syndrome.

Despite taking awhile, Jodie was eventually able to drift into a light sleep.

She had no idea how long she was asleep, before a cold draft woke her up again. Part of Jodie that had been warm previously, now wasn't. She wondered if maybe Troy had moved, had changed his position. Then there was a sensation of movement across her skin, and the cold patch got larger. Her sleepy mind couldn't comprehend what was going on, not before Troy's did, anyway.

"Hey!" Troy shouted, suddenly scrambling to get upright. His shouting and thrashing legs very quickly woke the others. "What do you think you're doing?"

Jodie's eyes flew open and the light momentarily confused her; she had forgotten that the blue now glowed. Her mind instantly turned to Ed. He was trying to kill Troy again, he was going to murder him!

Troy was already on his feet by the time Jodie managed to get up on her knees. Ed was dead of course, there was no way he could be trying to kill Troy or her or anyone else, but a struggle *was* ensuing. When Jodie was able to focus, she saw Troy and Denzel having a mini tug-o-war over Jodie's backpack.

"This doesn't belong to you!" Troy shouted into the larger man's face.

"I'm taking back the dog food!" Denzel roared back. "He certainly doesn't need it!"

Jodie realized then that this was about Eric. Troy had suspected that Denzel wouldn't give Jodie any water for Eric in the morning, but no one had thought that he would attempt to steal back the food in the middle of the night.

Denzel tried to pull the bag from Troy with a swift series of tugs. Although Denzel was bigger, Troy had a much better hold on the bag, his arms wrapped around it, and Denzel's jerks succeeded only in shoving the younger man around. With the men's feet shuffling all about, Jodie grabbed Eric and sat him upright. She held on to him, trying to keep him out of harm's way without touching the blue herself.

"It's not yours to take back!" Max had gotten up now, but didn't try to get near the scuffle.

Nina had crawled into the doorway opposite Jodie and Eric, where she cowered and whimpered in fear. Ian was helping Mandy get up and back out of the way.

"He doesn't need it!" Denzel screamed.

"Denzel! Stop this! Please!" Ian pleaded, perhaps hoping that as the person who was responsible for getting the food delivered, his voice carried more weight. It didn't stop Denzel in the slightest.

Toward the back of the train, people had been woken up by the shouting. They all looked on, dazed, unsure of what was happening. It seemed that Denzel had made this decision on his own.

When the struggle continued, and Denzel began shaking the bag back and forth hard enough to lift Troy's feet off the floor, Max joined in. Once Denzel left an opening, Max ran at him, driving his shoulder into Denzel's exposed ribs. All the air in the hydro worker's lungs escaped him in a single whoosh. His expression changed from fury to shock as he lost his balance, one of his legs giving out from under him. He fell toward Jodie and Eric, prompting Jodie to wrap her arms tightly around the unconscious man and to bury her face in his shoulder. Denzel didn't fall on top of them, but it was a near miss. Instead, he collapsed into the space between them and the side barrier, where he came to rest with his head and arm against the blue.

The silence that followed was filled only by a wind blowing against the side of the train. At first Jodie thought that maybe Max had killed Denzel, the way Ace had killed Stan, but then she remembered that this had apparently happened to her when she had touched the blue.

Denzel lay completely still, his jaw hanging slack, and his eyes staring out at nothing.

Troy was panting, still clutching the backpack as tightly as he could to his chest. "He was trying to take Eric's food," he said between gasps. "I couldn't let him."

"You did the right thing. We both did." Max placed a hand on his shoulder, letting Troy know it was over, and that it was okay to ease his hold on the bag.

"At least now he can't bully anyone else," Mandy commented.

Jodie turned and frowned at her. "You don't intend to keep him like this, do you?"

"Why not?" she shrugged. "He can't harm anyone like this, and we can just move him away from the wall once the rescue people show up."

"Because we don't know what it's doing to him." Jodie gently laid Eric down, turning her attention to Denzel. "The stuff is glowing now, who knows what else has changed about it? No, we can't leave him there."

Grabbing the cuffs of his pants, Jodie tried to heave Denzel away from the wall. He was very heavy though, and she wasn't very strong, especially with her lack of sleep and small meals.

"Won't someone help me?" she looked around at the others. Not even those at the back of the train moved to assist her. They had all given up on Denzel the moment they realized they could.

Frustrated with everybody, Jodie went back to pulling. She gritted her teeth and put all her weight into it, nearly falling over when her shoes lost traction.

Troy dropped the bag behind her with a thump, then stepped up alongside Denzel, careful not to step on Eric, and grabbed the large man's belt.

"On three. One, two, three."

With Troy's help, they dragged Denzel away from the wall so that no parts of him were touching it anymore.

"How long until he wakes up?" Jodie asked Troy. She had no experience watching this side of things.

"I don't know. It took you several minutes, and you weren't touching it for as long as he was. We don't know if it has some sort of cumulative effect." Troy picked up Jodie's backpack and handed it to her. Other than a few new scuff-marks, it was unharmed.

No one moved or spoke while they waited. Not many people from the rear of the train had gotten up to get a closer look, but all of them were leaning into the aisle and watching.

When Denzel's hand twitched, Troy gently nudged Jodie to stand behind him. Jodie went willingly, slipping her arms through the straps of her backpack, so that she was wearing it on her chest. If Denzel still wanted the bag, he'd have to drag her with it. Max stepped up alongside Troy, ready to take on Denzel.

"Where is she?" Denzel blinked, dazed. "Where is she?" As he sat up, tears quickly welled in his eyes and then spilled over to carve tracks down his face.

Jodie peered at him between Troy and Max's shoulders. "Where's who?"

"Isabelle. Wh-wh-where is Izzy? Where is my si-si-si-sister?"

"She's not on the train, Denzel."

"She was ri-ri-right here. We were t-t-t-talking. There was turkey, an-an-and she was helping me with mmmmmmy stutter."

Jodie suddenly realized that it wasn't emotion that was causing his hitching voice. She pushed between Troy and Max, both of whom had relaxed considerably. Denzel looked like a child in a man's body, his expression completely different from when he had been fighting with Troy.

"Where were you?" Jodie asked him. "What year was it?"

"I was five." Denzel's voice changed a degree. "I was five, and it was Thanksgiving. My sister was there. The one who died a long time ago. Leukemia."

"Your stutter is gone," Jodie observed.

"Yes. She helped me."

"So when you touched the blue, you were five years old again and having Thanksgiving dinner with your sister."

"Yes." Denzel glanced back at the glowing blue wall, his expression a mixture of fear, awe, and longing.

"And you know where you are now? And... what you had been doing?"

"Yes." Denzel turned away from the wall and stared sheepishly at his hands.

He stood up so suddenly, that Troy quickly pulled Jodie up onto her feet and placed himself slightly in front of her, turning so that he could keep an arm around her.

"I'm sorry," Denzel muttered, then turned and walked back to the rear of the train.

"That's it? You're sorry?" Max shouted at his back, but got no reaction or response.

"Leave him alone." Jodie wiggled herself free of Troy to put a restraining hand on Max's shoulder. "I don't think he's going to try anything else tonight."

"How do you know? How do you know it isn't just some act?" he challenged her when he couldn't get to Denzel.

"I don't know, not really. I just... I feel like he won't."

"I'd rather not rely solely on your gut," Troy told her. "Max, you and I can take shifts staying awake and keeping an eye on things."

Max briefly ground his teeth, but then agreed.

"You okay, Nina?" Troy asked as he helped her to her feet.

"Just a little shocked," she told him, quickly returning to the floor to straighten out the blanket that had gotten twisted and bunched. "Seems we can't have a single night on this train without something awful happening."

"Well, we should try to get some more sleep anyway. Who knows what we'll need the energy for tomorrow?" An involuntary shudder raised gooseflesh all along Jodie's limbs, as a cold draft wafted by. The wind outside was definitely finding its way into the train.

Troy insisted on taking the first shift and told Jodie he'd watch over Eric, so she crawled underneath the blanket beside Nina. Although Jodie felt certain that Denzel wouldn't try anything, she kept her backpack strapped to her chest, just in case. With the bag at her front, Nina's back against her own, and Roxanne's blazer draped over her, Jodie was able to build up a considerable bubble of warmth. If she had a soft surface to lie on, or maybe even just a soft pillow, she'd practically be comfortable.

Sleep came fairly easily, yet it never seemed to stay long. Every time Troy and Max changed shifts, which seemed to be rather frequently, their shuffling around always managed to rouse Jodie. Once they settled, however, she always found herself back in the land of dreams within a minute or two. She kept dreaming of the beach.

30

JODIE AWOKE with the sun shining in full force. It had risen completely over the horizon, but it was still early. Even with the light of the sun, Jodie would have slept on if everyone else hadn't decided to get up. Their movements woke her, and she didn't want to be the only one left sleeping on the floor. Once they were all up, Nina folded the blanket and set it on the seat beside her.

"What do you think is going to happen today?" Mandy wondered around a jaw-popping yawn.

"Hopefully, nothing," Ian replied, slouching in his seat.

"Does anyone else here know how to play Broken Bridge?" Max asked.

"I do." Nina raised her hand slightly.

"Cool. I figure we can teach the others and finally play a card game better than Crazy Eights."

"After breakfast," Nina suggested.

Jodie glanced toward the back of the train. Most of them seemed to be awake, but a few were still stirring, trying to hide from the sun to steal a few more winks.

"Looks like the clouds have completely gone again," Troy commented, peering up and out of the window.

"I liked those clouds," Jodie sighed. "You could feel the temperature drop every time one passed over the sun. So I take it nothing else happened last night? I woke up a few times, but didn't hear any problems."

"Nope, your cop instincts were right," Troy teased her.

"I don't have cop instincts." Jodie tried to be annoyed, but couldn't.

When the breakfast pipe was rung, it wasn't Denzel doing the ringing or the bellowing. Fatima wailed the wrench on the overhead bar, while Ace called everyone to breakfast. The line promptly formed and moved in an orderly fashion. Denzel still aided the process, handing out everyone's food, but he was quiet and withdrawn.

"Here's Eric's," he said to Jodie, handing her an extra bottle of water before she could ask. "I'd give you an MRE for him, but I don't think he'd be able to eat it."

"I don't think he could either." Jodie wasn't entirely sure if she agreed with that, but the MRE's rubbery texture would certainly make it difficult. The dog food they knew they could dissolve.

Returning to her seat, Jodie finished the last of her water from yesterday and was about to crack open the next bottle when a sound stopped her.

"Did you hear that?" she asked Troy who was just sitting down.

"Hear what?"

"Listen."

They sat quietly, those who had already started to eat pausing to see if they could hear what Jodie heard.

"There it is again," Jodie said when she heard the sound.

"I heard it that time, too," Mandy agreed.

"Same," Ian nodded.

"It came from outside somewhere." Jodie got to her feet, leaving her breakfast on the seat behind her, and began searching out through the train's windows.

All throughout the train, people heard the high-pitched chirp and abandoned their meals to locate the source.

"It's getting louder," Max observed, his face pressed against the window with his hands cupped around his eyes to block out any potential glare.

"There! There! People!" Alison started shouting at a window toward the back of the train. "There are people out there!"

No longer caring about their self-imposed separation, Jodie and the others rushed to the back of the train to gather around the window. Alison was right, there were people outside, at least a dozen of them walking up the Allen Expressway. The one in the lead periodically blew on a whistle, which was the sharp chirp they kept hearing.

"Here! Over here!" Sydney started yelling.

Soon enough, everyone had joined in, and was waving their arms. Simon knelt in front of the crapping hole and was braving the stink to shout through it.

As the people on the road got closer, the efforts became more robust. Fatima started hitting the overhead railings with the wrench again, while others smacked the windows. Some of the people outside were clearly military with their uniforms and weapons. In the middle of their group, they dragged large wagons that rolled on rugged-looking tires and were burdened with equipment.

Finally, the lead man spotted them and pointed in their direction. The troop of people headed toward the fence nearest to where those in the train had gathered; one of the few sections of fence not covered in blue.

"Hello there! Are you folks all right?" the whistle man asked as he got closer.

"Are you here to rescue us?" Simon asked, his voice strangely high-pitched.

"Yeah, we're here to get you out."

There was a brief moment of silence as everyone let that sink in, and then a great whooping cheer erupted. The trapped passengers started jumping up and down, hugging one another and crying. Jodie and Troy had latched onto each other, laughing as they rocked back and forth. Jodie felt like her heart was about to burst with pure joy.

Outside, the men and women were smiling as they watched the explosion of happiness inside the train. The joy of those inside was infectious, no matter how many times the rescuers had seen it before.

By the time Jodie was able to get herself under control, the troop had already set to work. With two pairs of bolt cutters, they began snipping their way through the fence and separating the wooden panels from it. Others started walking along the road, checking out the length of the train car and commenting on areas to one another. Two men were investigating the nearby vehicles, while a third went straight to the doctor's buried car; the doctor's arm was waving limply out his hole. While the remainder checked over their equipment, a woman brought out a camera and started taking pictures.

"This is how it's going to work," one of the men cutting through the fence began talking to them. "We *will* get you out of there. If you are badly injured and in need of medical assistance, we will help you get to the hospital. If you are not injured, you're on your own. I'm sorry, but we don't have enough time and manpower to escort everyone to an evacuation site."

"Evacuation?" a few people murmured, looking at one another. No one had heard about an evacuation.

The man outside seemed to realize their confusion. "The city is being evacuated, albeit slowly. We can give you maps to the various sites. With the roads as blocked off as they are, we can't get enough supplies into the city to sustain everyone. If you choose to stay, and the military finds you, you will be detained and then removed to one of the less nicer evacuation sites. We're starting in the downtown core and working our way outwards. It'll be awhile before we reach the outer suburbs."

It seemed that the rescue worker was anticipating that everyone would want to go home, and was letting them know that, so long as they didn't live downtown, they'd be able to do so without getting into trouble. They just wouldn't be able to stay there.

"Do you have any food for us?" Simon asked.

"I'm sorry, we have nothing to spare. If you have anything left, I recommend you divide it up now. Get your stuff together."

Everyone turned toward the food, wondering how much they would get.

"Orderly! Let's do this orderly!" Ace quickly shouted, looking and sounding a little frightened. A riot over the remaining food was the last thing they needed.

With much jostling and a few grumbles, everyone managed to form a line. Jodie didn't really care how much food she got, she was virtually vibrating with the idea of getting off the train. She couldn't stop smiling, like a kid about to be let into Disneyland.

It seemed the rescue workers had come just in time. It

turned out that everyone was given only one more MRE and one more bottle of water. They had just about run out. No longer needing to fear people attacking each other—at least that was the hope—Denzel handed back people's pointy objects. Jodie's art scalpels were returned to her.

Coming back to her abandoned breakfast, Jodie was virtually bouncing. Until she saw Eric, that was. Would the rescuers save Eric? She had no idea. She had promised she wouldn't leave without him.

"I can still come with you, right?" Troy whispered, drawing her attention.

"Of course you can," she told him, her smile returning.

They packed their supplies into Jodie's backpack.

"Do you want your portfolio?" Troy asked, fishing it out from under the seats.

Jodie quickly shook her head. Even if the bag had protected the contents from absorbing Joa's blood, she didn't want to touch it. She didn't even want to look at it again if she could help it. Troy kicked it back under the seats.

"What should we do about Roxanne's blazer?" Jodie asked him quietly.

"Take it with us."

"Do you think we should?"

"Why not?"

"I don't know. Isn't it disrespectful? It's stealing."

"I'm sure she'd want you to have it if she knew. Take it to remember her by. Maybe we can find a family member one day to give it to."

"Okay."

Folding it carefully, Jodie placed the blazer in her backpack. With a lot of folding and crushing, they then jammed Troy's coat on top. It still didn't fit completely making it so they couldn't close the backpack, and forcing part of it to stick out.

Once the bag was packed with everything, Jodie stood still and looked about the train. Those who had things to gather had done so quickly, many of them checking, and rechecking the contents of their bags. Nina had taken their blanket and was currently giving it to Carla. Jodie couldn't tell who had taken the rest of the blankets. The sisters, Bailey and Sydney, sat side by side, holding one another and crying silently with grins on their faces. Alison and Ian were talking excitedly together, their difference in voting forgotten. Max was checking over his bike, probably intending to ride it as much as he could to get where he wanted to go. Denzel was actually going around and handing out a few of his tools.

"If things are as bad out there as those forum guys said, you may want this," he told Troy as he held out a chisel.

"Thanks." Troy accepted the gift and pocketed it.

"What about him?" Denzel looked down at Eric.

"I'm going to stay here until I know they're going to free him," Jodie told him.

"We both are," Troy added.

"That's good." Denzel then moved on to give something to Mandy.

As the workers got through the fence, the passengers began to migrate toward them again.

"Keep back, please!" one of them shouted. "And cover your eyes!"

People were quick to obey, not wanting to interfere with the rescue operation. Through quick glances, Jodie was able to determine what they were doing. They used a blowtorch in short bursts on the blue covering the door that Denzel had dented. Once the blowtorch was pulled away, a second man stepped forward and wiped at the spot with what appeared to be a paper cup, which he then discarded and stepped back for the man with the blowtorch to resume. The process took awhile, but the workers seemed to know what they were doing. At one point, there was a sound like sliding ice and a small crash. A chunk of the blue had come off, no longer attached to the larger section of itself.

"Keep back!" one of the workers eventually ordered again.

As everyone watched, they jammed a Jaws-of-Life into the opening. The jaws easily widened the opening further, now that some of the blue had been dealt with.

"Okay, come on out. Watch your step. Orderly now!"

The mob inside the train was a lot less orderly getting off than they had been when getting their food. Jodie wanted to join them so badly, to get outside, but she held back. She returned to Eric and sat down beside him. Troy joined her. Together, they watched as the people they had spent far too much time with got off the train. No one took one last look.

Shortly, after all of the other passengers had escaped, two men climbed aboard.

"Are you hurt?" one of them asked as he spotted them, quickly making his way over.

"No, but Eric's trapped."

The two men knelt down to look him over.

"I told him I wouldn't leave without him," Jodie explained.

"I'm not sure we can do anything." One of the rescue workers shook his head. "He's too far in."

"There must be something!" Tears gathered in Jodie's eyes. "I promised him."

"I'm sorry, ma'am." The more military looking of the

two shook his head as well. "He's too far in for an amputation, and we can't waste our fuel carving him out."

"Down!" Troy suddenly said, perking up.

Jodie turned to him, as confused as the other two men.

"Cut out the floor from under him, isn't that what you told Eric once, Jodie? Based on the way the blue slid down the door after you cut it, it's not actually sticking to anything, right?"

"No, it doesn't stick. Once the blue stuff hardens, it retains that shape like a sculpture. A few cars that only had their hood or trunk covered, we've been able to just slide free."

"So if you cut the floor out from under Eric, he should just be able to slide out, shouldn't he? I mean, the blue isn't sticking to him," Troy sounded rather excited about the idea.

Jodie had forgotten she once mentioned that to Eric. The idea got her hopes up.

"We don't know what the underside of the train is like. The blue stuff could have gathered beneath it." The rescue worker sounded like he pitied Troy and Jodie.

"I can at least check it out," the military man offered.

"Please, could you?" Jodie begged him.

"Yeah. Greg? I'm going to at least look. I mean, the other guys are going to take awhile getting that doctor free, we might as well try while we wait, right?"

The rescue worker, Greg, sighed. "All right. Go look."

The military man got up and jogged over to the opening.

"How many people have you saved?" Troy asked while they waited.

"More than I can remember," Greg told them.

"Is it as bad out there as the forum people told us? With the looters and stuff?"

"Yeah, that's why the military with us are carrying weapons. Want me to wash that wound for you?" Greg gestured to Troy's arm, where there was still blood dried to it.

"Could you?"

"Yeah. Come here."

Troy shuffled over to Greg, who proceeded to squirt some water on it and wipe it down with a clean cloth.

"How did this happen?" Greg asked as he worked.

"Bit of a long story, but we had a murderer on board," Troy told him.

"Murderer?" Greg glanced around the train, his eyes lingering slightly on the remains of the duct tape still stuck to the pole.

"We moved the dead into the driver's cab." Jodie pointed to it.

Greg nodded. "They'll have to wait, but someone will eventually come to collect them. I'm sorry you had to deal with that, although you weren't the only ones."

"Really?" Jodie shuddered.

"Quite a few people snapped after being trapped for a few days."

"This guy didn't snap," Troy shook his head. "He knew what he was doing. He had been pretending to be blind before he even got on the train."

"Seriously?" Greg raised his eyebrows. "Jesus. What happened to him?"

"He's in there, too," Jodie told him with a small gesture of her head.

Once Troy's wound was washed, he shuffled over beside Jodie and placed his arm across her shoulders.

They waited quietly until the other man returned.

"Hey," he called to them as he slid back into the train and walked toward them with a smile on his face. "I think we can get him out."

Jodie stiffened, hoping the man wasn't yanking her chain.

"Is the captain cool with it?" Greg asked him.

"He says we can try."

Jodie shot to her feet and rushed over to hug the man.

"Whoa there, easy." He gently pushed her off him. "Do you know the guy?"

"His name is Eric. We've been taking care of him since he got stuck."

"That's kind of you. You realize he won't wake up when we free him, though."

"What do you mean?" Jodie felt the colour drain from her face. "We've had people get knocked out by the blue and they woke up." She decided it was best not to mention that she was one of them.

"People who've only touched it for a short period of time are fine. People like Eric, who've been trapped since the beginning... none of them have woken up yet," Greg told her.

Jodie was crushed.

"We'll still get him out," the military man was quick to tell her. "We'll take him to the nearest running medical centre. We haven't given up on people like him. The doctors there will give him fluids and take care of him. I believe they're working on transferring people like him to a handful of hospitals outside the affected area, where they can be cared for as long as need be."

"Okay," Jodie nodded, still feeling rather sullen. She had hoped to walk off the train with Eric.

"This is going to take us awhile," Greg told them. "You two should get going and make the most of this daylight. Trust me when I tell you that you don't want to be caught outside at night."

"All right." Troy got up. "Come on, Jodie."

"Just a second." Jodie put her bag down and dug out her piece of paper that had the six voters' contact information, including her own. She located Eric's briefcase and slipped it inside. "This belongs to Eric. Will you make sure it stays with him?" Jodie asked the military man, handing him the briefcase.

"Sure," the man nodded.

Jodie had no idea if he would or not, she just had to trust him. She then knelt down beside Eric. "Bye Eric. It was nice meeting you. Make sure to call me or something when you wake up, okay?" She swept his hair away from his forehead and gave it a quick kiss.

"You ready?" Troy asked as Jodie stood back up. He had put on her backpack and was waiting patiently.

"So, he'll end up being evacuated too?" Jodie asked for clarification.

Greg nodded. "It might take awhile, but he'll be kept safe."

"Okay." Jodie turned to Troy. "I'm ready."

Troy held out his hand and Jodie took it.

"Tell the captain we're going to try to free this man. And get a map to the evacuation centres while you're at it," Greg told them.

"We will," Troy nodded. He held out his free hand to each of the rescuers, shaking theirs and thanking them.

Turning away from Eric and the two men, Troy and Jodie headed for the opening in the train. Apollo's blanket lay in a crumpled, dirty heap next to the exit. Beneath the opening, a flat sheet of blue, presumably the piece that had been freed from the door, covered up their waste. Scattered around it were smaller pieces of blue inside paper cups.

"The blowtorch makes it liquid again, but it hardens soon after cooling," Jodie said, remembering what she had seen on the internet and pointing to the cups. "Before it cools, they must scoop it up into the cups so that it doesn't just gather in the way some place else."

"I know." Troy had seen the internet as well. "Let's get off this train, shall we?"

"Yeah."

Helping each other down onto the blue, Jodie and Troy disembarked. A light breeze tousled their greasy hair. Once on the gravel beside the blue, both Jodie and Troy stopped. Everything looked weird, almost wrong. The sky was pink, and for a moment, Jodie thought it was because that's where the blue came from, as if it were the colour of the sky itself that had trapped them. Then she realized it was because of the blue, but for a completely different reason. Her eyes had adapted to the tint in the train so that when she left it, her eyes weren't properly seeing that colour anymore. Jodie remembered it happening when she had spent too much time watching the penguins at the zoo through the underwater viewing area, and explained what was going on to Troy. It was taking her eyes a lot longer to correct themselves than that day at the zoo. Despite this, Jodie and Troy enjoyed the unfiltered sun and fresh air for the first time in roughly four days. They were free.

31

AFTER PASSING along Greg's message and being handed a map each, Troy and Jodie had a decision to make: did they follow the Allan Expressway or the subway tracks?

"We're going to your place, I'm leaving it up to you," Troy decided.

Jodie looked down the road, and then down the subway line. "We'll take the tracks as much as we can. I rarely ever drive, so I don't know the streets that well. I know the subway line."

"All right. Tracks it is, then." Troy stepped back through the opening in the fence.

Jodie glanced along the expressway before following after him. Sparks of light came from the back of the doctor's car, matched by similar flashes from the train. Between them were the people trapped in the blue, those who couldn't be saved.

"Jodie?" Troy worried as she stood there for too long.

"Coming." She quickly turned and walked through the fence.

Having watched the forum people and Apollo's dad,

they knew to walk through the train car behind the one they had been trapped inside. Jodie couldn't help but feel jealous of the people in this car as she passed through it. They had been able to escape at the start of things.

"When do you think we should stop to eat?" Troy wondered. "I didn't finish my breakfast before all this happened."

"Neither did I. How about when we get to the first station?"

"Sounds like a plan."

It took them a lot longer to get there than Jodie had thought it would. Not only was walking a lot slower than riding on the subway, it also wasn't a straight and simple hike. They were constantly weaving around blobs of blue stuff, sometimes having to backtrack as they ended up down blind alleys of it.

"I wish we had gloves and protective clothing," Jodie complained as she carefully squeezed her way between some blue and a fence. "Then we could attempt to climb over some of this."

"That would be nice," Troy agreed.

"What will we do if we find we can't go farther without touching it?"

"We'll figure something out. Maybe we can tear up my coat or find a way to use your paper to protect our skin."

At last, they made it to Yorkdale station. Troy gave Jodie a boost up onto the platform and then scrambled up on his own. The station floor was gloriously free of blue, the glass ceiling above having protected it. They went to the first bench and sat down, with Troy shrugging out of the backpack to get at their food and water.

"What do you think the mall is like?" Jodie asked

conversationally, pointing toward the stairs that were the subway's exit.

"No idea. We can go check it out if you want. The whole way from here to there is covered, so there shouldn't been any blue gunk in the way."

"Do you think we should?" Jodie accepted the MRE that Troy handed her.

Troy shrugged, passing her a water bottle and then straightening up after taking his own bottle out of the bag. "Maybe?" He cracked open the water bottle. "I mean, there might be more food and water in there. More importantly, there would be protective clothing. Gloves and things we could use to help us get around."

"But the place has probably been looted."

Troy nodded. "And there's likely still looters inside. We could easily run into trouble."

Jodie sighed as she picked at her rubbery food. "We're in danger if we go, and we're in danger if we don't."

"That's the crux of the matter."

"Let's finish eating, then decide."

"Okay."

They continued picking at their meals in silence. Jodie couldn't stop enjoying the fresh air and the open space that the station provided. She hadn't realized it at the time, but now she felt sure she had been becoming claustrophobic inside the train.

Once the MREs were done, both Jodie and Troy crumpled up the silver packaging and tossed them toward the tracks. Littering didn't seem like a big issue when the city was drowning in a mysterious blue substance.

"How many more stations are there?" Troy asked after several minutes had passed without either one of them making a move.

"Two. There's Wilson and then Downsview, which is the end of the line and not far from my place."

"Is any of it underground?"

"Just before reaching Downsview it'll become a tunnel."

"So there's likely to be a lot of blue on the tracks."

Jodie nodded.

"And at the end of the line, we're probably not going to be able to see anything without flashlights."

"Probably not."

"Sounds to me like we *have* to check out the mall."

Jodie sighed. "Sounds like that to me, too."

"Come on then." Getting to his feet, Troy put both of their unfinished water bottles back into the backpack and then swung it on.

"Do you want me to carry that for awhile?" Jodie offered. "You carried it the whole way here."

"No, it's all right. I got it. It's not that heavy."

They walked side by side to the other end of the station, which would lead them into the mall.

"I've carried that bag a lot of times, I know it's not *that* light."

"Really, I'm good. Maybe we'll be able to find you your own bag that you can carry if you really want to."

Jodie realized that Troy was teasing her and lightly punched him in the arm.

At the far end of the subway station, they were confronted with a set of stairs leading down. It was darker down there, as the sun shining through the glass ceiling reached only so far. Jodie and Troy paused at the top of the staircase.

"Do you think we should take out your scalpels?" Troy asked.

"I think that would make me feel a little better," Jodie admitted.

Putting the bag down, Troy poked around inside until he found the blades. There were two of them, one larger than the other. He handed the bigger one to Jodie, and placed the smaller one with its protective cap in his front pocket. He decided to wield the larger but duller chisel that Denzel had given him.

"Where do you think the others are right now? Do you think any of them headed into the mall?" Jodie asked, delaying their descent.

"I don't know. It's possible. Come on." Troy boldly headed down the stairs, leaving Jodie hurrying a few steps to catch up.

At the bottom, they climbed over the turn-styles and stepped through the doors on the other side. They were in the darkest part, beneath the Allan Expressway. Troy took Jodie's free hand within his own, and led them toward the light. Jodie couldn't stop imagining what might be in the corners she couldn't see.

Out from under the expressway, the sun returned through an arched, glass ceiling like the one in the station, except it was much lower. Still holding hands, Jodie and Troy climbed a set of steps back up, which led to a suspended tunnel that would take them over another road and into the mall. Partway through the tunnel, Jodie paused and stared out the glass side.

Most of the glass ceiling and sides were clear of the blue except for a thin dribble, just past the center point, that reminded Jodie of a string of spit. The road that travelled near the bridge didn't fare as well. In the intersection next to them, was a large flat pool of blue that had to be at least seven feet deep, and expanded a ways down each road, swallowing everything. No cars were trapped inside the actual intersection, suggesting to Jodie that both lights had been red when the blue struck. Cars were trapped at its edges, however, forever sitting patiently as if the light might still change. Jodie thought she could make out the corpses inside, but wasn't sure. She could definitely see the ones closer on the sidewalk, frozen in similar positions as those outside the subway train. It was strange how unaffected she was by the sight of them. By the time they were rescued, Jodie didn't even see the bodies trapped in the blue anymore.

Farther out was the mall's parking garage, which also had globs of blue clinging to the sides of it. Everyone who had been in the lower sections would have been safe, while those on the highest level would have had nowhere to hide. Jodie found herself thinking about Sandra for the first time in awhile, wondering where she was when the blue hit. Wondering if maybe she was alive and trapped somewhere like Jodie had been, or if she was sealed in blue like a statue. Jodie no longer had the energy to cry for her missing friend.

"Come on," Troy urged Jodie onwards.

They passed a glass-enclosed staircase that led to street level, and walked down a small handful of steps beyond it to enter the mall.

The first stretch of hallway they entered was empty. Jodie had come through here several times in the past, and it had always been crowded. The absence of people was disturbing.

"Let's be as quick as we can," Troy whispered.

Despite his suggestion for haste, neither Troy nor Jodie moved very fast. They glanced into the shop fronts on their left, the sun lighting the way for them through the windows on their right. Most of the shops, like the convenience store they first came across, were locked up tight, the employees having closed up and gone home once the emergency had started. They passed a dark security office, a dental centre, and the Go Transit office. After what happened on the TTC, Jodie had a feeling she wouldn't be riding public transportation again for some time.

"Ugh, I'd kill for a coffee," Jodie whispered as they walked by a Tim Hortons doughnuts and coffee shop.

"I don't think so," Troy whispered back.

Jodie wasn't sure whether he was negating her statement about murdering for coffee, or if he was saying they weren't going to check out the place. Either way, he was right. The Tims wasn't locked up like the other places they had passed, the employees most likely not caring enough and wanting to get the hell out of there. Toward the back of the powerless doughnut shop, it quickly got dark, but even in the weak light Jodie could see that someone had been there ahead of them. Chairs were knocked over, stale doughnuts were strewn across the floor, and torn-open coffee bags had left trails of beans. It was the first confirmation of looting they had come across.

Continuing to the end of the hall, where the windows stopped, they came to The Source. The place had clearly been broken into, its security cage bent and twisted out of shape.

"There'll be flashlights in there if no one's taken them already." Troy stopped next to the opening.

Jodie hesitated. It was even darker in there than it was in the Tims, and electronics had been scattered all over the place. "I don't know."

"Come on, we have to. I don't know where else in this mall they might have flashlights, and even if I did, I want to stay as close to the subway as we can." Troy slipped through the opening in the cage, entering the electronics store.

Jodie continued to hesitate, watching Troy through the bars. He stood there, waiting for her in the semidarkness. Gripping her scalpel tightly, Jodie slipped through the opening.

"I'm going to check by the registers," Troy told her. "They usually have small things around there."

"Where should I check?" Jodie didn't often find herself in electronics stores. Todd, Amber's fiancé, was far more interested in these things and was often the one buying her parts and cables. Anything Todd didn't pick up, Jodie ordered off the internet.

"Search around here," Troy suggested, pointing around the immediate area.

Jodie didn't say anything, but she was happy to stay where it was brighter. She suspected that Troy knew that, and that was why he told her to search the front.

Poking around, Jodie came across a lot of camera and cell phone accessories. Most of the cameras themselves were gone, stolen to be sold later. As she poked around, Jodie found a lens she had wanted for her own camera. A flash of thought crossed her mind, telling her to take it, but she quickly put it down. It was one thing to steal what they needed, it was another entirely to just take what she wanted.

"I think I found something," Troy hissed in the darkness. "I'm not sure it has batteries though."

"Check where the batteries go in," Jodie whispered back, moving closer to his position. "Sometimes there's a tab you have to pull out."

"You're right, there is."

With a soft click, Troy filled the store with bluish LED

light. He pointed it at the floor between himself and Jodie so that she could quickly make her way over to him.

"They aren't exactly flashlights, but they'll do nicely." Troy handed her one.

The thing was the size and shape of a hockey puck with twenty-four LEDs imbedded in the top. A button on the side turned on the lights, and on the back there was an adjustable hook that popped out, as well as a magnet. The thing was clearly meant to be placed or hung somewhere to provide constant light while someone worked in a dark space, such as behind a computer or TV or something. It wasn't really meant to be carried around, but it was good enough for Jodie and Troy.

"How many are you taking?" Jodie asked as she watched Troy pick up several more.

"Three for each of us. I don't know how long the batteries in these things last, or how much we'll be using them," he explained. As he grabbed the extra lights, he popped out the hooks and hung them from his belt loops. "Now all we need are gloves, long-sleeved shirts, pants for you, and probably a better pair of shoes as well."

Jodie glanced down at her slip-ons. They didn't have much of a grip, and wouldn't be very good for crawling over blue stuff.

"There's a Footlocker just up ahead at the first intersection. I think we might be able to find all that stuff there."

Troy grinned. "I'm glad I'm with a girl."

Jodie punched his arm, barely missing his injury.

"Ow, what was that for?"

"That was a sexist remark."

Troy raised an eyebrow at her. "Seriously? I think we still have bigger problems than me accidentally saying something sexist."

"I know that. Just... Come on." Jodie led the way back out of the store.

"Sorry. Would it make you feel better if I said I'm glad I'm with a fashion student? Is that less insulting?"

"Better." Jodie knew she probably shouldn't have bothered calling him out on his remark, but it was instinctive. Her dad was always calling people out on racist or sexist remarks like that, and so both his daughters had learned to do the same. Some people found it really irritating, because they saw themselves as neither sexist nor racist, but after making an accidental and mostly harmless remark, they felt like they were being accused of being one.

Jodie rolled her shoulders and refocused her mind. Troy was absolutely right when he said they had bigger problems at the moment. There was no sense in arguing about small things now, when they weren't yet safe. It was then that Jodie realized just how comfortable she was around Troy. She wanted to discuss larger topics like sexism with him, which was something she usually did only with her family and close friends.

Clicking out her light and hanging it from her skirt band, Jodie freed up one of her hands. She reached it toward Troy and took hold of his wrist. Without looking at her, Troy hung his last light on his belt loop, then took her hand within his own. Together, they walked down the hallway.

Although the mall was darker now that they had passed the wall of windows, sunlight still led the way. Skylights and a few windows up next to the ceiling let sunbeams shine down. A few of the beams were blue, where the glass was covered with the stuff.

"There it is." Jodie pointed out the store they were looking for.

Walking up to it, they found the employees had made an attempt to lock up. From what Jodie could see, it looked like they had drawn the security gates, but had failed to lock them, the lock merely hanging open off the bracket. Looters had discovered this and opened the gates enough for a body to slip through.

Releasing each other's hands, Jodie and Troy each took hold of their lights and turned them on. The store wasn't as bad as The Source had been. People weren't as interested in stealing sports clothing and shoes it seemed. A few things lay about, and a handful of mannequins had been defaced with spray paint, but most of the store appeared more or less intact, just dark and void of life.

"You go find a pair of shoes, I'll look for gloves," Troy suggested.

Jodie agreed and headed for the women's shoe section. She didn't care what the shoes looked like, she just needed to find some that fit. Going through every shoe that was displayed, she hunted for one that would fit her. Eventually, she found a stack of boxes for a bright pink running shoe and located her size among them. Runners in hand, she crossed the store to find Troy, following his light.

"I found gloves," he whispered as he saw her light coming toward him.

"I got shoes," Jodie whispered back. She looked at the gloves that Troy had found. They were for football players and had good grip along the palms and fingers.

"I think this size might fit you." Troy held out a pair.

Jodie tried on the gloves. They were a little loose, made for a man with more meat on his hands and fingers, but the length was good.

"So now all we need are the clothes," Jodie smiled.

"I think I might also grab a few shoelaces and tie them together in case we need some form of rope."

"You should also find new shoes. Yours look pretty worn down."

Troy peered at his feet and lifted one up. The sole of his sneaker was worn flat. "Suppose you're right."

"I'm going to check out the bathroom while we're here. I kind of need to pee."

"Go for it. I'll be over by the men's shoes."

They separated again, each searching for what they needed. Jodie located the employee bathroom, and discovered a key was needed to get in. Assuming the key would be behind the cashier's counter, she headed in its direction, checking out the clothing as she went. It took her a minute, but Jodie turned out to be right when she found a key with a large plastic fob labelled washroom. Returning to the bathroom, Jodie snagged a long-sleeved running shirt, a pair of tight running pants that should fit her, and some socks along the way.

Sitting on a toilet to relieve herself was surprisingly satisfying. Even better was when she got to use proper toilet paper, but the best part was that when Jodie used the handle, the toilet flushed. Having her waste get whisked away by running water actually made her feel giddy. Turning on the tap, she found it was also still working. She took the time to scrub her face, her hands, her arms, and even soak her legs a bit. There wasn't much she could do for her hair without shampoo and a brush, but she wet it back from her face. Not yet ready to turn off the tap, Jodie took a long drink. She told herself to grab Troy once she was done, so that he could get a drink of cold water as well, and they could refill their water bottles.

Finally, Jodie turned off the tap and changed from her

skirt to the pants. There was something comforting about wearing long pants again after having spent so much time in a skirt. She sat on the toilet while she put on the pink shoes, happy to have socks on. Her toes had practically given up on being warm, even during the hot stretches on the train. They were always the first things to get cold and the last to warm up. Once she pulled the shirt on, Jodie was ready to go. Bundling up her slip-on flats in her skirt, Jodie held them under one arm while she took her scalpel and flashlight from the edge of the sink where she had placed them.

Jodie opened the bathroom door and froze. More than one beam of light was moving about the store. She and Troy were no longer alone in here. When a man whooped and kicked over a mannequin, Jodie quickly ducked back into the bathroom. She pulled the key out of the lock, where she had left it, and sensibly brought it into the bathroom with her. Once inside, she locked the door behind her and cowered in a corner.

Where was Troy?

32

JODIE SAT on the floor next to the sink, curled up and afraid. She had no idea how long she had been sitting in the bathroom, but it had been long enough for her to stop checking her watch. It reminded her of trying to sleep after watching a particularly scary movie. Time dragged on as you lay in your bed, imagining the danger lurking in the darkness.

Jodie had real, physical beings that she could attach to her fear, yet she was still imagining the danger. She had no idea if the men outside would harm her or not, but she wasn't going to take the risk. It was safer to stay in the bathroom, her scalpel firmly in hand.

She could hear the men outside. She was assuming they were all men, as she hadn't heard any female voices yet. If she had to guess, she'd say they were drunk. There was a lot of senseless shouting, and frequently things crashed to the floor. Based on what she heard, Jodie suspected she wouldn't see a single display left standing if she ever got out of the bathroom.

"I gotta take a piss!" a voice alarmingly close to the bathroom door called out.

Jodie crunched up tighter against the sink, turning off her light. She kept turning her light on and off throughout her time in the bathroom. Not knowing how long the batteries would last, she didn't want to drain them, but when she turned the light off, it was pitch black. All too often she pictured some creature in the dark ready to pounce. She would tolerate the dark as long as she could, and then turn the light back on, positive it would reveal some hideous face in front of hers.

The doorknob rattled as the man outside tried to get in. He thumped into the door a few times, Jodie's whole body twitching with each strike, but it held.

"Anybody find the key?" the man outside called.

A distant voice replied that he hadn't.

"Well help me find the damned thing!"

"Just use the one next door!" a third voice told him.

There was a grumbled response that moved away from the bathroom. Jodie finally released her breath. After what felt like several minutes, she clicked her light back on, once more confirming that she was alone in there.

Jodie thought that by now she should be used to being trapped in a confined space without much to do, but she wasn't. She was bored whenever the voices weren't near the door and nothing was crashing to the floor. A few times she risked turning on the tap to get a drink and she peed again, but she didn't dare flush the toilet, afraid that the sound would find its way to the ears of the men outside. In the bathroom, there was no one to talk to, no cards to play, no sketchbook to doodle in. She almost wished she was back on the train. Almost.

A soft tapping on the door made her jump so badly she came close to hitting her head on the sink.

"Jodie," a barely audible voice hissed through the door. "Are you in there?"

It could only be Troy. Throughout her confinement, she had carefully listened for the sounds of confrontation that would indicate Troy had been found, but she had heard nothing like that. Scuttling over to the door, she gently released the deadbolt. Cracking the door open, she peered out to find Troy's face level with hers near the floor, a variety of battery-operated lights around the store making his features visible.

"Get in," Jodie whispered, latching onto his shirt and yanking him through the opening.

Once Troy had scrabbled inside, Jodie quickly closed and locked the door behind him. Troy turned on one of his lights and set it in the middle of the floor so that they could both see.

"Where have you been?" Jodie whispered, worried. She couldn't stop herself from examining him for new injuries. He was wearing a new shirt and running shoes, but otherwise looked just the same as when she had last seen him.

"I got trapped in the storage room," Troy whispered back. They kept their heads close together, talking in the softest voices they could. "None of the display shoes were my size, so I went back there to find some. A few of those guys kept wandering in and out. This was my first chance to get away. Are you okay?"

"I'm fine. I have the key so that they can't get in."

"Good."

Jodie threw her arms around Troy, happy to see him. He hugged her back. They sat together for several minutes before Troy disengaged himself.

"The water here works. You should get a drink, and we should fill up the water bottles."

Troy was more than happy to get a drink from the sink. He also took a piss in the toilet, his bladder having been full for awhile. Jodie gave him as much privacy as she could by sitting in the opposite corner with her back to him.

"We have to get out of here," Troy stated the obvious.

"We have to wait for them to leave," Jodie told him, not wanting to risk going out there.

"And how long will that be?"

"I don't know. They'll get bored eventually. It sounds to me like they've just been knocking a bunch of stuff over and drinking. Once all the displays are down, there won't be much to hold their interest."

"I hope you're right."

"I hope so, too." They both knew that drunken individuals could easily spend a lot of time in one place, finding inane things with which to amuse themselves.

They passed the time by carefully repacking Jodie's backpack to optimize space. Jodie suggested leaving a few of her art supplies behind, but Troy wouldn't hear of it. All of their things were coming with them, including their old shoes. Troy even managed to fit a roll of toilet paper into the bag. Once that was done, they spent time braiding shoelaces together. Troy had taken a shoebox full of packages of them before getting trapped in the storage room. After Jodie showed him how to do it, they braided and tied the shoelaces to make a stronger rope out of them.

"We should check outside," Troy urged, after they had finished winding up their makeshift rope and carefully placing it in one of the backpack's side pockets.

"Let's just wait a little longer," Jodie suggested.

"It's been pretty quiet out there," Troy pointed out.

"I know. I just want to wait a little longer."

Troy sighed, but gave in.

Several minutes later, even Jodie couldn't wait any longer. She duck-walked over to the door and pressed her ear against it. Troy sidled up next to her and did the same.

"Do you hear anything?" he spoke as quietly as possible. "I don't."

"I don't, either."

"Let's open the door then."

Jodie paused for a minute longer, listening intently. Finally, Troy got impatient and gripped the doorknob himself. Jodie shuffled back as he threw open the deadbolt and then gently cracked open the door. Moving slowly, Troy stuck his head through the opening to look around. He must not have seen anyone, because he began to crawl out, gesturing for Jodie to follow him. After grabbing the backpack, she did.

The store was in a chaotic state compared to the way it looked before Jodie had entered the bathroom. From what she could see, every display shoe had been pulled off its shelf and thrown every which way about the store. Large racks of clothes had been knocked on their sides, or turned completely upside down. Mannequin parts were strewn about, like the aftermath of a low budget horror film that couldn't afford any blood. A head near Jodie's feet had its face bashed in. Only three mannequins remained standing. One had been rearranged to have a man's head on a woman's body and legs in place of arms. The other two had been positioned together in an obscene pose. They were showcased by one of the three remaining battery-powered lights, all of which were motionless. The one that Jodie could see came from a large orange box that she guessed was meant for roadside emergencies.

As they huddled against a stand meant for a mannequin, Troy took the bag from Jodie and slung it over his back. As he did this, Jodie noticed a small pile of toques nearby. She reached out quickly, snagging two of them. After pulling one down over her greasy hair, she handed the other to Troy and he did the same. For now, they weren't wearing their gloves but had stuffed them into the backpack's side pocket, opposite the shoelace rope.

Once they determined there was no movement in the store, Troy led the way around the stand and through the debris. As they neared the front, they slowed down, not knowing where the men had gone.

A loud snort startled them both. Jodie and Troy both whipped around to face the source of the sound. A man was sleeping—or rather passed out based on the empty liquor bottle by his feet—in a pile of shirts, shoes, and pants. A dog lying next to him raised its head, looking at the pair of escapees, but it quickly assessed that they were no threat to its master and laid its head back down on its paws. Jodie's heart was in her throat, but Troy urged her on, even quicker now that he knew a drunk was so close and could wake up at any moment.

At the security gates, Troy immediately risked sticking his head out and checking down all three hallways of the T-junction where the store was positioned. When he didn't see anyone, he took Jodie's hand and pulled her out of the store. They headed back toward the subway station, but just before they got out of the intersection, Jodie spotted a guy stepping out of a store down the hallway that was not in line with theirs. He was out of sight before she could tell if they had been spotted.

Jodie and Troy moved as quickly as they could without squeaking their shoes or slapping their feet too hard against the floor. They moved at an awkward jog, Troy leading Jodie by the hand while she constantly twisted around to see if they were being followed.

When they reached the section of the mall with the one glass wall, they spotted movement up ahead. Troy quickly redirected them into the Tim Hortons. There was no time to find a proper hiding spot, so they simply rounded the corner and huddled up against the wall next to the door. If anyone came in to check the place, they'd likely be found

Coming toward them from the direction of the subway was the clomping of many footsteps, in what sounded like heavy boots. Above that noise, was a metallic scraping, that made it easy to track their progress. It put Jodie's teeth on edge. As the group of people walked past the Tims, Jodie could see their backs. There were at least two dozen of them, and they were all carrying blunt weapons in their hands. The metallic rattle was the end of an aluminium bat being dragged along the floor.

"Hey!" someone from back toward the intersection shouted. "You know this is Tom's territory!"

"We're here to tell him otherwise!" a woman in the new group shouted back as the last of them finished passing by Jodie and Troy's hiding place.

Troy grabbed Jodie's hand and pulled her around the wall, into the hallway. He ran for the subway entrance without looking back. Jodie couldn't resist glancing over her shoulder. Two people from the new group were looking back at them, but must have decided they weren't important or dangerous, and so ignored them.

After dashing up the steps into the tunnel over the road, Troy and Jodie froze upon reaching the top. A few teenagers, a small handful of children, and one adult were blocking their way. The adult was pointing a pistol at them.

No one moved or said a word. No one seemed to breathe for several seconds.

"Are you with them?" The man with the gun gestured toward the mall with his head.

Troy and Jodie both shook their own in response.

The man continued to consider them, his eyes roving up and down, but then, after a minute, he lowered his weapon. "Go on then, get out of here. Kids, make way."

A gap opened up between the teenagers and children, allowing Jodie and Troy to get through.

"Wait." Jodie stopped Troy just as they passed the crowd. She pulled out her evacuation map and held it out to the man with the gun. "You should really consider going to one of these places instead of fighting over a mall."

"You clearly don't know what's happening here." The man shook his head, but accepted the map. "It's probably better for you to remain ignorant. Get going now before I change my mind about you two."

Jodie turned and grabbed Troy's hand again. Together they quickly crossed the remainder of the bridge, then headed up into the subway station.

"All right, gloves on." Troy hastily shrugged out of the backpack so that they could get the gloves out.

"What do you think that was all about?" Jodie wondered as she pulled on her pair.

"I don't know. And like that guy said, it's probably best that we don't." Once Troy had slipped his own gloves on, the backpack was returned to his shoulders. "We need to get moving. We spent a lot more time in there than we meant to. We might get caught out in the dark."

Jodie hadn't realized just how much the sun had crossed the sky while they were inside. As they clambered back down onto the tracks, she saw they had only about an hour before it hit the horizon. It had taken them a long time to get to the station, and an even longer time was wasted in the mall. It was only a moment later that Jodie learned it wasn't wasted time, but time well spent. Almost immediately after stepping out of the station, they found themselves walking, crawling, and climbing over blue stuff. The gloves were a big help, not only because they protected their hands from touching it, but because of the rubber grips. The rubber skidded less across the blue than the fabric covering their knees and elbows did.

As the two of them started to cross over the 401 highway, Jodie couldn't help but be distracted by it. Nearly ten lanes across and stretching for miles in either direction, it held a vast number of vehicles. Had it been rush hour, the highway would have been absolutely covered with barely moving vehicles, but even in non-rush hour times traffic was always heavy, as it would have been with the lunchtime crowd when the blue hit. Globs of blue dotted the highway everywhere, burying vehicles of every shape, size, and colour. Some had escaped entombment, only to be boxed in by those that hadn't. Here and there, car doors stood open, but most of the vehicles were closed and probably locked as well, their owners hoping to be able to get them back. Jodie was fairly certain no one was going to get their vehicles back. She didn't think they were going to get their *city* back. It was lost to the blue. There was just so much of it, heaped up all along the highway and clinging to the sides of just about every building that Jodie could see. She couldn't imagine anyone in the world being able to clean up this mess.

"Come on, we should keep moving." Troy eventually tugged on her hand, prompting them both to turn away from the highway.

It was hard work moving around and over the blue. Jodie found herself sweating from the exertion. It was different from sweating in the train, though. There was a breeze out here that Jodie could stop and appreciate every once in a while. Out here the air moved.

About half way across the bridge, they came across a spot devoid of blue. The low grade of the blue hill they had been climbing sloped down fairly steeply toward the bare patch, making sliding on their butts the best way down. Jodie enjoyed the ride down, mostly because it meant she didn't have to do any work. When she looked at the slope ahead, however, her brief joy turned sour. It wasn't as steep as the one they had just descended, but it was even higher.

"That's going to take a lot of effort," Jodie groaned.

"Yeah, it is," Troy nodded. "What do you think? Should we spend the night here?"

"What?" Jodie turned to him.

"The sun is setting soon. I was hoping we could get to the next train station before that happened, but I don't think we're going to make it. Here seems pretty safe. We could spend the night here, and tackle that mound tomorrow morning."

Jodie considered his suggestion. It did seem they were in a fairly safe location. Anyone sneaking around at night would have a hard time getting to them with the blue hills on either side, and it didn't look like it was going to rain, so a roof overhead didn't seem necessary.

In the end, it was the weariness of Jodie's body that made the decision. "Yeah. Okay. We'll stop here for the night."

Troy shrugged out of the backpack and sat at the side of the tracks, leaning against the concrete barrier that separated them from the drop to the highway. Jodie plopped down beside him.

"I really wish I had spent more time working out," she commented.

"I know what you mean. We should eat." Troy opened the bag and began carefully unpacking it, searching for the MREs.

"Last one, right?"

"Last meal we have, yeah."

"So no breakfast in the morning."

"No breakfast. Unless you want to drink water-softened dog food."

"I wonder how he's doing? Eric. Do you think they freed him?"

"I'm sure they did."

Jodie opened the MRE that Troy had handed her. She ate slowly, wondering if she could trick her stomach into thinking it was full faster, so that she could save some of the food for the morning. She thought of Eric while she ate, wondering where he had been taken and if he'd ever wake up.

"Where do you think the others are?" Troy asked after awhile. "Nina, and Mandy, and them."

"No idea. Somewhere safe, I hope. Home."

"They might be. They must have chosen not to follow the tracks like we did. I figured we would have come across one by now, unconscious from accidentally touching the blue gunk."

Jodie looked up at the sloping blue, following its curve over one side of the bridge. "You know, if we accidentally touched the blue, there's a good chance of ending up splattered on the highway below."

Troy followed her eyes. "Yeah. We got lucky. Tomorrow, we should tie the rope around our waists. That way, *if* one of us slips or something, the other might be able to save them."

"Or get dragged over the edge as well."

"Or that."

In the end, Jodie hadn't been able to save any of her food. Together, she and Troy sat and watched the sunset in silence. When darkness came, the blue stuff started glowing once more.

"Does it seem brighter to you?" Jodie wondered.

"No. Why? Does it seem brighter to you?"

"I don't know. Maybe." Out of curiosity, she stood up and looked at the highway again. A long trail of glowing patches lit up the night.

"It would be pretty if I didn't know people were trapped inside," Troy commented, standing up next to her.

"Yeah."

They stared out at the blue a moment longer then sat back down. Preparing to sleep, Jodie pulled her hat as tightly over her head and ears as she could. She and Troy curled up next to the tracks together, using the backpack as a pillow and Troy's coat, Jodie's skirt, and Roxanne's blazer as blankets. Despite being outside the shelter of the subway train, it was the warmest Jodie had been at night since the blue came. She still wished they had taken more warm gear from the mall, but then they hadn't expected to be outside another night and hadn't thought about it.

The warmth and her exhaustion put her quickly into a deep and dreamless sleep.

33

AS WAS THE NORM NOW, Jodie was awakened by the sun. She continued to lie still, but opened her eyes and stared up at the crisp, blue sky. That blue was so much more familiar, so much more comforting, and yet that was where this other stuff had come from. Jodie began thinking about the story of Chicken Little and how, after today, it might be told differently.

"I have to piss," Troy interrupted her train of thought.

She hadn't known he was awake as well, but wasn't surprised to learn that he was. Untangling himself from the clothing blanket and Jodie, he walked to the far side of the bridge where he could relieve himself in relative privacy. Jodie also had to pee and was wondering where she could go. In the end, she pulled her skirt back on and used it as a kind of curtain while she squatted by the tracks.

"Do you want to try the dog food water?" Troy asked when she returned to the backpack, skirt once more removed.

"No thanks. I'll stick to regular water for now."

She had a breakfast of water and Troy did the same.

"You ready?" he asked as they finished and packed up the bottles again.

"I guess. Let's get going."

As they had agreed the night before, they each took an end of the braided shoelace rope and tied it to themselves. Troy volunteered to climb the grade first, and call out good handholds. The rope wasn't long enough to put a lot of distance between them, but it was enough that Jodie didn't have to worry about being kicked in the head.

They took to the blue wall like spiders, lying on their bellies and pressing as much of their limbs against it as they could without risking the exposed skin of their faces. It was slow going, but once they reached the top, things got easier.

The blue was rarely flat, but nothing else on the bridge got as steep as the sides of the valley in which they had spent the night. Even though they remained tied together as a precaution, they hadn't needed to, as they managed not to slip and fall at any point.

"Look, there's a train." Jodie pointed to the end of the bridge. On the north bound tracks meant for trains headed in the opposite direction from the one they had been riding, the rear end of a train with a glob of blue attached to its side was visible.

It wasn't long before they were walking alongside the train. It was one of the newer ones that had enclosed, accordion-like, moving sections between the cars, which allowed passengers who entered from the front to walk unimpeded all the way to the back. Jodie couldn't help but be envious, and even a little angry. If they had been in one of these new trains, they would have been able to escape as soon as the blue stopped falling, just like the people in the car behind theirs. Her jealously didn't last long.

Like their train, this one had ploughed into freshly

fallen blue, but it had had more dire results. Based on what Jodie saw, it looked like the front end of the train had been lifted clear of the rails. It had bent and then rolled sideways, pulling the attached cars with it and twisting metal. Some of the movable sections that connected the cars were shredded.

Parts of the train had crossed to their side of the tracks, but not enough to block their way. Thinking that she could have been on a train like this, or that her own train could have just as easily been popped off the rails, Jodie couldn't resist peering in through one of the windows. There were bodies inside. Some of them had probably been killed on impact, but based on the poses and states of a few others, she didn't think all of them had been. A few of the passengers had just been too badly injured to move. She wondered whether they had been abandoned by those who could move on, or whether the healthy had promised to come back. No one currently left in the train appeared to be alive.

Just past it was the next station. It was the last one before the end of the line. The passengers who had suffered in the crash had been so close to safety. If the blue had fallen just a little later, the train would have been under the shelter of the station roof and they would have been safe.

"Should we take a short break?" Troy asked as they stepped out of the sun. It was turning out to be another hot and sunny day. It felt like summer now, as opposed to spring. Jodie wondered if the blue had anything to do with it, but couldn't see what the connection might be. If only the nights would warm up in equal measure.

"Yeah, all right." She was tired from their walk. If the route had been flat, she would have been fine to keep going, but it wasn't, and so she needed a rest.

Troy boosted her up onto the platform and then

climbed up himself. They sat on the edge, upon the yellow band that warned people not to wait so close to the tracks, with their legs hanging over the edge.

"It's farther between this station and the next one," Jodie told Troy as they drank some more water.

"No more bridges though, right?"

"No, no more bridges. It's pretty open actually. If I remember right, we're farther away from the roads, and I think there's a train depot or turn around section or something. I never paid too much attention to the scenery outside."

"Open sounds good. If there's more space between the fences, we should be able to walk around more of the blue gunk instead of having to climb over it all the time."

"Yeah."

"Think we should untie ourselves?"

Jodie shrugged. "Sure. Let's pray we don't have to climb any more steep spots."

After they untied the rope from around themselves, Troy carefully bundled it up to put back into the bag.

"Do you want me to carry that for awhile?" Jodie asked, pointing to the backpack.

"No, I got it."

"You sure?"

"Yeah, I'm sure."

"You're not doing this just to be manly, are you?"

Troy laughed. "No. The way I figure it, you're helping me by letting me come to your place, so I'm helping you by carrying your stuff for you."

"You don't have to."

"I know, but I want to. I feel like I need to do something, and this is pretty much the only option."

Jodie took his gloved hand in her own. They sat there for several minutes longer, just slowly swinging their feet.

"It's the silence," Troy eventually said.

"What is?"

"I've been trying to figure out what I find the most strange about all of this. There's the emptiness, the stillness, the tension and fear. But it's the silence that affects me the most. No electric hum, no cars, no people out on the streets. Have you noticed there's almost no bird song? No bugs? I bet a lot of animals got buried in the blue gunk. And those that didn't, might be getting knocked unconscious by touching it, just like we are. The helicopters don't seem to be flying around anymore, and I haven't seen a plane travel overhead since this started. Can't blame them. Since this stuff came from up there, they probably closed off the airspace. I wouldn't be surprised if air traffic all over the world shut down at least for a little while. This blue gunk has muffled everything."

Jodie hadn't thought about it, but he was right. There was a silence over everything that she hadn't noticed. Even when they were talking to one another, they spoke barely above a whisper, as if something might overhear them.

"Let's keep going," Jodie decided, not wanting to think about it anymore, "in case there's another detour. I don't want to get caught out in the dark again."

Troy nodded.

The pair climbed back down onto the tracks and walked on them the rest of the way through the station.

It wasn't long before they came across another body. Just a few feet from the other side of the train station was a man trapped in the blue. Based on his clothes, he was a transit employee of some sort. A glob of blue had managed to grab his right half, his leg and arm trapped inside. He had probably tried to pull himself out before it solidified, but hadn't been fast enough. When Jodie and Troy first spotted him, Jodie assumed he was unconscious. As they got closer, it became evident that he was dead. He must have been alone out here, or abandoned. He had most likely died of thirst, or maybe even exposure. The man's skin was drawn, dry, and chapped.

"I think he might have tried to chew or claw his arm off at some point," Troy commented, pointing to the spots of blood on his shoulder. "Or maybe he had a tool." There were a few drops staining his pants as well.

"I didn't need to know that."

"Sorry."

There wasn't much blood, just a few small, dried circles. The man wouldn't have been able to get at his own shoulder very well, or even his leg. His teeth and fingernails wouldn't be very effective, but even with a tool, the pain would probably have stopped him fairly quickly.

Jodie and Troy kept moving, trying futilely to push the dead man from their minds. They didn't come across any more dead people trapped in the blue. The tracks had been clear of workers for the most part. As they were led farther away from the road, Troy and Jodie couldn't even make out the cars.

"What is that?" Troy pointed as they rounded another mound of blue. They had been able to walk around most of the blobs since leaving the station.

"I don't know."

They could see something through the side of a blob, but it was just far enough and distorted enough to make it hard to identify.

"Do you think we should check it out?" Troy asked Jodie.

Jodie looked ahead. They couldn't even see the tunnel to the final station yet, but it wasn't that far out of their way. "Yeah, sure. Let's go take a peek."

As they rounded to the other side, it became obvious what it was. People had touched the blue and fallen unconscious. There were three of them, and it was impossible to tell how long they had been lying there.

"They didn't know not to touch it." Troy pointed out their bare arms revealed by T-shirts and their bare hands. "I'd guess they tried to use this gunk to get over the fence."

Jodie nodded. There were two males and a female. Judging by their variance in ages, dress, and the lack of a family resemblance, they had probably been strangers to one another before the blue came down.

"Well, we can't take them with us," Jodie sighed. "Let's at least move them off the blue. Maybe they'll wake up on their own."

"Maybe."

Working together, Jodie and Troy dragged one person after another as gently as possible and left them side by side away from the blue.

"Do you think we should wait?" Jodie wondered once they were done.

Troy shook his head. "Based on the sunburns, they've probably been there for some time. It'll take awhile before they come to. We should keep moving. We can alert someone to their whereabouts later."

"Okay."

Jodie found it a lot easier to walk away from these strangers than it was to walk away from Eric, even though they might die of exposure out here.

By the time they finally reached the tunnel, the only other notable things they had seen were a few empty trains on some side rails, and one unfortunate racoon completely buried in blue. His posture wasn't violent and thrashing like the people's poses had been. The poor thing probably didn't realize what had happened until it was too late. The racoon was like a penny in a Lucite cube, except it was formerly alive and tinted blue. Jodie shuddered imagining it on some CEO's desk.

They paused before entering the tunnel. Part of the top was blocked by a hanging curtain of blue, but it was still open enough for them to walk in without any trouble. The tunnel was a black, gaping maw, refusing to let them know what was inside.

Without saying a word, Troy and Jodie stepped into it, clicking on their flashlights as they went. Troy turned on two of the lights hanging from his belt loops, essentially turning them into headlights. They highlighted most of the tunnel, while the one Jodie held in her hand lit up the rest. Not far from the entrance to the tunnel, they came across a spot that seemed to have been a campsite. Empty water bottles, tin cans, foil wrappers, and a long dead fire were all that was left. The campers had moved on, but the rats and mice hadn't.

It wasn't a terribly long walk through the tunnel, at least not compared to the rest of the journey, before they came to the station.

"I'm almost home," Jodie whispered, tears unexpectedly springing to her eyes as she took in the familiar station walls.

Troy helped her up onto the platform, where she turned around and helped him up in turn.

"I understand you're probably eager to keep moving, but I would like to take a water break."

Jodie nodded. She wanted to run the rest of the way

home, but she knew she'd collapse from exhaustion long before she made it.

Sitting in the dead and dark station was a little spooky. Unlike the others, there were no windows here to let in the sunlight. Although their hockey-puck lights were bright and revealed much, dark shadows persisted in all the corners.

"All right, I'm going for it."

"Going for what?"

Jodie's question was quickly answered as Troy spun the top off the water bottle with the dissolving dog food in it. He took a large mouthful, getting one of the remaining gelatinous kibble bits. It remained in his mouth for a little while as he smushed the bit with his tongue and then swallowed.

"And?" Jodie prompted him when he didn't say anything right away.

"Could be better, could be worse," he shrugged. "I definitely wouldn't chose it over a cheeseburger, but it doesn't make me want to vomit. You want to try?"

"No thanks, plain old water is still good enough for me."

As if to prove it wasn't terrible, Troy took another swig of the kibble water before returning it to the backpack, and then drank more of his normal water.

Jodie was a lot less interested in sitting around this time. As soon as Troy looked like he was good to go, she got to her feet. Troy was more sluggish getting up, but get up he did. Once he got the backpack on, Jodie led the way out of the subway station and to the surface. The sun still shone brightly, almost blindingly after the darkness of the tunnel.

Taking Troy's hand, Jodie directed them along the street. They had finally left the subway's yellow line and she was headed home.

The way was as winding as it had been on the tracks.

Blue blobs covered the road here and there, but Jodie and Troy could always find a way around them. Jodie was impatient with how long it was taking. She knew these streets, and knew she could have covered twice the distance they had if it weren't for the blue.

Her eager urge to run home was kept in check by a sense of eerie disquiet. She saw no people, no shops or stores open, and no cars or buses driving down the street. Jodie had lived in a relatively busy area, thanks to the proximity of the subway line, but now all was still and quiet. As her building came into sight, she suddenly felt apprehensive.

"What's wrong?" Troy asked her, noticing that she had slowed her pace.

"What if there's no one there? What if my sister has moved on to an evacuation site?" She didn't dare voice her concerns for her dad.

"That's fine. We'll rest up, resupply, then head to one ourselves. I can't imagine they wouldn't have set up a program to help families find one another."

As they reached Jodie's apartment building, they saw that the doors had been blocked by blue, however, a pane of glass next to them had been smashed out so that they could walk inside. There wasn't any broken glass on the floor; it must have been busted out awhile ago and someone had since cleaned it up. Jodie briefly wondered if that had happened before or after Amber had gotten there.

The lobby was dark, but Jodie got them to the stairs quickly. The battery-powered emergency lights were all dead, but their hockey-puck lights provided more illumination than those old boxes could anyway.

Climbing the stairs, Jodie convinced herself that Amber was gone, that she had left for an evacuation site. Troy was right though, they could rest here and then move on to one themselves. Amber would have left a note saying which one she had gone to, and they could find it on Troy's map and head there, once they had gathered more food and water. Jodie also wanted to grab a second bag to carry this time.

Finally reaching her floor, Jodie headed to her door, in the unfamiliarly silent hallway. There was no reason for the door to be unlocked, so she turned to Troy and gestured for him to turn around.

"My key's in the bag," she told him, her voice unusually quiet to match the stillness of the building.

Having reorganized the backpack during their semi-disastrous side journey to the mall, Jodie knew exactly where the keys were. As she plucked them out of the side pocket, she used her free hand to stifle a yawn. She was so tired, and being so close to home only seemed to make her weariness worse. Her bed was only a few feet away.

In the dark, with tired eyes, Jodie missed the key slot on her first attempt, the tip of the metal skittering around on the strike plate. Once unlocked, she tried to open the door and was confused when it refused to budge. Then she realized that Amber must have also thrown the larger deadbolt before she left, so Jodie located that key as well and unlocked it.

The smell of her apartment as she stepped through the doorway caused Jodie to pause, blocking Troy's entrance behind her. The place smelled as it always had, and Jodie hadn't known just how much she had missed it, trapped in that awful subway train. It was such a clean smell.

From down the hallway came the grumpy yowl of Rusty. Jodie turned to see what was wrong with him, but instead saw Amber. Her sister was half frozen with surprise, only her arms moved as they drifted down toward the floor from over her head. The stillness broke when their dad's wooden baseball bat slipped out of Amber's hand and clattered on the hardwood floor.

"Jodie," Amber wheezed. Before Jodie could figure out that her sister had thought she was someone breaking in, she was swept up in a tight embrace. Amber's hands kept patting along her back, and after finally releasing her, she started touching Jodie's face as well, making sure that she was real.

Having convinced herself that Amber would be gone, Jodie was equally surprised and couldn't find her voice.

"Hey Amber, so the guys on the radio say they've found evidence that the stuff is from space. Apparently, they-" Todd, Amber's fiancé, cut himself off as he walked in from the balcony and spotted the girls by the doorway. His hand first twitched defensively toward a hockey stick leaning against the nearest wall, but then his eyes recognized the face beneath the hat. With a few long strides, he crossed the living room, depositing a windup radio on the table that he passed.

Jodie found herself quickly swept up into another hug, this one threatening to squeeze the wind out of her, but thankfully it was blessedly brief.

"I'm so glad you made it back," Todd smiled, yet there was something odd and forced about it. The man's eyes then quickly darted past Jodie, locking onto something behind her. That's when she realized that Troy was still standing in the hallway.

Disengaging herself from her family, Jodie turned to Troy and gently pulled him through the doorway.

"Amber, Todd, this is Troy. He helped me get home, but doesn't have anywhere to go himself right now, so I said he could stay with us. Troy, this is my sister Amber, and her fiancé Todd."

"It's nice to meet you," Troy mumbled, clearly unsure what to do with himself.

"Sit down, sit down." Amber ushered them both to the couch. "I'll make you some sandwiches." Before heading to the kitchen, however, Amber first closed the door and made sure that both locks were engaged.

"Are you all right? Are you hurt?" Todd asked as Jodie collapsed onto the couch and Troy sat more carefully. He was in a strange home and didn't know what to do with himself.

"We're fine. Just tired, hungry, and very dirty."

"Yeah, there's a bit of a stink coming off of you," Todd chuckled, although it was briefer than usual. His eyes darted to a pair of bags in one corner before settling back on Jodie.

"We caught you just in time, didn't we?" Troy figured it out before she could.

Todd shuffled uncomfortably.

"I wanted to come find you," Amber spoke from the kitchen, able to hear them through the open doorway. "I really did."

"It's just so dangerous out there," Todd continued. "We both wanted to come get you, but there's the blue, and the gangs. It's madness out there."

"It's okay," Jodie spoke in Todd's direction, but her words were meant for both of them. "I didn't expect either you to come find me. Even if you did, there wasn't much you could do." Jodie knew that they could have done *something*, but she held her tongue on that point. Both of them clearly felt badly enough as it was. Besides, she was too tired to be angry.

Amber returned to the living room with simple sand-wiches and glasses of water.

"I'm sorry, you're not allergic to peanut butter or anything, are you?" Amber paused before putting down the plate in front of Troy. Jodie barely noticed as she proceeded to wolf down the peanut butter on bread she had been given.

"No, no allergies here." Troy's eyes were locked onto the food and he managed to wait until Amber put the plate down before snatching the sandwich off of it.

"Where's Dad?" Jodie asked around a sticky mouthful. She feared the answer, but had to ask it.

"In a hospital. He's all right, just a broken leg. I didn't get to learn much before he had to go, so I don't know how it happened. He'll be brought to an evacuation centre with the rest of the patients when it's possible." Amber perched on the armrest of their dad's lounger, watching with sad eyes as the pair ate. "We were just about to head to one ourselves."

Jodie nodded, swallowing her mouthful. "That's where we planned to go if you guys weren't here. I figured you had already left, but I'm glad you didn't."

The sisters smiled at one another, with genuine smiles, nothing forced or hidden behind them.

"We'll get some extra bags and pack up some more supplies. May I?" Todd pointed to the backpack that still hugged Troy's shoulders, forcing him to sit on the very edge of the couch cushions.

Tory paused for a moment, unwilling to release the bag at first. He had been protecting it long enough that it was difficult to let go of now. After swallowing another bite of sandwich, he slipped his arms out of the straps and gave the bag to Todd.

"I'm exhausted," Jodie told her sister once the food and water had been consumed.

"Why don't you rest then? We don't have to leave right now. I'll wake you when it's time to go."

When Jodie left the couch, Troy followed hesitantly behind her to her room, where he stopped in the doorway. Jodie forgot about him for a moment as she spotted Rusty. He was inside his travel crate and was looking angrily out through the cage door. It explained his grumpy complaint when she had first entered the apartment.

"Oh, Rusty, come here, boy." Jodie opened up the door and pulled the cat out, cradling him to her chest as she went and sat on her bed. She knew it would be hard to get him back in there, but right now she needed a snuggle.

Troy shifted in the doorway, finally drawing Jodie's attention back to him.

"It's okay. You can come join me on my bed. We're all adults here," Jodie smiled. Putting down Rusty, she crawled beneath her covers, kicking off her new shoes in the process.

Troy came over and sat on the other side of the bed, leaning against the headboard, clearly too wary to sleep, unlike her. Rusty walked around a bit, glad to be free of his cage, and then gave Troy a thorough sniffing. Satisfied, the cat then curled up against Jodie's legs, seeming to be as happy to have her home as she was to be there.

"Troy?" Jodie whispered, her eyes already heavy enough to make it hard to open them. The warmth and comfort of her bed, combined the familiar surroundings and the soft voices of Amber and Todd talking down the hall, were very quickly lulling her to sleep. Everything that had happened was falling away, at least for the moment.

"Yeah?" Troy whispered back. He didn't sound tired, but when Jodie placed a hand on his arm, she could feel him slowly relaxing, slouching down farther. He'd probably be lying down soon enough.

"We made it."

"We still have to get to an evacuation site," he reminded her.

"Yeah, but we made it."

Jodie didn't know if he answered or not, as sleep finally overtook her. Everything else could be dealt with when she woke up. For now, the fact that she was finally off the subway was enough. She was finally back home.